# HEROES OF ANOTHER AGE

© 2024 All rights reserved. No part of this publication may be reproduced, distributed, or transmitted in any form or by any means, including photocopying, recording, or other electronic or mechanical methods, without the prior written permission of the publisher, except in the case of brief quotations embodied in critical reviews and certain other noncommercial uses permitted by copyright law.

ISBN 979-8-35097-857-5 eBook 979-8-35099-366-0

**For Alex and Sam**

*With enough passion and dedication,*
*any dream is possible.*

Other books by B.L. Mostyn

## The Guardian Series

*Heroes of Another Age*
*A Glimmer of Hope*

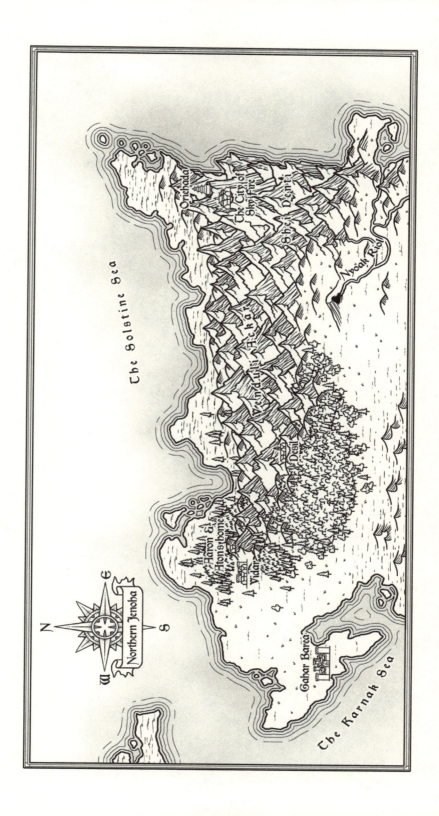

# HEROES OF ANOTHER AGE

**B.L. MOSTYN**

# CHAPTER 1

## *More Than Human*

Aaron sat among the sheep, listening to them bleat and chew their grass, while he thought again, *Why aren't they terrified?* They should've been terrified of all of them: him, his brother, and his mother. They were predators after all. That was supposed to be the way of things, and yet, for some reason, these sheep didn't seem to know it. He didn't know if they just couldn't smell the danger, if they'd somehow become desensitized to the threat, or were just too stupid to comprehend the whole situation in the first place. Of course Aaron also couldn't have said for certain that they were any more dangerous than a typical human, even if they were...

"Werewolves," the boy said aloud as he leaned back, propping himself up on his arms, hands disappearing into the long grass up to his elbows.

The spring day was brilliant, the skies a robin's egg blue, the new grass so light green Aaron could almost see how soft and tender it was. The sheep certainly seemed to like it, munching the fresh blades with gusto after their long sojourn in the lower winter field. Though Aaron hardly noticed, his mind still wandering down familiar paths.

Their mother had been the one to tell Aaron and his brother what they were, though at six years old, neither he nor his brother had ever gone through this mystical "Shift" she'd told them about, the one where the boys would be able to magically change their human bodies into those of wolves'. She'd said they wouldn't have their first shift, or at least be able to control it themselves, until they'd come into their "maturity", whatever that meant.

She, as their mother and alpha, supposedly could've forced them to change shape, but wouldn't. They'd never even seen her shift, though not for a lack of asking. They'd pestered her constantly once she'd revealed the ability to them, only she responded the same way to every entreaty. She would shake her head patiently and say that it was too dangerous for her to reveal them as different in case the "normal people" ever caught wind of what they were.

"Not that there are any 'normal people' anywhere near here," he said to the sheep. They of course didn't reply.

The three of them lived isolated and all alone, save for the sheep, in their tiny little cottage perched atop a mountain peak. The nearest town, Vidar, where their mother sold their wool and cheese to those "normal people," was all the way at the base of their mountain and a good ways walk from the road down. It wasn't likely that anyone would hike the whole way up the steep mountain track only to catch them in the act of shifting, especially if they shifted inside, in the middle of the night, once.

Aaron never thought of himself as special or different, especially not sitting in the middle of a flock of sheep that weren't even afraid of him, and yet he knew his mother wouldn't lie to them either.

"So I'm a werewolf," he said on a sigh. Several of the fluffy, hungry, and unbothered sentient-clouds strolling around gave a bleat, which Aaron took to be agreement.

"Aaron."

A familiar voice, lyrical as the larks in the bushes nearby, called his name. The boy turned to see his mother exiting their little home.

Taller than the boys by half, thin and strong as the apple tree that grew on the hill, their mother walked over. She dried her hands on a kitchen towel before tucking a stray strand of flaxen hair, much like his own, behind her ear. She leaned down, her familiar green eyes meeting his upside-down violet ones as he craned his neck to look at her from his sitting position.

"Aaron," she said, tucking the towel in the pocket of her cream apron that she wore over her soft purple dress, "have you seen your brother?"

The boy frowned. "He was supposed to be brining the cheese."

"I didn't see him at the vats," she said, one hand on her hip, the other reflexively tucking a strand of hair behind her ear, though no more had come undone. The ring on her left hand caught the light and flashed as she did so. The flash pulled Aaron's gaze from his mother's face, to just over her left ear, but something else was there.

He jumped to his feet, pointing behind her. "There," he shouted.

She spun to look.

Behind their little cottage, the stone and timber freshly whitewashed for spring, above its thatched roof, rose the very peak of their little mountain. Though much of their land at the summit was mainly flat, there was a gentle slant to the plot, covered in a delectable, sheep-loving grass. There was also a little crag of stone that the boys called the true peak of the mountain that jutted up on one side. More a high protrusion, the peak was just a pile of stone that Aaron's older brother, Aton, was currently climbing.

"What is he doing?" his mother asked no one in particular, her hand going to her lips. She picked up her skirts, revealing her sturdy leather shoes and a flash of her light-colored leggings, and rushed toward the crag, Aaron right on her heels.

They raced around the house, passing their front vegetable garden and flowered window boxes, both just starting to bud. Aaron was quicker, passing his mother, turning the corner of the stable, and skidding to a stop right in front of the tower of stone. There was a tiny cave in its base, just big enough for the three to enter while ducking, though not at the same time, into the cool interior of the spire. It was where they stored their fermenting cheeses. It was where Aton should've been, putting away wheels of cheese just freshly brined. Instead, he was more than halfway up the stone bluff and clambering higher still.

Their mother had told them not to climb the crag because she worried about the stones coming loose and the boys falling and hurting themselves. They'd done it anyway of course, from time to time, but never that high. They'd made an agreement with each other to never go above the halfway point so that their mother couldn't get too mad at them. So why had Aton changed his mind and gone so high?

Aaron saw his brother scrambling over a particularly ragged ledge, one arm, then the other, but his foot slipped and a rock came tumbling down the steep side. Aton was hanging on with arms alone, his small legs flailing out into open air. Aaron found himself holding his breath, too scared for his brother's safety to even gasp, even as Aton found another foothold and recovered. The other boy was reaching for something—another handhold? Reaching—

"Aton," their mother gasped when she caught up to him.

Aton fell backward, spinning out as he tried to hold on to the ledge with one hand. He slipped, unable to support himself. Aaron watched with horror as his sibling tumbled through nothing then struck a rock hard with one leg, which sent him spinning in the other direction before he landed with a sickening *thud*.

Both Aaron and his mother shouted as they rushed to the boy's side.

Aton was laying out, the dirt his landing had kicked up falling all around him through shafts of sunlight. Their mother reached him first, laying a hand on his head. For a terrifying moment, Aaron didn't think his brother was breathing.

Aton coughed.

"You just got the wind knocked out of you. Try to breathe slowly," the boys' mother said with evident relief. "Tell me what hurts." She was careful not to move him yet, lest she injure him further with an unthinking embrace.

He only responded with more coughing.

"Slow breaths, little breaths," she soothed, fingers delicately examining him for broken bones.

Aaron watched her search for greater injuries, then a little wisp of wind carried a metallic tang to his nose. Then he saw the red.

"Blood," he said, pointing to the pool forming under Aton's knee.

Their mother spotted it too, her nimble fingers lifting up the ragged cloth covering the wound.

Aton gasped and then coughed again, tucking himself into a ball in reaction to the light graze against his injury.

"I'm sorry," she said, smoothing his dark hair back from his face.

"I'm fine," he grunted.

Aton clearly wasn't as badly injured as Aaron had feared. Aton rolled onto his back and push himself up to his elbows to better look at his mother and brother. The little climber bent his leg, but snarled and winced when it was less than halfway bent.

"Easy, easy," their mother said gently. "You'll be okay."

Their mother didn't sound concerned anymore, but Aaron found that once he'd seen it, he couldn't take his eye off the ragged tear in his brother's pants through which he could see the hole in his knee. The skin had been ripped away like the fabric beside it, revealing the soft, bloody mess beneath. There was only a thin layer, through which he could see the white gleam of bone. He swallowed hard past the lump in his throat. It looked like it hurt, a lot.

"You'll be alright." Their mother repeated the phrase while running her fingers through Aton's dark brown hair in constant, soothing strokes, keeping the strands out of the sweat blossoming on his caramel skin.

Aaron watched in fascination as first the blood stopped flowing and then the white of the bone started fading right before his eyes, though he knew from experience that the pain wouldn't be gone yet.

"Thank the gods for werewolf healing," their mother said with a sigh. "It'll close up completely soon, but we'll get you back to the house and bind it up, just to make sure you don't get anything nasty in it while your body's healing." Her voice turned stern. "Now, what were you doing up there anyway? You know how I feel about you boys climbing the—"

Before she could finish, Aton leaned to one arm and extended the other toward her, his fist clenched around a tuft of grass and the stem of a single, dark purple flower.

"The first violet of the season," he said. "I thought you'd like it."

She stared at the bloom, her bright green eyes, nearly the shade of the new grass, focusing on the tiny gift. She began to laugh, the laugh of a spring brook rushing down the mountain. It was such a joyous sound.

Taking the flower from him, she said, "Thank you," and kissed the top of his head. "That was very thoughtful of you, but you shouldn't have climbed up there just to get me a present. As punishment you'll wash and darn those pants you just stained and ripped." She kissed him again then added, "Once your leg is better."

She scooped up the injured boy into her arms and gave him a hug. Then, despite her slight frame, she stood upright with him in her arms as though he weighed nothing and started walking back toward the cottage.

"Aaron," she said, finally turning her attention back to him.

"Yes?"

"You get back to the sheep while I get your brother cleaned up, alright?"

"Do I have to?"

"Yes," she said. "I'll call you when it's time to pen them for the night. Then you'll wash up and come in for dinner."

"Fine." Aaron frowned.

She leaned over and kissed him on the top of his head. "Good boy. Now, go on."

The younger boy jogged ahead of his mother and brother, trekking back around to the front of the house, toward the field. He looked back over his shoulder on his way. His mother had reached the door and was disappearing with his brother into the shadow of the house's interior, but through the opening Aaron caught the warm smells of garlic and cinnamon dancing to the rhythm of their mother's cooking. The garlic, he knew, was from her rabbit stew. Aton had caught a pair of rabbits the day before. The cinnamon, though, he hoped, was part of some dessert.

## CHAPTER 2

## *Treasures*

That night, with bellies full of rabbit stew and warm cinnamon bread, the brothers got ready for bed. They shared a room, their little one-story cabin too small for more than two bedrooms, a kitchen, and a hearth. Not that they minded. The brothers had their own beds set into opposite sides of the chamber, a window between them and a chest of extra blankets sitting below that. The windowsill was lined with objects—a pinecone found in the winter meadow, a lark's feather trapped under a pretty stone, three sheep teeth, and a strange, twisted root they'd pulled from the garden—their shared cache of treasures.

Aaron pulled a sleeping shirt over his head. Aton was taking a brush to his teeth when his younger brother spoke up. "How's your knee?"

Still brushing, Aton pulled up his pant leg to show his brother the appendage in question. He'd taken off the bandage to wash himself before bed and their mother hadn't bothered to tie a new one. The wound was smaller with a hard, dark, red-brown scab crusting over the top of it. Aton let the fabric fall, covering the leg again and turning his attention back to his teeth.

Aaron had known it was a deep gash when he saw the bone. Most of their scrapes barely lasted a few hours, but this one might linger for a whole day. Not that it mattered. Aton would heal just fine. Aton wouldn't even have a scar to show for it. It was just Aaron couldn't stop thinking about what his mother had said—"Thank the gods for werewolf healing"—and on the same day he'd been wondering about the sheep not being afraid of him, about being a werewolf.

"What were you thinking anyway—climbing the peak?" Aaron asked the question more harshly than he'd meant to, but his brain was buzzing with something, only he couldn't have said what, nor could he knock it loose. It grated on him, making him irritated.

Aton turned after spitting into the basin below the sliver of mirror on his dresser. "Jealous?"

"That you get to wash and darn your own pants? No."

"That I was brave enough to get that flower for Mother."

Aaron's fingers stilled in the action of adjusting his shirt as he considered the question. "No," he said after a moment, going back to his clothes.

"Liar," his brother chuckled, pouring a little water over the brush to wash it before setting it next to the basin.

"Am not. Mother may have been happy about the flower, but then she was mad at you. Then you got hurt on top of being punished. If that's what bravery gets you, you're welcome to it."

It was Aton's turn to pause, looking at the lighter-haired boy. "Really?"

"Yes," Aaron replied firmly, putting his day clothes in the basket by the door to be washed.

"Aren't you two asleep yet?" Their mother came in, a fist-sized sunstone hanging from a cord around one wrist, giving the room just that extra bit of light.

"Just about to," Aaron said, diving into his bed and pulling up the covers. His brother did the same a little less quickly.

Their mother nodded, taking the dark, heavy blanket from the hook on their wall and throwing it over the larger sunstone sitting by the open door, smothering the light and plunging the room into near darkness. The only light left was a thin beam cast through their open window by the sliver of the crescent moon and the cheery, orange glow radiating from the palm-sized sunstone around her wrist.

"To sleep with you both; you've had a full day today." She leaned down and kissed Aton on his forehead before going over to Aaron. "Tomorrow's market day, so I'll be gone till sunset unless I sell out early. You'll both need to weed the garden before letting the sheep out." She smoothed a fringe of hair away from Aaron's brow before planting a kiss on it. "Keep them out of trouble, won't you?"

Aaron smiled and nodded, though if she was talking about just the sheep, or his brother too, he wasn't sure.

Walking to the door, she turned at the threshold. "Good night." Blowing them a kiss, she left them to sleep, taking the last of the warm glow with her.

# CHAPTER 3

# *Different*

As their mother had left with the sun, breakfast had been strips of salted mutton and leftover slices of the cinnamon bread slathered in butter. It was an excellent way to start the day, Aaron thought, though the weeding afterward in the pale light of dawn had been less enjoyable. His back ached and the chill of winter still lurked in those early hours. Of course, neither discomfort had lasted too long.

"A werewolf fur coat would've been nice," Aaron chuckled to himself.

His brother either hadn't heard or hadn't cared as he opened the gates for the foolish flock to begin grazing. The sheep ran out of the pen in a wooly avalanche, bleating all the while and jumping on top of one another to be the first to the fields.

Aaron found a sunny spot in the soft grass still glistening with recently melted frost. He watched their livelihood munching their own breakfasts and sighed. Living on a farm as they did, there were always other things the boys could've done besides watching the sheep. There weren't any predators on the mountaintop, besides themselves, to protect the sheep from, and one boy could've made sure that the sheep didn't wander off the pasture, only their mother liked to give them an easy day whenever she went to market. Maybe she felt guilty that she wasn't there to share in the burden, though selling their cheese and wool was a different kind of work.

Aaron thought Aton should be brining cheese, as he'd failed to do it the day before in favor of flower picking.

Aaron turned around to tell Aton so but saw that the older boy wasn't sitting and watching the sheep like he was. His big brother was standing a little way off, looking out pensively at the rest of the mountain range.

Aton did that sometimes—gazed off into the mountains with a look in his eyes that said there was something out there, something more than what they had on the farm. Aaron never looked, at least not with anything like burning curiosity or the desire to see more. He liked their little home, their little family, and their flock of woolly headed sheep that moved around him like he was a rock in their river, even if he did think they should run away from him.

He knew that Aton did too. He loved him and their mother and even their sheep. Only every once in a while, he would gaze at the range for a little longer than just a passing glance, and Aaron could tell that his brother was wondering about what lay beyond. Those glances made him wonder if the wolf in Aton somehow pulled at him more strongly than his own seemed to.

"What are you looking at?" Aaron called, tired of his own thoughts.

"Nothing," Aton said with a shrug, turning away from the view, but away from Aaron too. His dark hair reflected the light, looking more chestnut than its typical umber.

"We are so different." Aaron mumbled his thought softly.

Aton had been born only a minute earlier than him, but they were far from identical twins. With Aaron's fair hair and skin nearly the color of milk, he was almost as bright as the sheep's wool, while his elder twin was like his shadow with skin that darkened at the slightest kiss from the sun and rich brown hair. The contrast in their appearances was striking. Only their eyes were the same, deep violet.

Aaron clearly took after their mother, while, in theory, Aton took after their father. It was probably where their shared eye color had come from. They'd never met the man to confirm this, of course, and their mother would get a wistful expression on her face whenever he was mentioned, so the twins had learned not to bring him up. Not that it stopped the questions that burned on their tongues. At night sometimes, Aaron and Aton would stay up and wonder about him, giving a voice to their questions, none of which they could answer with certainty. What sort of man had he been? Had he been a werewolf too? What had happened to him? Why wasn't he there? When they got to that final question the conversation usually petered out. They had asked their mother the last question when they were very young and before they'd learned better, but she'd said only that he was gone. He loved them all very much, but he couldn't be with them now. As an explanation it hadn't been enough to quell questions, but the tears that'd come to her eyes when she spoke about him had stopped them from asking again. Their little family shared everything they had from chores to sweets, but there was so much more to wonder about, so many more secrets—

A harsh little bleat caught Aaron's ears, and he turned to see one of the spring lambs wandering off toward the rockier parts of the pasture, closer to the edge of the plateau.

"I'll get him," Aton called and jogged off after the escapee.

Aaron watched him go for a pace, seeing him gain on the wee little beast with hardly an effort. With an exasperated sigh, Aaron threw himself back into the grass. Trying to block out the questions running around his head, he pictured the pursuit in his mind. He heard his brother and the lamb's footsteps. They were close. There was a pause as his brother pounced, then the serenity was shattered with a burst of indignant bleats. He had to smile, imagining his brother tangled in a pile with the little fluff ball protesting so adamantly.

Only, in the next moment, the bleats turned into terrified screams. At once, Aaron was on his feet, sprinting across the grass toward the sound. He skidded on the bare patch of dirt, arriving at where he'd heard the commotion.

The lamb lay in the turf nearby, thrashing and shrieking in obvious pain and panic, unable to rise, but Aaron was looking for Aton. His brother was sitting nearby, back to him, hunched over on himself.

"Aton!" He sprinted around to look him in the face.

Sweat coated the older boy's forehead and upper lip above his gritted teeth. Aton pressed his hands to his right thigh, where a trickle of bright red blood passed through his fingers. Aaron knelt down, shoving Aton's hands away to get a better view of the wound. Two little circular punctures greeted him through a torn patch in his brother's trousers, red soaking into the fabric. Their mother would be furious that he'd ruined another pair of pants.

It wasn't as bloody as the wound he'd gotten the day before, but it seemed far more sinister. Aaron's twin hadn't gotten a cut like that tripping over a rock or fighting with a sheep. "Aton," he said again, a tremble creeping into his voice.

"Go." Aton grunted, pushing at his shoulder.

Aaron barely heard Aton over the sound that came from behind him. The noise was harsh and brittle, like a gale gusting through dried leaves, though with no wind, Aaron understood that it was something else. He spun from the bloody holes to find himself face-to-face with a pair of predatory eyes, a black, forked tongue, and a diamond-shaped head as big as the boy's fist. The head was poised atop a long, thick, sepia-colored body. Reared back as it was, it would've been almost as tall as Aaron's waist had he been standing. Crouched down, their eyes were level to one another's. The snake's cat-slit pupils fixed themselves on his face, the skin of which he knew was becoming paler by the moment. Aaron was transfixed by those eyes, whose hues ranged from amber, to copper, to honey, struck through with those two black chasms, waving to and fro, but always locked on him. He felt horrified and fascinated at the same time, though not in equal portions. His shoulders came up and he hunched in on himself, feeling small and fearful, still staring at those eyes.

"Go, run!" his brother roared.

Aton pushed at him with one hand, keeping the other on the puncture. It didn't help though; Aaron couldn't run. His legs felt like ice—frozen to the spot.

The snake watched them, tongue tasting the air, tasting Aaron, and apparently decided it liked what it sensed. It struck. Lightning quick it came, with inch-long fangs extended toward his cloud-pale skin.

Only the bite never landed. Aaron blinked as the creature hung in midair, snapping and coiling and hissing mere inches from his face. He glanced up and saw Aton holding the snake around its neck. He'd caught it mid-strike. His older brother looked down at him, and Aaron saw his own astonishment mirrored in his twin's face.

The snake, still struggling to be free, writhed in the hand that held it. The older boy brought his fist down and pinned the animal to the dirt. Aaron saw him frantically searching the ground with his free hand, trying to find something to restrain the serpent with. It was bucking and squirming, and his brother nearly lost his grip on it twice, and then his hand bumped into a rock just big enough to fire in his palm. Aton seized it at once and hoisted it high into the air, but there he hesitated, his fist trembling above his head. His dark twin looked up to meet his eyes, the twins of his own. Both sets were wide and uncertain. Aton looked at Aaron and Aaron gazed back, both boys struggling under the weight of fear and revulsion and indecision.

A moment of resolution flashed in Aton's eyes, steel setting his features before he brought down the rock. A terrible cracking noise rung out as the stone struck the thrashing snake. He raised the stone again, smashing it over and over onto the skull of the creature, each successive blow emitting a progressively wetter and squishier *thud*.

When the stone came away, dark crimson, the snake had stopped thrashing some time before. Aton stopped, letting the rock fall to the dirt with a much more muffled impact. The dark-haired youth looked at the bloody mess he'd made on the ground and then to the same coating on his hands, studying his grisly handiwork with a strange detachment. Finally, he looked back to Aaron. Cold metal shimmered in the older boy's gaze, a gaze Aaron could describe only as determined, grim. Aaron had never seen his brother look like that before and it sent a shiver racing up his back.

Then it was as if all the strength fled the burgeoning warrior at once. Aton fell backward onto the ground, catching himself before he collapsed, trembling from head to toe.

Aaron, freed from the trance, scrambled on hands and knees to his brother's side. Looking back to the injured leg, he saw the wound had turned an ugly shade of purple-red. Sweat was back on his brow and lip as if they'd never left. In the adrenaline-fueled surge of unbelievable speed and strength it must've taken to catch the snake, his brother had forgotten about the poison. Now that the danger had passed, it reminded him. Aton clutched his leg, heat radiating off the limb, breath coming in hard gasps, his whole body shaking, tears welling in his eyes.

Aaron was shaking too, but for a different reason. His eyes glanced to the lamb, which had been the snake's last, unfortunate victim. It lay quietly twitching in the grass, dead, or very nearly so. This wound wasn't like the scrapes they'd gotten, wasn't even like the terrible gash in his knee—this was a snakebite. Could werewolves heal from a snakebite? Looking on his brother, thrashing with the pain, he didn't think so. His own tears burst forth with this certainty. Aton, like the lamb, was going to die.

"Go, Aaron," his brother said through clenched teeth.

"Go?" he stammered. "Go where?"

"Go get Mother."

"She's at the market. It would take me forever to get to town and then her spot. It'd be just as long getting her back here. Aton, are you going to be alright?"

"Go get Mother," Aton growled again.

Aaron knew his brother was trying to protect him by sending him away so that he wouldn't have to watch what came next. Aaron knew this, but he couldn't just leave Aton there to die alone. He didn't want to lose Aton. He didn't want his brother to leave him. He wanted the three of them to be together always.

Aaron could hardly see through the tears as he placed his hands on the injured leg. It was burning hot, the skin feeling like it had live coals just below its surface. Still he kept his hands over the wound, as though his touch and will alone could heal the affliction. He squeezed his eyes as tight as he could, the tears leaking through, and willed his brother to heal himself just like he had when he'd fallen off the peak.

His brother screamed. Aaron fell backward, eyes wide with surprise and anguish that he'd caused his brother so much pain. "Aton, I'm sorry, I—"

But Aton wasn't looking at him. His face still covered with sweat, his normally tan skin an ashen gray, he was staring wide-eyed at his leg. Aaron followed his gaze and was struck dumb by what he saw. Aton's leg looked completely healed. The punctures were gone, the surrounding skin smooth, no longer an angry red and swollen. It had returned to its olive hue without even a scab or a scratch to tell the story. It was fixed, faster than even their advanced werewolf healing could've done. His brother was whole and completely healed.

Aaron looked down at his hands then and saw them glowing with a pale spring-green light. He tottered backward for the second time in as many minutes. Staring at his fingers, so familiar and yet so strange, cloaked in this new hue, he had to wonder—had he done it? Had he healed his brother? His fingers were tingling, not uncomfortably, as the soft light began to fade. He turned the appendages over and over, checking for any sort of permanent change, but with the light gone they looked as they always had.

Aaron looked up and met Aton's eyes. Both sets of eyes shared the same wide surprise, but as confused as he was, Aaron's chest swelled with relief and gratitude for whatever had just happened. His face split into a wide grin before his vision started to blur. All at once a lightheaded feeling took over and he felt exhausted, too tired to even keep upright. The last thing he saw before he passed out was the worry on his brother's face.

## CHAPTER 4

# *Slanted Shadows*

Hours later, Aaron woke. He was in a bed, but not his; it was too big. Without looking around he knew he must be in his mother's. She did that when he or his brother had a bad dream. He hadn't had a bad dream, though. He'd passed out. This was the first time he'd ever remembered passing out.

Maybe he was sick. Did werewolves get sick? He knew human kids did. He'd talked to the boys in town when his mother had taken them to market from time to time. They'd mentioned sick siblings or parents, though Aaron hadn't understood and had asked his mother about it. Her explanation was that werewolves rarely got sick and never from the sorts of things that humans contracted all the time, colds and influenza and the like. So he probably wasn't sick.

He took stock of himself, trying to mentally examine each part of his body. He was still tired, but not exhausted. He wanted to feel his forehead. A boy he knew had mentioned that he'd get a fever when he was sick, but when he shifted his position, he found Aton curled up next to him. Maybe that was why he'd woken up in their mother's bed—they could both fit. His sleeping twin was pressed in close, holding his hand protectively. He was always protecting him.

Aaron sat up with only a little effort, pulled in his knees, and took his hand out of Aton's grasp gently. It must've been the middle of the night because the house was still and dark save for the moonlight casting long shadows as it poured through the open windows. He didn't feel hot, or in pain, or in any of the other ways he thought he should feel if he were sick. So he wasn't sick.

His head buzzed, recalling the events—the snake, the poison, and the light. He couldn't be sure what that last had meant, but he thought he knew.

"Magic." The word came out of him so quietly that it felt more like a puff of air than speaking. But that was impossible. He couldn't have magic. Magic was a story from Rahovan, the continent across the sea to the west, the land of myth and monsters. There was nothing like that on this continent, on Jenoha. An entire sea, the Karnak Sea, separated their home from its sinister sister continent. There were demons, monstrous dark things, in both places, but they were all over the world, including the other islands that were supposed to be out in the world, but that was it. On Rahovan, though, there were twelve-foot-tall bears, alligators big enough to swallow a man whole, and eagles so huge that they could pick up a ten-year-old child and fly off with them. Aaron had never heard of any of them on Jenoha.

Of course, they'd said there were werewolves over there too. They were "savage, hungry beast-men that would just as soon eat you as look as you." He hadn't known he was one of those when he'd heard the stories. His mother had told them what they were only last year, when they'd been five. They hadn't been to town since. If werewolves existed in Jenoha without anyone knowing, maybe magic did too.

He didn't want magic. Having magic would make him even more different, even more strange and dangerous, even more of a monster according to the "normal people" of the town. Their mother always said that if they found out that they were werewolves, it would mean big trouble. Now if he had magic…

"I'm so dead." He thumped his head down on his raised knees. He squeezed his eyes tight and tried to focus. "I don't have magic," he whispered to his kneecaps. "I don't have magic. I don't have magic. I'm not different. I'm not different from Aton or Mother." If he said it enough, maybe it'd be true.

He turned his head to rest his ear on his knee and sighed. He began studying the moonlight to distract himself from thoughts of werewolves, of magic, and of being some sort of monster. He blinked. Focusing closer, he found that the moonlight was wrong. The beams were brighter than they should've been. Thinking back to the night before, he remembered that the moon had been a crescent, nowhere near full, nowhere near large enough to cast that sort of light. He was pretty sure that even if the moon had been full, the hour was so late that the shafts shouldn't be coming in through the window at the angle the shadows implied. Strangest of all was its color. It was green as a new blade of grass.

With his heart pounding, Aaron slid out of bed. The motion woke up Aton, who snorted at the sudden disturbance, but noticed his odd behavior and followed him in silence as the younger twin tiptoed toward the kitchen. They had few actual doors in their little home, so there were no barriers as they snuck from their mother's room through the hearth room and into the kitchen. There, seated at the table that was a makeshift divider between kitchen and hearth, staring up at the millions of stars above them, was their mother. Between her hands she held a great glowing sphere of bright green light, the same color as her eyes. The boys both stared, silent and still with mouths hanging agape, watching the ball of magic softly pulse and throb. She turned to look at them then, green light illuminating her soft features and lips, which were pulled up in a lopsided smile. She shifted the orb to one slender hand, held up a single finger on the other, and pressed it to her lips in a gesture for silence. The moonlight glinted off her ring like another tiny star. Perhaps, Aaron thought, he wasn't so different after all.

**CHAPTER 5**

# *The Eight*

Sleep was a foreign concept to Aaron that night. Back in his own bed, he'd shut his eyes and tried to will himself into unconsciousness, but thinking about that light between his mother's fingers just made his lids fly back open every time. He forced himself to be still, lying next to his brother, who appeared just as ridged on his own mattress when he glanced to the other bed, until the first rays of dawn touched the walls with a rosy glow.

As though the light had been a signal, he threw off his sheets and bolted toward the open door. Aton had obviously been in the same frame of mind, springing from his own sheets a second later, but bounding to the door so quickly that the twins nearly collided in the narrow archway. They raced through the small house in a matter of moments, only to half-tumble at the base of the kitchen table.

Their mother was sitting in the same spot where they'd found her the night before, a crisp morning breeze ruffling through her light hair while she drank a steaming cup of tea. She smiled at the boys, who were jostling for position and gulping for the air to speak first.

There was something a little sad in that smile, Aaron thought, but he was too excited to truly pay attention as he blurted, "You can do magic?" There couldn't be any other question in the whole world save for that one.

And then he found more. "And I have magic too? Does Aton have magic? Is that why he could catch that snake? Can all werewolves use magic?"

"Sit," his mother said, pointing to the bench with an indulgent smile on her lips, her ring flashing with the movement.

The brothers rushed to obey, muscles fairly trembling with their anticipation.

She set down her cup, the smell of lavender curling up in fragrant wisps, and picked up a small book. Aaron recognized it. Books were expensive, so they had only a few. Still, she'd said it was of the utmost importance that both boys knew how to read. He knew without looking at the cover, from the size and color, that this one was called *Prayers to the Five Gods of Eris*.

Opening the little volume, she began to answer his questions in order. "Yes, I have magic, and, yes, so do you. Aton, it would seem, didn't inherit that particular gift, but has found a different one all his own." Her green eyes flicked up to regard the darker boy with a clever smirk. "Aton, as demonstrated by his handling of that snake, appears to be much faster than any six-year-old boy, werewolf or no, has any right to be."

"What does that mean?" Aton spoke, a frown etched into his youthful features.

Her smile widened. "That you're special."

Aton's frown softened, but didn't completely leave his face. He just stood there, looking thoughtful.

Their mother's voice pulled Aaron's attention back to her smiling face. "Not all werewolves can do magic. I've heard it's quite rare in all species, especially here on Jenoha."

"What about on Rahovan?" Aaron asked.

She thought before answering, placing the open book down in front of her. "On Rahovan it must be more common. Most of the stories about magic that I was ever told as a girl, outside of our own family histories, were tales from that place, tales of magic and of whole packs of werewolves living alongside even greater beasts," she added, showing her teeth menacingly. Rather than scaring the boys, the expression only served to crinkle her nose in a comical way.

"Did our family come from Rahovan then? Did they take a ship over the sea? Were there sea monsters? Did they use their magic to slay them?" Aaron asked on a single breath.

"No, no," she laughed. "As far back as we've traced, my side of the family has always lived on Jenoha, just as the magic has always been in our blood."

"And the werewolf part too?" Aaron chirruped.

Her smile slipped just a touch. "No, your werewolf part came from your father. Jenoha doesn't have many werewolves. That's what he'd always told me, anyway."

Aaron refused to let the melancholy take over this monumental conversation. "Maybe he just didn't know where to find them. We've got elves and dwarves on Jenoha too, just not around here, and there have to be nokken out in the Karnak Sea."

"You're probably right." Her smile recovered some of its joy.

"Do they have magic too?"

Aton piped up. "Elves are the best at magic. That's what all the stories say."

"You're right; many of the Eight have casters, on both continents. Werewolves, humans, elves, nokken, and dwarves all carry the potential for the magical gift."

"But not the other three." Aton spoke, his voice a shade darker.

"Yes and no," she replied. "The First God—"

"Varro!" Aaron yipped, happy to add to the conversation however he could.

"Yes, Varro. When he created the dragons, he made them strong, powerful, and huge with invulnerable scales, the power of flight, fire, and teeth longer than my arm. He decided that they didn't need any more gifts."

"What about the Ancients?" Aaron asked.

"The Ancients are all dead," Aton replied.

"I know that," he shot back.

"Yes, Varro's first race, the Ancients, are all gone. So we don't know if they could use magic or not, but it's likely that they could."

"And demons." Aton's voice dropped even lower. Aaron could feel his shoulders creeping up just a little, a shiver running through him.

"The demons have their own tricks," she answered. "The story goes that a group of demons stole power from Varro while he was busy creating the other Eight. Only when they touched the magic, the power soured. It poisoned them, leaving them twisted, terrible things, the power they stole becoming terrible like them in turn."

"Those were the greater demons," Aton said with a bit more conviction.

"Yes," their mother said in a breathy voice. "The stories say that those first few demons may have been Ancients once. Then they took the power and turned to terrible monsters. They thought themselves gods too and gave a bit of that tainted power to some lesser beasts, to the animals they could find in the fields and seas. The ones they touched turned into lesser demons and became the greater demons' own craven servants."

"But Varro died. He fell to create the world. So how do we still have magic?" Aaron asked, trying to steer the conversation back to his new talent.

"Varro didn't die," she corrected gently. "He sleeps beneath our feet, so his magic is all around us." She spun the book on the table so the familiar title faced them. "Also, he left the Five Gods here to take care of everything while he's asleep, each of them in charge of an element."

"Indris for fire, Pendry for water, Belkis for wind, Arden for stone, and Enoch for light," Aaron said by rote.

"Correct."

"So they give us the magic?"

She picked her teacup back up and sipped, readying herself before replying. "I think we should save the rest of this explanation for your first magic lesson."

"What? Why?" he whined.

She chuckled. "Don't worry; we'll start them soon."

Aton frowned.

"And don't you worry either," she said, reaching up and brushing his hair down where it had been tussled from the sleepless night before. "Market day is coming soon. I'll have something ready for you too just after that." She stood and kissed the top of Aton's head, pulling Aaron over to do the same to him. "Now go and get on with your chores."

## CHAPTER 6

## *The Five Gods*

"What spell am I going to learn first?"

They were in the kitchen, Aaron and his mother, sitting at the little table under the window turned golden by the afternoon light. The kitchen felt warm, drying herbs hanging from the ceiling perfuming the air with scents of thyme and rosemary.

Aaron had left Aton outside after finishing his chores, his twin looking moodily over his fluffy charges as they grazed. It had given Aaron a thrill to be different, to be special, and he tingled with excitement, waiting for his mother's next words.

"We're not ready for spells just yet," she replied, eyes trained on her task.

She was laying objects out on the wooden surface, each in a tiny bowl—a feather, a smooth pebble, a pool of water, and a lit candle. Behind the items she set four tiny carvings, odd forms that didn't look like anything in particular to Aaron, but each with a particular form and pattern that made them unique from each other.

His shoulders slumped. "We're not going to pray, are we?"

"No," she replied with a chuckle. "I brought these out to remind you of each of the domains within the world and the gods that oversee them. You'll want to think on them as we move along in your training."

One carving sat alone, without a bowl. It was just a little bigger than the others.

"Why doesn't Enoch ever get an offering?"

"Enoch is the God of Light."

"Yeah, but if you use a feather for Belkis's wind, couldn't you use a sunstone for Enoch's light?"

"Enoch's offering is a little more special than that." She had a little smirk on her lips as she said it.

This got his attention. "What is it? I've never seen it."

His mother opened her hand. Just as it had happened the night after the snake, a ball of bright green light appeared above her palm. This was a smaller sphere, but no less brilliant. It was then Aaron noticed a smell. He couldn't name it, but it did seem familiar. It was clean and sweet.

"We are. Enoch's light lives in each of us."

The verdant light reflected in the boys wide eyes. "Wow," he whispered.

She closed her hand, dousing the glow, the scent lingering, but dissipating soon after.

He shook his head, trying to gain his composure. "Enoch is the strongest then." It was a statement instead of a question.

"We Enochists think He is."

This was the first time he'd heard the label. "Enochish?"

She laughed. "Enochists," she corrected. "It's a religion, believed mainly by humans, that holds Enoch as the first of Varro's Five Gods, his heir. The old god then created the other four to serve him, to take care of this world, Eris, while He takes care of us."

"There are people who don't believe that?"

"Not everyone believes as we do."

"What do they believe?"

"From what I was told, most of the other Eight—the elves, dwarves, and nokken—believe mainly in Varroism. Of course, I have to imagine some of them could be Enochist." She gave a little shrug.

"Varroism? Like the old god?"

"Yes. Varroism believes that the Five Gods are just greater elementals, taking care of the old god's body till he wakes again. They need only worship Varro himself to gain his blessings."

"Greater elementals?"

"There's a lot to teach you." She ran her hand through his hair. "Spirits and elementals are the servants of the gods. They're in the water, the air, the ground beneath our feet, the flame." She blew a little gust toward the candle, making the fire dance on its wick. "They live in their element and tend it, like you tend the flock, making sure it's healthy and safe."

"But Enoch doesn't have any elementals or spirits?"

"We're his spirits. We tend the light within ourselves."

Aaron sat with this new information. His tiny brow creased as he thought hard about what his mother had said.

"So." His words came slowly as his thoughts formed. "You said that the people below were afraid of things that were different, like they would be afraid of werewolves. But if humans think Enoch's light is in each of us, they wouldn't be afraid of people who can use it." His words became stronger as he reached his conclusion. "So I don't have to worry about them finding out that I can use magic." He grinned as he thought about showing the other boys, the next time he went into town, the incredible spells he was going to learn. They would think he was amazing.

Her smile faded. "No."

His smile fell too. "Why not?"

"Most Enochists, the ones who can't use the power, believe that all magic belongs to Enoch. The light within us is supposed to help us live our lives, have children, flourish, and give Enoch thanks for our strength and is protection. To use the power for more, to light a fire or water a field, to make our lives easier, is a terrible insult to him. To those Enochists, people who warp his power, the magic of Enoch, are evil and must be stopped."

"Stopped? How?"

When she didn't reply he felt his shoulders creeping up to meet his ears.

"So they kill them?"

"Even more readily than they kill werewolves."

Aaron gulped audibly.

"But don't worry," she said, laying a warm hand against his cheek. "I lived my whole life hiding what I am, even from you two for a while, and no one ever found out. No one down in the town knows we have power, just like no one knows we're werewolves. As long as we keep it hidden and only practice inside, we'll be just fine."

Her reassuring smile helped settle him a bit.

"How can you be an Enochist?" He wanted to know. "You can use magic, but you're not supposed to."

She let her hand fall back to her lap. "I am an Enochist. I believe that Enoch gave us his light, but my mother told me that not everyone understood his intentions very well. She said that those people, the ones who couldn't use magic, were jealous of the ones who could, so they were the ones who made up the rule that no one should use it, ever. She said that Enoch wouldn't have given us the power if he didn't want us to use it. But because there are many more people who can't use magic, opposed to those who can, I was taught to hide my skill. I behaved as any other proper young woman would—learning needlework and attending prayers. It was only at night that my mother would teach me about casting and using the spirits. Maybe that's why I'm so close to fire, as we were always whispering and learning next to the hearth at night."

His mother got a faraway look in her eyes, as though she were looking back on that hearth, next to her own mother. Aaron wanted to give her a moment with her memory. He looked to the table, to the statues and their offerings, to the prayer book. He picked up the book idly and opened it. Past the cover and title page, he looked to the first spell and blinked. He'd seen the book before, of course, but something new had struck him.

"Mother," he said, breaking her out of her daze. "If this book is Enochist, why isn't the first prayer to him?" He pointed to the first page, where a prayer to the Five Gods was shown, each god's symbol scrawled in the corners and below the bottom line.

"That book isn't Enochist, though there are prayers to him in there. I left my prayer book with my other things when I left home. This particular book is filled with prayers from The Order." Then, quietly, she said, "It was your father's."

This information launched the boy into a new flurry of questions. "My father? What's The Order? Is it a holy brotherhood? Was my father a knight, fighting for the gods?" He pantomimed holding a sword, ready to do battle.

"I think I've been reading you too many stories before bed." She smiled, but it was still a bit sad. "No, The Order is the third religion on Eris. They believe that the Five Gods are equal, in power, in importance, and should be held so in our esteem. That's what Bain, the first werewolf, taught his children."

"The first werewolf." Aaron's eyes widened, the mere thought of a first werewolf activating his youthful imagination. "What was he like?"

"We'll save the origins of the Eight for another day." She set her hand on his head and ruffled his hair before continuing her explanation. "The Order says that we must pray and thank *all* Five Gods for their contributions."

"Does The Order think that it's wrong to use magic too?"

"No, only Enochists believe the power belongs to Enoch alone."

His voice dropped as he spoke till it was just above a whisper. "So a werewolf caster wouldn't be in trouble if they lived with a group that followed The Order, or Varroists?"

She looked at him, and he knew his face showed his concern.

"I know this is hard to understand," she said gently, "but we're human."

"I thought we were werewolves."

"Werewolves are still half human. We can't breathe under water like nokken. We can't live away from Enoch's light, burrowing in tunnels, like the dwarves."

"But the elves?"

"I don't know," she sighed, resting her cheek on her palm and stroking his hair with the other hand. "My mother told me that elves didn't think much of humans. I believe she even said that elves found humans 'brutal, barbaric, and backward.' Though she also said that werewolves were 'savage monsters that would eat me up if I ever met one,' and yet your father loved me." Pain flashed across her face for only an instant, but Aaron saw it. "So she could've been wrong about the elves too. Maybe you'll meet an elf one day; then you can tell me what they're really like."

"What about Father's pack? You said he believed in The Order, and he must have had a family. We could go live with them."

"I used to think we would, but your father came from far away." Her voice was a little softer.

"Far away? From Rahovan?"

She turned her head, looking out the window, maybe to hide tears, maybe to check on his brother. Aaron wanted to know more but, a little late, he remembered their rule about discussing their father.

"So what spell am I going to learn first?"

She turned back to him, letting out a little sigh and giving him a weak smile. "First, you'll need to get a handle on your energy, how it flows through your body, and how you can move it to one part of you. Using it will come later."

"But I can use spells already. I healed Aton," he protested.

"I know." The next smile she gave him was a genuine one. "I'm so proud of you. I don't even know any healing spells, but just because you did it once doesn't mean you can repeat it without practice."

He ducked his head before asking his next question, afraid to meet her eyes. "Why did-why did it hurt him?" He remembered his brother's yell when he'd touched the injury with his light and healed it. It was like he'd opened a new wound instead of closing one.

His mother slid from her chair to kneel on the floor before him, taking his smaller hands in hers. "Do you remember when you helped me fix the sheep pen and you got that splinter?"

"Yeah," he replied, confused by the change in topic.

"Do you remember telling me that it hurt you more when I took it out than when you'd gotten it?"

"Yes."

"Maybe healing magic is a little bit like that. It has to hurt a little to heal." She kissed his fingers and Aaron remembered when she'd done that before, that day she'd pulled the wood from the pad of his thumb.

"Now, let me tell you a little more about how you can use that light within you."

## CHAPTER 7

## *Sources*

"It's not fair," Aton said. The larger boy's arms were crossed over his chest, his face clouded with a dark expression as he said it.

It'd been less than a week since the snake incident, but Aton was different. Aaron could feel it. His older twin had always been quieter than him, more serious, but he hadn't smiled in two days and the steel had never really left his eyes. Of course he could just be jealous of all the attention the younger brother was getting.

"Sorry," Aaron said, not feeling sorry at all. "Mother says I have another magic lesson today."

"While I have to tend the sheep and finish up the chores by myself."

"You just need something to keep you busy. Have you fixed your pants yet?"

Aton's scowl deepened. He laughed, turning his back on the other boy, and sprinted toward the house.

They'd spent the morning piling bundles of wool and rounds of cheese into their cart, then covering it with an oil-soaked hide to keep any rain off, in preparation for their mother's trip to town on the following day. After the cart was loaded, the next task was for Aaron to give their cart horse, Apple, a good currycombing. Apple was a quarter horse, just the kind of sturdy breed you'd want on a farm for hauling things. She had a lovely yellow palomino coloring with three white socks and a blaze that ran from her forelock to her pink nose. Her favorite treats were of course apples, when they were in season, hence her name.

"You've got a few more months till I can get you a fresh one," the boy said to the horse, straightening her forelock. To appease the animal, he pulled a small, slightly wizened apple from his pocket. "Sorry," he said, holding out the fruit.

The horse didn't seem to mind, reaching out with her black-and-pink velvety lips and her big wet tongue to scoop the offering into her mouth, crunching down on it happily. He pet her absently with one hand as he grimaced, wiping his other hand on his pant leg, rubbing off the horse saliva that had pooled there.

Under their one tree, which sat on another little rise in the pasture across the plateau from the peak, was one of Aaron's favorite spots to sit and think. With it being nestled in a particularly deep pocket of rich soil, and with their mountain being at the tail end of the range, so the winters didn't last too long, the tree did well enough. It wasn't the tallest or the straightest, bending against the frequent winds, but it never failed to bloom every spring and give the sweetest fruits every fall. They could see it from the kitchen window, so it was a constant reminder to the twins of tasty apple pies and cobblers, but Aaron thought he liked the tree best in spring, when it burst with tiny white blossoms that lent the breezes a beautiful perfume.

It wasn't far from blooming time now, he thought as he ran into the kitchen. His mother was sitting at the table again, a basket at her feet, folding the laundry she'd just brought in.

"That time already?" she smiled, tucking a strand of loose hair behind her ear.

"Yes," he chirped. "And look." The boy stared down at his hand, his eyes focused, his face creased in heavy concentration. Sweat broke out on his brow when his tiny digits began to glow a dim, faint, spring green. It flickered and wavered, but continued for the count of twenty, that same sweet smell seeming to envelope him.

Letting out the breath he'd been holding in a huff, the light vanishing with it, he looked up at his mother with a big grin splitting his face in two. "Did you see?"

She clapped her hands. "I did; that was very good." She reached out and enveloped him in a hug. "And with only a few days of teaching too."

"And when I did it before," he corrected once she'd released him. "I remembered how it felt when all of my light went into Aton's leg that time."

"Of course." She nodded to the chair opposite her. "Sit down and we'll practice some more."

He did, nodding his head respectfully to the five little statues of the gods sitting on the far end of the table, out of the way but present to oversee the proceedings.

"Since you're progressing so quickly," she said with a smirk, "should we try to do something with that energy?"

"Yes!"

Just then the door banged open and Aton shot past them and over to the counter.

"Oh, Aton," their mother said. "Is everything alright?"

"Fine," the older twin grunted just as his fingers closed around one of the sharper kitchen knives. Holding it firmly but carefully, Aton hurried from the kitchen, closing the door behind him.

Aton's mother and her second son watched him hurry, without running, back out to the sheep field. He sat down in the grass and picked something up. He began to fiddle with it studiously, turning it this way and that, though Aaron couldn't see what it was.

They watched for a few minutes more, but when Aton didn't move again, his mother directed Aaron back to the lesson at hand. "Ready to try a spell?"

"Yes." His response was a little less exuberant after the interruption.

She opened her hand and a diminutive flame appeared, hovering just above her palm, not touching and not burning the alabaster skin.

"That's amazing."

"You've shown me you know how to call your power to your hand, but you'll need more. You need the energy that's all around you. If you can, feel it and then try to pull it toward yourself."

"What do I do with it?"

"Let the energy you pull decide that for now."

Aaron didn't really understand what that meant, but he tried to comply anyway. Calling his own energy was familiar, though in no way easy. It felt a little like trying to get water to all go down in one stream over a rock—slippery, evasive, inevitable—but he could get some to go the way he wanted. When his hand lit up again, he felt around him. They'd practiced that the day before, and he'd found he could feel all sorts of energy swirling around him. He didn't know how to recognize types—wind from water, or from stone, fire, or light even—but there was energy there, a lot of it, coursing all around him, like he was swimming in it. He tried pulling at some, but it resisted. It was the same slippery, elusive feeling that his own power had, only stronger.

Eyes still closed, he said, "I can't get it."

"You'll have to pull at it. Enoch will make you work for it."

He tried again, tugging and then pulling with all he could. He visualized taking great handfuls of the currents and dragging them toward himself. One strand gave way, and he held it, pulling the energy to him and squeezing it together with his own that he had gathered in his hand.

He heard his mother gasp. Opening his eyes, he saw that a tiny flame had appeared above his own palm. His eyes wide and his grin even wider, Aaron felt a surge of pride well up inside him. He'd done it. He'd used magic on purpose. He was on his way to becoming a caster like his mother.

The flame in the dish before Indris popped and went out, the room feeling a little colder for its absence despite the trail of smoke drifting from the extinguished wick. It so surprised Aaron that the little fire in his own palm vanished in turn.

"What is it?" his mother asked, trying to see what he was looking at.

"Indris's candle." He pointed to the pillar that still dripped wax into its dish.

"Oh." She smiled, flicking a finger and relighting the offer. He definitely noted a distinct chill in the air. "No need to worry."

"But why did it go out?"

"Because you pulled the flame's magic to you. I shouldn't be surprised that you'd have a fire affinity like me."

"But why did it go out?" he repeated.

"The energy you pull," she explained, "it has to come from somewhere. You pulled the energy from the flame on the candle to make your own fire in your hand, just like I pulled the warmth from the air to spark it alight again."

"I made the fire go out? So I took the fire's energy?"

"Aaron." She put a hand to his cheek. "It's fine. You pulled the power you needed."

"But when I called light to my hand the room didn't get darker."

"Because Enoch is the strongest god and we're His spirits. We have His light within us that we can call whenever we like. Only, like the fire's energy, it has to come from somewhere. It's not unlimited and when you use it, it gets released back into the world. You can only work with as much energy from yourself as you have to give; that's why we borrow more from the world when we need it."

Aaron thought about this. Taking stock of himself, he found he did feel tired, very tired. The effort of moving his energy and then pulling the fire's had taken it out of him. It was important to know that this power had a cost, that there were limits. Still, looking at the newly lit candle, something felt off.

In the pensive silence, Aaron caught a sound coming in from the open window—a harsh scraping that raked at his ears. His mother must've heard it too, because she craned her neck to look back out the window. Through the portal, he saw Aton. He'd moved his position. He was now sitting cross-legged on a rock, the sheep grazing placidly around him as he worked. In one hand he held the kitchen knife and in the other he held a large branch that must've come from their woodpile out back. They weren't going to cut down their apple tree, so often their mother would trade for wood in the market.

Aton was running the sharp metal over the stick, peeling off layers of bark and thin wooden veneers, coaxing it into some shape, a shape whose one side held a long, thin edge.

His mother shut her eyes and sighed. "It's a good thing I'm going to market tomorrow."

## CHAPTER 8

# *Training*

On the following day, their mother left with the rising sun, as she did on every market day. The boys stood outside the kitchen door and waved to her and Apple as they made their way carefully down the steep mountain road toward town.

They used to go with her, when they'd been really little, but now that they were six and almost grown, she left them home on most market days to continue their chores. They still went on occasion, but they no longer tagged along on every trip.

Still waving, Aaron was surprised to feel like he should be going with her this time. Was it because he knew she was a caster and thought he should protect her? He shook the thought away. That would have been Aton's thought.

As though he'd sensed his thought his brother said, "No magic today then?"

The comment struck the very nerve he'd been thinking about. "Shut up," Aaron snapped.

The cart turned the corner and was lost to sight.

"No, I'm sorry." The older boy stopped waving, letting his hand fall to his side and turning to face him with a frown. "I know you like it. I'm sorry you'll have to miss it."

"Yeah." Aaron looked down, his anger vanishing as quickly as it'd appeared. He kicked a rock with the toe of his boot.

Aaron picked his head back up, pushing the topic aside. "What were you doing yesterday?"

He'd meant to ask when they'd gone to bed the night before, but magic was harder than he'd thought it'd be, and Aaron had fallen asleep without saying anything to his brother.

Aton grinned, and Aaron thought there was something feral in his brother's expression. Without a word of explanation, the dark-haired boy took off toward the house, his lighter twin on his heels—through the kitchen, past the dining table and the hearth, and into the bedroom they shared. Aaron's older brother dropped to one knee, reaching his arm below the crisply made bed, and retrieved the object, holding it aloft in triumph.

The whole thing was long, over two feet, and made of a pair of sculpted branches. The first was thicker, carved straightish, thinning to an edge on one side; the other, shorter piece had been tied on two-thirds of the way down the first.

"It's a sword," Aton proclaimed.

And it did look like one. They'd played swords a few times when they'd both been in the pasture and watching the sheep, but that'd only ever been with plain sticks, hardly more than twigs, they'd find under the apple tree or by the thicker brush. This creation, while not completely straight or sharp exactly, was sturdy, heavy, with a mean-looking edge that when swung looked like it would do damage.

"Why?" the younger asked.

The smirk turned to a frown in an instant. "You said yourself I needed to find something to do."

"But why a sword?"

Aaron's older brother studied his handiwork, as though he'd never considered the question before, and maybe he hadn't. Finally, he replied slowly. "Because of the snake, you know?"

"In case there's another in the field?"

"Sure. Or a coyote, or a mountain lion, or a demon—"

"A demon?"

Aton looked at Aaron with all seriousness. "It's dangerous out there, Aaron, and it's my job to make sure we stay safe."

"Why—"

His brother spoke over him before the question could fully form. "You have magic, but I'm stronger and faster than you are. My talents can be useful too."

They'd separated after that to do the chores and tend to the animals.

Typically, on market days, their mother left with the rising run and returned just before it set. No one wanted to travel the mountains in the dark, after all. So that was why the boys were so surprised when they heard the *clip-clop* of hooves on the trail around noon.

They rushed over to see what was happening, Aaron from the garden, Aton from the stables. Riding up the path, with her wagon mostly empty and Apple puffing in the lead after the long hike, their mother appeared with a sweet smile on her lips. Only she wasn't alone. Behind her cart came another, this one pulled by a stout gray horse, a man in the driver's seat.

Aaron recognized him vaguely as someone their mother often traded with at market, though his name escaped him. Aton stepped forward a pace, almost aggressively, while Aaron stayed in place, watching the carts pass them to pull into the flattish dirt area in front of the barn.

"Aton, Aaron," their mother said, climbing down and walking over to them. The big man strolled up behind her. "You remember my friend Captain York?"

"Ex-captain," the dark-haired man said in a low voice that sounded just a touch embarrassed. "Hello again, boys."

"You've met him a few times at market, and you'll not have known this, but he was once the captain of the guard for Colm, a town to the east of here."

"And then got old," he added. "I came here to get some quiet and warmer weather."

Aaron studied the man a bit closer as he spoke. Some gray glinted around his temples and beard, mixed in with his thick, umber-colored hair. Crow's feet gathered around kind eyes, next to a scar on the left that ran nearly from his temple to his jaw. York had called himself old, but to him, the man still looked plenty strong. Even more striking was his stature, tall and thick as an oak, especially when standing next to their willowy mother.

"York," she continued, "has offered to teach Aton swordsmanship."

That made Aaron and Aton take a step back. Their mother had never brought someone up their mountain before, and now she wanted Aton to spend time with this man? He was barely more than a stranger. It seemed so reckless after all the warnings she'd given them over the years about hiding themselves, not getting too close to anyone, not making real friends with the town's children. Now she wanted Aton to spend time learning from him. Where, in the sheep field?

Their visitor got down on one knee so that he could address the twins at their eye level. His scar shone like a smooth, pale ribbon on his sun-darkened skin. "Your mother tells me you've been making something. I'd like to see it," York said, not unkindly, to Aton.

Aton hesitated, darting a glance to their mother. She gave him a gentle smile and a nod, confirmation that their guest wasn't here to cause trouble. The elder twin turned back to look at the man again, staring at him warily but steadily, then turned and loped back toward the house.

York turned his attention to the second son. "Aaron," he nodded, still on his knee so that he didn't tower over the boy. "Are you interested in learning too?"

Aaron's mouth flopped open, though he didn't know why. He should've jumped at the chance but instead he had no idea how to reply.

Before he had to, his mother spoke up. "Aaron has other talents, ones that I'll be guiding him in."

York looked back at the youth, running his eyes up and down his frame, clearly guessing what those talents might be. When he'd reached his conclusion, he grunted a laugh. "If she's grooming you to be a merchant, you'll find no better teacher in negotiation, that's for certain."

"Oh, York," she protested, though her smile curved a little more at the edges.

Aton reappeared then, wooden sword in hand, blade bared and ready. Still on their level, the old soldier opened his calloused hands and the boy laid the weapon flat against his palms. The instrument that had appeared so long and threatening in the boy's hands looked like the toy it really was in the man's. Yet York ran his eyes seriously along the length of it, not dissimilar to how he'd examined Aaron. He weighed it, held it in one hand, and looked Aton right in the eye as he asked, "You made this?" His voice was soft but serious.

Aton nodded.

"It's decent work. It's heavy and a bit off balance, but I can right that when I come back."

"Come back?" Aton asked.

"As I said," their mother said in her lyrical tone, "York has offered to teach you."

"I'll be coming by once a week, after market, to give you a lesson. Just be mindful to practice what I teach you from week to week and, in time, I've no doubt I can make something of a fighter out of you."

He handed the sword back to Aton and straightened with another grunt, using his knee to stand. Aaron wondered briefly if the man had other scars that they couldn't see. Could he really turn his brother into a warrior?

He looked to his brother and found Aton staring up at the ex-captain, face open with eagerness. If they really were werewolves and Aton had been in wolf form, Aaron didn't doubt that his tail would be wagging.

"Now, why don't you show me what you can do with that twig?" York said, nodding to his new pupil.

# CHAPTER 9

# *Dark Stories*

"And those boys, the sorriest bunch of layabouts you'd ever seen, had the gall to say that I was past my prime. I tell you they weren't calling me old after we ran that first mile in padding—padding mind you, not even armor. They collapsed in the yard, covered in mud and sweat and a few other things more foul-smelling than that, puffing like bulls in the springs, and there I am holding a tankard and smelling like daisies. They were missing their hoes and plows after that, that's for certain." The room shook with his booming laughter while York slapped the table in his mirth, making the plates and cups clatter.

Aaron wanted to plug his ears. It wasn't that he didn't like his brother's teacher; it was just that he'd come to dread his visits. York's arrival after market day always meant twice as much work for him while his twin spent the day under the ex-captain's tutelage. Also, he couldn't practice while the older man was around. Their mother trusted him around the house and to eat the weekly meal with them, but she still told them both not to utter a word about magic or werewolves while he was around.

Aton smirked at his teacher's antics, their mother giving a serene smile as though they were discussing knitting or the weather, as opposed to trouncing young men, as she passed the peas in his direction.

"No, Marilyn," York continued. "You did right to ask me to train Aton up when you did. Boys need to learn to work hard when they're young if they want to get anywhere." The big man took a deep gulp from his cup, glancing at the older boy and then the younger. "When are you going to let Aaron join the fun? What do you say, Aaron? Swordplay's a whole lot more rewarding than balancing books. Trust me; I've done both."

"That's alright," Aaron muttered, taking a sip from his own cup.

A little bit of the joviality fell from the ex-captain's face. He looked down, cutting up his lamb. "Besides, it's important for a boy to know a bit about weapons, not just to man a guard post one day either. He's got to defend himself and his family." The younger twin looked up, curious about his change in tone. "Maybe you ought to let me start training Aaron when I come by next."

He nearly choked on his mouthful of water.

"Aaron's gifts are different," the boys' mother replied smoothly. "Aton's the one with the knack for fighting."

The man studied her and frowned. "They're not going to be together forever, Marilyn."

Both boys looked at him. "One day they'll live their own lives, and even if Aaron takes over the farm, it's still not a bad skill to have if someone tries to mug him in an alley on market day."

Their mother sat, her face peaceful, her eyes dedicated to watching her slender hands cutting her food into small bites. "They'll be together when it matters."

They all stared at her, but she returned none of the looks directed her way, only continued to serenely eat her meal.

"I guess they are still young," York said finally to fill the silence. "They'll be together up here a good long time yet. And you're right enough that Aton was born to this, strong, fast, and quick to learn. Enoch crafted him for the blade sure enough." He touched his brow to show respect as he uttered the God of Light's name.

York didn't know the half of it. Since the day with the snake, Aton's strength and speed had only continued to grow. Now he could haul whole feed bags by himself, carry a halfdozen wheels of cheese, and throw a fully grown sheep over one shoulder and get it to the shearing pen before the dumb beast realized it wasn't standing in the field anymore. Of course his brother downplayed these talents while the captain was around. Though York was something like family, he was still a human.

"Aton will be able to handle himself and you all should a little trouble come your way."

"Trouble?" Aton asked.

"Bandits, thieves." York waved his fork dismissively. "The usual sort of no-goods."

"We're at the top of a mountain and herd sheep," their mother replied, giving the man a dubious glance. "We'd not be worth the trouble for bandits to hike all that way. I barely convinced you to make the journey once a week."

"That's true." He nodded, shoveling another forkful of meat into his mouth. "But there's more than one type of trouble in this world, you know."

"What trouble?" Aton still wanted to know.

"Demons." The old man's eyes narrowed, his voice a dark hiss as he said it.

Aaron shivered while his brother leaned in to hear more.

"York," their mother said, a note of warning in the single word. All of them ignored her.

"Have you seen a demon?" Aton asked.

"This is hardly a topic for the dinner table," she said, laying down her cutlery and looking a little sterner.

"They want to know. They should know." The man gave a half shrug and spoke plainly. "I have."

Both boys' eyes grew wide.

"Where?" Aton asked.

Aaron was glad Aton had asked. He wasn't sure if he had the breath to ask any questions himself.

"Out at my old post. It was deeper in the mountains, deeper in the trees, a land of shadows. Demons love the dark places of the world."

They wanted to hear more. "What kind of demon was it?" Aton pressed.

"A lesser demon. Not I, nor anyone I know, has ever crossed paths with a greater, and you pray to Enoch that you never do either."

"York," their mother said again, but her protest was weaker.

"What was it like?"

"Like every story I'd ever heard—dark, shadowy, threatening. We couldn't see it clearly for the trees that surrounded the town, and we were high on the walls, but we could smell the rot drifting from the dark and see its red eyes glaring from the gloom. Like twin coals in a smoldering hearth, they were intense and hot."

Aaron's shoulders crept up, his head sinking to meet them as he thought of a ruby-eyed shadow smelling of rotting meat and fangs and claws reaching out to grab him.

"What did you do?" his brother asked.

"Stayed inside the walls, of course. I ordered every man at his post to hold an arrow, ready to knock, should the thing think about partaking of the tender flesh past our wooded wall."

"Did it try?"

York's frown deepened. "It certainly thought about it. The eyes came nearer, and I saw it start to exit the cover of the canopy."

"What did you do?"

"I pulled my bow and shot at the shadow, a half dozen of my men with me."

"Did you kill it?" Aton was standing half out of his chair, meal forgotten, while he and his mother stayed silent and listened.

"No." York shook his dark hair, silver streaks reflecting the candlelight. "It was fast. Turned and ran the instant it understood the danger. We hurt it, though."

"How do you know?"

"The next morning—in full light, mind—we checked the spot where we'd seen it and found a black pool of blood, still steaming, on the ground."

Aton's excitement turned to a bit of confusion. His head cocked to one side, he asked, "Steaming?"

"Demon blood is a foul thing. It'll burn anything it touches. The arrow that had struck it wasn't more than a lump of metal lying in that puddle, the shaft looking like termites had gotten at it—full of holes and breaking up."

"What would've happened if it did get into the town?" Aaron asked, his shoulders taut with the tension.

The captain looked grimly at the two young boys. "Nothing good."

"Would it have eaten people?" Aton guessed.

"Demons eat magic." Their mother corrected Aton, but looked right at Aaron as she said it.

"They eat His light," York corrected her, "out of His creations. Though they aren't particularly delicate on how they go about getting at it. They don't eat flesh, but they tear their victims apart to get at His light. Death is death, whatever the intent."

Now Aaron's shoulders were brushing his earlobes as he asked, "Have you ever seen a demon near Vidar?"

"No," York said, sitting back more easily in his chair. "We're at the end of the range here, out of the deep wood and the darker crags. The demons don't come this far west—not enough cover, not enough darkness to slink around in, and too many people. Like any predator, they like to single out their prey. With Vidar being as big a town as it is and Gahar Barea not too far away, it's too crowded with people to present good hunting. Still, it's always a good idea to be prepared, if not for today, for when you start to make your own way in the world."

Aton nodded at this piece of wisdom.

"Not to worry; we've got plenty of time to train you up before that day comes."

## CHAPTER 10

## *Broken*

"Be good." The twins' mother kissed Aton on the top of his head. "I'll be back early tomorrow." She kissed the top of Aaron's head. Aaron smiled, noting she no longer had to bend so far to do so.

Since his twin had started weapon lessons with the ex-captain nearly six years ago, it'd been their mother's habit to spend the night in town on market days, so that when she returned with York at first light, teacher and pupil could have the full day together to train. Now, at nearly twelve, the boys were used to the routine, yet her goodbye never differed, even if their heights had.

She climbed onto the bench of their wagon, which was laden with wool and cheese. The elderly Apple was hooked up to the lead. She'd been pulling the cart since well before Aaron could remember. In his earliest thoughts he saw her prancing around the fields; now her hoof falls were a little less light and her sighs after a trip quite a bit heavier.

Turning in her seat, their mother gave them a smile that outshone the dawn in brightness and warmth. "I love you both. See you soon." She blew them both a kiss.

"We love you too," they chorused, unable to keep smiles of their own from spreading across their features in return.

Then she was off, clucking to the mare and giving the reins a jostle to get the old girl's attention. The wagon began to roll. In a clatter of hooves and jangle of tack, it pulled away from the yard and down the trail toward town. The boys stayed, waving to her departing back. It was their tradition to stay and wave until she was out of sight, though these days that seemed to take longer and longer the older the old horse got.

To fill the time, Aton started up a conversation. "York's bringing his bow tomorrow," he remarked, still waving, still watching.

"You're onto the bow now?" Aaron asked reflexively without looking at his older twin. He was still watching his mother too per usual, hand still rocking, only this time he found himself thinking. He knew his brother wanted him to be excited about his latest change in training and expected more than just the one comment. Without really thinking, he added, "This'll be your third weapon?"

Aton grunted. "Fourth."

Aaron knew he'd annoyed his brother, but his thoughts were buzzing and he couldn't concentrate enough to correct himself. "Sorry; I just couldn't remember if it was two years per weapon type or a bit less."

That seemed to be the wrong thing to say. "And how's your training going? In the six years since Mother started training you, I'm not sure I've seen you do more than light the kitchen hearth fire."

That comment pricked Aaron enough to get his full attention and he finally looked at his twin.

"I'm sorry. A stick and a table knife make you threatening to who? A roast chicken? At least my training with the sword, quarter staff, and dagger will be useful out in the world. Pulling water from the air will get you thrown in a cell at the least, tied to a stake more likely."

The twins glared at each other, the hard look in their violet eyes exact reflections even as their coloring made them exact opposites. Over another half decade, the twins' appearances had shifted even further away from being identical. They'd both grown taller in the six years training and tending to the farm, only while Aaron had achieved mainly height, looking lean and stretched, Aton had gained bulk too. He wasn't unnaturally large for a near-teenage boy, but he looked closer to fourteen or fifteen than he did eleven, with solid arms and legs and a torso to match. The constant days of practicing fighting techniques in the sunlight had taken his skin from olive to chestnut, his hair remaining dark with a bit of a wave. Aaron practiced much of his magic outside too, where the elements he studied naturally occurred, only he usually did it with his shirt on. Magic didn't work his body into a sweat the way that swinging around a sword would. And he liked to do his work in his favorite place under the apple tree—quiet, out of the way, and exactly what he needed to concentrate on the complex weaving of energies. As a result, his naturally pale skin remained, seeming almost to glow along with his bright hair in the sunlight.

In Vidar, on those rare occasions he and his brother were allowed to go, the human girls of the town would call him "cute" between giggles. His features, still a bit rounded with youth, were too angular now and his height too great for them to refer to him as "pretty." When they saw Aton, on the other hand, they'd whisper "handsome" to each other on deep sighs whenever he passed them by.

Despite their differing descriptions, Aaron garnered more female attention, though not for his own sake. Perhaps they found him more approachable, but the gaggle of Vidar girls always asked him why Aton was so brooding, so mysterious. He too had noticed this change in his brother's demeanor over the years. His twin had grown more stoic, more serious, with every year he gained. Though some of that was just natural from growing up, he'd tell the interested females that it was all due to York's military discipline and training to become a steadfast soldier. To himself he'd add to that his brother also possessed a focus on getting stronger, faster, better, to fully capitalize on his natural gifts and finally find their limitations. Though, in the moments he allowed himself to remember that far back, he'd recall that Aton had really started to change right after their encounter with the snake, when he'd had to save his little brother by...

Shaking himself out of his thoughts, Aaron turned back to the slope, the sweet horse still plodding along. The cart turned the bend, taking the equine and woman finally out of sight. Aton's hand fell and he turned away from the road without another word, bound for his daily chores. Aaron hardly noticed. A feeling he couldn't name was rolling around in his gut, his thoughts buzzing noisily within his skull every which way, without a clear direction. He just stood, eyes not seeing the road ahead of him, while he tried to listen to that buzz. What was the cause of his unrest? Why did he feel so unsettled?

"Aaron."

The other voice cut through the noise in his head. He blinked rapidly, shaking his head again, and glanced over his shoulder at the speaker. "What?"

"We have work to do, unless you'd like to stand there uselessly staring off into the clouds all day."

"Right," he said, not rising to his brother's tone.

His body turned to go, yet his eyes felt pulled against his will again to the spot where the yard turned to road, to the path on which his mother left and returned from the market once a week, and there was that buzzing again.

The day passed slowly, each degree of the rising and setting sun feeling longer than an hour. He and his brother, after their verbal scuffle that morning, had seemed to agree to limit further conversation. Not that Aaron noticed much. He performed his chores with a mechanical rhythm, still trying to catch his flying thoughts, trying to cope with his aching stomach.

That night, Aaron couldn't sleep. He watched the moon sail through the star-filled sky out his window, passing just as slowly as the sun had.

"Why aren't you sleeping?"

Aaron didn't even twitch, his eyes trained on the sliver of silver. "Something feels wrong."

"What does?" his brother asked from the other bed.

"I don't know."

"Go to sleep."

"You sleep. You'll need your rest, what with York coming in the morning to teach you the bow."

"I intend to." The larger boy rolled over, pulling up his blanket over his shoulder.

Maybe Aton expected further conversation, but Aaron said nothing further. His eyes were wide, soaking in each weak ray of crescent light, and his stomach churned within him like a beast with cold, clammy, claws.

"She's late," Aaron said, squinting against the morning's early light.

"Hardly," Aton replied, looking to the sun for confirmation. It was only a little after breakfast time.

They'd heated themselves some porridge their mother had left them. Despite the blueberries and honey she'd added to sweeten it, the food hadn't tasted like anything to Aaron that morning.

"She should be here."

"They're probably getting breakfast, buying some fresh bread for us."

Aaron didn't respond. The mention of more food sent further ripples through his middle unpleasantly.

"Come on." He could hear the irritation in his older brother's voice. "We still have work to do."

He did go to his chores, but he was distracted. He pulled a parsnip sprout instead of a weed, which he quickly replanted. He pricked his finger deep while darning his socks. There wasn't any blood; his body healed the injury nearly as quickly as it took to pull out the needle, but the tiny pain wasn't enough to encourage him to pay any more attention, and he stuck himself twice more before the sock's hole was patched.

Aton rounded the house, a basket full of wet sheets in one hand. Laundry was one of those tasks their mother typically did on sword training days. Aton had already finished it, taking it over to the drying lines.

"They're not back yet," Aaron pointed out again.

"I know." His older brother walked to the line and pulled a sodden bed linen from the basket.

"Why aren't they back yet?"

"I don't know." Aton tugged on the corners to even the sheet out into nearly even halves over the line.

"York only has the one day a week to train you."

"I know." The darker twin jerked the sheet taut to remove the wrinkles.

"Should we go look for them?"

The older boy let the next sheet droop back into the basket. "I think—"

He stopped mid-sentence, his head jerking up, listening. Aaron did the same. There was a noise—a rhythmic *clip-clop* coming from around the house.

Laundry forgotten, Aton leapt over the basket and ran. Aaron discarded the sock and thread to follow.

The brothers stopped in front of the house, their full attention aimed at the head of the trail, both standing stock-still, not breathing. Only it wasn't the palomino mare they saw coming up the path.

York had traded in his old gray gelding a few years back for a strong, younger colt, only now the spry black pulling at the cart's lead felt like a harbinger of ill tidings. The familiar driver, holding the reins loosely, looked anything but with his head hanging heavy. York had claimed to be an old man the first time he'd come to train Aton, but this was the first time in six years that Aaron had ever thought it himself. Icy fingers traced themselves up his spine, and he ducked his head reflexively as this older version of York drew near.

"Hello, boys," York said, climbing down from the bench.

"York," Aton replied.

The questions burned on Aaron's tongue, only his mother's lessons in manners held him back from outright demanding her location from the man.

"Can we go inside and talk?" York asked.

"Of course," Aton answered. "Aaron, take care of the horse."

Aaron would have liked to have argued, to have said he wanted to know what York had to say that minute, but he only nodded mutely, watching the pair disappear into the house. He noticed the way the growing shadows swallowed them as they crossed the threshold, and the image made his shoulders creep up just a bit more.

He shook himself, turning his attention to the horse. The animal huffed great breaths after its long climb, and he went to loosen the bit to allow it to graze. It shied at his approach. The beast had always been a bit skittish. Maybe, unlike the sheep, it could tell what they really were, except, on this day, it seemed even more agitated than usual. He tried twice more without success, the horse constantly dancing away from his hands. Finally giving up, he grabbed the reins, walked the animal over to the trough, and hitched it to the post there, so at least it could drink and rest.

Aaron gave the bed of York's wagon a quick glance as he passed. The whole thing was covered with an oilcloth, vague shapes of boxes and bushels supporting it from below. He strode into the house and saw that Aton was already serving tea to the old soldier, the slightly floral scent filling the room. His twin didn't pour any for him or himself as he took one of the seats across from York. Their guest's face was unreadable as tree bark as he stared at the steaming liquid without focus. The light twin sat down beside his brother, his breath coming in tiny gulps he tried to hide.

The ex-captain wrapped his hands around the steaming cup, warming them even on so mild a spring afternoon. The boys waited, sitting at attention, silent with anticipation.

With a heavy sigh, the older man began. "Boys, this'll be hard to hear, but Marilyn—" He swallowed. "Your mother has passed on."

The words rung out in the empty house. That simple pronouncement, stated in the most banal of terms, stunned Aaron to his core. The world gave way beneath him. He felt like he was falling, his mind swirling, making him unable to focus on any one thought. He'd suspected, had outright known on some level when York had appeared alone, that their mother had been injured in some way. Hearing that it was even worse than he'd suspected made his already twisted stomach spasm. He swallowed hard, trying to breathe, trying to focus, the effort making sweat blossom on his brow and upper lip.

"How?" The flat, toneless word came from his older brother.

"I was waiting at market," the soldier began again. "She'd asked me to get some things for her, and I was eager for her to see what I'd bought. Only when she didn't come by, I got worried. I went to the path. I had to search for nearly the whole day, but—" He took a breath. "You knew that old nag wasn't as young as she used to be, not as sure-footed." Sucking in another breath, he finished. "It looks like the horse slipped and pulled the wagon and Marilyn off the cliff with it. They died quick when they hit bottom." His eyes were unfocused as he stared at the mug, looking at it like he was seeing the scene all over again.

The silence that fell over them felt heavy, smothering, and Aaron had trouble breathing past the emptiness.

"Did you bring her back?" Aton asked at last, only his words weren't as solid as they'd been a moment before.

The head, which had gathered even more gray over the years, bobbed. "She's in the bed," York said into the cup, unable to meet their eyes.

Aton stood, uneasy on his feet at first, walking through this nightmare, and left the room. The weapons teacher rose a moment later, then him, last and the least sure-footed.

Out in the yard, the shadows were lengthening. When the horse saw Aton approach, it danced nervously, perhaps dreading, as Aaron did, what the boy meant to do. His older twin ignored the restrained animal, whipping off the tarp with one yank. And there she was.

Among the bushels of wool, the boxes, and a bag set out neatly beside her, lay the body of their mother—small, twisted, and broken.

Then he was sick. He fell to his hands and knees before his mutinous stomach gave up its contents, retching into the grass beside the cart. Over and over his body spasmed and shuddered. Grief, panic, and bile poured out of him with each contraction of his guts. The state of her—limbs lying not quite straight, her clothes tattered, and one shoe missing—was an image Aaron knew he would never forget.

Aton stilled, frozen to the spot, York behind him, a deep grimace etched into the older man's weathered features, while Aaron knelt on the ground retching.

When he could purge no longer, Aaron dug his fingers into the soft soil and gritted his teeth. He forced himself to stand, the acrid taste of stomach fluids still on his tongue and stinging his nose. Steeling himself, he looked again at the body. York had thought to throw an extra bit of cloth over her face, and with the unnatural shapes implied beneath, Aaron was glad of it. She must've hit her head when she fell. It was one of the only sure ways to kill a werewolf. They were stronger, faster, and heartier than most of the other Eight, with a healing speed nearly ten times that of a typical human, but they were still people, still mortal.

Even the bite from the snake that day wouldn't have been deadly. Aton was uncomfortable, the pain doubly terrible due to the nature of werewolf healing as it tried to burn the poison off so quickly that it conversely ended up amplifying the toxin's effect, but Aton had lived. Poisons were even more dangerous to their kind due to that quirk in their healing process. Aaron's sudden spurt of healing had saved his brother from a prolonged agony, shrinking the time down to just one unbearable moment, but that was all.

Werewolves were tough despite their toxin sensitivity, no doubt about that. Only their mother hadn't been poisoned. Her skull had been crushed. Fast healing didn't matter if the organ that was to direct the effort was lost.

He would've liked to fool himself into thinking that it was someone else beneath that cloth, that through the horror of finding a mangled corpse, York had somehow gotten it wrong. Only the thin strands of blood-specked, yellow hair, so like his own, poking out from beneath the edges of the cloth made that hope evaporate instantly. There could be no doubt.

"Help me bring her inside," Aton asked in a hollow tone that pulled Aaron back to the moment. Only the young warrior wasn't talking to him. The older man nodded and stepped forward.

Aaron moved aside as best he could to give them room. Any of them could've moved the body on their own, as light and birdlike as their mother had been. Aton, at only eleven, despite looking older, still didn't want to display too much of his unnatural strength to this man. Despite the fact that the twins had come to regard him as something like an uncle, York never learned the truth. Similarly, the ex-captain never would've presumed to patronize his student in such a way as to imply that he needed help to shoulder this burden. So Aton asked for York's aid in the task, saving them both.

Together, the two lifted the thin frame from the wagon. Gently, reverently, they carried her inside and set her down softly on their small dining table. Aaron watched from the doorway and saw that their mother didn't quite fit. Her bare feet hung off the edge, her other shoe lost in the transition. The sight of her corpse on the dinner table was even more surreal, and Aaron was glad when York spoke, distracting him from his vertigo.

"Do you need help burying her?" The teacher's voice was low, as though the twins were wounded animals he was trying not to spook.

"No," Aton replied.

York nodded. "Do you want some company tonight?"

"No," Aton said again. "Thank you, York, but it should be just the three of us tonight."

The phrase made Aaron worry that he'd be sick all over again. The statement was a gross perversion of one of his happiest thoughts—just the three of them, up on their little mountain, their little life.

"I understand." And maybe York did. "Should you boys ever need anything, come and find me in town. Marilyn, she—" He had to swallow again. "She was a great woman, a great friend, and you boys—" His emotions made his words come out strained. "I'd lend you any aid I could. Don't forget that and don't you doubt it."

Aton returned the statement with a nod. "Thank you, York."

Dismissed, the big man turned to leave. Aaron looked from him to his brother and back again, finally following York out into the dwindling late afternoon light.

The man was issuing calming noises to the black horse, running his calloused hands over its long face.

"Thank you, York," he said at last. He couldn't quite squeeze out anything else past the lump in his throat.

York looked at him with a frown, the lines on his face deep, and moved around to the back of the cart, reappearing with the sack that'd been lying next to their mother in his hand. It was brown with a rough weave, the kind of bag animal feed was stored in.

York held the bag out to Aaron. "Marilyn gave me some coin a while back and asked me to pick up a couple of things for her. I think she meant to give them to you both for that birthday you've got coming up." He shook his head. "So this should go to you." He handed Aaron the bag. It was heavier than it looked, though with his werewolf blood and farm living, it wasn't too much for him to take easily. "I meant what I said. If you boys ever need me, you just ask, for anything."

Aaron nodded numbly for a moment, looking at the sack, studying the brown threads that made up the weave. He felt the man's hand on his head, then it slid off to rest on his shoulder. He didn't look up when the soldier said, "Take care of each other."

The hand squeezed his shoulder and fell away. The ex-captain took his horse by the bridle and turned him around, walking down the slope instead of riding, maybe afraid of a fall himself, back toward the village. He didn't turn. York was leaving them alone, to say their goodbyes in their own way.

Aaron watched the cart go for a long time before Aton walked out from the side of the house, interrupting the stillness. The older boy took the bag from his hand and replaced it with a shovel.

"What's this?" he asked, looking over the tool with bewilderment.

"We need to bury her."

He felt like the spooked colt. "Bury her. But—"

"Unless you want to sleep with her on the table all night."

He thought about that for a moment and felt a shiver crawl up over his shoulders. The thought of trying to sleep with the corpse of their mother laid out in the kitchen was too terrible to contemplate, the shadows of night creeping in, the thin moonlight bringing little relief.

Aton must've seen his shudder, because he nodded as though Aaron had agreed. His brother put the bundle by the door and trooped up the hill toward their lone apple tree. He walked quietly behind him, past the docile sheep bleating in their pen, and mimicked putting shovel to dirt as the older boy started to dig beneath the shadow of the canopy.

## CHAPTER 11

# *Lengthening Shade*

They dug, deeper and deeper, for hours. The sun, making its slow progression to the west, stretched the shadows into tall wraiths and painted the world in bloody shades of red, and still they dug. He'd lived on a farm for his entire life and had never felt so tired or sore as he did in digging their mother's grave. The sun set and the moon rose, a sick little sliver of a thing, providing them with next to no light, and still they dug.

When Aton finally called a halt, Aaron looked up to the lip of the hole and wondered if he had the strength to pull himself out or if he would have to sleep in the cold, damp ground. His brother didn't let him wonder for long, nudging him toward a rope he'd brought and tied to the apple tree for this purpose. Once they'd both emerged, Aton led them back inside the house, making sure to wipe his dirty boots off before crossing the threshold.

Aaron stopped at the door, staggered by the vision before him. The angles and misshapen profile of her shrouded form were thrown into even sharper contrast by the little moonlight, twisted and unnatural.

His brother didn't seem to notice, standing near her head and studying her as though she were a problem to solve and not someone he'd loved and lost. He spoke calmly enough. "Get the tablecloth."

The request was so sudden and unexpected that Aaron complied without question. The linen wardrobe where their mother had kept all the extra bedsheets and other household fabrics stood in the hearth room. In the bottom drawer, she kept a white linen tablecloth. It was one of the nicest pieces of textile she owned; it was a lovely thing with little blue flowers sewn into the corners. She'd only ever pulled it out for the nicest of occasions, usually on their birthday, and whenever it came out, Aton and Aaron were always mindful to eat very carefully lest they stain it. He pressed the fabric to his nose and breathed deeply, his strong senses detecting notes of its story—of washing soap, traces of good food, and her.

He came back into the room and held the object out to his brother with something like reverence. Aton took it with hardly a glance and began to spread it out on the floor next to the table.

"What are you doing?" he asked.

"We'll use this to lower her in," the other boy answered as he straightened out the creases.

His insides gave another turn, but it made sense. His brother could carry her easily on his own, but they had no way to set her gently into the ground without some sort of sling.

"Wait." Suddenly alert, his brother had clearly just thought of something. Jumping up, the older twin moved to the body's left hand. There, on her third finger, was the ring. York truly was a good man for not taking such a prize. The heavy gold band, decorated with intricate swirls, was set with a large, light green emerald and would've been worth a fortune, possibly as much as their little cottage and all the land it sat upon. It'd been given to her by their father, the only tangible memento of him she'd had, and now it might be the last memento of her.

Aton carefully removed the ring, holding the pale hand as delicately as a butterfly as he did so. He held it out to Aaron. "You should take it."

Aaron looked at the ring as though Aton were offering him her finger along with it. "What? Why?"

"Because she would've wanted you to have it. It's the same color as your magic."

The magic that they'd shared, he didn't say. Aaron kept shaking his head. It was a piece of her. It felt wrong to see it off her finger, where it'd always been, as far back as he could remember. "I don't want it. She should keep it."

Aton's expression darkened. "She wouldn't want it in the ground."

"Then you keep it," he snapped back without thinking.

His older brother's scowl deepened, but rather than continue the argument, he walked over and set the ring on the bookshelf. "It's yours." He went back to spreading out the sheet. Satisfied, he looked up at Aaron and ordered, "Take her feet."

Aaron looked at the corpse and felt queasy. He was going to have to touch the thing on the table, the thing that had once been their mother. Struggling to breathe slowly and easily, he moved to the feet dangling just off the edge of the table. Reaching out tentatively, he watched Aton take her by the shoulders. Aaron moved likewise and touched her ankles, his hands recoiling at once. She was cold to the touch, colder than anything should've been on so warm a spring night, and her skin felt waxy, unreal, more repulsive than he ever would've imagined. He didn't know how, but he could tell just by that touch that there was no life in the flesh, and its absence made something primal within him revolt.

Except his brother was already moving her shoulders. He didn't want to let the rest of her fall. Seizing her ankles, fighting his revulsion, he helped Aton lower her to the cloth. Once she was on the cloth, the older boy made to arrange her. Aton folded her arms over her chest and made sure the fabric over her face hadn't moved. He stood back and rubbed his hands on his pant legs, trying to dislodge the chill her flesh imparted to his own skin. "Take up those corners."

Aaron did as he was bid, his sibling doing the same. They lifted her between them, the moonlight revealing a long shape under the folded cloth.

Even though he knew he was only taking half her weight, the younger twin marveled at the lightness of her. Their mother had seemed so strong, so vivacious in life, and yet in death, she seemed greatly diminished, delicate and fragile, as they carried her out into the pale starlight and up the incline.

The wind blew through the branches, rustling the leaves and the last few blossoms on the apple tree. It took white petals off the flowers and swirled them in the night air, sweetening the scents and adding a bit more brightness to the gloom. He imagined the tree to be weeping, as he felt he was too stunned to cry himself.

Together they maneuvered her body over the hole they'd dug and slowly, gently, lowered her in, placing their mother delicately into her grave. They dropped the corners of the cloth once she'd reached the bottom, letting them flutter and fall as they may. The small pale bundle was a mere smudge inside, the white of the tablecloth the only light within the impossible dark. He felt himself pulled in toward that abyss from a great height, unable to tear his eyes away, when Aton came around to stand beside him. His older brother placed a warm, solid hand on his shoulder, steadying him, haunting the pull he felt. Aton held a fistful of soil in his other hand.

Aton's words trembled just a bit. "Thank you, Mother. Thank you for always being there. Thank you for loving us and keeping us safe. Aaron and I will always remember what you taught us. We'll keep training with our gifts, but don't worry; we'll keep them hidden too. We'll stay safe and well, and we'll take care of each other." He paused. "I'll take care of Aaron. I promise." Closing his eyes, he breathed in a shuddering breath. "And know that we'll always love you. We'll never forget you. Sleep now." His voice thickened the longer he spoke. It was the longest speech Aaron had heard him give in some time, each word a greater and greater effort to speak. A last deep breath came and Aton opened his hand, letting the dirt spill through his fingers. The flecks of soil spun and tumbled and fell into the depths of the grave, landing atop the body and the white tablecloth.

Seeing the dark dirt marring the bright fabric, realizing what his brother was doing, that he was burying their mother, Aaron snapped. He dove for the edge of the grave. Aton, in his shock, still managed, just barely, to catch him before he flung himself into the hole.

Aaron couldn't let Aton bury her. They couldn't leave her alone in that terrible place.

"No." The word tore from his throat in a mad half-scream.

"Aaron, Aaron." His brother tried to soothe Aaron as he grappled with him. The older twin had always been stronger, but in Aaron's mania, he could feel his brother strain to hold him back. "Aaron, she's gone."

"She's not gone. She's not. I can save her," he screamed.

"You can't save her."

"I can."

"Aaron, you can't. She's dead, Aaron. You can't bring her back."

The finality, the certainty of the statement caused the younger twin to whirl on his brother with bared flat teeth. "And how would you know that? You don't even have magic. So how could you possibly know what it can do?"

Not rising to the barb, Aton replied, "Aaron, it's not possible."

"Says you," he shot back. "I'll show you. I'll bring her back. You just watch me." He spun on his toes and stalked toward the house without so much as a backward glance.

He strode right into the room where the books were kept and began to tear them from their shelves. He discarded the books on shepherding and gardening. He threw the book on history and the little book of prayers to the Five Gods of Eris. He knew their mother would've been too careful to keep an actual book on magic in the house, even if such a thing existed. Instead, Aaron turned to her tome of stories and folktales. Even if it didn't give exact instructions on how to perform a resurrection, it might give him enough of a clue that he could puzzle out a spell.

The book he grasped was thick and tall, full of wondrous and fanciful stories that the three of them read by sunstone light before settling down to sleep. The leather cover was smooth with much use, the smell of warm hide clinging lightly to its surface. Sitting cross-legged on the floor, he resolutely opened the book, flipping through the first pages. He had to focus hard to block out the sound that carried through the open kitchen window, the sound of Aton's shovel filling in their mother's grave.

## CHAPTER 12

# *The Seer's Deck*

When Aaron awoke, he wasn't on the floor, surrounded by books, where he'd fallen asleep. Instead, he was in his bed with the sheets pulled up around his chin. Aton wasn't in the other bed, or anywhere else he could see. He sat up and looked down at himself, noticing that he still wore the clothes and dirt from the night before. Tossing off the bedding, he walked into the kitchen and looked out the window toward the apple tree. The grave had been filled in. A slightly raised mound of freshly turned soil marked its location. At its peak, a bunch of bright yellow daffodils were planted, waving in the early morning breeze.

He knew he'd passed out on the floor while pouring through the fairy-tale book. There'd been plenty of death in the stories—soldiers slain in glorious battles, wicked kings cut down by noble heroes, and lovers taking their own lives so as to be reunited in another world. Only the common theme seemed to be that, when someone died, that was the end. They stayed dead.

He turned to give an accusing glare to the books, scorning them for their failure to give him any hope whatsoever. Only they weren't on the floor either. He saw that the volumes too had been neatly put away. They sat on their shelves in a neat row, just as if the tragedy of the night before had never occurred. It was then that something else caught his eye, a wink of light sitting atop the short bookcase.

Walking over, he saw their mother's ring, shining brightly in the early rays. The green stone reflected the illumination and glowed like the orb their mother had held between her hands the night she'd told them that she'd had magic too. Tears burned at the backs of his eyes for the first time as he remembered the scene, so ordinary and so fanciful in the same instance.

This was the last thing they had that'd truly been hers. The house, the clothes, the land, all of it would hold ghosts of her, but this was a piece of her. He reached out a trembling hand, meaning to touch the smooth surface of the bright green stone, wanting to see if her warmth still lingered there—

"Aaron."

The sudden shout made him flinch and he knocked the ring to the floor. It bounced off the wooden floorboards and skidded beneath the shelf. He cursed himself and fell to his knees, reaching as far under as he could, but his fingers met something that wasn't the wooden flooring nor the metal of a ring. He traced blindly over the object and realized that it was some sort of paper envelope. Sliding it out, he saw the ring sitting on one corner and a deep red wax seal greeted him upon his inspection. Putting the ring aside on the floor, he flipped the envelope over and saw the words '*Aton & Aaron*' written in their mother's flowing script.

Without thinking, he cracked the seal, red wax crumbling and falling away. The whole note was penned in her same handwriting, delicate but confident. He sat down, hard, and read.

My dearest Aton and Aaron,

I know that you'll only be reading this letter if the very worst has happened. I'm sorry. Please know that I love you both, that I have always loved you and enjoyed you more than anything I have ever had in my entire life. I feel blessed to have had you both. I'm sorry I can't be there to comfort you and help you through this awful, unthinkable time. I'm sorrier still to let you know that you can't grieve for me long. I only hope that you're old enough and strong enough to bear what I have to tell you.

For you to understand what I'm about to tell you, I first need to explain how I came to know it. A long time ago, a little less than a year before you were born, I was living in Gahar Barea, in your grandfather's house. He was a wealthy merchant, a trader in all sorts of exotic gems, woods, and spices, with a fleet of ships always sailing between Rahovan and Jenoha.

As a daughter of the upper class, ve attended all sorts of parties and functions, but I was never one for that and I loved going into town or out to the coast to watch the ships sail in and out of the harbor. It was there that I met your father.

I know you'll want to know more, but I don't think I have the heart, or enough paper, to tell you about our first encounter or about how I had to sneak out at night to see my lowly sailor. We had so little time together, but despite the brevity, we fell in love and confessed everything to each other on those stolen nights, even that I was a caster and he a werewolf. I can't tell you here about the night he proposed to me and how I demanded that he turn me so that I might be a part of his family, his pack, or about the night of my first shift, running with him across the silvery beach, stars above and reflecting below us like we were running through the skies.

He told me he needed to take one more voyage to honor his debt to his captain, but he promised when he returned we would run away and start a family of our own. He gave me the ring before he left, an heirloom of his own line and a vow to join his life with mine forever.

This promise had to be a secret between us alone—my family would've never approved of our union—so I wore his ring on a chain around my neck, under my dress and close to my heart. I watched him sail away, thinking that I would see him again in a few months, not knowing that I would never see him again.

While he was gone, I had to pretend that everything was the same as it had been, only everything had changed for me and I felt restless. Two days after his departure, I asked one of the kitchen girls if I might go to the market and do the shopping instead of her, for want of something to do and an excuse to stretch my legs.

I'd gotten a rack of lamb relatively quickly, but I wasn't ready to return to pacing my rooms quite yet. I kept wandering the markets, past spices from Rahovan and perfumes all the way from Mirea Shainel, when I heard a voice: "Know your fortunes. Behold your future."

The voice was from a woman dressed in dark blue silks that were embroidered in white and silver thread; her raven hair was shining nearly blue itself in the bright noon light. Her skin was a deep caramel, darker than that of the local Gahar Bareans, but it being a port town, the city attracted all walks of life, so this was nothing new. I'd seen dwarf craftspeople, nokken sailors, even the occasional eln merchants walking those streets, so her clearly human appearance and slightly darker coloring did not surprise or concern me—it was what she'd called that piqued my interest.

Now, you have to understand that in Enochism, only the priests of Enoch may speak of future events, illuminated for them by the God of Light. Especially in the smaller towns and tiny villages, such a thing as selling visions for coin would be punishable by death. However, in a big port city like Gahar Barea, having a person pretend to see your future is seen as something of a humorous diversion by the more affluent class, those who often have more money than sense.

"You," she called out, pointing a bejeweled digit in my direction. "Do you wish to know your future?"

"I don't," I told her, walking on without giving her a second glance. I needed to save all my money as your father and I would be running away as soon as he returned. "My future already looks bright, thank you." I was thinking of the ring next to my heart.

"I fear not all of your days will be as bright as you hope."

"No one's ever are," I told her. I was near to turning and crossing the street when she said something that arrested my steps.

"Hidden love is a fine thing, but there's always a price to pay, always the threat of secrets exposed, especially considering his breed."

I spun to look at her. I remember that she was leaning up against a pole supporting the tent behind her, a tent I'd failed to notice when I'd first passed by. It was a riot of reds, yellows, and all the hues in between, all made of various heavy fabrics embellished with images and patterns that were illegible from where I stood. I don't know how I'd missed it before, but as bright as it was, the woman captured all of my attention. One arm was stretched above her head in a languid pose, her silk sleeve falling to reveal bare skin the color of burnt honey and decked in a series of golden bangles. Her black waves of hair cascaded over her other shoulder and her other hand was planted on her generous hip. She was all soft curves and lithe lines, though her full lips were no longer smiling. She stared at me, all charm and play having fled her face, waiting for my reply.

When I didn't move, she spoke again. "If not your own, there are other futures that should be told." She nodded curtly in my direction, only lower than my face. I followed her gaze and clutched at my belly. I was pregnant then, or thought I was. I'd not said as much to even your father, but my cycle was late and I'd started to suspect that I might be.

The woman vanished inside the red and orange fabrics and I followed before I could think better of it. The inside was dark as a cave, the thick cloth blocking out the sun's illumination. It was warm too, smelling of sandalwood smoke and, somehow, the dry breeze off a desert. Past a few layers of curtains, the woman led me to a low table with cushions set around it, lit candles upon it lighting the rose-colored room, and a deck of cards.

I wasn't sure what I'd been expecting—runes, a reflecting pool, a looking glass—but cards hadn't been it. I'd heard of a fortune teller's deck. Many of my fellow debutants called them a seer's deck or cards of destiny while placing gloved hands over their giggling mouths.

The woman sat behind the table on a pile of the pillows and extended a hand for me to sit across from her. I left my basket, the meat safely wrapped in paper, by the entrance and sat on the jewel-tone cushions as instructed. Everything looked eerie in the flickering candlelight.

"Shuffle," she ordered, pointing to the stack of cards.

Each one was larger than my open hand and there were many, but I took them up. As I shuffled, I could've sworn I smelled the clean, sweet smell I always did when I was casting by the hearth, just under the sandalwood smoke. My fingers were numb when I handed the deck back to her and maybe they were shaking too.

She pulled the top card and studied it, then turned inky, dark eyes to me, saying, "Your past," as she laid it on the table. It showed a chest, so intricately drawn that even the wood grain seemed expertly rendered, filled with a variety of gemstones—rubies, diamonds, emeralds, and more—all glowing like sunstones.

"'The Ten of Jewels," she proclaimed. "You've lived a privileged life, one of plenty, of safety and indulgence."

I wrinkled my nose at her words. I'd been born to a wealthy family, but that wasn't hard to see by the way I was dressed or my smooth hands. I didn't think her very good at the façade of drawing the customer in with tantalizing visions of mystery and delight, as the other girls had claimed they'd received.

She drew another card. "Your present." This card showed two open books, partially overlapping, thick and ancient-looking manuscripts. I noticed one was held by a youth, a boy, painted as a yellow silhouette on a black background, and behind the second appeared the inverse of the image, a black silhouette on a yellow field. "'The Two of Tombs. Duality."

"What does that mean?"

"Two choices, two paths." Her eyes drifted back to my belly. "Two futures." She placed the second card below and to the left of the first, drew yet another, and placed it directly next to the two of tombs. "'The Queen.'" And the card did look regal. A woman sat on a throne, straight and proud, a scepter and a sword crossed across her lap and a crown set atop her auburn curls. "Responsibility. Duty to guide and to guard."

I still didn't see any truth in her words, but the sneer had left my lips. I waited perfectly still for the next card, curious about how she thought duty and duality played into my current situation.

"Your future." She laid the first card in the third row and I felt a chill race up my spine. "'The Moon. Secrets.'"

The card was beautiful, showing the round face of the glowing moon, and I could've sworn it was tinted green. Behind the moon and just below it stood a wolf so intricately rendered I felt I could reach out and stroke its fur. The wolf stared out at the viewer, challenging, daring them to look away, daring them to deny the truth.

The fortune teller picked up another card, laying it next to the moon. "'The Castle. Safety, or the illusion of it.'" There might've been a stone fortress atop a high crag, a single road running from its gates, but I couldn't take my eyes off of that wolf.

"And the last," she announced. "'The One of Hearts.'" Her voice became even more sober as she added, "Isolation."

"What?" I asked, looking to the last card she'd placed. The heart was a deep red, almost burgundy, and it sat alone atop a parapet, a raging gray sea crashing against its walls, desolate and empty. The flesh of the organ had been scored and from the wound wept rich, crimson blood, painted so cleverly it appeared wet to the touch.

"What are you talking about?"

"Your future, your path, has been set out before you. You'll have to leave your life of comfort and exchange it for a different sort of existence."

"I was going to anyway," I remember saying, feeling sick in the hot tent, incense in my nose, and all these thoughts in my head. I was planning on running away with your father.

"But which path to take?" She placed a blue-tipped finger on the Two of Tombs. "The choice must be made wisely, in full knowledge of what it will mean." The finger with the dark blue nail, matching her silks, tapped the Queen next.

"There's only one path," I insisted. I'd be running away with my husband and we would start a new life somewhere far from Gahar Barea.

"There are two," she argued, "and you must choose the correct one." Her hand moved to the third row, three cards representing my "future." "The responsible, right path will lead you down a difficult road, one filled with secrets and the want for safety, and one that you will need to walk alone."

"And if I choose not to take that path?" I fairly spat at the woman.

"I see nothing." And the look on her face was grim, as grim as though she were pronouncing her own demise.

"Nonsense," I spat. The heat was becoming oppressive, the scent was overwhelming, and her ridiculous predictions were making me irritated. "Given your elaborate setup, I would've expected an expert charlatan like yourself to know the sort of readings your audience would appreciate. Try giving your next customer one of those. I've no doubt it'll earn you a higher tip." I stood to leave, but she grabbed my wrist in an insistent grip.

"I told you it was not just your future I would show you." Her eyes darted back to my belly and I covered it with my free hand reflexively.

"I don't want to hear any more of your false prophesies," I remember growling at the woman, but she wasn't listening. Still holding my wrist, she swept the cards from my reading off to the side and flipped the top card of the deck.

It was a picture of the sun shining in a sky with a few puffy clouds, only it was upside down. I hadn't flipped any cards in my shuffling, and I'd wondered at the time if she'd put the cards back on the table that way.

"A reading of their purpose." Her words came in a breathy hiss. "The first card represents the circumstances, the location. The sun is inverted. The sun is depicted at its zenith; inverted it could be rising or setting. Given its position in the reading and the newness of the subject, it must be rising," she said with confidence. Then she flipped the next. "The second card: endeavor, action. The Caster. Inverted."

The card showed a man, his head wreathed in a glowing light. He held fire in one hand and stone in the other. This card too was upside down and I was sure that she'd done it when I'd stood to leave.

"It means power, only inverted it is not the gathering of power, but the sharing of it. And last, the outcome, the stakes." She flipped the last card and stopped. The picture paused a few inches from her face as she stared. She let go of my hand.

"What?" I demanded.

She placed the last card on the table and my eyes were greeted with the sight of a grinning skull. This card pointed upward instead of being inverted. A sword sat beneath the bleached bone and ravens flew in the background.

"Death?" I whispered.

"Perhaps," she answered, recovering herself but looking at me with round eyes. "The Skull means danger, terrible danger, but death—"

She let her words trail off, but I knew the truth. Looking into those hollow eyes and at the flashing teeth, I knew death was in the prediction, and not the type that comes gently while we sleep. I told her I didn't believe her, that everything she'd said was a pack of cruel and twisted fantasies. I stood, angry, but feeling a cold pit in my stomach just underneath the heat. I went to pick up my lamb and leave. She got to her feet too.

"You must believe me." Her voice was so full of confidence it only served to enrage me further.

"I don't."

"Please." A note of begging in that proud voice made me hesitate. "The life you carry has a heavy future, heavier than I have ever felt before. There are people, many people, many innocent lives, who will depend on that salvation, on your choice to follow the path that I have shown you."

"A path filled with fear and secrecy and isolation?"

"Yes. You will have hardship and trials, and you will need to hide and keep secrets, alone. Only life is never so cruel that it affords us no joy."

"Only denies us the ones we want—a husband and family to help me raise this child?"

"Yes, you will have to do this alone, somewhere far from here. You will need to hide and protect that which you carry, so that one day they both may grow and fulfill their own purpose, and that purpose will mean so much to so many. Your sacrifice will let them do that."

"No." And then I ran. I picked up my basket and fled from that tent, from the oppressive heat and heady smell and promises of dark and terrible things.

I didn't sleep that night, laying in bed, hand on my stomach, swearing that I could feel the life stirring inside of me, yet the only thing I saw whenever I tried to shut my eyes was that grinning skull. I went back to the market the next day to see if the woman had tried to trick some other young girl with tales of danger and loneliness, only I discovered her tent was gone, replaced by a man selling soaps and oils. Three more nights I lay and dreamed about all of the images I'd seen. Sometimes it was the rising suns, another night it was crossed swords and bleeding hearts, but each night I'd see that skull and I'd wake in a sweat.

On the fourth day I made preparations to leave. Your father and I had already started making arrangements for our own escape; now I knew it would only be me running away. I packed what clothes I could carry and sold everything I could rightly call my own and made ready to depart. Before I did, however, I had to let your father know what had happened. I had to leave him a letter. It wasn't dissimilar to this one. I told him about the fortune teller, that she'd confirmed what I'd only suspected, that I was with child, our child, and now I needed to run and hide to protect our baby. I hid the letter where we'd promised ourselves to each other, where we'd had our private wedding, and where he'd turned me. I cut my finger and pressed it to the stone covering my missive so that there could be no chance that he would miss my farewell, and then I left.

I left Gahar Barea, left my family without a word, and traveled east. I found Vidar, a tiny scrap of a town under the shadow of a low mountain. I used the money I had to build our cottage, my fortification from the world, and set myself up with a flock so that I could earn some income.

There were nights when I doubted myself, when the wind would scream and I'd huddle up next to the hearth alone. Only my swelling belly and the image of that skull kept me focused.

When you were born and I saw you both for the first time, it wiped away my doubt. You were twins, and twins as different as night and day, or like the Two of Tombs with its silhouetted children, one dark and one light. Only then did I remember the fortune teller saying, "so that they both may grow…" She'd known I would have two children.

As you grew, my attention on the fortune faded for a time. For who could think of skulls and death when I had a pair of rambunctious twins to clothe and feed and clean, on top of tending my little farm? And then you turned six and you met that terrible snake, the danger that brought out your gifts. I saw it then, how the two of you could fulfill that future as it'd been foretold one day. I could see the difference you could make, the lives you could save, and I felt at peace with my choice. It was then that the Skull came back to me too.

I'd known on the day that I'd seen it that the card foretold death, and not just far-off death, of strangers who might meet their end if you weren't there to save them. I'd seen my own death in that painted card. I still don't know when you'll be reading this note, how many more years we'll have together, or how I will inevitably meet my end, but I am writing you this note now realizing the truth of all of it, and I need you to know how we came to this and why.

Aton, you are so strong, and not just in your arms, or the skills you're learning from York, but in your heart. You are steadfast and true, dedicated, and always know what is right.

Aaron, you have a gift for magic stronger than my own and it makes me proud to see it, but your kindness and thoughtfulness make me even prouder.

I know I'm only seeing a glimpse of the gifts you'll share with the world and of the heroes you'll become, of the men you're turning out to be, and it all makes me so happy and so proud.

There's something else the fortune teller told me that was true—that "life is never so cruel that it affords us no joy." I've had joy, so much joy that I can hardly express it here: Aton catching his first sheep for shearing, Aaron's first steps, the two of you making me a cake for my birthday. In all of my years of life, I've never had more joy than what I've experienced with the two of you. My life on this mountain, in our cottage, with my sons, has been worth every moment of fear and struggle and hardship. It'd have been worth a thousand times more.

You've both given me more than I could ever ask for, and so I could never ask you anything in return, but I would suggest that you think about my story. There are people out there, people you've never met, who may be very far away, who will need your help. I don't need any cards of destiny to tell you that the road to them will be hard and dangerous, what with humans' fear of werewolves and casters, of elves, dwarves, or nokken distrust of the humans you appear to be, of long roads and bad weather, and of demons lurking in the dark forests and crags of the world. No, this path will not be easy, and I will not ask you to walk it. I will leave the decision up to you as it'd been left to me. My only wish is that you both stay well, stay together, take care of each other, and, whatever you do, find happiness for yourselves, whatever choice you end up making. That's all a mother can ever wish for her children. Know that I will always love you, I will always be watching, and I will always be with you.

    Your loving mother

*Marilyn*

## CHAPTER 13

## *Choice*

"Aton," Aaron called, still unable to look away from the papers in his hands. The older boy jogged in a moment later, looking him over with concern. Pale and wide-eyed, Aaron extended the letter to Aton with trembling fingers. Aton took it, confusion plain on his face until he saw the handwriting. He read the letter and then read it again before passing it back to Aaron. The older boy's face was a mask completely void of emotion or reaction, save for the unfocused gaze as he stared out the kitchen window.

Aaron took back the note without a sound, but kept his own eyes trained on his twin's face, silently willing him to tell him that it was all nonsense. Of course there wasn't a story about them being needed to save a whole group of people. Of course two not-even-teenage boys could not be responsible for deciding who lived and who died.

When his brother spoke next, it wasn't the denial Aaron had been expecting. "Start packing."

"Packing? You're joking."

"You read the letter."

"Yes, I did, and it talked about hardships, dangers, and demons. Why on Eris would we want to do any of that?"

"Because it's what we were meant to do. Our purpose. Our destiny."

"Are you listening to yourself? Destiny? You don't believe that."

"Why not?" Aaron's brother stood a little straighter. "Mother did. That's why we're on this mountain. She was preparing us to go on this journey."

"This journey to where?" Aaron demanded.

"The card said the location of the rising sun, which is to the east."

"East? East isn't a destination; it's a direction. And what are we supposed to find in the east?"

"People who need our help."

"What people? Where? How?"

"We're to share our powers with them." Aton offered an answer for only the last question.

"Which power? Your strength or my magic?"

Aton shrugged. "Both."

"So they'll need you to chop down a tree and me to light the hearth fire so they can make bread, thus saving the town from starvation? Aton, we've never done anything significant with our powers."

"I've been training to fight," he growled.

"And how many fights have you actually been in? How about York?"

"You know about his battles—"

The younger twin cut off the older. "Yeah. Against humans. You're proposing we go out into a world thick with demons. Even York only saw the one, and half a dozen men only scratched it."

"It's what we're meant to do," the larger twin insisted.

"I'm not going." Aaron crossed his arms over his chest, though he was in no way as intimidating as his brother.

"The letter talked about the Two of Tombs, two twins, one light and one dark. It has to be the two of us."

"That was part of Mother's reading, her choice. Who knows? Maybe the reading was just about you. You're the one who feels so strongly about 'destiny.' You go find it."

Aton's voice softened a touch. "You want to stay here alone for the rest of your life?"

Aaron turned his head away from his brother's serious face, nose in the air, trying to seem resolute and aloof. He looked out over the land that had been his home for his entire life. Through the window he could see the pastures filled with fluffy sheep, and the hill with the apple tree on it, and yellow flowers waving in the breeze.

It startled him to realize that he didn't want to stay there, not anymore, not as things stood. Their house and fields and silly sheep would always remind him of happier days, but the fresh grave on the rise would be a constant reminder of their loss. No, he didn't want to stay, but neither did he want to trek halfway around the world and possibly run into demons that would try to eat him, destiny or no.

Aton must've seen him waffling because he added, "It's what she wanted—for us to go and become heroes."

That stung. He glared at his brother for the jab, but the older boy looked neither abashed nor apologetic.

Aaron knew his brother was right. Even though she'd written that she'd never choose for them, their mother had followed the advice of the fortune teller and had said she would be proud of the heroes they'd one day become. She wouldn't have trained him or asked for York's help if she wasn't expecting them to leave. She might not have even written the letter at all if she'd meant to spare them from that future. Only she had written it.

Or was the letter and the training just her doing the best she could? Was she only trying to be as brave for her sons as they would have to be one day, the day when their destiny came calling? If she believed none of them could avoid it, then maybe she could rise to meet it and take pleasure in every bright moment leading up to it. It was clear that, for her sons, she would do anything and everything she could to make sure that they were as safe and prepared as she could make them in the face of this inevitability. In that spirit, Aaron could hardly do less.

"What's your plan?"

"Gather our things. Whatever we'll need on the road and anything that'll fetch a price. And then—" Aton paused, looking out the window toward the mountains. "We head east."

## CHAPTER 14

# *Vidar*

The following morning, Aaron and Aton were loaded down with heavy packs. The elder twin had taken the shepherd's hook from the wall and they'd hiked up the slope to the fresh mound of dirt. They stood for a moment, silent, gazing at the daffodils dancing in the early breeze. Aaron's legs felt heavy and cold, just like the lump in his chest.

Finally, Aton broke the silence. "We're going now, Mother. Heading out to face our future, just like you said. We'll make you proud. We love you, and thank you for everything." The older boy stood, the same breeze blowing his dark hair around his set features, which might as well have been carved from stone. Even though he wasn't even twelve yet, in that moment, he looked every inch the stoic hero they were supposed to become.

Aaron didn't feel like a hero. He felt he should speak too, but he couldn't think of the words to say. Even if he had, a tightness closed his throat in an icy, iron grip. Fear, guilt, sorrow, and anger were so tightly balled up within him that he could barely breathe, let alone utter a sound.

Then Aton added after taking a beep breath, "And you don't need to worry. I'll take care of Aaron. We love you."

After that, the older twin turned and walked toward the fluffy herd of bleary-eyed sheep, hook in hand, intent on wrangling them into some semblance of order.

Aaron watched him go. The anger in his gut dimmed, but guilt and sorrow welled up to fill the vacated space. He turned back to the grave. "We'll miss you," he squeezed out, hindered by his unshed tears. "I know you didn't want this for us either. You wouldn't want us to be sent into danger for something as vague as 'destiny.'" He watched the flowers nod along with his words. "But if you could be brave and strong for us, and you were, and if you could make the sacrifices you did, then I suppose I can too. I don't know how yet, but I'll make you proud. And I'll take care of Aton too," he hastened to add. "I love you." He gave a shaky little smile, the wind, filled with the scent of apple blossoms, tussling his hair.

Adjusting the straps on his shoulders, he turned back and found Aton waiting for him at the head of the path leading down the mountain. He spared one last look around at the cottage, the fields, the peak, and the apple tree. He was sorry to be leaving, but his brother was right; it was time to go. There was nothing left for him in that place save ghosts and memories. He jogged the last little bit, catching up with his brother as they started down.

Driving the sheep along the mountain road was a precarious business. They had nearly twenty of the beasts, and even though they couldn't easily run away on so narrow a path, they kept getting dangerously close to the edge. Aton's quick action with the hook saved more than a few fluffy heads from jumping into a cloud.

Once they were on flat ground things became easier. The elder led the way while the younger, armed with the hook, kept the flock moving. They herded the animals along the road in the direction of Vidar, a path both familiar and strange for the lack of a chaperone.

The light twin heard and smelled the town well before he saw it and knew what to expect when he entered the main gate. Stalls and stores lined either side of the wide main street, teeming with people crammed in together shoulder to shoulder. On market day, the population of Vidar seemed to double. From every quadrant people talked and shouted over clacking hooves and clattering wheels. His ears ached almost at once. He always forgot how loud market day could be. Smells of every sort, from baking bread to animal leavings and worse, mingled in his nose to the point that it became too numb to tell one from another. Everywhere there were people, specifically humans, as far as he could tell—farmers, like them, come from far-flung fields, merchants and peddlers from even farther, bringing with them scents and sights, some of which he'd never seen.

As Aaron looked, Vidar looked back. All eyes fell upon them as they led their flock through the center of town. The animal yards were on the outskirts, but it would've taken them all day to circumnavigate the perimeter, and Aton was in too big a hurry for that. Nasty looks and curses from people trying to get past followed them on their parade, but none of it deterred the older boy, who led them straight as an arrow like he knew where he was going. Though, Aaron suspected, he was only following his nose. They walked on, noticing the merchants turn from ones selling silk to ones selling wool, the jewelry shops fall away to be replaced by farriers, and the bakeries substituted by butchers.

At the north edge of town lay the beast markets. Pens and corrals on every street blocked the view of the rest of the surrounding countryside. Each pen and corral was filled with goats, pigs, and horses all pawing and calling out in their own way, making a din loud enough to rival the auctioneers. They'd never had cause to be in this section as their mother had acquired their sheep before they were born, and Aaron was glad they'd passed it earlier. It was by far the worst part of town according to his theoretically heightened werewolf senses.

When Aaron and Aton entered the quarter proper with their wooly stock, they garnered everyone's attention in a new way. The crowd no longer held sneers of annoyance; instead their stares were tinged with a hungry edge. His brother's glower kept most of the older predators away, implying they'd be no easy mark for swindlers, all except for one ancient and wizened old man. Walking with a bent spine and leaning heavily on a stick, the cadaverous codger tottered up to the twins.

"Why, hello there, boys." He gave them a wide smile devoid of most of its teeth. "It looks like you've come here to sell. You're lucky I found you first. These old jackals around here would as soon bite you as give you a proper trade. Yes, I'm sure we can come to an arrangement that would suit us all just fine." He settled both hands atop his cane and a gummy grin spread through the wrinkles as he waited for their reply.

When it came, it was brief. "We're looking for a man named York," the darker boy said.

The joviality fled from the old trader at once. He stood a little straighter as he asked, "What do you want with York?"

"That's our business."

The man's face creased even more as his frown deepened. "He's not real reputable if you get my meaning." Then he clarified. "He'll swindle you if you give him half a chance."

"Thank you for the warning," Aton replied without warmth. "Now, where can we find him?"

"I'm telling you, you'll not get a better deal with him than you will with me. Ask anyone around here and they'll tell you the same. Just ask them about Old Jaspen."

"We'll take our chances with York."

The old man turned his head and spat a glob of something thick and yellow. "On your own head then."

Aaron wasn't sure that they'd get anything more out of Old Jaspen, but the man pointed one gnarled and nubby finger down a street. "He's that way, but when he robs you blind, don't say Old Jaspen didn't warn you."

"Thank you," Aaron's brother replied with a brief nod before walking in the direction Old Jaspen had indicated, thankfully away from the animal yards. He hurried to drive the sheep after his twin.

They found York a little way down the indicated road. He was leaning against a barrel in front of an open shop door with a knife in one hand, carving an apple he held in the other. When he saw the twins approaching with their herd, he dropped the fruit in surprise. Stowing the knife quickly, he hurried over.

"Boys," he said. "What in Enoch's name are you doing here?"

"We've come to sell our sheep," Aton replied.

"By His light, why?" the ex-captain snapped. Then he said more gently, "You need those sheep."

"We can't take them with us, York."

"With you? With you where?"

"We're leaving. We've got some family in the east we're planning on visiting."

The brothers had talked about it. They knew lying to York wasn't right, but he'd never help two children wander off into the mountains by themselves with nearly no goal in mind aside from heading east. He'd been the first to tell them to stay out of the woods for fear of the demons in the shadows. They needed him to think they had a plan and people to take care of them, though it still didn't feel right to Aaron.

York looked dubious. "Boys, I know you just lost your ma, but that's no reason to be racing off into the wilds. You need time to think about this, time to—"

"We're leaving, York. You said if we ever needed anything we should come to you, but if you won't help us, there was a toothless trader, Old Jaspen, back there who seemed eager."

"Alright, alright." York put up his hands in surrender. "I'll help you as much as I'm able. How much are you looking to get?"

"As much as we can."

York cast his eyes appraisingly over their heads at the flock. He'd obviously seen them wandering around during his visits, but never with the eye of acquiring them for his own. With a sigh he said, "Come with me."

He led them back over to the shop door. A sign hanging over it bore the name *York's Cellar* and depicted a wheel of cheese with a knife plunged into it and a frothy mug of beer next to the cheese. Aton followed York inside while Aaron waited on the doorstep to watch the sheep.

They'd of course visited York's store in the past. A kind of shop during the day, it turned into a small alehouse in the evenings serving fresh bread, sausage, and sheep's cheese. It was why their mother and the ex-captain had become friends in the first place.

The building wasn't all that large—it held a handful of tables pushed to the sides during the day and a counter that doubled as a bar. York stepped behind this and pulled a heavy-looking metal box from underneath. He drew a key from within his shirt and unlocked the box, then scrutinized the contents thoughtfully.

"I can give you seventy-five for the lot," he said.

"Done." Aton nodded immediately.

They'd known York long enough to understand that he was an honest man. He'd become something of an uncle to them over the years and there was genuine affection between them all. Whatever deal he'd propose, it'd be as good as he could make it.

"There's something else." Aton started digging in his bag. "Aaron, get them out."

From his own pack Aaron produced two books. Aton, holding the three he'd gotten out, collected the other two from him. They'd kept one, the book on edible plants, in case it proved of some use on the trek east, but the older twin stacked the other five on York's counter.

"What? What's all this?"

"We want to sell the books too."

"Boys, I'm not a bookseller. I wouldn't have any notion of how much—"

"Just give us whatever you've got," Aton pressed. "You'll make it back and then some."

York looked at his apprentice with concern in his eyes. "Do you really need to leave so soon?"

"The sooner we get started, the better."

York's frown deepened, but he produced a bag, heavy with coin, from the depths of the box. "Go on and take it, for all the good it'll do you out there."

The young swordsman took the bag, feeling the weight of it, but not bothering to look inside. "Thank you, York, for all you've done for us and our mother."

"I don't think I'm doing you any favors," he said, crossing his arms over his wide chest. "But since it doesn't look like I can stop you, then at least I can make your way a little easier."

"You have. Thank you again, and goodbye."

Not waiting for the older man to reply, maybe fearing he'd try to stop them anyway, Aton passed Aaron in the doorway, turning back toward the stockyards. York came to the doorway too, watching the dark-haired boy stride his way through the crowd.

The younger twin started to follow but spun back, remembering to hand the shepherd's hook to the man. "Thank you, York, and be well."

"Aaron." There was hurt in the ex-captain's eyes, but Aaron didn't wait to hear more, trotting off to catch up with his brother.

Aaron took a quick look back. York was standing there, hook in hand, twenty sheep milling around his feet. He looked grim, the emotion pulling at his face, making the wrinkles a little deeper, pulling at the scar as the light caught the gray hair at his temples. He wondered then if they'd done York any favors either. They'd given him the far better end of the deal on the books they'd brought, but how many worried and sleepless nights had they given along with them? He hoped it wouldn't be too many.

## CHAPTER 15

# *The Run*

"Why are we going north? I thought we were supposed to be headed east," Aaron asked aloud as he forced his way through another thicket of brambles.

"Because we're getting off the roads," Aton replied.

"I can see that, but I'm sure there are forests a little further south too."

"There probably are, but there are most likely more towns too."

"And that's a problem because…?"

"Full moon's in two weeks."

Aaron tripped over a protruding root, his heavy pack shifting him to the left and causing him to fall with a heavy crash into the scraggly undergrowth. His older twin, neatly ducking the next branch, didn't even pause to wait for him to disentangle himself. Once free of the grasping cover he jogged to catch up. "You think something's going to happen?"

"Probably."

"Just because it's our first full moon without—" His throat slammed shut, making him unable to complete the sentence.

"We'll be twelve."

"It's not like twelve's a magic number or anything. It's supposed to happen whenever we reach our 'maturity whatever that means."

"Can't you feel it?"

Aaron was quiet. His brother must've taken his silence as confirmation, because he didn't elaborate. Did Aton feel something? Aaron wasn't sure. Plenty about his life had changed. He was colder, hungrier, and grumpier than he could ever remember being, and his guts still churned with thoughts he refused to let surface, but was there something else? His twin seemed to think so, but he wasn't sure he cared to look just then. There was too much he was and wasn't dealing with already.

Days later, still hiking directly north with the moon growing fatter by the night, they'd reached the true start of the Venduli Ackar, the range their old peak had been at the tail end of. Their little mountain had hardly been worthy of the title compared to those giants still untouched by the spring thaw. They'd turned northeast then, following the edge of the mountains, content at last that they were far enough from anything that could be reasonably called civilization.

A few more days on and they found that, whether or not they'd turned up into the mountains themselves, the terrain still rose in elevation. Aaron felt the change in pressure in his ears the higher it went. It felt like they weren't just leaving their false-normal-human lives behind, but the spring too. The farther they traveled the colder and darker it became as the trees grew thicker and the snow extended further down the slopes, and still they traveled on.

On the day of the full moon brother called a halt around midafternoon, wanting to settle in. The forest was a sea of dark green pines, all the starker for the contrasting shin-deep snow. They'd dug a little place and erected their tent, but they hadn't started a fire. They didn't want to draw any attention to themselves, especially not on that night.

With nothing left to do, they sat and waited. Aaron watched his breath curl from his mouth in the dying light, pale ghosts against the verdant pine needles. He was shivering terribly, his teeth chattering so hard he felt they might shatter. Of course that was probably due to the fact that he was dressed in only an old shirt and rough leggings. Aton was so sure that something was going to happen that he insisted that they wear their worst clothes and as few of them as possible. He'd thought it idiotic at the time, but now he found that his chattering teeth weren't loud enough to drown out his thumping heart ringing in his ears like a festival drum.

He'd realized that he hadn't really felt anything when Aton had asked him before, two weeks back, but he couldn't deny something was different now. Besides his bucking heart, there was a stirring inside him, a feeling like something was going to happen. It was like the feeling he used to get on Midwinter's Day, the morning after the longest night of the year, when he'd wake up knowing that his mother had baked sun-raisin sweet buns for their breakfast. She'd have a small gift for both of them to celebrate the birth of a new sun and a new year. It was a sense of something good coming their way, of anticipation.

His steadfast brother stood nearby. Similarly dressed in simple and tattered clothes, Aton wasn't visibly shivering. Even though they'd never shifted before, their mother had warned them that the first time was always the hardest on the shifter and their wardrobe. Hence Aton's instructions about the tattered garments. Aaron wished he could've wrapped himself in a bedroll or heavy cloak, something he could simply cast off if needed, but they had no idea what would happen, and his brother wouldn't let him risk it.

Aaron turned his face toward the sky. The sunset's pinks melted into the darker purples and blues, the snow took on the cooling tones around them, and the scent of pine and cold pricked at his nose. "S-s-so," Aaron tried to say, clamping down on his rebellious teeth. "When does this all happen?"

"Soon." The word sounded as solid as his brother looked.

"H-h-how do you know?"

"I can feel it."

"We've felt good on full moons before. A deeper voice and a little chest hair don't mean the wolf just springs up."

"The shift isn't being pushed down anymore."

Aaron's back straightened. "You're saying s-s-she—"

"She told us she was."

"That doesn't mean tonight—"

"I can hear your heart beating from here."

Aaron bit down on his teeth again, not willing to admit he could hear the echo of his own heart in his brother's chest too. He rubbed his arms, trying to get life back into them, but found that they weren't quite as cold as they'd been a moment before.

As the light dimmed further, he found he was growing warmer, not colder. The ever-present chirping of birds and scurrying squirrels had disappeared at some point in the evening, though he couldn't have said when. Sweat was breaking out on his forehead, the night suddenly feeling more like summer somehow, despite the snow. He felt his blood heating, felt his muscles tensing on their own, felt his body readying itself for something. Fight or flight? His head started swimming. He felt dizzy and turned his eyes back to the sky, his pupils opening too wide, searching for the light. "Aton." The word was a sigh, his lungs pulling in breath like a forgeman's bellows, trying to pull in enough air.

His brother didn't respond. In the next instant Aaron saw him fall to his knees in the snow, a nearly inhuman roar tearing from his throat, arms wrapping around his shoulders, hunching in on himself. His screams echoed terribly.

"Aton!" Aaron took one step toward his brother when the first rays of the moon met the yawning maw of his widening pupils. The light held him, pierced him, entered him; it was like no sensation he'd ever felt before—being filled by that pure, cold, clean, white light. And then the pain came.

He screamed, falling, just as his brother had. All of his muscles spasmed at once, jerking and twisting. Sharp snaps and flashes of agony flared as his bones began popping and shifting positions, pulling the sinews with them. He tried to hold himself together, tried not to feel like he was tearing apart, but the pain was too great. He threw himself sideways into a snowdrift. Boiling on the inside, every inch of him felt set alight by the intensity of the pain, and in his addled mind, he imagined steam coming off his skin as he writhed in the white powder.

Besides the heat—and it was almost impossible to think beyond the heat—he found he could barely breathe. His clothes were too tight, suffocating him. He had to get rid of them. He tore at the fabric, frantic for a handful of heartbeats. The ripping was as audible as their screams and his exposed skin prickled everywhere the air and light touched.

He stretched and he broke, and everything *moved*, in ways, he was sure, they were never meant to. His eyes bulged in their sockets and his vision went white with hot torment, his very skull warping around them.

Aaron was lost to the shift for what seemed like days, and yet when he finally collapsed, panting and exhausted, he saw that the moon hadn't yet even cleared the trees. Gasping for air, he saw the shafts of moonlight filtering past the branches and marveled at its brilliance, like shattered diamonds hanging in the air. Everything seemed brighter and sharper and deeper, like he'd been looking at the world through water until just that moment. He heard the wind blowing on the mountaintop and felt his ear turn to hear it better, turn on top of his head. He smelled things, warm scents scurrying away through the pine forest. He could tell the size of the things by their scent alone, and how far away they were, and the traces of their last meal lingering on their breath.

He pushed himself up, the agony from a moment ago disappearing like a dream, like his steaming breath, and he looked around. The world was the same and yet changed, much like himself.

Standing in awe with a dancer-like grace, balancing on toes in the snow, he held up a hand, examining it with his new eyes. He still had hands, the configuration of four fingers and thumb familiar to him, only altered. They were now covered all over with short, sleek, silvery fur, each digit tipped with a long, hard, black claw. Turning it over, he found rough, black pads at the tips of his fingers and covering his upper palm and a pad at the base of his thumb. They were just as dexterous as they'd ever been, but much sturdier and pulsing with new strength.

His gaze traveled down his arm, to his shoulder, and then down the length of him to the tip of his new tail waving behind him. All of it was covered in varying lengths and shades with silver-gray fur. Circling on two new legs, he noticed that they were a little further from human. They bent at the knee and then again at his extended heel, hock-like, similar to a horse or dog. He couldn't feel the cold through the padded and insulated toes that he wiggled in the powdery crystals. They were more canine too, bigger, thicker toes, with more claws poking out through the fur, no doubt with more thick pads beneath. Glancing behind, he saw his footprint looking just like a wolf's, though far, far larger.

He stared back down at his hands, flexed his fingers, and breathed. "I don't think I believed it."

His ears swiveled, directed toward a large crunching sound coming from behind him. New thoughts and knowledge flew through his mind in less than a moment. The sound he'd heard was big enough to be a threat, and close. His twitching nose detected snow, pine, and then a deep musk of fur covering muscle and blood. His own muscles bunched, his mind getting ready for what came next, until…

He relaxed. His nose also detected apple blossoms and wool—the smells of home—and something else unnamed but equally familiar.

Aaron looked around, but almost missed seeing Aton against the dark forest backdrop. His brother had come through the shift like a piece of the night itself. With inky black fur, with only the slightest variations in dark gray, Aton was even bigger than he'd been before. Aaron hadn't noticed, but his own vantage point had elevated by at least another head. His twin, on the other hand, had turned into a small boulder. All of the muscles he'd honed in his training with York had grown alongside his general height. He stood solid, immovable. They'd always been different, but in that moment, more than ever before, bright silver and black, they looked completely opposite. Except for their eyes, Aaron noted. Their violet eyes were still the same, a shared family trait.

"Aton," he said, noting his voice's deeper tone.

"Yes," the fuzzy boulder replied, grinning, teeth startlingly white against all the black.

"It's true. She was right."

"You doubted it?" A deep chuckle rumbled through Aton.

"I didn't know." Aaron looked at his padded hands again, thinking.

Aaron's brother didn't let him wallow. Aton took off like a shot, leaping into the trees and vanishing at once. Startled, but not wanting to be left behind, Aaron followed, plunging into the slightly brighter forest.

Aaron felt fast, so fast, so strong, as he whipped through the trees like a beam of moonlight himself. He could see flashes of the dark wolf ahead of him and pushed his new legs, gaining even more momentum. The hulking beast, as large as a bear, kept just a pace ahead. He laughed at the challenge, at his new strength, at the freedom, pulling in great lungsful of cold, sweet air. He ran and ran, never losing his brother, who must've been holding back for his sake, leaping at him only for the other to dodge away.

He jumped logs and brambles, dodged trees, and ducked branches as though he knew where each impediment lay. Hopping up on a tree, broken mid-trunk, standing on its exposed core, Aaron threw back his head and howled a long peal of ringing delight. All of his feelings—his joy, his sorrow, his fear, and his exaltation—were poured into the one note. His brother lent his own voice; their song echoed away from them into the deep forest, into the dark sky. They'd been in hiding for their entire lives, but there, out in the forest, under the bright moon, they could be free. They could be different and make no apology for any of it.

## CHAPTER 16

# *Gifts in the Moonlight*

They'd ran until the night grew thin and Aaron could almost smell the approaching dawn. As far as they'd run, it wasn't hard to find their camp again, not when everything they owned had a touch of sheep smell to it. They collapsed next to their bags with wide grins.

"That," Aaron said, tongue lolling out and steaming, "was amazing."

His brother chuckled in agreement.

Aaron was ready to curl up and fall asleep right there—no need for a tent—when he caught sight of the scraps of his clothing littered about their campsite. "We'll need to buy bigger clothes."

When his brother didn't comment Aaron turned, only to see Aton rummaging in his pack. "I hope you're looking for breakfast," Aaron said, letting his head flop back to the snow. "I think we scared away everything with a heartbeat for thirty miles."

His fellow werewolf still didn't reply, continuing to dig. Aaron sat up, watching him, and when his brother emerged with a bag, he was disappointed to see that it wasn't food. Instead, it was the sack that'd been in the cart next to their mother on that terrible day.

Aaron suddenly lost his appetite. "Aren't those the gifts Mother asked York to buy?" But of course he knew they were. "Why are you bringing them out now? Our birthday was a week ago." They'd both let the day pass unremarked. There hadn't seemed to be much to celebrate. "Wouldn't it have made more sense to open them then?"

"It felt right to save them till now," was all the answer he received as the older boy undid the drawstring on the bag. Aaron saw his twin's eyes grow wide as his fingers alighted on something.

Aaron sat up a little straighter to see. Aton's dark fist emerged holding a sword and scabbard. Reverently the black werewolf parted the steel from its casing. It was a short sword that spoke of years of use, judging from the nicks and scratches that covered it. It might as well have been covered in gold the way Aton's eyes were fixed to it. The larger boy weighed it in his hand, sliced it through the air, and looked all the more appreciative. It must've been a good blade, despite how rough it looked to Aaron's ignorant view.

"No wonder Mother needed York." Aton's eyes were still fixed to the weapon as Aaron spoke. "York would've known what to look for. He'd have gotten you the best sword in Vidar."

The larger wolf gave it another swing, the steel singing as it sliced through the early-dawn air. It looked tiny in Aton's larger, lupine digits, but Aaron didn't say so as he took up the bag from where it lay.

"I hope he didn't get me a sword too." Aaron tried to joke, smile lopsided at best, only Aton still wasn't listening.

One last object sat heavy in the sack. It was solid, but clearly nowhere near the sword's weight. Aaron's hand met something solid and rectangular. Pulling out the object, his heart picked up its pace once again.

"A spell book?" Aaron wondered aloud, then his ears drooped in realization. "It couldn't be. There'd have been no way she could've asked York to get a twelve-year-old a spell book. She'd never even mentioned magic around him. Besides, there's no way he'd be able to find something like that in Vidar."

He traced his fingers over the cover, leather dyed forest green, smooth and unmarked. There was no title on its spine either, no hint to its contents. Aaron opened the cover slowly, gently, and paused. He flipped the first page, then the next, then the next.

Finally able to tear his eyes away from his own gift, Aton asked, "What is it?"

Aaron held out the book to Aton wordlessly. Aton strapped the new sword and scabbard to his belt, leaving his old, wooden blade forgotten in the snow as he walked over. Aton took the book, opened it, and then flipped through the pages. "Blank?"

Aaron nodded. There wasn't a single scribble to indicate what their mother had been thinking in giving him this present. It was possible that she'd meant to write something in it, only she'd never gotten the chance. Books, even blank ones, were expensive, so there must've been a good reason for such a gift, but what?

"Maybe she wanted you to fill it." Aton shrugged, tossing the volume back to Aaron.

"Fill it? With what?"

Aton shrugged again. "I imagine that'd be up to you."

Aton turned away and settled down in a snowbank below the base of a tree and reexamined his new gift, clearly more taken with it than he was with Aaron's.

What had their mother been thinking? That she'd gotten Aaron a gift at all showed that she cared about him, but what was he supposed to do with a blank book? Record spells in it? He could read and write, she'd seen to that, but he didn't know how to write a spell. He threw up his hands and shoved the book into his pack. He'd give it more thought later. As he lay back in the snow, watching the moon set and his mind reeling, sleep took him quickly and completely.

## CHAPTER 17

## *Three Sides*

Aaron's foot, despite being padded, slipped out from under him on an unseen patch of ice. Skidding face-first into the snow, the hare dashed under a thornbush and disappeared from view. Snarling, Aaron pushed himself up, raising his left hand, which began to glow spring green, the air cooling further and taking on the familiar sweet tang as he readied to burn the thicket, rabbit and all.

"Let it go," his brother said, walking up behind him.

He didn't lower his hand right away, his palm still pulsing with soft illumination before it faded. He stood brushing the snow from the fur of his face and chest.

"Let's get back to camp."

Aaron was still in the middle of ridding himself of the evidence of his latest failure when his nose twitched. Looking back at Aton, he saw that his brother had a pair of hares and a pheasant slung over one shoulder.

"How?" he stammered.

"Wolf form gives me speed."

"And flight?"

"The bird was eating berries off a bush."

Aaron's muzzle scrunched and his ears drooped, but he didn't comment further and followed his big brother back to camp. Since he'd shifted into this half-human-half-wolf shape, the cold barely bothered him anymore, his thick double coat better than any woolen one he'd ever owned. The sentiment must've been shared, because, without talking about it, the brothers hadn't bothered setting up their tent in days and only made fires when the black wolf caught them something to eat.

As soon as they sat down, the hunter got out his knife and started skinning one of the hares. Aaron sat across from him and took the second rabbit begrudgingly.

"I hate this part." Aaron's borrowed, smaller knife sliced through the skin with ease.

"You've done it plenty before," his brother said, without looking up.

"It was bad enough with the spring lambs, and that was before I had a wolf's nose." He crinkled his muzzle for emphasis. "There's got to be a better way to do this."

"Like what?"

"Burn it off."

"You'd ruin the meat."

"Or blow it off, or soak it, or I don't know." He raked the metal through the center of the animal, spilling its blood and marring the white snow.

Aton didn't respond, only setting down the cleaned carcass in clean powder and then taking his knife to a stick, intent on making a roasting spit.

Not even halfway through his task, the younger brother put down the hare. "I'll go start the fire."

He piled sticks on a bare patch of ground they'd cleared for the purpose. The light came to his hand readily, Aaron relishing in the familiar warmth and scent, the fire leaping into being a moment later among the kindling.

"You're getting better at that," his twin said, handing him the second cleaned rabbit, already skewered and ready for roasting.

They sat in silence, the only sound the popping fire and sizzling meat. Had the brothers not been two massive werewolves, Aaron might've worried that the smell would attract larger predators, but so far anything larger than a squirrel had given them a wide berth.

"I smelled smoke earlier."

The sudden conversation caught Aaron off guard. "And?"

"There's a human town up ahead of us."

Aaron's hands stopped rotating his dinner. "And you know it's humans?"

Aton nodded.

"How close?"

"We'll reach it tomorrow at the pace we're going."

"What are we going to do? Can we go around it?"

"We could," Aton started. Then he added, "Or we could go through it."

"Through the town? Like this?" Aaron gestured with his free hand to the fur covering him from head to tail under his clothes. They weren't sure if werewolves wore clothes, and the clothes they had didn't fit well at all, especially not the pants, but it felt strange to go around without anything covering them. A town would give them the opportunity to pick up better options. Was a new set of clothes worth the risk?

"We'll have to shift back."

"And you know how to do that?" Nature and the full moon had forced them to shift and seeing as it had been a boon for dealing with the cold and in getting extra energy for hiking, neither boy had even mentioned getting back to their human shapes.

"Can't be that hard."

"Why would we want to go through a town?"

"We could get supplies, more rope, cord, maybe some bread and cheese."

"You'd risk a bunch of humans skinning us alive for some cheese?"

Aaron's brother gave him a flat look. "We're less likely to get skinned walking through the town as humans than we'd be sneaking around it as werewolves."

Aaron shrugged. "Fine. Change back then."

The black wolf stared.

"You want to go to town? You go first."

Aton stopped cooking and stuck his spit, meat up, into the snow. Closing his eyes, breathing steadily, he appeared to be applying all of his concentration to the task. "I can feel...myself," the dark wolf said after a moment, eyes still closed. "The boy I've always been." His eyes scrunched and his brow furrowed. "There's something else."

"What?" Aaron was instantly on alert.

"Something different. Me, but—" Aaron's twin didn't finish the thought. Doubling over with a lupine snarl and gripping his sides, the dark werewolf started to shift.

Aaron thought he might be sick as he heard the first of his brother's sinews start to pop. He'd not seen his brother shift before—he'd been going through it himself at the time—but the sight made him want to retch. It looked like something was crawling under the black fur, making the muscles squirm and move into new configurations, like worms after a rain. He heard the jarring snaps and cracks and watched joints bend in ways they weren't supposed to. If they'd actually gotten a chance to eat the rabbit, he was sure he'd have lost it right then, but through the disgust he knew that something wasn't right.

The growls and snarls weren't turning to shouts. The fur wasn't falling out or shrinking in and Aton's body was condensing in on itself, not lengthening. Aaron leaned closer to get a better look, hoping to make sense of what was going on, but not too close, in case he received a flailing claw in the face for his curiosity.

When Aton stopped struggling, growling, and thrashing, he sat in the snow panting, his long pink tongue lolling out of his long dark muzzle.

"Aton," Aaron said, staring at his sibling, "you're a wolf."

They'd always been part wolves inside, and more recently they'd changed into a sort of human-wolf hybrid. Only in front of Aaron now was a huge, black, normal-looking wolf, sitting on its haunches, its forepaws on the ground supporting its upper torso, just like any dog he'd ever seen. His brother was clearly far larger than the average wolf and the clothes that he wore draped off of him in odd ways, a clear indication something was off, but otherwise he was indistinguishable from the normal variety of wild dog.

The lupine looked down, lifting paws that hid in sleeves too wide for his arms. He then sprang to all fours and turned around in a circle, trying to see all of himself at once, but only looked like he was chasing his tail.

Aaron saw the violet eyes that stared back at him were bright with excitement and the mouth was hanging open in a wolfish grin. His brother was enjoying this. "What does it feel like?" he wanted to know, still unable to fully grasp that the animal in front of him was, in fact, his older twin. If he hadn't just seen it for himself, he'd never have believed they could have a third form. Their mother had certainly never mentioned it.

The black wolf chuffed at him.

Without understanding any words, he understood the intent. "Me?"

The transformation had looked painful, and if it was anything like what the first shift had been, it absolutely would be. Did he really want to do that again?

The wolf at Aaron's feet struggled out of his human clothes, exposing his glossy black coat fully to the night air, then lowered himself back to his haunches. He sat, staring at Aaron. The look was so penetrating that it didn't even matter that he apparently couldn't speak in this new form. Aaron looked away, not meeting the wolf-Aton's eyes. The animal bowed down, front paws outstretched, tail high in the air, stare still challenging.

"Stop it," Aaron said. "I don't want to play."

The wolf growled.

"No."

The wolf growled deeper.

"Fine." He growled back and the wolf started panting again, still in the playful pose, the smile back on his muzzle.

Sighing deeply, Aaron closed his eyes to begin searching within himself for the "other him" his brother had mentioned. Of course he couldn't "see" anything save for the blackness behind his eyelids, and he could only feel the steady rhythm of his own breathing—in and out. And then there was something else. If he thought about it, he could almost hear the sheep and smell the apple blossoms and feel the wind on his bare skin. It was like he was that boy again, sitting in the afternoon sun and watching the flock move by him like fluffy clouds. Turning away from the sensation, he felt something darker, but richer too. That way was the forest, the soil, leaves under paws, the scent of fur and mountain breezes, heat from muscles, running under the cool moon's light. It was like the night of their first shift. He mentally moved in that direction.

Instantly his body was jabbed with red-hot agony again. This too was like the night of his first shift, only without the full moon shining down on him. Pops and snaps and creaks and whines filled his ears as his body went through the intensive process of changing forms.

When it was over, he slumped over in a drift, glad for its cooling touch, and watched his breaths leave his maw in icy puffs. His darker half padded up, crunching the icy crust with every footfall, and nudged at his shoulder with his nose. He got to his feet.

It was strange, even stranger than becoming the half-and-half version they'd just been. He was on all fours and there didn't seem to be a way to straighten up. His legs felt longer, but his vantage point was much lower. There wasn't as much power in him either, more than human certainly, but nothing compared with the strength of his in-between shape. Though, after examining everything he could about his new shape—and it seemed impossible—but his senses, especially his hearing and smell, had gotten even better.

The black wolf nudged him again, this time with his whole head. Aaron looked at him. Grinning like the excited twelve-year-old boy in a wolf's body that he was, Aaron's twin took off into the trees again without even a yip. He paused to look around the camp at their packs and their forgotten dinner, and sneezed at the ash that drifted into his nostrils. As though that had been the jolt he'd needed, the silvery wolf followed the black, just like before, running into the night and leaving it all behind.

## CHAPTER 18

# *Fangs of Steel*

Near dawn they returned to their camp, their fire long since dead, their energy well spent too. Aaron laid down heavily by his pack while his dark wolf brother collapsed by the hare he'd not finished cooking earlier. Without apparent thought or preamble, Aton sank his teeth directly into the still red and glistening flank of the carcass. Aaron wrinkled his nose, listening to his brother crunch through the small bones like a handful of nuts. Instead of ripping straight into his own raw rabbit, the younger twin thought of lamb chops and their mother's roasted carrots and parsnips, thick with the scent of rosemary—

Aaron's body spasmed. As he crouched down, a whine tore from deep in his throat. Muscles and bone moved; the hair that covered his whole body retracted beneath the skin, like growing in reverse, until he was no more than a twelve-year-old human boy, shivering and naked in the deep wood.

The black wolf cocked an ear at him while he worried toothily at the hare's spine.

"It's great that we have a third form and all," Aaron said, reaching for his clothes, "but we can't travel that way."

His brother sat up, the bloody ruins of his meal between his paws.

"How could we carry our packs? And even if we could figure out how to squirm into them, you think the people around here wouldn't notice? We might as well travel in our were-forms."

The wolf flattened his ears and looked to their bags, letting out a side-heaving sigh. Taking one more mouthful of the near-raw hare, Aton tensed, readying himself for the shift.

Aaron looked away, distracting himself by putting on his pants. Watching a shift wasn't quite as bad as going through one, but it wasn't pleasant either.

Once the transformation had ended, blood still coating his lips, bared olive skin faintly steaming in the chilled air, Aton dressed too. "It hurts less the third time," said Aton as he pulled clothes from his bag.

"Did it?" Aaron hadn't noticed. But maybe it had been quicker by a pop or two.

"You're right," his brother said, only slightly muffled as the shirt went over his head. "We can't travel that way. The wolf is faster, but not stronger. If we run into any demons we'll want the best balance."

The next shiver that went through Aaron had nothing to do with the snow. In their human shapes, bundled against the biting cold they'd nearly forgotten while traveling in wolf-fur coats, the boys approached the town in the early morning light of the new day.

Upon second glance at the throw of buildings, Aaron found the settlement wasn't really worth the name. Smaller than Vidar by a considerable margin, the place only had one main road, and that a muddy rut, cutting through the length of it. With few permanent structures and another smattering of tents to fill in the gaps, the place looked like a trapper's camp more than anything else, partly for the tents, but more so for the smell of animal blood and innards permeating the air.

Few people stood outside, chatting with puffs of steam to indicate which one was speaking at the moment. All were bundled so tightly in dense fur coats, hoods, and gloves that their faces were the only exposed patch of skin. It was impossible to tell much else past all the trappings, but every one of them looked hearty and tough, men and woman used to a rougher way of life. The fruits of that life stretched out tanning in the sun next to each tent—skins. Everything from deer hide, to beaver pelts, to wolf coats was spread out in a macabre display.

"I don't think you'll be getting any cheese here," Aaron said.

Every person and surface they could see was covered in the grisly handiwork, not a scrap of cotton cloth or weave of wool anywhere, only beady eyes staring out at them from beneath hoods of skin not their own.

Aaron had felt eyes on them in Vidar too, but back there they'd only needed to worry about being stoned to death. Here he could be killed and then actually end up as someone's coat. His mental hackles started to rise and he worried that something of his wolf might be showing, his shoulders creeping up at the thought.

Aton of course showed no concern walking straight into the town. Passing the locals without even a glance, concentrating all his attention on the permanent buildings along the main thoroughfare, the dark-haired boy gazed up at the signs hanging in front of each door. Having found what he was looking for, he stopped outside one of the buildings, a length of rope and an ax carved into the wooden plaque above its door.

The older boy pushed open the portal and they were greeted by the sounds of tiny chiming bells. The younger was surprised by the delicate sound in so rough a surrounding, staring at the tiny silver objects hanging like an exotic bouquet of wildflowers just inside the door. The shop itself was cozy and warm and smelled of woodsmoke, all supplied by the hearth blazing merrily in the corner. The walls were a white stucco and covered nearly end to end with gleaming metal tools—shovels, hatchets, pickaxes, and knives.

"Be out in a moment," said a feminine voice from somewhere behind a curtain hanging in the back of the shop.

Aton gravitated toward the knives on the walls while Aaron saw a table closer to the back, little jars and tins covering it that smelled strongly of herbs. He picked up a tin and opened it, revealing a yellowish paste. Giving it a quick sniff he recognized pine, rosemary, and primrose oil, plus something else he just couldn't place, something rich. He closed his eyes and breathed deeply, trying to think of it—

"Not seen you around before."

Aaron set down the tin hastily, seeing a woman behind the counter. Too engrossed in the question of the paste's secrets, he hadn't noticed her come in. Her accent was thick, and one he'd never heard before. Looking at the woman herself, he saw her face was round and wide with a generous nose and mouth to fill it. A brown braid, streaked with white, cascaded over one shoulder, and crow's feet, accompanying her deep smile lines, crinkled at the corners of her bright eyes.

"We're passing through," Aton replied.

"On the way to where?" the woman asked. "Desil is about the furthest point from anything."

"We've family to the east."

"What family?" She laughed. "You all are related to dragons then?"

Both brothers stopped and looked at the woman, who was still grinning at her own joke.

Aaron piped up. "Dragons?"

"About the only thing, besides demon-infested forests, between here and the sea."

The younger twin swallowed at the mention of the creatures, but his older brother had picked up on a different part of her statement.

"Are there a lot of dragons that way?"

"Hundreds I shouldn't suppose." The woman shook her head. "One of their great strongholds is in the high mountains, I've heard, damned hard to get to, I'd imagine, if I know anything about the breed."

"A whole fortress of dragons?"

She raised a brow at Aaron. "That's what I've heard. You know, they're not the dumb beasts you all think they are."

"Of course not." Aaron shook his head quickly, hoping his brother hadn't insulted the woman.

"We're here to get supplies," Aton said, changing tact.

"Of course, of course," she said, raising broad and calloused hands. "You must be prepared for that long hike to see the family after all. Feel free to take a look around. I've got the best work anywhere due east of Gahar Barea."

"You made all of this?" Aaron asked, looking again at the odd-smelling jars.

"The metal, yes. Not that mush." She frowned at the vessels on the table. "That comes from an old herb woman who lives just a little south of Desil. Herb-infused rodent fat, or some such nonsense, but it'll heal cracked skin, too long in the cold, quicker than anything. I sell it here as a favor, and it does work, just smells awful. The demons must think so too, because she's not missed a week's delivery yet."

Aaron had to work his dry mouth before asking, "Do you see many demons in Desil?"

"Aye. We'll get the odd Fouldeer or Picker, drawn by the smell of blood and meat, no doubt. Except Desil's business is death; when you get right down to it, we take care of them quick enough. The townspeople used to see bigger, nastier things out in the woods before my time. Word is they've all been coming less and less. Tired of being killed, I should think." She shrugged. "You two ask a lot of questions. Look, tell me what you need, and I'll see what I can do."

"We need rope and cord or twine if you have it," Aton answered for them.

"I do have those." She ducked behind the counter. Aaron thought she must keep such things under there in a drawer. Only a moment later she came walking around to them, standing just below the counter's height.

"What're you staring at?" she asked, putting hands on ample hips covered by trousers made of deerskin, though her top appeared to be cloth. Both boys looked down at her, unable to speak. "You never seen a dwarf before?"

"No," Aaron said.

She sniffed. "You must have family in these Varro-forsaken mountains to be so sheltered. Is this going to be a problem?"

"No," Aaron said again, quicker this time. The dwarf woman may've been shorter than him, but he wouldn't count that against her. She was thicker than he was and not with fat. Given that she'd made all of the metal tools in the shop, it made sense when he noticed that her arms were as big around as his thighs. He'd just not noticed when she'd been behind the counter, on a step stool most likely.

"Good." She nodded, apparently glad to have that settled. "What are your names?"

"I'm Aton; he's Aaron."

"Well, Aton and Aaron, you can call me Brywyn."

"Why are you out here?" Aaron put a hand to his mouth, hoping that hadn't been as rude as it'd sounded. "I mean, I thought dwarves lived underground." He tried to cover his gaff, then wondered if he'd actually made it worse.

"We're not moles, you know." She snorted again, speaking while walking. "True, most of our finest cities are under the crust, but commerce flourishes on both sides of the rock, so here I am. And speaking of which, here's your rope and deer leather cord," she said, pulling the items from a bin at the side of the shop. "Anything else?"

"A knife," Aton said.

"Fancy yourself a dragon hunter then?"

"For my brother."

Aaron looked at his twin sharply. The woman regarded him in turn.

"Skinny," she pronounced. She looked back to Aton. "You look like you could take down a deer with your teeth, but him?" She frowned.

The brothers stilled. Did she know?

"Well," she said after a moment. "I suppose we could all stand to be a little careful in these trying times."

She walked with a rolling gait over to the other wall where knives were hung in neat rows. Long knives, short knives, choppers, and kitchen knives—a vast array of metal glittered up on the wall like jewels. She looked at them, a frown curving her full lips, until her eyes sparked, gazing at a particular blade. Standing on her tiptoes she plucked it from its hanger. "Here we go, a simple skinning knife, but enough of a flash to give most pause."

The thing was massive to Aaron's eyes, though not quite the length of Aton's short sword. "I don't think—" he began, but his brother cut him off.

"Thank you." Aton reached out for the tool. It didn't look so big in his palm as he tested the weight of it.

"You look like you might know what to do with that bit of scrap on your hip. Looking for something better? Desil doesn't have much use for proper weapons, but I have a few in the back."

"No," he replied. "I don't need another sword, but we'll take this knife."

The dwarf shrugged. "Suit yourself. Just the knife, rope, and cord then?"

"And some bread."

"Ah, Ginny's the baker in town." She walked back behind the counter and popped back up where they'd first seen her. "Just two houses down from here. The girl makes a decent enough loaf and will give you trail crackers if you've got far to go, a whole pouch for a mark. Not much to them, flour and water by my understanding, filling if bland, though eat them with tea or you're liable to break a tooth."

"Thank you; we'll go there next." Aton stepped up to the counter, pulled out the bag of coins York had given them, and placed the appropriate number of coins on the counter. The woman scooped them up in a flash and stowed them in a box below the wooden barrier.

"Nice doing business with you both, and you boys best be careful. Fouldeer and Pickers are bad enough, but I've heard tales of too many types of monsters, even if I haven't seen them, to believe that's all that's out there."

"Thank you," was all Aton said as he turned and led the way out of the shop.

Two houses down, they did find the bakery, the sign above the entrance a loaf of bread, though they couldn't clearly smell the baked goods till they were inside. The baker was a pretty woman, older than them, probably in her late twenties. She too had a braid over one shoulder, without the streak of white, and wore bright clothes, still leather, only with painted flowers tooled into the hem.

The twins skipped the trail crackers and bought two loaves of golden-colored, crusty bread. Aaron was surprised when his brother also asked for one of the sweet buns sitting out on the counter. The woman happily put it in a bag for him and put the bread in another. They left town after that, leaving the rest of the fur-clad townsfolk to watch them melt into the shadow of the trees.

# CHAPTER 19

# *Demons in the Deep*

"Why did you buy this?" Aaron asked once they were well on their way. They hadn't shifted back yet, though the cold was already seeping through his layers and wrapping icy fingers around his bones. He was regarding the knife, turning it over in his hands. "Am I supposed to stab the foretold trouble coming to those people with a skinning knife?"

"Coming to the dragons."

"What?"

"The trouble coming to the dragons," his brother repeated.

"Wait, wait. You think we're supposed to head east to save a city full of dragons?"

"Yes."

"From what? What could you and I possibly help a dragon with, let alone a whole city of them?"

His brother shrugged. "Something magical?"

"Why would you think that?"

"Because dragons can't use magic."

"So I'm supposed to do something magical for them? Then why are you here? No offense, but you're not as strong as a dragon."

"Maybe I'm supposed to get you there." The bigger boy kept on walking, now not even looking at Aaron.

Aaron changed the subject. "I don't even know how to fight with this."

"Maybe you should learn."

"So there's more to it than 'put the pointy end in something else'?"

"A bit."

Aton suddenly stopped, tilted back his head, and sniffed the air with his dull human nose.

"What?"

"Do you smell that?"

Aaron tried. Now that he had experienced being a wolf, smelling as a human was like trying to hear through a wool-knit cap, everything muffled. Though he did think he could smell something. He scrunched his nose in disgust. "What is that?"

"I don't know. Let's go look."

"You want to get closer to that?" But Aton was already moving, the snow hardly an obstacle, leaving a clear path for Aaron to follow.

The smell grew stronger—sharp, acidic, and somewhat sweet too. It hurt Aaron's face for the way it made his nose want to retreat inside his skull. His brother slowed, each step exact, as they started up a small rise. He followed, trying to mimic his twin's example, but each footfall sounded clumsy to his own ears. They reached the top and the older boy crouched behind some scraggly undergrowth thickened by drifts of snow. Creeping up next to him, Aaron could see movement just down the other side. He tensed, glad that he was still holding the knife they'd just acquired. They hadn't taken the time to shift before, but he wished they had. It was too loud and took too long to do it in the moment, but he would've felt a world better for it.

The thing below stepped between bushes, half hidden in the shade of the canopy, head sniffing the ground, topped by points poised on four thin legs. It was a deer.

Aaron let his breath go in a puff. "All that for a de—"

His brother gripped his arm. The animal picked up its head at the sound of Aaron's voice and turned in their direction. Out of the shadow, bright, red eyes glared up them.

Aaron stopped breathing. The demon looked like a deer, only wrong. Aside from the unnatural gleam in those eyes, its wide crown of horns was the color of charred logs. Rotten strips of hide hung off of it in shades of dark, sickly green, exposing darker meat beneath. It took a deep sniff of the air, wrinkling its nose, and as it did, it exposed sharp teeth and a set of vicious-looking fangs. He felt his heart ratchet up another level, pounding painfully beneath his ribs. How ironic it would be for a pair of wolves to be eaten by a deer.

It took a step nearer and the snow sizzled, burning beneath its hooves. Its wet, black nose tested the air, drawing nearer to their hiding place. Aton's hand drifted slowly toward his hip and the blade concealed there.

In an instant decision, the demon-stag turned and fled into the trees, away from the brothers, leaving only an acrid scent and melted hoofprints in its wake.

"What was that?" Aaron whispered.

"A lesser demon," his brother answered just as quietly. "Probably the Fouldeer Brywyn mentioned."

"There are more of those?"

"I think we'd better assume so."

"Aton." He swallowed. "What are we doing out here?"

"Heading east to save some dragons. Come on."

More weeks into their journey and Aaron had to admit to himself that he was getting sick of the mountains. True, there were places he could shift and run, as long as there weren't any humans around, and the further they marched the fewer humans there were to avoid. The next settlement they found had only one permanent structure, a general store, the people there looking more like beasts than men for all their fur and facial hair. The last place they'd passed over a week back had been only a circle of tents housing a dozen or so men clutched bows and sharpened knives. They'd gone around that one. Since then, they'd been able to travel exclusively in their were-forms.

Of course, as the humans had thinned out, the demons had become thicker. Herds appeared of more Fouldeer and Pickers, which were small impish things with bulbous eyes and lipless mouths full of sharp teethhough only the size of a squirrel., the Pickers were mainly a threat to rodents and song birds. They could be aggressive to larger animals; Aaron had seen a swarm of them attack a wild goose that had picked the wrong pond to rest in, but not them, even though the blacksmith had said they caused trouble for Desil. They saw other things too, creatures with too many red eyes and legs creeping in the hollows of trees or in rotting logs. The lesser demons, unlike their sheep, seemed to smell or sense what they were, even when they traveled as humans, and gave the twins a wide berth.

It wasn't the demons, the humans, or the shifting they had to do in response to both. That was getting easier each time, if only a little. No, Aaron was getting tired of the mountains because of all of it—the constant snow; the constant ups and downs over crags, through bushes, or down ravines; and the constant chores. The chores, all of which were important to their survival, never ended, whether it was finding food and scaring off the demons to keep it, or finding a place to bed down that wasn't already occupied, or making sure their pouches were filled with fresh water. Being werewolves, their systems could handle most things, but they'd learned the hard way not to drink downstream of a herd of Fouldeer. The water tasted sour and caused terrible stomach pains if they drank too much, the creatures' poison clearly present in their saliva or somehow dripped from their hides. But shoving snow into a canteen wasn't all that easy either, so getting fresh water was harder than it sounded.

It wasn't that Aaron was unused to chores, having grown up on a farm. He was just not used to ones that his life depended on while they were constantly watching their backs. Even though the demons seemed to instinctively fear them, that didn't mean they were too scared to steal food, and he didn't trust them not to take their chances if both of the brothers were asleep. So they took turns at night sleeping and watching for red eyes in the dark. They certainly never had to worry about the sheep suddenly attacking them back on their mountaintop.

"This looks like a good place," Aton announced.

Aaron let his pack slide off his shoulders to land in the snow, following suit a moment later to rest himself.

"Do we need a fire?" Aton asked, setting down his own pack.

"Yes." Aaron grunted as he rolled over, opening his bag to grab a pan.

"You know we can eat the meat raw."

"I don't like it cold."

"It's not cold if you eat it fast enough."

Aaron shuddered. "We're half human, you know."

"And half wolf." Aton smiled even as he stacked wood for a fire.

Aaron frowned, turning back to his pack to see if they had any potatoes left from their last contact with humans.

He thought he'd found a tuber, only to realize it was a pair of socks, when his brother said, "Light it."

Aaron flicked his eyes to the pile, then turned back to the bag, stuffing the socks down. He gave a wave over his shoulder without looking at the wood. A flame, just a small one, popped into being at the heart of the stack. His next breath was cooler for having taken that bit of heat from the air to spark it. Not that it could get too much more miserable, he reflected.

The ember sputtered and flicked, and Aton had to blow on it gently to encourage it to take hold.

Aaron could've made it bigger, only his heart wasn't in it. All he could think was that there must be months more of this tedium and forced trudging yet to go. They were going at a fast clip, not having anything else to do with their days and their werewolf stamina much better than their human bodies had been capable of, but they were crossing a continent. Brywyn had said the dragons were in the east, in someplace nearly unreachable, and while these mountains were cold, arduous, and full of nightmarish creatures, unreachable they were not. Heck, this place was practically a playground for his strong, agile beast of an older brother. He spared a glare for Aton over his shoulder. "How long till we reach these dragons?"

"So you believe it now, that we're going to help dragons?"

"Brywyn said there was nothing between Desil and the coast besides dragons. After the humans' towns peter out, and knowing that the nokken live in the sea, and that the elves prefer warmer weather, unless we stumble across a city of dwarves, I think dragons are the only 'people' out here."

The fire grew, Aton still dutifully feeding it twigs and brush to coax it further. Aton replied, "I don't know. I don't know where we are now."

"I suppose a map wouldn't have done us any good. Even if a group of human explorers—who'd be the only ones mad enough to come out here—drew up a map, I doubt they'd have marked a dragon city on it."

"Unless they were dragon hunters and wanted to mark a good spot. Maybe humans are the 'darkness' we're supposed to save them from."

"I don't care how much horns and hides go for in human markets, no hu—"

Aton's hand shot up, cutting off Aaron's next words. The larger twin left off the fire and stood. Turning in a circle, Aton picked up his lupine head, ears alert, nose twitching, eyes searching the trees.

Aaron heard it too—something big, really big, crashing through the trees. He got to his feet, staring at the forest, the sounds of splintering wood getting closer and closer.

Out of the shadow a massive creature lept directly between them. It landed on four wide paws, each the size of a dinner plate and tipped with wicked-looking curved claws. With its short fur a study in gray from light to dark and speckled, and ropes of taut muscle bunching under its coat ready to spring, the beast looked like a mountain cat, only as large as a bull. Its mouth was open, its dark gray tongue licking long, feline teeth set beneath red eyes bright as gemstones. There was no mistaking this monster.

"Demon," yelled Aton, turning and lunging for his short sword, which was propped up against his pack.

The demon-cougar whipped toward the dark wolf, its long tail thrashing in annoyance, and hissed like a winter's gale. Aton held little interest for it, though, as its nose began twitching, searching the air for something. Twin spots of carnelian fixed on Aaron and the demon's mouth parted, its breath coming out in puffs of putrid fumes. It wrinkled its nose again, testing the air, its tongue curled between double sets of fangs now on full display, distinctly dark green at the gumline. Full of purpose and malice, it stalked toward Aaron.

Aton didn't hesitate. The larger werewolf came from the side, his short sword drawn and aimed for the predator. He slashed. The blade missed, only an inch away, as the creature, quick on its feet, leapt nimbly to the side. It gave an indignant growl and swiped out with a paw the size of Aton's head in retaliation. The counter had been half-hearted, and Aton was able to dodge in turn. While his brother had distracted the demon, Aaron had used the opportunity to put distance between himself and the monster. The demon, like a true mountain cat, only this one appearing to be made of fluid granite, was drawn by his movement and sprang instinctively at the younger twin.

Aaron had not gotten far enough away. The mountain cat would catch him. As he scrambled, energy sprang to his palm, the adrenaline pulsing in his veins pushing his power all the quicker. Without time to plan or even think, he flicked off a shot of wind. The spell was badly formed and smaller than he knew himself capable of, but Aaron was confident it would knock the demon off its mark.

The seconds it took the mountain cat to leap at him stretched as he watched his blast of air spiral toward its mark. The spell was on target, sure to hit, and then, inexplicably, it slid to the left. It struck a tree, showering them with a hail of splinters, but doing nothing to the beast's trajectory.

"What?" Aaron stumbled in his surprise, falling to the ground. The tumble saved him, the demon-mountain cat sailing over him and landing just ahead, its paws empty of prey.

Aaron used his momentum to roll up to a crouch, dodging around his traveling pack, scrambling to get out of the way. He meant to make it to the fire, back past his brother who was charging at them. He made to leap, like the mountain cat had, over the fire to put some sort of barrier between them, when his foot slipped out from under him. He tumbled painfully to his knees. He glanced beneath him, where the mountain cat had initially landed in their clearing, and saw that the top layer of stone beneath him had melted into a gritty slurry in twin patches side by side, the size of dinner plates.

He heard those padded paws, tipped with claws that scratched and scraped as the demon ran at him again, only they weren't alone anymore. Aaron's brother leapt over him, still crouched on the ground, and brandished a very different weapon in his hand. Aaron turned to see those claws and teeth bearing down at him again. Their frying pan, pushed through the air by Aton's considerable strength, sailed over him and let out a loud *clang* as it struck the demon's skull.

Momentarily dazed, the beast staggered, shaking its head and giving a low, moaning growl. The black werewolf took a step forward, standing between Aaron and the demon, ready to swing again. Trusting his brother at his back, the caster grabbed for his satchel, still near at hand. He dug through the contents quickly, carelessly tossing out shirts, cord, and anything else that got in the way of his search. Finally, his hand found the hilt of the knife Brywyn had sold to them. He pulled it free of the bag and then from its sheath. The metal glinted in the firelight, ready to do its work.

He heard another loud *clang*. Turning, he saw that the demon-mountain cat had come back to its senses and had swiped the frying pan out of his brother's hands, sending it halfway across the clearing. Aton was still uninjured, but he was also unarmed. Despite this, Aton wasn't backing down. His teeth were bared, his fists were up. He threw a punch, but the beast was ready for him. It raked four-inch-long talons through the air and scored a cut in the boy's forearm, at the same time injuring him and turning the blow. Aaron cringed to see his twin's blood, but the dark wolf was made of sterner stuff. He used the momentum of the strike to spin and smashed the back of his other fist into the mountain cat's face, right below its red, shining eyes. It yowled, turning away from the force. Aton pounced on it, throwing his arms around its neck. The big wolf swung a leg over the thing's back as though he intended to ride it and pulled, jerking the demon's head back.

Aaron wasn't going to get a better opportunity. Knife brandished above his head, he ran.

His brother saw him. "Aaron, no."

The beast must've sensed the attack coming. It slashed forward with a hind leg, catching the distracted werewolf on its back in the left thigh and opening a long, bloody gash. The warrior lost his grip and the demon bucked free of its attacker. It jerked its head, ears pinned, fierce eyes locking on the rushing youth.

Aaron had to strike, had to stop this monster. He plunged the knife down toward the beast's face, only it swung out with its massive paw again and batted him away like a dandelion puff on the wind. He tumbled hard. The knife skidded away, toward the campfire and out of reach.

Aton, bloodied and bruised, sprang back into action. The older twin jumped again up on the dappled back of the mountain cat, arms wrapping around its neck from a new angle. The mountain cat bucked and thrashed to dislodge him, but Aton was strong.

Aaron searched from the ground for his weapon and saw it glittering in the light. He dove for it, his fingers wrapping around the handle. He'd do better this time. He had to. Springing to his feet, brandishing his blade, he once again charged at their struggling foe.

*Slash. Swipe. Stab.* Aaron couldn't connect. The mountain cat and his brother wrestled and rolled and jerked, and Aaron couldn't get a clear shot at the demon without endangering his twin.

"Get back," Aton snarled when he had a second to draw breath.

"No!" Aaron's reply came through gritted teeth. He struck out again, only the demon's wildly slashing talons found his hand in mid-strike. Claws raked through fur and flesh, drawing bright rivers of blood and knocking the tool from his fingers again.

The demon, maybe scenting the new blood, tossed Aton in a burst of new speed and energy. The older twin flew off, rolling with the momentum to the side of the clearing. Instead of following up its attack, instead of pouncing on the clearly larger threat, the demon-cougar rounded back to Aaron. He wasn't sure if it was because he was smaller and thus weaker, but the demon was clearly intent on the younger twin as its preferred prey.

Aaron didn't have the time to think about it. The demon came again, fangs bared, fetid breath heavy. He ran. He ran to the other side of their little campfire, insufficient as it would be as a barrier. At least it might buy him a second to think.

Lucky for Aaron, his brother didn't take being ignored very well. The fighter had found his short sword, and the beast had to abandon his charge to avoid the path of the weapon. Now reengaged by Aton, the demon wouldn't be after Aaron again for a few moments at least. His knife was gone, and with his slighter frame, he was unlikely to do much damage with his claws, not when his big brother was barely keeping up with their adversary. He'd have to try his magic again and pray to the Five Gods that it worked this time.

Pulling the magic to his hands, the caster began, using their fire as a focus. The air around him dropped drastically in temperature, each breath becoming painful in the icy air. He could see the branches of the nearby pines freeze solid, and still he pulled the energy into himself. As the light collected in his open palm, he felt the weight of it and smelled the clean, sweet odor of the magic, like a lightening storm just before the strike.

The demon-mountain cat's head snapped up immediately—eyes bright, nose twitching, staring at the younger twin. It was attracted by Aaron's magic. Of course it was. His mother had told him that demons ate the magic in all of them, and here he was flinging spells. It was like when they threw apple cores to the sheep as a treat; the sweet smell brought them running every time. Aaron had practically rung the dinner bell for this thing. Still, if the spell was big enough, maybe he could use it to hurt the demon.

The demon turned and sprinted from the dark wolf, gave chase, but even with his speed the mountain cat was faster, reaching the little campfire in two bounds. Without even pausing it sprang over the tiny stack of burning sticks.

Aaron was ready this time. He threw both palms skyward. The campfire burst into a raging bonfire. The demon disappeared, instantly obscured by flames of red and gold consuming all traces of gray. A scream rang out and echoed off the mountains, the scream of a creature not a part of this world. The smell of burning fur and flesh wafted across the clearing as the animal's momentum carried it through the inferno to land on the other side. It lay in a heap, unmoving, smoke rising off of its body in long tendrils.

The demon was still alive. Aaron could see the thing's sides heaving, but he was sure that his attack had done considerable damage. If it recovered enough to stand, it would realize that this prey wasn't worth the effort and run off.

Aaron was exhausted. Besides all the running and fighting, he didn't think he'd used that much magic at once before. If the mountain cat did recover and didn't run, he wouldn't be able to repeat the fire trick. It was then that Aaron noticed the frying pan lying not too far from the fire. It looked a little dented, a little worse for wear, but his brother had hit a demon with it, and it'd been effective. It was close, but it was also close to where the still-smoldering demon lay. The beast was definitely down for the moment, most likely so hurt that it wouldn't be able to twitch its tail even if he got close. He should grab the pan, just in case that changed later on. Ever so slowly, he slid one foot toward the pan, the fire, and the demon-mountain cat.

"Stay back," Aton called to him from the other side of the fire. Aaron's older twin looked rough—fur askew, blood still dripping from the deepest cuts—and he was favoring his right leg. He'd be fine of course, they were werewolves after all, but he didn't look in any shape to keep fighting demons.

"It's still alive," Aaron confirmed, though the beast continued to lay perfectly still, aside from the breathing.

"All the more reason to get away from it," the dark wolf growled, making its way around the fire and past the melted pools of rock.

"I'm just going to grab the pan. If it twitches so much as a whisker, we'll hit it back down."

"Don't—"

His brother didn't finish, and Aaron never reached the pan as the demon suddenly pushed itself upright and spun around to face him. Those red eyes locked with his again, pain and anger smoldering, rotting clouds of steam escaping from its jaws in labored breaths.

The younger twin dove for the pan, but his brother hadn't been faster than the mountain cat, so he certainly wasn't. He'd been so sure he'd downed the beast, but his spell hadn't been enough. That thought rang through his mind as he tried to pull back from the pan to dodge the creature, only for one of the gigantic paws and its long, curved claws to snag his leg. Blazing pain shot up the appendage when the talons found purchase past cloth and muscle and hooked into the bones that made up his ankle.

Aaron's momentum instantly arrested, he fell, crying out with the pain. He was caught. Scrambling, crawling, grasping at grass and roots in an attempt to find a handhold, he couldn't get away, the demon hauling on his leg with unthinkable strength. As the thing dragged him closer he tried calling another spell, only he couldn't think past the agony—not that he had enough strength to do anything substantial. His magic was useless. It was then that he spotted the gleam. The dwarf knife was right there, nestled in a tuft of grass. Pulling on his own bloody leg, Aaron reached out just a little further, the mountain cat pulling back. He grabbed the knife.

The demon pulled Aaron in, raising its other paw to strike. He drew himself inward, aiming to jab the knife at the paw stuck in his leg. And then Aton was there.

The dark wolf rammed his sword into the side of the demon's throat, right up to the hilt. Black blood gushed from the gaping wound like an ink spill. The monster jerked and pulled, but it couldn't flee, not only for the steel lodged in its neck, but because its forepaw was still caught in Aaron's leg. Aton threw all of his weight on top of the guards and the grip, pushing with all his considerable might, causing the weapon to slice downward through the jugular, the trachea, and the skin holding it all in. The sword passed out of the gray fur, soaked in the black deluge of its blood. Its jaw worked, its red eyes bulged, and it collapsed to one side. The giant demon-feline convulsed and spasmed as it tried unsuccessfully to draw breath.

Throwing the knife aside, Aaron worked at the paw in his leg, pulling out the hooked claws one at a time even as the demon thrashed. He moved when the last claw was freed, pushing himself with his good leg as far back from the injured demon as the terrain would allow.

The black wolf stood, covered in gore, his blade still held tightly, on guard in case the demon healed the wound and came after them again. It didn't. The gray and blackened mass of fur's movements slowed, blood loss and suffocation making its end come quickly, until the werewolves were the only two living things left in the clearing.

Letting out a heavy sigh, the warrior let his shoulders fall, turning his back on the corpse, and limped over to inspect what damage had been done to Aaron. Aton frowned at the ruin of Aaron's leg. "That looks bad."

"Does it?" Aaron snapped, the pain burning a bright path up his nerves.

"We need to get you bandaged up."

"I'll do it myself." The caster looked down at the appendage. The ribbons of muscle gleamed sickly through shredded skin next to the grisly white shine of bone. Red flowed from the wound, but gazing at the exposed inner workings of his leg, Aaron noticed something worse. A milky substance oozed out with his blood and looking to his ankle bone, he could see where it came from. The demon-mountain cat, like the Fouldeer, clearly had an acidic substance that seeped out of it, causing damage wherever it walked and, apparently, to whatever it touched. The feline's footfalls had melted stone; melting bone and flesh would've been a far simpler process for the toxin.

"You won't die from it, but you should do something," Aton urged.

"I said I'll do it."

Even though Aaron was a werewolf and would heal faster than anything else he knew about, a wound this bad was going to take a while to heal, and the acid would probably slow the process down even further. There was no telling how long it'd take to heal on its own. Aaron had never healed himself before and he remembered Aton's screams when he'd healed him after the snakebite.

He looked around their ruin of a camp. The dead demon lay in a pool of its own onyx plasma. The fire, having been the center of his spell, had burst. Nearly extinguished now, there were traces of the blaze far from the initial pit, to the odd cinder still burning at the parameter, making Aaron think of the demon's red eyes. Their bags were toppled, his supplies spilling out, but luckily nothing was on fire. He noticed a roll of liniment lying near the bag and he stretched out to snap it up. There was so much more he should be doing—cleaning the wound for one—but he just wanted to hold it together for the moment. He wrapped the injury as tightly as he could, crimson staining the white fabric on every layer. When he reached the end of the roll, he tucked it in and turned up to look at his brother.

"That doesn't look done," Aton observed.

"I don't want to cast anymore here. There might be more of those things out there. My werewolf healing will fix it up. We should get moving."

"Mountain cats are lone hunters."

"You want to take the chance that demons are like that too?" Aaron snarled, his fists clenched. Aton was always correcting him. The little brother was always wrong. "If only the fire had worked, if only I'd gotten it with the knife, it wouldn't have gotten me this bad."

"It's a good thing you didn't cut the demon."

Aaron looked up and finally noticed that his brother had been wearing a grimace. He thought it might've been the sight of his ugly wound, but the larger boy turned and walked a few paces off, dropping to one knee next to an untouched snowdrift. Aton stabbed his sword into the snowbank and started rubbing his arms with the white powder.

"What are you doing?"

"It burns," Aaron's brother replied, not turning away from his task.

The sorcerer blinked. "What does?"

"The blood. The black blood burns where it touches."

Aaron's eyes opened wider in realization. It walked on acid—of course its blood would have similar effects. He glanced back to the corpse. Where the cat had walked, small puddles of stone had formed, but he'd not noticed that the corpse of the demon was sinking, the rock beneath it pitting and breaking up. The blood seemed to be even more corrosive.

"Can you get the waterskin?"

Brought back to the moment, Aaron cast about, leaning over and snagging his pack to do as his brother asked. He pulled the water canteen first, thankful it was mostly full, and then dug in its depths for a cloth they didn't mind wasting on cleaning off acidic demon blood. A clatter sounded on the stone next to him and he watched their mother's ring spin where it'd landed after falling from his pack. The gem glinted weakly in the dim light.

Aaron wore a grimace of his own looking at the jewelry. Aton had made him take it when they'd packed their few belongings, but he'd kept it buried at the bottom of his things, unwilling to look or even think on it.

Leaving the memento on the ground for the moment, Aaron got laboriously up on his good leg and limped over to his brother with the deer-hide pouch and a rag. He poured the clean water over his brother's arms while Aton rubbed at his fur vigorously with the scrap of cloth.

When his brother stopped scrubbing, Aaron took the pause to look over the damage. Aton was missing patches of fur, the skin beneath angry and red. It was painful looking, but nothing dangerous.

"Better?"

"I'll be fine," Aton replied, then he turned to his sword, pulling the weapon from the snow and examining it. "I'll need to get out the whetstone when we camp next. The blood's taken the edge off."

"Is that why you didn't want me to stab it?"

Aton's brow creased. "If you'd stabbed it while it had ahold of your leg, the blood could've gotten into your wound."

Aaron pinned his ears thinking about it. His leg was still screaming, and that'd just been a little acid. If he'd gotten the demon's blood in there, blood he was pretty sure wasn't just acidic, but poisonous too...

"It stung enough on my skin. Hate to think what it would've done inside," Aaron's sibling added unnecessarily.

Aaron limped back a step and half fell back to a sitting position. Aton limped over to the discarded knife, which looked undamaged for all that it'd been thrown about that night.

"Do you want me to heal your leg?" Aaron offered. He meant it as a peace offering for snapping at Aton when Aton had just gone through all the trouble of saving him.

Aton stilled and Aaron saw his ear twitch. "No."

"Alright." It was good. Aaron really didn't have the energy to spare, but he wondered if his brother was also remembering his healing on that day.

The black werewolf came closer and picked up something else before approaching the younger boy. When Aton was back in front of Aaron, he presented the knife to his twin.

"You still want me to have that?"

"It's never a bad idea to have a weapon."

He'd proven that statement false. Aaron had almost poisoned himself trying to stab that demon, but he took it anyway.

Aton held up the second object in his other black fist—the golden ring. "You need to be more careful with this."

The younger brother scowled at yet another reproach. He didn't reply.

Aton's frown deepened as he palmed the ring and walked to his own pack. The caster saw him reach a hand in and pull out a length of the leather stripping that they'd bought in Desil. Coming back over and slipping the leather strap through the metal circle, Aton presented it to Aaron. "Wear it around your neck."

"What? Why?"

"So you don't lose it."

"Can't I just strap it to the bottom of the pack?"

Violet eyes, the twins of Aaron's own, glared daggers at him. Aaron's face darkened and he snatched the ring out of the air. He tied the thong around his throat sulkily, the golden ring nestling into his silver fur.

Clearly satisfied, Aton turned a circle, surveying the camp again. "We've got some gathering and repacking to do before we can move on." Then his gaze landed on Aaron. "We should get you someplace safe first. Give that leg time to heal. Stay here for bit and I'll find a place."

"Are you sure you—" Aaron broke off. He'd been about to ask if his brother thought it was a good idea to head out there by himself now that they knew demons were about, but why should Aton worry about that? He'd been the one to kill the demon after all. Instead, Aaron said, "See you soon."

## CHAPTER 20

# *A Voice in the Dark*

"We'll stay here tonight," Aton pronounced, helping Aaron limp to a little patch of bare snow, where their bags and supplies were already stacked.

Hopping the last few steps, Aaron sat himself down on a cleared rock, sniffing the air as soon as he did. "I smell smoke. Are people close by?"

Aton nodded. "Another trapper camp, over the next hill."

"We're too close."

"Nothing for it. We'll need to shift."

"Shift?"

"You said it—we're too close." Aton bowed his head, wrapped his hands around his arms, and began to change. Aaron turned away the moment his brother's body started making noises of its own.

After all they'd done already that night, he felt too tired to shift. All of his werewolf stamina had been poured into his one, failed spell. Anything he gained now should be put toward his natural healing ability so he could get back on his feet. Still, the last thing he wanted was for a human to come across an injured werewolf. Their presence might be enough to deter the demons, but they were still a threat. He had no choice. He had to shift.

He closed his eyes and initiated the shift. It hurt, of course, only far worse than before. His leg spasmed and radiated near-intolerable pain as the injured bone and shredded muscles moved back into human configuration. He was fairly sure the shift had ruined any of the repair work his body had already achieved.

Shift completed, Aaron sat naked, shivering, and bleeding in the snow. "Now what?"

"Get warm and turn in."

"What about a fire?"

"We don't want to draw attention to ourselves. We go without."

"But—"

Aton turned his back to Aaron and started getting dressed, ending the conversation. That was abrupt. Was Aton angry with him? The larger boy crawled under his blankets and made to sleep, his back still turned. Aaron dressed as quickly as his injury would allow and got under his own blankets, the snow making for a soft, if chilly bed.

Wounded and cold, Aaron found sleep difficult. His frustration gnawed at his stomach and his mother's ring hung around his neck like an accusation. He knew that Aton was the strong one, the more capable woodsman, the born hero, but now he'd learned that his own gifts, his fantastical magic abilities, were worse than useless, that they were dangerous, actually able to attract lesser demons. It made him sick and it made him angry at himself. What good was he? Why would the dragons need his powers?

He chuffed a quiet laugh at the thought, as if defeating a lesser demon were something he ought to be able to do. Only Aton had. His big brother had had to save him from a normal snake, had had to save him from the mountain demon, and now Aaron was supposed to save a city of dragons against some coming darkness that they weren't capable of dealing with, but he was? The thought seemed ridiculous. They'd picked the wrong brother.

His mind whirled, but eventually his exhausted body won out. Leg throbbing, muscles aching, and eyelids drooping, he fell asleep, darkly chuckling at the joke the gods were playing on him.

Hours later, in the thin time before dawn, something woke Aaron. The half-moon had set, and the stars were hiding behind clouds, making the world a study in shades of dark. It took him a moment to confirm if his eyes were actually open. They adjusted, and he could see dim white snow contrasting with the darker trees and rocks in the gloom. Still, he lay, frozen, not daring to move, as he listened for the sound that'd roused him from his deep sleep. Had it been another demon? Another mountain cat? Was his luck so bad or his power of smell so good that he could've attracted another? Did they travel in pairs or in packs?

He held his breath as the sound came again, and he nearly growled in exasperation. It was Aton's voice. His brother was talking in his sleep.

"He's doing fine." The other boy's voice was hushed, like an echo of a conversation taking place in a dream.

Aaron let out the breath he'd been holding. He wanted to chide himself for jumping at the sound of his own brother's voice, but he also wanted to roll over and shake his twin awake to get him to stop talking in his sleep. He was about to when he heard someone answer Aton.

"He's lost out here. You can see that." The voice was dark, deep, and dry, like the scraping of leaves against a stone floor. It set every hair on Aaron's neck to standing on end, but he dared not move, dared not draw attention to himself, not until he understood what was going on.

"He's getting better," Aton said a little more forcefully.

"Yeah, sure." The voice laughed lowly, quietly, and darkly. There was something else about the voice besides making Aaron want to crawl away—something intriguing, something that made him want to listen. "That was a pretty pitiful showing with that mountain cat. It's way too dangerous for a kid like him out here. How long is it going to take the shepherd to turn into a warrior? How long before the puppy becomes a wolf?"

Aaron's eyes, facing away from the voices, stretched wide. The voice had called him a puppy. Was he in wolf form? He couldn't remember. He tried to flick his tail but had none. He'd shifted into a human before they'd gone to sleep. How did the voice know what they were? How did it know about the demon-cat?

The voice laughed again. "Even his puny parlor tricks aren't doing anything for him out here."

"We'll take care of each other. We'll make it through this, together," Aton said confidently but still quietly. Both parties still spoke in whispers so as not to wake Aaron, clearly not wanting to involve him in this conversation.

"Yes, I can see that you're taking fine care of him—you killed the demon, after all—but what is he doing? How is he taking care of you?" The question was asked in an off-handed manner, but the pause that followed sat as heavily as a stone.

The other continued. "It's not his fault, of course, for slowing you down. He just wasn't made for this life of struggle and adventure. Not like you. You know, you'd do just fine out here all on your own."

"No, we won't stop. We're going to go on, together." Aaron's brother tried to emphasize the word *together*, only it sounded a little less confident this second time.

The other made a thoughtful noise. "Maybe he's not the one afraid of being alone." Aaron could hear the smirk in the voice's words.

"I'm not going to leave him." This time Aton delivered the declaration with a hint of a snarl.

"No, no, of course not," said the other breezily.

Aaron nearly shrieked when he felt a thin, skeletal hand pat the hair on the top of his head. The owner of the voice was touching him, and his touch was as cold as snow and as soft as twisted branches. "Even if you did, he'd never make it out of here on his own. He'd get snapped up by the first thing with red eyes or a bow. No," the voice said sadly, "he'd never make it back to civilization. Knowing that, would you be willing to take him back there?"

Another silence Aaron's brother didn't fill.

"I mean you keep talking about going on, about forging ahead. Whatever you're doing must be important. Are you willing to sacrifice that future glory so that your little brother can go back and keep pretending that he's human?"

This time the pause was longer, and when Aton did speak, the answer was a strangled "No."

"Then you have a decision to make." The voice sounded sly, like it was grinning.

"But our mother—"

"Your mother would've wanted one of her sons to survive," the voice said, cutting Aton off. "Is it going to be him or you?"

"I can't—"

"No. Of course not. You can't abandon him out here, leaving him scared and alone and just waiting for something to gobble him up. You're not that kind of a monster. But you can't abandon your mission either. What will you do?"

The voice let the question hang before he said, "There is another option."

"There is?"

"You could end it for him."

"What—"

"Listen, listen. Do you think your brother wants to be out here in this godforsaken forest? Do you honestly believe he wanted to be touched by this 'destiny'? Can't you see how he's drowning in all of this? Only you can save him. Only you can take his fear and pain away."

"Take away his pain?"

"It's the least you can do for him, if you're any sort of a brother, if you care about him the way you claim to."

Aaron had stopped breathing. He couldn't believe what he was hearing, what the voice was telling his brother to do, though he couldn't deny anything it was saying about him either. He'd had the same thoughts about slowing his brother down, about not being fit for this mission, but to kill him? Aton wouldn't do it. He didn't believe for a minute his brother would murder him in his sleep, and yet his body refused to move, refused to keep breathing. He lay completely still, waiting for his twin's answer.

He heard someone shift, then the clink of someone picking up the short sword; it must be his brother then.

"Yes," said the voice softly, soothingly, hypnotically. "Make it all go away."

Aaron heard the blade scraping against its scabbard as it was drawn. Aton wouldn't do it, couldn't do it. Aton was not going to kill him, but still his body refused to move. He was in a dream. He had to be in a dream. He heard footsteps behind him. He couldn't turn, couldn't see what was happening. He couldn't believe it. Was he going to—

A shriek shattered the silence of the night. Aaron sat bolt upright, shedding his blankets, and turned to see Aton with his hands on the hilt and pommel of his sword, the blade embedded between the skeletal shoulders of a demon.

Black blood dripped to the snow below, turning it dark and sizzling, melting it away. Aaron's brother had struck true, pinning the nightmarish creature where it crouched. The being pulled up its head, mad red eyes fixing on Aaron, as a wide, sinister slash of a smile spread across its twisted features.

"Well, that didn't work." And it laughed, actually laughed. "I have to hand it to you; you caught me off guard. Not bad for puppies." It was clearly undisturbed by the weapon spearing through the center of it, its voice still conversational without even a hint of pain or discomfort. "But that's not enough." The demon slid from the sword, passed right through it as though the weapon or the creature itself was composed of no more than smoke. It straightened, standing to its full height, smile still etched into its dark, lipless face, and towered over the twins.

Aton still crouched, blade still embedded below the snow, while he looked up, possibly calculating his next move. His younger twin, by contrast, was still in his blankets, blinking dumbly at the monster with them, not knowing what to do.

The thing was tall, thin, and vaguely human shaped, if stretched out of its usual proportions. Its skin looked like charcoal half-spent, the darkest of grays. It had no hair anywhere on its form. Its head, more a skull than anything fully fleshed out, was smooth while the rest of it was composed of sharp angles, ending in innumerable points. Its fingers concluded in straight claws like daggers, spikes jutted out at every joint like a thornbush in winter come to life—dark, twisted, and sharp. It looked down at the pair of werewolves with a thin sneer on its slash of a mouth filled with teeth pointed and numerous. "A valiant effort."

"I'll put more effort into my next strike." The warrior snarled, pulling his weapon from the ground and brandishing it at the intruder, despite how ineffective it'd proven to be.

The demon looked at the boys, head cocked to one side, studying them like an unfamiliar pair of insects. It shook its head before transforming entirely into black smoke. The wind broke up the demon-shaped cloud and blew away tendrils without a sound. It simply disappeared into the night in lethargic black wisps, leaving only two thin footprints in the snow to attest that it had ever even been there.

"You should be grateful that I've tired of this game." The disembodied voice of the demon emitted from all around them, making it impossible to discern its location. "Had it gone the way I'd planned, I'd have painted these stones a shade darker with your insides. Still, there's always next time. Good luck, pups. When your night terrors come for you with red eyes and daggers, you can now put a name to them—Kaliton. Till then, farewell."

The last word echoed and faded away, taken by the wind, like the demon's smoke-body. They couldn't have said what had changed to indicate that the demon had truly left, but a pressure eased from the campsite as the echo died away. It was still a long moment before either brother could make himself move.

Aaron looked down at his blankets. Kaliton had tried to make his brother do a terrible thing, but not everything he'd said to motivate Aton had been wrong. His twin didn't need Aaron to be the hero he was destined to be. Their guess was that the dragons needed Aaron because of his magic, but the seer had mentioned his brother too. Maybe they both had the power to help, and if that was the case, he knew which one of them was the more likely champion.

Guilt, shame, and frustration washed through Aaron, burning in his guts. He'd been dragging his feet, sniping at his brother, and complaining all the time, and all because he didn't feel up to this challenge, didn't feel that he was up to his brother's level. He'd taken out his frustration, his anger, and his grief on his brother, and somehow Aton still hadn't turned his back on him.

His head jerked up, mouth opening and closing without sound. He wasn't sure how to convey all the warring emotions inside himself. He wanted to tell his twin that he was sorry, sorry for making things harder than they had to be. He wanted to tell him that he would do better, that he would become better. That he would become worthy. "Aton, I—"

Aton cut Aaron off with a hand on his shoulder as he sat down on the bedroll next to him. "We'd better get some sleep. We've still got a long way to go in the morning." A smile spread across the larger boy's features.

Aaron felt his throat squeeze with emotions. Looking into his twin's violet eyes he could see understanding. No words were necessary. He returned the smile with one of his own, along with a sharp nod. "Right."

## CHAPTER 21

# *Lights in the Mist*

After that last trapper camp, which they'd neatly skirted around on the following morning, they stopped detecting humans—no more towns, no more camps, not even the smell of smoke from a cooking fire. Not that the twins could blame the people. The overall elevation they traveled was becoming steeper, colder, and rougher. It was prime demon country if Aaron had ever pictured it, only they didn't see as many demons as he thought they should. The trees were thinning with the change in altitude, so maybe the demons sought the shadowy crags and crevices of the mountain peaks, trying to find hiding spots to ambush from. Maybe they felt more exposed to an unknown danger that he refused to think about, because if it could scare a demon, he knew he didn't want to meet it.

Overall, Aaron was glad for the isolation. Trekking across the frozen roof of Jenoha, not having to give up his werewolf form with its warm coat, extra strength, and energy, was a real boon. They continued that way until they reached the end of the Venduli Ackar mountain range, the stately spine of the continent falling away, snapped off by mountains running perpendicular to them—the soaring spires of the Shei Denti.

"Whoa." Aaron breathed, his eyes trying to encompass the wonder before him and failing. He'd lived on a mountain all his life, a tiny one at the end of the Venduli range, and he'd spent months traveling alongside the peaks, their majesty growing with each mile, only the Shei Denti were something else entirely. It was like living next to a lake and then getting a view of the ocean—the difference was something he couldn't have imagined without seeing it in person.

He'd heard that Shei Denti meant Gods' Teeth in one language or another and he could see why. While the Venduli Ackar ran west to east, the Shei Denti ran north to south, cutting off the other range instead of being an extension of it. The former range touched the clouds in a series of stately pyramids. This new one speared through the clouds, and not in gentle cones, but almost in jagged spikes, all cliffs and bluffs, just like the teeth of some god or great beast, maybe like a dragon.

"This is what real mountains look like." Aaron's brother smirked, putting a hand on his shoulder.

Aaron didn't respond right away. He was still looking at the mountains, each peak wrapped in a heavy mantle of clouds.

"How will we know which one to climb?" he finally asked, not tearing his eyes away from the expanse. "The dragon city must be on top of one of these, but how could we possibly know which one?"

The larger wolf shrugged. "Hard to tell with all the clouds. We'll just have to pick one and climb it."

Aaron looked back at his twin, incredulous. "Just climb one? To see what? What clouds look like from the inside?"

"You think the dragons will live in the clouds? I say these mountains are so tall that they stretch above them."

Aaron looked out again at the formidable terrain and shook his head. "That's a long climb."

"We'll take it in sections. I'll climb, reach a ledge, you climb to it too, and we do it again. Just like the peak back home."

Aaron thought back to the crag their mother had warned them to keep off of. That had been a hill of pebbles compared to these towering giants, but there was nothing for it. Aaron had sworn to himself he was going to try harder—now was the time to prove it. "Let's go."

It wasn't quite as simple as climbing the first mountain they saw. First, they had to get down off of the cliff they were on, what Aaron thought of as the broken edge of the Venduli Ackar. Then they had to scramble through the broken valley to reach the side of the closest peak. Opposed to what it first looked like from the cliff, there was a bit of a tricky, if even slope for the first part of the mountain that they could trek up together.

The sun had passed its zenith by the time they reached an end to the ground over which they could hike and they were presented with nearly sheer cliffs. The brothers sat and ate something like a late lunch of dried deer meat and fresh spring water, wanting to recoup as much energy as they could before the next part.

"Alright," Aton said, standing and looking up at the clouds, which were still as thick as sheep's wool. He shouldered his pack. "I'm going up."

"And what am I supposed to do?"

"You stay here. I'll climb up, find a ledge, and then drop you the rope."

Aaron looked again at the sheer wall. "And if you fall before you reach that first ledge?"

His brother shrugged again. "Then I guess the seer was wrong."

"You could still be a hero after all your bones have finished healing."

The larger wolf gave him a half-lidded glare and frowned. Without another word, the warrior adjusted his pack and started forward. "I'll drop the line soon."

"If you do fall," Aaron called after him, "please yell as loudly as you can, so I know to get out of the way."

Aaron watched as his older sibling, strikingly dark against the pale stone, began to climb the cliff face. Aaron didn't make a sound or call any words of encouragement that might distract his twin as he entered the gray mist. He only said a quiet prayer to the Five Gods that Aton would reach the next ledge in one piece.

When the warrior finally disappeared and he couldn't hear him bouldering anymore, the caster grabbed his own pack and moved up to the cliff. He didn't sit directly under where his brother had started to climb, but close enough that he'd see the rope when it fell, and also to keep out of the blustering wind. He nestled as comfortably as possible into the rock face and settled down to wait. The wind blowing through the mountains was the only sound.

Aaron didn't know how long he sat there, but he began to wonder if the rope they'd bought off Brywyn would even be long enough, if it were taking this long for his brother to find a suitable ledge.

He shook his head. His brother would drop the rope down soon. In the meantime, he just needed to relax. They'd been on their hike for so long, without pause, that he found the quiet mountainside rather peaceful. True, it was cold and windy and mainly barren of anything living, but there was a stillness, save for the wisps of clouds that occasionally dislodged themselves from the solid cover to drift lazily by him like translucent fish in a stream. Unsurprisingly, he found himself dozing.

As Aaron drifted in and out of his stupor, he experienced firsthand how fickle the weather at higher altitudes could be. He knew from a lifetime of experience that mountains create their own climate and they could turn from sunny skies to a downpour or even a blizzard in the next instant.

It was growing colder and the clouds were getting heavier with every degree lost. They fell upon him like the cover of night that descends after the sunset, blanketing him and his senses in their muffled white. He wasn't concerned, though. The clouds weren't heavy enough for a real storm, and a little fog was hardly something to get agitated over. As long as the weather held its precipitation, they'd be fine.

He was resettling himself, laying his head back to resume his dozing, when a sound caught his attention. He leapt to his feet, now fully alert. It hadn't been a stone dislodged by the climber, nor was it a rope hitting the rock next to him. It'd been louder than that.

Aaron flattened his ears and pulled his shoulders up, pressing his back to the cliff as he cast about for the sound's source. The world was only swirling white, and he couldn't see more than a few paces in front of him. He dearly hoped that whatever was out there was having the same issue and couldn't see him either.

His imagination jumped first to the demon from all those weeks past, Kaliton, stalking out there somewhere in the gloom. He immediately dismissed the thought with a shake of his head—the noise had been from something much bigger than a person. The thing in the mist had sounded enormous, and he didn't relish the prospect of fighting a giant monster all by himself, especially not if it was one of the gray acid cats, which he might never see coming through all this cloud.

The sound came again, and he understood that it was claws clacking against stones. Something big, on four legs and with huge claws, was coming closer. He nearly laughed when he realized that the sound hadn't come from a demon-mountain cat, and he felt the blood drain from his face because it sounded even bigger.

He strained all his werewolf senses to penetrate the barrier, but could see nothing through the thick fog, smell nothing through the heavy moisture, and hear nothing through the muffling clouds. Yet he knew something was out there. He could hear it whenever it moved. If only he could see it.

Aaron couldn't take the suspense any longer. Calling to the power within himself, he drew his energy to his palm, forming a globe of spring-green light. His heart twisted in his chest as he thought about the night his mother had first shown them this trick. The sweet smell of the magic always brought a further reminder, but he didn't have time to dwell on it. Whatever was out there would see the light; he just hoped he saw it first.

The bright illumination of his power reflected back to him as two blazing yellow-orange disks burned through the white like tiny twin suns. He froze, transfixed by the great shining circles. They hung still, the only movement caused by the pulsing energy in his hands. He held his breath, not knowing what to do next. Both of the orbs were as big as his head, spaced apart by a distance longer than his torso. If those were eyes—

The twin disks surged toward Aaron through the mist. He stepped back, his fear overcoming his concentration, and the light disappeared—not that he needed it anymore to see what was coming. The creature's movements ripped apart the clouds, revealing a set of teeth, the largest he'd ever seen. He dodged to the side as the resounding snap of jaws echoed against the cliff walls.

Spinning back to get a view of his aggressor, Aaron saw that it was still mostly shrouded in the fog. Thick chunks of cloud floated in drifts, even as the complete cover had been shredded and obscured, and then revealed his attacker. Yet the young caster still found the creature no less impressive for the limited visibility.

Its head, the part he could see the clearest, was larger than he stood tall. Its eyes blazed out of a face covered in bright yellow scales and surrounded by a mane of white fur. It pulled back reptilian lips to expose the glistening teeth he'd almost become very familiar with while long twin whiskers floated about as though on their own private breeze.

This was a dragon—he had no doubts about it—and, if his brother was to be believed, one of the very people they'd come all this way to see. Of course, now that they'd finally arrived, he was about to be eaten by one.

Aaron had to speak up. He had to convince this dragon of their purpose, but he had no idea what to say. The massive creature angled toward him, jaws half-parted.

*Now or never.* "Great dragon—"

It surged again without waiting for him to finish.

"No! Wait!" He backed up, but lost his footing on loose gravel, banging against the cliff face and limiting his options for escape. Those bright eyes came at him like a charging ram in springtime, only equipped with fangs longer than his forearm. He crouched down, hoping to spring out of its path at the last moment.

From above them, out of the clouds, plummeted a dark object. Like an avalanche, it fell heavily, landing squarely on the charging dragon's head. The impact caused the dragon's chin to hit and then bounce off the stone, halting its forward momentum. Before the leviathan could register what had happened, from his new perch, Aton grabbed one of the dragon's deer-like horns and leaned on its temple. He reached out his paw, claws on full display, and held it mere inches from the dragon's left eye.

"Stop it now." Aton's voice was dark but calm. "I don't want to blind you, but I will." It was not so much a threat as a statement of fact.

"So, it's a pair of thieves, is it?" rumbled the dragon's deep voice, dripping with disgust.

"We aren't thieves," the younger boy called up, indignant surprise coloring his words.

"You're much too small to be hunters." The serpent chuckled, and Aaron felt the very ground reverberate with its laughter.

"We're not here to hurt anyone," he declared.

"Oh?" the dragon asked, arching the brow Aton currently sat on, Aton still holding his claws threateningly close to its eye.

"You struck first," the dark wolf said.

"I was only scaring him off." The dragon's body shifted in what might've been a shrug.

"That was a pretty near thing if you were only trying to scare me."

"You don't get as big as me with bad aim." The dragon laughed again. "If I'd meant to eat you, you'd already be stuck in my teeth."

Aaron wasn't sure what to say to that.

The dragon's eyes rolled upward, looking at Aton and then back to Aaron. "Werewolves?"

"Yes," the older twin replied, still not moving his hand.

"I don't recall seeing any of your lot around here before. I'd recommend going south. Better hunting."

"We didn't come here to settle," Aton replied.

"No? Then why are you here?"

"We came to help," Aaron called up.

"Help? Help who?"

"You," the older twin answered.

The dragon let out a long, deep laugh, a rich sound that echoed and seemed to fill the peaks, not with mocking, but with surprised disbelief and delight.

When it finished laughing, the dark wolf remaining in his spot, the dragon said, "Well, thank you for making the trip, but why do you think we need your help?"

"A seer told our mother you would need us. She said you'd need my brother and me to stand against a great darkness," the caster replied somewhat defensively.

"Ah," the dragon said, stretching out the sound. The laughter was gone, but the light in its eyes remained. "Destiny, is it?"

He nodded, praying it was true that the dragons were the ones they were supposed to help.

"We know something of destiny here." There was a touch of hushed reverence in the dragon's voice alongside the mirth. It directed its next statement to the werewolf on its head. "If you'll come down, I'll see what I can do to help you in kind."

The older twin looked dubious. Aaron asked, "How do we know you won't try to eat us again?"

"If it's your destiny to help us later, then you know I don't eat you now." Its jovial tone belied the gravity of the statement. If it were mocking them, the dragon would snap them both up as soon as Aton's feet were on the ground, but if it did believe, and, more importantly if they truly believed, they'd know their story wouldn't end there.

Slowly, reluctantly, the warrior climbed down off of the dragon and came to stand at his twin's side, whether to be eaten or aided Aaron wasn't sure.

With the black wolf off of its head, the daffodil-colored dragon settled down, laying on its belly to bring it closer to their level, if only a little. The rest of its body was still obscured by the heavy cloud cover. "Now that we know I won't eat you and you're not threatening rightful vengeance, should we introduce ourselves?" The dragon laid one massive palm on its chest. "I am Yielle, and you?"

Aaron had not been sure before, but after talking to the dragon and hearing its name, he was inclined to think it a female. He hurried to answer before she thought them rude. "I'm Aaron, and this is my brother, Aton."

Yielle studied one twin and then the other. "You said you're brothers?"

Had he not had his fur on, Aaron might've blushed. "The similarities aren't all that much clearer when we're human."

The dragon continued to stare. "Hmm, maybe around the eyes—" She trailed off before shaking her head. "Not important. Now, let's see about helping you two. You said a seer told your mother you would help the dragons?"

"Yes." Aton nodded.

"Sort of," the younger twin corrected. "The seer said we'd save many people from a coming darkness, but she didn't say who. The only clue we had was that they'd be located toward the rising sun."

"So you came east," she finished for them.

"As far as we could." The dark wolf nodded again.

"I see. The sun does rise out of the Selist Mar, and assuming you're not here to save the nokken that live beneath it, we dragons are the only ones on this corner of Jenoha." She looked down on them with a thoughtful expression. "And you came all this way because of these words?"

"Yes." The older twin nodded.

Then she nodded, as though coming to a conclusion. "Then to thank you for your treacherous journey on our behalf, I will take you to someone who might be able to tell you more about your destiny."

The brothers' faces lit up. The younger spoke for them both, tail slightly wagging if he were honest. "Really? Who?"

She chuckled again. "All in good time. Follow me."

Yielle stood, turning back into the fog, but Aaron could still see the long body curving in an echo of the movement, a long sinuous side glimpsed only as a sunny haze through the gray. They followed the movement themselves into the mist for only a short time before the other creature stopped, glancing back at the pair. Aaron walked forward to ask why she'd stopped, and almost fell off of the cliff edge. Pebbles skittered down the sheer drop, clattering far longer than he could track their progress.

"Hold on," the dragon said, reaching out to catch him if necessary.

Aaron's brother put a hand to his shoulder to steady him.

"You'll never make it on foot," rumbled their guide.

"Then how—" Aaron let his words fall away as an upward draft pulled back the veil of mist and showed them the mountains. There were mountains and mountains and nothing else stretched out as far as he could see, only fog filling in the spaces between them.

"I told you I would help you," Yielle said.

"But—"

It was the only warning Aaron received as he was snatched from behind. A talon large enough to hold him from ribs to knees wrapped around him as he was propelled forward. His heart, already in his throat, climbed higher still as the dragon didn't even pause at the edge. She threw herself over the precipice and into the open sky. He watched in stunned horror as the rest of the animal materialized above them. Her body was like a waterfall of yellow scales, with white fur along her spine, impossibly long, cascading out of the clouds. With a further spike of panic, he realized nothing was breaking up that waterfall. The dragon had no wings. She'd jumped off of the cliff, holding him and his brother, with no means of surviving the fall.

A scream threatened to tear itself from his throat when the wingless serpent inexplicably began to pull upward. Without feathers or webbing, the dragon was suddenly soaring through the sky. He heard another deep laugh of delight as the dragon dipped, rose, and returned to where they'd been, dipping again and catching up their packs with a hind talon before veering off once again.

Their guide moved gently from side to side through the sky, swimming more than flying. Her antics were more like those of a sinuous fish as opposed to those of a bird in flight. He couldn't understand how, but the dragon just floated as she went, navigating through the unseen currents of air, seemingly oblivious to the miracle she was performing. Only the smug smile on her lips suggested she may have known how amazing this all was to her poor ground-walking passengers.

Aaron looked to their transport's other talon to check on his brother. The black wolf's eyes were wide, but there was a smile on his face, a look of pure wonder. Now that he wasn't plummeting to his doom, Aaron realized he felt the same—just as filled with wonder, just as in awe. They'd lived much of their lives close to the clouds and now they were soaring above them.

The setting sun turned the sky as pink as an apple blossom and the clouds strolled by like puffy white sheep. It was almost funny to be thinking of their tiny hilltop while surrounded by all this majesty, but maybe he'd thought of it because the warmth of feelings welling up inside him reminded him a little bit of home.

Aaron saw his twin suddenly tense in the dragon's claws and lean forward as much as the talons would allow, intent on some new sight. Aaron followed Aton's gaze, only he didn't have to look long to know what had caught his brother's attention. They'd come around one wide peak and there, built upon the summit of a colossal mountain, was a sprawling city. The setting sun at their backs turned the pearl-white walls pink and deepened the shade of each red roof tile to the deepest claret. The city looked to be glowing, as if the sun itself were setting down to rest within this impossible fortress in the sky. He forgot to breathe in that moment. When he took his next breath, he let it go with a sigh of relief. They'd made it to the dragons' city, one step closer to their destiny.

## CHAPTER 22

# *City in the Clouds*

Yielle angled toward a massive platform set right before a wide set of open gates. Aaron imagined the gates to be mainly ornamental, as there was no path leading up to them from the ground, nor was there any way to reach them at all without flight. Of course, if the visitor could fly, there was nothing to stop them from simply flying over the gates and into the city even if they were shut. Still, the grandeur and scale of them were immense, larger than their dragon companion by another head.

She set down their packs first, then the werewolves, before settling herself. Instead of flying, she strolled through the gates without preamble. The brothers grabbed their bags and hurried after their guide, who strolled casually into the streets.

As striking as the city had been from the outside, the interior was all the more amazing. There were more white walls and red roof tiles, but it was the inhabitants that brought the full spectrum to the metropolis. Like bright streamers, dragons of every hue and shade swam through the air about them. Some stood no taller than the brothers, while others were as large as the one accompanying them.

"Off you go." Yielle laughed as a cloud of the smaller dragons flew around her head. "The younger ones like to be in the way." She smirked as she said it.

Music filled the air, plucked strings and piping flutes, notes soaring like the dragons themselves. The huge houses they passed all looked big enough to fit their new friend comfortably but would swallow the werewolves without a thought. Each was painted with intricate designs they hadn't seen from the air—swooping lines, bright flowers, and birds in soft colors. New smells wafted from the open doors, strange herbs and spices, warming despite their novelty. They saw a pair of dragons, both with a massive set of horns, clearly male, drinking soup from bowls sold by a dragon standing behind carts. They stood on three legs while conversing, holding the bowls in one free hand and drinking it as if out of a teacup. Aaron could just see glimpses of whole vegetables, and possibly the legs of some wild game, sliding past the teeth and down the gullet of one predator.

The werewolves received quite a few stares in return from the inhabitants they passed. The citizens seemed curious, not hostile, but the added attention still made Aaron want to squirm. They'd stop in mid-conversation, or while trading for fish or eating delicious-smelling baked goods Aaron longed to sample, to stare at the tiny strangers. Their sunny companion paid the onlookers no mind, however, humming a tune while walking calmly toward the largest structure in the megalithic metropolis.

Up at the height of the city, the trio stopped before another set of gates, this one closed to visitors. Aaron still wondered at the efficacy of such a structure, but he supposed it was more of a message to stay out as opposed to an actual barrier to a flying species. Then there was the guard.

Another example of the dragon species sat in front of the doors. Body coiled around itself like a snake, this one was just about the size of Yielle, so probably around the same age, only with deep plum-colored scales. It had shorter, less extravagant horns, so again, Aaron guessed it was female.

The gate guard looked at the three of them with narrowed, disapproving, bronze eyes. She addressed Yielle. "What is this?"

Aaron didn't like the disgust that dripped from her tone, nor the sharp glare she turned on them.

"I found these two wandering in the mountains," their escort explained.

The other dragon sniffed. "I believe wolves are often found wandering in the mountains."

"They were trying to come here."

"Why?" The word sounded acidic and her lip curled in further disdain.

"A seer told them they would aid the dragons."

"Aid? Them?" The plum dragon pointed a clawed digit, the same color as her bronze eyes, in their direction and gave them another look. "They're werewolves and infants." Her snout wrinkled, her whiskers trembling.

"We're not infants," Aaron heard himself say, though he regretted it in the next moment. Still, he'd spoken up. "We're twelve and we've spent the past four months trekking from the Karnak Sea to the Selist Mar to get here."

A long tongue—he was surprised to find that it wasn't forked—licked absently at her reptilian lips as she stared at them more thoroughly. Though her reply still wasn't for them. "And so you wish them to be shown to the seer for confirmation?"

"Visions are a serious matter." The yellow dragon's shoulders rolled in a shrug-like motion, feigning indifference. "Though I leave the choice to your discretion, Steward Hiensun."

The gate dragon pinned them with her metallic stare once more before replying slowly, unhappily. "Indeed. The gods may have granted the possibility for the Sight in all their people. However, we cannot guarantee it is equally strong or accurate in each. Still, I will take them to the seer."

"Very wise." Yielle bowed her head deeply. "And you two," she said, turning to face the twins, "may Indris watch over you, and perhaps our paths will cross again."

"Thank you for your assistance," Aton replied formally, bowing as they'd just seen the dragons do. This caused their sun-colored companion to chuckle again.

"Yes, thank you." Aaron hastened to follow his brother's example and bowed.

"There is no need to thank me. It is we that should be thanking you for coming all this way to help a species not your own." Yielle's eyes sparkled as she gave them a grin filled with more teeth than Aaron had ever seen in one place. "I'll look for you two on the day the darkness comes." With one final nod she turned to leave, heading back down the street and into the crowd of swirling bodies and riotous colors, a cloud of youngsters descending around her horns almost at once. They heard her laugh and then she was gone.

"Come along then," the plum dragon snapped. The sound was something akin to a tree cracking in the forest, and both werewolves stood at attention. The reptile pushed open one side of the gates and slithered through. Aton and Aaron had little choice but to follow or be left out in the yard, so in they trotted.

This massive structure of the dragons was astounding, and that was even compared to all the wonders they'd already seen that day. It had been built on a scale that staggered Aaron to think about, so large that both Yielle and the steward probably thought it was spacious. Only as opposed to feeling cave-like, the building felt open and airy. With pale walls and surrounding clouds that drifted through open windows, the corridors made them feel like they were walking through the sky, forgetting the also pale roof so far above their heads.

Aaron thought the palace should've been freezing, as high in the mountains as they were and with so many openings in the walls, but warmth drifted up from beneath his feet. Upon a second inspection, he saw vents carved into the stone floors, warm air emanating from them, balancing out the chill. If he closed his eyes, he could almost imagine them on their own mountaintop in late spring, right before it turned truly hot in the summer months.

There were other wonders too—paintings in bright colors, long rugs with intricate designs, ornaments in every shade of metal or polished wood, and sculptures carved from the same pale stone—only there was no time to look at any of them as their escort hurried down the halls, giving no thought to her charges' shorter legs, let alone their interests. The smaller beings had to jog to keep pace, passing room after room of treasures beyond their imaginings. Each of the rooms stood open, their doors, great circular stone barriers carved with intricate designs and pivoting on silver hinges, pressed against the adjoining wall. All, that is, except for one.

At the end of the hallway, a door as brilliantly designed as any of the others stood mostly closed, ajar only the merest crack. The steward stilled her steps so quickly that the brothers nearly stepped on her tail, trimmed neatly in soft lavender fur. Like a rabbit smelling a fox, the dragon did not move for a long moment, her bronze eyes widened by some surprise.

"He is expecting you." She'd whispered it, but Aaron still heard the words clearly, and the shock in her tone.

It'd been obvious from her reaction when they'd first arrived that the steward hadn't believed the brothers' claims about visions or destiny. Only the sight of a door, standing open just wide enough to fit one of the werewolves through at a time, had somehow changed her mind.

Aaron took a step forward. Was this really supposed to convey that they were expected? Maybe someone had forgotten to close the door fully in their haste to be somewhere else. He peered at the space beyond the opening. While the hall they stood in was still flooded with the last rays of the sun, the space beyond the door looked completely lightless. The silver wolf pressed his ears back against his skull and hunched his shoulders just a bit. They were supposed to go in there? A warm breeze flowed through the opening, carrying a scent he didn't know, but he couldn't avoid the comparison to a wide, breathing maw, ready to devour them whole.

"Go on," the dragon said in the same hushed tone. When neither brother moved, she rallied, repeating more forcefully, "Go on. You mustn't keep him waiting."

Aton walked to the door first and Aaron saw his nose twitch. Aton had smelled what Aaron had, only Aton didn't hesitate, stepping over the threshold and into the hot darkness. Aaron followed his twin's lead, swallowed the lump in his throat, and walked in without even a look back.

Inside the door, Aaron tried to take in their surroundings, but couldn't actually see anything. Even with the light cast from the hallway behind them, their shadows melted into the greater gloom seamlessly without actually revealing anything, and then they were deprived of even that as the dragon steward closed the massive stone door behind them, shutting them in total black.

## CHAPTER 23

# *The Importance of a Name*

Dread clutched at Aaron's throat and guts as they were sealed into the dark room, encased, as though they were within a tomb. He focused on his breathing, trying to keep it steady, while he strained his ears to hear any sort of movement since his eyes were useless. He told himself he needed to be braver, stronger.

A hand materialized out of the shade and clapped him on the shoulder. Aaron jumped and spun to look toward the owner of the arm. His twin was nearly impossible to see, merely a darker outline in the dark sharing similar coloring. Only there was a difference, even if just a slight one. As his eyes began to adjust, Aaron realized there was some light in the cavern. It was red and sickly, diffused by wisps of moisture that floated through the hot hall, but it was there.

The shadow that was his brother nodded and, with no other option, the pair walked toward the light. Almost at once he felt that the floor was angled in a steady slope downward. It seemed odd to him that the dragons would build their fortress high into the air, only to keep their inner sanctum buried below it. They weren't dwarves, after all.

The source of the light they'd seen was farther than it'd seemed upon their first reflection, the path descending all the while, and it took them a long time to reach it. Stranger still, he saw that the light was coming up from the floor, though the color was like no sunstone he'd ever seen.

He kept his ears alert, constantly swiveling this way and that, even as his eyes were trained on their objective, because despite the silence, he was sure they couldn't be alone. Then he did hear something, a bubbling or churning, less like a babbling brook and more like someone cooking a pot of stew, thick and viscous. With the first, he found a second noise, a constant, heavy *whoosh* like bellows. Were they headed toward the kitchen?

Wherever they were going, the light remained constant, radiating up from the floor, from somewhere, and then it shifted. Both brothers tensed, Aton going for his sword, Aaron pausing on toe-point, ready to move.

The beam's movement was accompanied by yet another sound, this one a grinding metallic noise, like many metal bars scraping against one another. Atop the light a huge mass of something was moving. It writhed, alternatively covering and then reviewing shafts of the sickly glow, struggling to make itself coherent. The mound produced a head on a long, serpentine neck that rose from the form on the cavern floor and rose and rose.

The leviathan was massive, longer than both Yielle and the steward, possibly put together. If size had something to do with age, then the being before them had to be older than the mountains themselves. This seemed to be confirmed by the state of him. The dragon was milky white in color, save for the fur at its lip, cresting its back, and framing its face, which were all a dull and dusty gray. The horns it sported were large, so it was a male, but one was half broken, the other missing some of its points.

Aaron stood on guard, not sure what to expect, when the dragon opened its mouth to speak.

"Greetings to you, Children of Bain."

Hearing the ancient creature speak was like hearing a thunderstorm from inside a cave—impressive, only not quite as vibrant. Examining him closer, the younger twin started to notice a few of the dragon's other imperfections. The dragon was missing a few teeth and a few scales too; still other teeth were cracked. His fur was not just gray, but sparse, and his whiskers hung on either side of his face, lacking the energy to rise and float about as they should. Most startling of all were his eyes. Pupil, iris, and orb were all varying shades of the same sickly white, matching the rest of his body.

"Come closer," the great beast requested. The elderly creature said it without looking at them, nor did it follow their progress as the twins drew nearer. With a start Aaron realized that this being couldn't see them, that his eyes were completely sightless. The title of Seer, if that was who this dragon was, seemed ironic, if not some sort of cruel joke.

They were nearly upon their host when they had to stop short. They'd come to the edge of the light and looking down, Aaron could see that it emitted from beneath a massive metal grate, and below that was something he couldn't believe. Deep, impossibly deep, was a channel carved all the way down into the very heart of the mountain. That heart was ablaze. It was filled with fire, accounting for the light, and some churning liquid that cracked and glowed sinisterly. It boiled and roiled before their eyes, each bursting bubble casting another blaze. He'd never even heard of something so bizarre—it was like looking into the gods' own forge.

This dragon, this white, near-toothless, blind worm, sat directly atop it, soaking in the warm rays like a snake in a sunbeam, and it was warm. Had he been in his human form, Aaron was sure, he'd be sweating; as it was, he was resisting the instinct to pant. While not oppressive, the heat was considerable, and now closer to its source his nose could detect the odor he'd smelled earlier, like ash and rotting eggs, again not overpowering, but considerable.

They were still a bit away from the seer, though the only way to draw any closer was over the pit. They could easily fall through the gaps in the grate, as they were as big as Aaron stood tall, only likewise were the bars nearly as wide as a thin alleyway, easily wide enough to walk on, one at a time, just to be safe.

The older brother went first, testing the metal with a paw. Showing no signs of pain, the black wolf strode forward without further pauses. There was nothing else for Aaron to do but to follow, across the iron crossbeams, over the pool of liquid fire boiling distantly below. Nothing to it.

A generous platform stood right in the center of the vent, right before the massive serpent, his audience deck of sorts, while the bulk of the dragon's form sat comfortably over the crossbars farther on. The twins gained the solid expanse of metal and stood side by side, staring up at the old prophet.

Up close, his decay was all the more apparent, and so were his magnitude and the weight of his age, calculated in centuries instead of decades. The seer then turned its head to gaze down at them, his smooth, white orbs unfocused but attentive. Aaron supposed, if this being was a seer, maybe he'd seen this entire scene play out already, and so he knew what they'd do and where they'd stand.

The dragon spoke again in his mountainous voice. "I am Sonju, the Seer of the City of Sky Fire."

Aaron blinked. This was the first they'd heard the city's name. With clouds drifting through the corridors, white stone everywhere, and this core of impossible fire, the name certainly made sense to him.

"Thank you, Sonju," Aaron's brother said with a similar bow to the one he'd given Yielle.

Aaron hurried to mimic him. He hoped he was at least polite in this dragon's future memory.

The older boy straightened and continued. "Our mother spoke to another seer before we were born. That seer said my brother and I would be of some help to your people someday." He faltered. "Sh-she seemed to think that time was now" His words trailed off. As his twin spoke of their mother, Aaron felt his own tears threatening and a tightness in his throat, but he shook himself and tried to stay as resolute as his brother.

Sonju nodded. "I too have seen you in my visions. I have seen the wolf brothers, silver and black, coming to our door, and that this would announce the coming of a great darkness."

"What darkness?" The warrior tensed beside Aaron.

"That I cannot see." The seer sighed. "Visions are seldom clear, glimpsed as they are through the thick mists of time and choice. It will take still more time to decipher all of their wisdom. It is not clear to me yet what danger you have come here to subdue, though it is certain that you are vital to that struggle."

"I knew it," Aton said, fists clenched at his sides, eyes bright.

"How?" Aaron blurted out. "How can we be of any use to you? My brother is an excellent fighter, but your people are ten times our size, and I—" He hesitated. "I know a little magic, but not enough. I'm nowhere near strong enough to fight a dragon, let alone anything that could threaten one."

"And yet the gods saw fit to send you," the ancient being said with a small smile, lifting a drooping whisker with the gesture. "Yes, the nature of your contribution is shrouded—"

"Then how can you know it's true?" Aaron was shocked by his own outburst. He'd promised himself he would get better, stronger, but for what? How could so many claim to know about their importance, but not one could tell them what form that importance would take? He tucked his tail a bit, embarrassed over his rudeness. He was frustrated, but that was no excuse for snapping at the seer.

Surprisingly, though, the old dragon seemed to take no offense; he only chuckled. "It can be very frustrating for the seer too," he told them. "Though it can bring overwhelming joy as well. As my eyes grew dim, my true vision grew stronger. I see much more with the sight than I ever could with these mortal eyes. I see glimpses of great happiness and also great sorrow. I see your small house upon the hill, but I also see the grave beneath the apple tree. The past is much more distinct than the future. The past is set while the future churns, though what is most important must always shine through. You two will be important—that I see very well, even though we do not fully comprehend how."

Aaron's shoulders let go of some of their tension as he resigned himself to a longer wait for his answers.

The dragon continued. "Before then, however, there is much work to be done."

"But I thought you said our arrival will bring the darkness," Aaron asked.

"Your coming here does mean that it is closer than before. However, we still have a little time, I think, time we will use to prepare you."

"Tell us what we need to do," Aton said.

Aaron could hear the eagerness in his brother's voice. His twin stood at attention, every inch the soldier York had tried to mold him into. He thought his sibling's apparent eagerness was due to the promise of more training and the opportunity to grow stronger, not the possibility of carnage and death, which was what he saw ahead of them. At least he hoped it was self-improvement that was making Aton smile like that.

As though there had been some unspoken signal, the door at the top of Sonju's cavern opened again, the brief glimpse of different, distant illumination the only indication. Then a new figure joined them.

There at the edge of the grate stood another dragon, only far different than any of the ones they'd seen up to that point. It was smaller for one, maybe only twice Aaron's size, which he supposed meant the newcomer was young, only he wasn't sure about the rules of this new breed. It had to be another breed, as this dragon walked on two legs like a human, or like a werewolf, considering the similar structure of its legs with two prominent bends and a long tail waving behind them. It had a broad chest with shoulders connected to arms and hands tipped with hard, black talons, and two bat-like wings. The wings were folded, tucked mostly behind the figure, but they looked massive; they'd have to have been to lift something so sturdy looking. Aside from the clear muscles and scales evident on the new dragon, his expression was the hardest thing about him. He looked like he was scowling even from all the way across the grate. He—Aaron guessed he was male because this type of dragon didn't have branching antlers, only two long horns jutting from the temples and aiming straight back—walked over the beam, claws hanging partially off the edge, and came to stand confidently before them.

Only after the dragon had stepped onto the platform and slightly to the side did the caster realize there was another figure behind him. This second being looked human.

"What?" he breathed. He couldn't contain his surprise at seeing a human in a dragon city, especially after the way they'd been greeted. So much inside him cringed to see an actual human. He was in his werewolf form, and his mother had drilled into him time and time again not to let a human see him this way, even though this human had clearly been accepted by the dragons.

The man strolling toward them, seemingly without a care in the world, was tall and thin with long, silver hair cascading past his shoulders and down to his mid-back. It was an odd color for human hair. It was a light, almost white silver, as opposed to his gray-silver fur coat, and fairly luminescent in the dark cave. Aaron had seen old men sporting tufts of gray before in the markets, but this man was not old. He walked the iron path like a dancer, completely at ease, a natural grace about his every movement. He too came to the platform and took up a place next to the new dragon, only coming up to the beast's shoulder.

"I present to you Dexus of the City of Stone Fire, our capital city across the sea," Sonju said with a nod to the other dragon in their midst.

It was hard to judge color in the shadowy cavern, but Aaron thought Dexus to be a deep shade of red, his wing membranes a slightly lighter shade he saw as the newcomer gave a deep bow in response to the seer's acknowledgment.

"He will be your sword master."

Aton's ears perked up immediately and his bright eyes grew a touch wider. It wasn't until that moment that Aaron noticed the weapons hanging on a belt around the new dragon's midsection. There were two swords, one longer than the other, but both were thinner than Aton's short sword, if the scabbards were any indication. Why would a dragon have weapons, and why swords of all things?

Dexus said nothing, only turned cold, hard eyes in their direction. Scanning both boys, he didn't look impressed with what he saw.

Sonju spoke again. "May I also present the Lukia Candose, Lotician of Veralucia? He will be instructing you in magic."

"Luka Cand-wha?" Aaron found himself trying to sound out the words.

"It's elvish for high sorcerer," the man smirked.

Aaron's mouth fell open. He couldn't help it. Now that they were closer, he could see long, delicately pointed ears peeking through the curtain of white-silver hair. Lotician wasn't a human at all—he was an elf. It made much more sense that he wasn't human, what with humans' reputation for hunting dragons, but did an elf make any more sense? Of course the dragons couldn't teach him magic. They couldn't use it, so they'd need another species to do it, and elves were said to be the best.

Sonju answered Aaron's unasked questions. "The elves and the Fire Race have been friends for a long time, since just after we began recording it, I believe." He chuckled at his own joke, and it sounded like a tiny landslide. "When we asked our allies for help, Lukia Candose Lotician volunteered at once."

"There were a few of us, high sorcerers, who volunteered," Lotician added with a smile and bow to the seer. "I was granted the privilege due to my seniority."

"Privilege?" The younger twin asked.

"Quite. Lord Regent Fen Ryok has graciously granted me access to the City of Sky Fire's great library. The dragons are truly meticulous scholars, you know," the elf said in a conspiratorial tone. "Many of my colleagues would've given their right ear for the chance at even a peek at their collection." Then he added more loudly, "And of course the honor of lending aid to our great and ancient friends alone would be worth the journey." He gave a flourish with his long, slender hand as he bowed again.

Dexus seemed less inclined to elucidate his reasons for being present, which intrigued Aaron all the more, though he found the dragon way too intimidating to ask him anything. As if it wasn't odd enough that they'd gotten a dragon to teach swordsmanship, they'd chosen one from across the sea, from Rahovan. Was fighting with weapons common for dragons on the other continent? They did seem to be smaller, so maybe they needed a new skill. Surely their claws, fangs, and fire would be enough for anything. Weapons almost seemed redundant.

Looking over at Aton, Aaron could see his brother wasn't thinking anything like that. The warrior was only staring longingly at the blades at his new teacher's side, no doubt wondering about their style and strength.

Sonju chose that moment to speak again. "If you accept this future I have seen and the tutelage of these masters, they will train you until the day the darkness comes. Yet before you agree, I would have you know this." Sonju raised a clawed digit. "Here in the City of Sky Fire, we believe that when a pupil is taken into training, it is very like being reborn. You came here with many memories, painful and joyous, and with habits, both bad and good. All of these will hinder your teachers' attempts to mold you in their image and to assimilate you into their ranks. Therefore, you must give up your old lives in order to gain a new way of being. To signify this, you must sacrifice your names."

"'Sacrifice our names'?" The younger twin echoed.

"As you are nameless in the womb, so you are nameless in your training. By giving up that symbol of who you were, you die to your old lives. You will no longer be Aaron and Aton. During this time, you will be nameless."

"But—" Aaron spluttered, though the dragon seer pressed on.

"Apprentices may regain the right to bear a name again only once they have proven themselves to their teachers and thus completed the first stage in mastering their art. Once they have been born again as full members of their clan, it will be up to the initiates what name they will take on the other side. These successful students may choose a new name to represent their rebirth or take their previous names to honor those who brought them to this path. Either way, this sacrifice must be made to open yourselves to this transformation. Do you agree to this condition and thus the training of these two masters?"

Aton strode a confident step forward and said without pause, "I do."

"At—" Aaron began, whirling to face his brother.

The older boy did not stop. "I will relinquish my name and my past in order to become a stronger warrior." The look of pure determination etched into his brother's youthful features frightened Aaron.

"Good." Dexus spoke for the first time, his voice gruff and rumbling. The sword master strode toward them, towering over the youths, and fixed Aton with a stare. "Had you hesitated, I would not have agreed to take you on. Life as a warrior is about focus, dedication, and resolve. If you lack these, there will be no future glory."

The dark werewolf youth did not reply, but his posture was rigid and his breath steady.

Dexus watched him a beat longer. "You seem confident. We'll see how long that lasts." The foreign dragon pulled up his head to address the seer. "I accept the responsibility of training this young pup in the ways of weaponry. He will pass this stage of his training once he can best me with the blade." He clutched the hilt of the long sword by his side for emphasis.

Aaron wanted to cry out. His brother was twelve and the beast next to him was twice his size with who knew how many years of training. How was his twin ever supposed to beat a monster like him with a sword? Surely the others in the room had to see that.

No one else questioned Dexus's pronouncement. The ceremony continued without missing a step.

"Then it has been decided." Sonju nodded. "Aton will be reborn to the life of the swordsman."

The ritualistic nature of the exchange filled the caster with unease, as though this was a point they couldn't come back from. His brother looked grimly excited, his features stern, but the hint of a smile peeked through. Did he understand what he was doing?

"And you?"

The voice surprised Aaron, and he twisted around to see who'd spoken. The elf, Lotician, had crossed the platform with almost no sound, making his sudden appearance by Aaron's side seem like magic.

"Do you wish to learn sorcery?" Lotician's tall, lanky form reminded Aaron of an acrobat he'd once seen in Vidar on a festival day as opposed to a fighter, bigger and more muscled. Yet his assurance even among so many giants made it apparent that the elf was more powerful than he appeared, or at least he thought he was.

Aaron hesitated. "I do. I just don't know if I'm strong enough to do what needs to be done."

"I can already tell that you have some talent," Lotician assured him. "And if you are a true believer in all of this fate and destiny business, you should be confident that the gods wouldn't have put someone unworthy on this path." He shrugged. "Still, it is up to you."

"I—" Aaron looked to the side, to his brother. Aton's expression had changed from determined excitement to disbelief that his twin was even questioning the obvious choice.

"This is why we came here," Aaron's brother reminded him quietly.

Aaron flattened his ears, feeling like he wanted to crawl inside his fur to get away from all the eyes staring at him. They'd come to help the dragons, and it made sense that they would need to get stronger before they could do that, but how long would that take? How long were they going to train, and what were they even training for? What was the darkness? And was there any way out of this destiny?

He flinched at that last thought. Ducking his head toward his shoulders, he felt ashamed of himself for even thinking it. He had the opportunity to help someone, to help a lot of people, and all he wanted to do was to go back up on his little mountain with his mother and his brother. Only his mother wasn't there anymore, and his brother was staring at him as though he didn't understand why he wasn't itching for the chance to leap into danger.

Having a teacher with the express purpose of training them to become stronger meant the coming darkness was going to be something truly awful. It had seemed less scary when he thought he could arrive as a novice magic user and fix whatever problem the dragons were having at that moment, but to train for an unknown amount of time showed that whatever this was, was much larger than he'd feared.

Standing there he heard the words of their mother's letter playing in his head, saw his brother's expectant look, and knew Sonju, Lotician, and Dexus were all waiting for his answer, all expecting something from him. The pressure was suffocating.

"A seer may tell you the future," Sonju said softly, "but he cannot force you to act, nor would he wish to. Though the gods sometimes make choices for us, we may take comfort in the fact that their plans are always for the better. The gods do not make mistakes when they choose their champions, though sometimes it is hard for the champions to see it themselves. You are strong enough to do what is right, whatever you believe that is."

Aaron looked up, uncertainty and doubt still pulling at his heart. He looked to his brother again and then to Lotician, who stood with his hands behind his back as though he were in no hurry to hear Aaron's answer.

The darkness was coming. This had been confirmed by two seers now, and they were supposed to fight it, whatever it was, and he had promised himself that he would get better. Only he still had a choice. He could pretend it wasn't coming and hide away until the trouble found him or accept the training the dragons were offering and become as strong as he could before it arrived. When he thought about it like that, there wasn't much of a choice. His mother and his brother had both made the same choice. He would be strong like them.

"I'll accept your training if you'll have me," he said, facing Lotician. His back was straight, his tail up, and his eyes as hard as he could make them. "I'll reject my name and past so that you may show me how to become more than what I am now."

"Brilliant," Lotician said with a softer grin. "I will accept you as my student, and I will train you to become an accomplished sorcerer. Your training, therefore, will end when I feel that you truly understand the elements and can use them to your advantage with ease."

He would get stronger. He would become braver. He would be a hero like his brother, like his mother.

"The path is set," Sonju said with deep gravity in his weary voice. "Aaron will be reborn to the ways of magic."

## CHAPTER 24

# *Rocky Beginnings*

"Wait. So you didn't know about the un-naming ceremony?" the silver wolf asked.

Aaron and his new eln teacher were in the grand guest chamber the high sorcerer had merited as his temporary residence. It was human sized, roughly average height for the Eight, which had surprised him until he thought back to when the seer had said the dragons were friends with the elves. Maybe they visited often enough to warrant a few rooms. They were staying in another, if lesser such room, after all. The grand chamber had three distinct sections—a bedroom, a washroom, and a sort of study, where they currently sat—all lavishly appointed in white stone, gold trim, and silks.

"Not until my arrival here," Lotician clarified. "This concept of apprenticeship and rebirth seems to be a ryong tradition. I suppose I see the parallels, but it's not the way elves treat their students. If you'd come to Veralucia and requested to be a Lukia, we wouldn't have asked for your name in return, only proof you were capable of becoming one. Though I don't suppose there've ever been any Children of Bain on Veralucia before, and certainly none that have requested an apprenticeship."

That one sentence brought up so many questions, Aaron almost didn't know where to start. "Sonju called us that too—Children of Bain. I know the first werewolf was called Bain, so does it just mean werewolf?"

Lotician paused in his perusal of a particular tomb and looked at the youth. It amused Aaron to see his teacher's ears perk up when he was surprised, like his own lupine ones. "You don't know?"

His own ears lowered. "No," he admitted.

"Yes, Bain was the first werewolf, the progenitor of your species. He was responsible for not only the werewolves' creation, though the other don't call themselves the Children of Bain. You should look in the dragons' archives if you'd like to learn more. I don't know that they'll have everything on the topic, but it's a place to start. What did your parents teach you about him?"

"My mother was newly turned, and we didn't grow up around many wolves." Aaron looked down at his hands. He didn't want to explain further.

Lotician shut the book he'd been pursuing with a snap, drawing back his student's attention. "History lessons later. For now, show me what I've got to work with."

At first Aaron didn't know what to show the elf. Was he supposed to impress him? Show him the most powerful or most complicated thing he knew how to do?

Closing his eyes, he knew what he'd show him. He pulled his power, felt it flowing from the center of his core in response. He gathered it between his palms and produced a sphere of magical light glowing brightly, gently pulsing, and almost as wide as his own chest, shining the same bright spring green.

His teacher nodded. "Good. It's well formed, stable, sizable, and bright." He nodded again. "You've had at least some training then."

Aaron gave a nod of his own. "My mother trained me."

"Did she teach you anything about the elements? Are you able to call any of them?"

"Yes." Aaron perked up. He was relieved that his new teacher seemed pleased. Maybe his training wouldn't be too daunting.

Absorbing most of the energy back inside of him—he always lost some from the effort of calling and moving it—he moved a portion of the energy to his right hand but kept it inside. Then he tried to find a source. The room was lit with sunstones, but there was still heat in the air. He pulled at that, felt the strings of fire interlaced with the ones of air, and tried to pull them apart. Once he had hold, he drew on the fire's energy. When he'd felt he'd stored enough, he opened his fist and a ball of fire bloomed into being, hovering a scant two inches above his palm.

He smiled and let out the breath he'd been holding. It came out as a cloud of steam, the temperature of the room having plummeted from his magical draw. He'd not been sure if he'd be able to pull off the trick. The fireball was small and somewhat unbalanced, but it was more impressive than a flicker would've been.

"Stop, stop!" The elf waved his hand, both words coming on clouds of their own.

In his confusion, the apprentice lost his concentration and the fire vanished. Lotician was looking skyward, as though asking the gods for help.

"What?"

"You were trained by a human." It was a statement, not a question, given as a groan.

"Yes," he replied, still not understanding.

"Don't you see the damage you're causing?"

He blinked in surprise. "You mean the air cooling?"

"Yes, the drop in the ambient temperature. And let me guess. When you call on the water the plants around you dry up, call on stone and the soil beneath you cracks?"

"Yes."

"You're damaging the world every time you cast."

"That's how magic works. You pull energy from the world to cast with."

"No." The one word and shake of his teacher's head was so adamant that it shook the silver curtain of hair over his face. Tucking it back, he said, "You need to ask the world to lend you its power."

"What?"

Instead of replying the elf opened his hand and a ball of fire, much like Aaron's own, appeared and then flew off, replaced by another and another. Soon enough half a dozen balls of fire floated slowly about the room, only their presence made the room warmer, not colder.

"How?"

"I asked the fire to aid me, and it did, and since it did so willingly, I didn't have to pull at it and force it to comply to my will, thus not having to break a part of the world to do it."

"That's not what my mother taught me."

"You said she was newly turned, meaning she was raised by humans. They don't know any better and refuse to be taught."

"Why do you say that?" He was trying not to snarl at his teacher, but it felt to him that the elf was getting close to insulting his mother.

The high sorcerer paused, watching his flaming orbs float about, momentarily lost in his own thoughts. At last he said, "I said we'd save the history lesson for another time." All at once, in a sudden flare, all of the fire dissipated. "For now, I'll teach you how to speak to Eris, to her spirits, and, eventually, to her elementals. I supposed the ryong have a point when they ask you to forget everything you were taught before."

"Talk to the elementals? Aren't they only larger spirits?"

"They are a race of great spirits that aid in the care of the world and move the elements through their power. When you're ready, you'll form a pact with one of each kind. It's pivotal in your advancement toward becoming a Lukia Candose."

"And I'll need to be a Lukia Candose in order to defeat the darkness?" His tone dropped at the mention of his ultimate obstacle.

Lotician sighed and placed a hand on his shoulder. "No one knows how long we've got. I plan to train you the way I would any other apprentice. Fate will sort the rest out."

## CHAPTER 25

# *Faces in the Wind*

True to his word Lotician started Aaron from what he called the basics. elven teacher had seemed pleased enough by how the silver werewolf was able to move the energy within his body. "For the moment," the elf had hastened to add, but he needed to start all over again with his element training.

This included spirit spotting. His mother had told him each god had servants that helped them, but he'd never seen them. Lotician taught him to do just that. The sorcerer taught him to see faces in the wind and strange, darting fins in the water, eyes in the stones, and hands in the fire, or any combination in any and all of them.

"They don't have true forms," Lotician told him.

The pair were standing out on the landing platform, the one that Yielle had brought the twins through when they'd arrived. They were gazing out at the Shei Denti, the wind whipping around them. He'd been instructed to search for air spirits while his teacher lectured.

"They may be part of their element and thus invisible, or they may choose to stand apart and show themselves to those with the power to observe them. They are each composed of their element, you see, and thus just as transmutable, but they like to play. There is no better game for a spirit than copying what they see, sometimes all the things they've ever seen at once."

"If they do this all the time, then why can no one see them?" Aaron asked, watching an air spirit swim past with the body of a fish but the head of a dragon.

"They need to be seen with more than just your eyes," his teacher replied, waving his long fingers through the air, where another wind spirit took on the shape of a snake and wove around them. "Every living thing has the essence of the world and thus the divine within it. Some call it power, or energy, or magic, but it's all the same. It's the lifeblood of the old god Varro, who fell to create this world of Eris, which he bequeathed as a gift to all the beings that have sprung from it."

"Even plants and animals?"

"Yes, I did say all things. Only the degree with which they may use it consciously will vary. That is controlled by the lineage of the parents, be they elf, elk, or elderflower, and by the luck of their birth, if they are one of the Eight blessed with the ability to use the power at will and to what degree. The will of Varro determines it all."

"The degree?" the boy asked, watching the air spirits dart in and out of being, one moment taking on a form of their own, the next merging back into their element and disappearing.

"If they are one of the races that may be born with the conscious ability to use magic, those being elf, were, human, nokken, or dwarf. There are then four degrees, or levels of ability, that they use the magics of this world—Herstia, Sustia, Lukia, and Crumem."

The elvish language was beautiful. It sounded like his teacher was singing instead of merely speaking, not that he understood any of the words. The only word he recognized was Lukia, which he knew meant sorcerer.

"Crumem," Lotician began, "means seer. It's a passive ability where an individual sees glimpses of the future and the past. These visions seem to be random, appearing only when something important has occurred or is about to."

Silver Wolf nodded.

"Herstia, on the other hand, is a more active power. Directly translates into the common human tongue as listener; this is an individual who can only hear the spirits."

"Hear?" The silver werewolf flicked his ears, trying to hear tiny voices in the wind, only he couldn't make out anything except the constant rushing of the breeze.

The elf shook his head again, gentler this time, causing only a silver strand to fall across his face. He cleared it away before replying. "The spirits don't use words as we understand them. When we say 'listener,' this is someone in tune with a particular element. This could look like a farmer who consistently pulls in a good yield, a woman who knows which herbs are good for healing instead of just flavoring a soup, a man who can track a dove through the forest. It can be subtle; often listeners might not know what they are doing, but it is the elementals aiding them and guiding them in the ways of the elements, though at their whim, not the listeners'.

"Sustia translates to speaker. These are individuals who can speak to the spirits, though usually only one type. This could be the forge master able to ask the flames to burn brighter and hotter, the fisherman who can ask the current to direct the fish into his nets, or the woman who harvests vegetables from the ground as though she were plucking them from soft snow."

That sounded a bit more useful. "Only one element?"

"Typically." Lotician shrugged. "Occasionally they have two types of spirits willing to listen. This is the level where the users of magic start to see the spirits, and only those that are in tune with the speaker. The last type is the Lukia."

"Sorcerers," the boy said.

"Yes, that is what a human would call them. Lukia, if you translate is directly, is commander."

"Commander?"

"This is the highest level of magical caster, one who may use all four of the elements on Eris."

"But if Lukia is the highest, then what is a Lukia Candose?"

"A Lukia may speak to and be obeyed by spirits of all four types. A Lukia Candose will have made pacts with all four types of elementals, the true movers of Eris, but it goes beyond just the pacts. To achieve high sorcerer status, the caster must have the blessing of the elementals and their trust that the caster will use only the power that they require, and then will give them thanks and aid in return should the need arise."

"And I'm going to become a Lukia Candose?"

Aaron's teacher smiled, still facing the sky and the world beyond. "Perhaps. It will depend on how much time we actually have. The condition for ending your apprenticeship was that you must have the ability to call on all four elements and use them with ease. This will require you to reach the level of Lukia, but Lukia Candose? We'll have to see."

## CHAPTER 26

# *Magic and the Way of Things*

Once the young werewolf had learned to see the spirits and hear the wisdom they chose to impart, Lotician instructed him that it was time to ask for their aid. He needed to progress from listener to speaker.

They were back in Lotician's guest quarters and study. Silver Wolf, as he was now called, was sitting cross-legged on the floor, a little pile of common mountain stones stacked in front of him. He was meant to use his power to shape them. No, he was meant to ask *them* to change their shape or to give him the power to make them change their shape. He was still trying to figure out which.

He focused on the stones beneath his hands, focusing his energy onto them, only not just his own power, but the power he was asking the stone spirits to give him. The rocks trembled, his hands hanging inches above them, but then the top stone fell from the pile, completely unchanged.

Silver Wolf snarled. He'd always had trouble with stone, even on the few occasions when his mother had been teaching him about that particular element. He wanted them to shift, to change, but they refused. Baring his teeth and pinning his ears, he redoubled his mental efforts, willing them to obey. The ground beneath the pile began to crack.

"Stop, stop! Human magic," Lotician said in disgust, his frown making him look like he'd tasted something sour. "It's like trying to teach a dragon to dance the Ludessa."

"Dance the what?"

"It's a graceful dance the elvish people do to celebrate the return of summer." He shook his head again. "It doesn't matter. You can't just reach out and take the magic, then try to force it to obey you. You know this. You'll never achieve the same level of energy if you're battling with its source. You need to ask the spirits for the power you require. I know you're half human, so that'll hold you back, but your other half should be closer to the natural world. This shouldn't be beyond you."

The apprentice sorcerer sighed and went back to concentrating on the stones. Spirits didn't use words, as Lotician said, so they didn't respond to verbal commands, only mental requests through emotions and visualizations. He tried to "talk" to the spirits, and when nothing happened, he fairly yelled at them in his head, his frustration trembling through their mental connection.

The rock wobbled again, this time from its place on the bare stone floor; it rocked and trembled, but didn't change one bit. Letting out a puff of breath, Silver Wolf released his gathered energy, falling back on his hands and groaning.

"Keep at it. You'll get it eventually," his teacher said, writing down a note the boy was certain had nothing to do with him.

"And you wanted to come here," the werewolf asked between puffs of breath, changing the subject away from his ineptitude, "just to teach me how to make different shapes out of rocks?"

"Of course not," Lotician said, setting down his quill.

"That and to read."

"The City of Sky Fire's library is extensive, enticing even, and certainly well worth the long journey here all on its own," the elf acknowledged. "However, curiosity played its part as well."

"Curiosity? About what?"

"About you. I've lived a long time, not long enough that I was around to witness the creation of species, but a long time, nonetheless. I've seen many Lukia, trained a few myself, but when the envoy of the ryong court came to our shores and asked for our help in training their god-chosen hero, well, that was something new. It piqued my curiosity. What would a god-chosen hero be like?"

"And how am I?" He sat up, legs crossed with his elbows on his knees, half eager and half worried to hear the answer.

"Young, impulsive, impatient." Lotician's smile broadened.

The wolf's ears flattened in consternation. "I get it."

"Unsophisticated and woefully mis-instructed," Lotician continued. "However, I am beginning to see hints of the gods' reasoning."

This made Silver Wolf's ears perk up again. "Really? What hints?"

"There is a natural order to magic. Think of your body and its ability to contain power as a jar." He plucked a glass vessel from the table. "And the level of magic within as a quantity of water." He opened a hand and the boy stared intently as droplets began forming out of thin air and collecting in a sphere right above the elf's open palm. When he had collected enough, he let it pour into the glass until it was about halfway full. "You may borrow power from the world and its elementals—once you've made the pacts, of course—to add to your own," he said, adding still more water. "However, you need to be careful not to exceed the amount that your body can handle." He added still more water to the jar, filling it to the very top, then exceeded it. The excess water flowed down the sides of the glass and dripped to the floor. "Do that, and the consequences are dire." The water continued to flow over the glass and Silver Wolf had to wonder what that would feel like, to have the power run loose, to have it overwhelm him. "Now, your jar may grow, as your body does, through the natural process of aging, and there are active ways of growing this container as well, like strengthening a muscle. Yet like with your physical strength, there are limits based on your form and mental capabilities. That is why it is paramount that we come to understand our own limitations." Lotician set the jar down.

"And being a human is a limitation?"

"No. They'll never be as adept with the power as, say, an elf, but they can be nearly as talented as a nokken or a dwarf, I suppose. They might even be stronger, if they'd stop stealing power."

"My mother wasn't a thief," he said, an edge to his voice.

Lotician raised a delicate hand. "Not her fault. It was what she was taught, what she taught you. Tradition is a hard knot to untangle. Stealing power takes less energy from the caster, but you'll never achieve the pinnacle of your strength until you combine your strength with a willing world's. Asking yields the greatest results. As a people, they've just not learned that yet."

"So what makes me different? You said you saw hints."

"Your jar is much larger than I would've expected for a boy of twelve. I'm not sure if that's because you're a werewolf and there's something of magic within your breed at the start, or whether it was because you were touched by the gods when they chose you, or it's simply natural talent and the reason you were chosen in the first place. Whatever the cause, it means your raw potential is perhaps the strongest I've seen."

"Really?" His eyes lit up at the unexpected praise.

"Really." The elf chuckled. "However, just because you have the potential doesn't mean you know how to use it. Now, ask the stone to smooth itself."

Silver Wolf bobbed his head thoughtfully and returned to the little pile in front of him. Eris was watched over by the gods but was taken care of by spirits and their higher counterparts, the elementals. He just needed to ask for the power, add it to his own, manipulate it, and put it back into the element to affect a change.

Staring at the stones, he could feel the threads just before him. In the past he would've mentally stretched out and pulled; instead he sent a wave of his own power joined with his will and desire toward the energy. A trickle of outside magic, not much, touched him, and he felt it flow into him, easy and growing stronger. He took hold of all the power within himself, molded it, and pushed it back into the rocks at his feet. Before his eyes, the stone lost its sharp angles. Just as though he'd taken a hot knife to a stick of butter, it smoothed.

A wide grin stretched over his features, his tail thumping on the stone floor behind him.

"Well done." Lotician nodded, flicking a finger at the recently smoothed stone. The rock immediately returned to its rough, jagged, original shape. "Do it again."

Grin gone, the student leaned back with a snarl. "I need a break."

"It's not that stone is unwilling to help," Lotician said. "It's just very slow to do so. Once you've gotten the knack of it, you'll be able to do so much more." The master sorcerer waved a hand, which pulsed with marigold light, the same color as his irises that surrounded his gray, cat-slit pupils, an elven trait. The room filled at once with the scent of magic—clean and sweet and electric—as the bright light swirled. The smell still reminded Silver Wolf of his mother, though he didn't have the time to notice the pain in his chest as he watched the spell his master worked. One of the stones began to hover, other smaller rocks rising to meet it. They clumped around each other, mixing and stacking until they had formed themselves into the shape of a very small tortoise, no bigger than Silver Wolf's fist. He leaned forward to look at the sculpture. It looked back at him with tiny pinpricks of marigold light and hissed. The wolf lurched back reflexively.

"What is that? A spirit? An elemental?"

"A construct," Lotician corrected, stroking a single finger over the tortoise's shell. "Similar to a spirit, it is a being composed of a particular type of magical element. The difference is, while you may think of spirits as an elemental's minions, as the elementals are for the gods, this one is mine, made from my power to do my bidding."

"And it's alive? It thinks for itself?" he asked, watching the little construct walk around in the space between the two sorcerers.

"It has the affectations of life and temperament, typical of its element, but it has no true thought or mind."

"No mind?"

"As far as we've been able to gather. They're never around long enough to tell. These creatures are sustained by a constant flow of the caster's energy and are thus quite taxing to maintain. They're called for a task and then dismissed." The Lukia waved his hand again and the little tortoise collapsed back into the pile of loose stones.

Silver Wolf felt a strange pang of sympathy for the little being as it crumbled back to nothing. "And I'll learn how to call these constructs?" the werewolf asked to distract himself.

Lotician smirked. "This is quite a high-level trick. You'll have to graduate from talking to spirits to making pacts with elementals first. You're not there yet. Once you are, however, we can start to teach you. It takes a long time to master, though I did know one apprentice who summoned a construct quite early in his training, accidentally of course."

"Accidentally?"

"Just as it takes concentration to gather and direct one's energy, a lack of it or an excess of emotion can cause it to run amuck in some quite unexpected ways."

"And this apprentice summoned a construct?"

"A water pike. The blasted thing nearly took his arm off."

Silver Wolf blanched under his fur. "But I thought you said it was supposed to obey the caster."

"If you're so entangled in your own emotions that you can't even form a coherent thought, how do you expect to control a capricious thirty-foot fish?" Lotician sighed, shoulders slumping at the memory. "For now, let's skip the carp and stick with smoothing out stones. Agreed?"

## CHAPTER 27

## *Timeline*

Hours later, Silver Wolf dragged himself back to the room he was staying in, the room the dragons had assigned to both twins. It wasn't nearly as grand as Lotician's, but that was fine with him. It reminded him a bit of their bedroom back at the cottage. Made from the same white stone as the rest of the city, with an open window and heated vent to make the temperature pleasant—though he shivered when he thought of where the heat came from—it had two single beds and a round table, complete with two chairs, and a washroom attached. They didn't really need anything else.

His head pounded and he felt completely drained of all energy. Even though he'd spent most of the day sitting down, he'd literally poured everything he had into his training. He plopped himself down in one of the two wooden chairs. On the table sat a stone bowl with a wooden lid, fragrant steam escaping around the edges, and a pair of ceramic bowls and spoons. He had no doubt that it was filled with an excellent stew. He'd been surprised when he'd first eaten a meal in the city and found he liked dragon cuisine. Every herb and spice had been an adventure, mostly with pleasant results, sometimes not. There was one dish—goat, he was fairly sure—that the dragons burned till it was nearly all cinder. He'd not been able to choke it down.

As good as he knew the soup would be, he wasn't much interested in eating at the moment. He was looking longingly at his bed when the door banged opened and the black wolf hauled himself through, not even looking at his brother as he fell onto one of the beds face-first.

"Tough day?" Silver Wolf asked.

Black Wolf grunted into the pillow but wasn't forthcoming with any more details.

Silver Wolf looked back to the food. As much as he wasn't looking forward to eating, he knew they both needed to recoup their energy. "We should eat. Do you think you can?"

"I'm fine," grumbled the elder twin, hefting himself up from his prone position and half-limping over to their little table, falling into the second chair.

When Silver Wolf pulled off the lid, the room instantly filled with the fragrant scents of the meal, a hot soup filled with wild edibles, root vegetables, and wild onions mainly, accompanied by large chunks of some kind of wild game, most likely ram or deer.

His mouth salivated as he ladled out the meal for himself and his twin. The warrior pulled the bowl over and started in slowly. His body clearly wanted to prioritize sleeping over eating, but appeared to change its mind as soon as the first spoonful reached his mouth. He finished the bowl with gusto.

"Is training with Dexus that brutal?" Silver Wolf asked after he'd finished his own bowl and started scooping out seconds, the tang of the pepper still lingering pleasantly on his tongue.

"I used to think training with York was hard."

The younger brother grimaced at the thought. He could remember his twin out in the sun with the old soldier for hours, swinging his blade over and over until his muscles remembered the correct forms, sweat flowing off him in rivers.

"What's so different about it?"

"The tail for one." Silver Wolf saw his brother rub absently at his wrist. "For another his standards seem to be higher than York's."

"Sonju did say he was a sword master."

"He keeps saying my stances are sloppy, my swings are wild, and my focus is lacking. Every point punctuated by his tail." The big wolf frowned. "And you? How's your training?"

The sorcerer's apprentice gave his own frown, adding a weary sigh. "Lotician has me going over the same spell until I can get it right every time. I must have changed the shape of that rock two dozen times today." He shook his head. "I know it's not the same thing as what you're doing, but it takes a lot of energy to cast. I'm exhausted."

His older brother nodded, still concentrating on his second bowl of soup.

There was more. "He said I don't have healing magic."

"What?" Black Wolf looked up from his meal.

"After I'd failed with the fire, I told him I could heal. He cut his own hand and told me to show him."

His brother watched him, waiting for more.

"I gathered the power and put my hand over the wound and" He trailed off.

"And?"

"And nothing. He said the only thing I was doing was pushing my energy into him. I gave him power but didn't instruct his body what to do with it."

"But you healed me."

"Apparently, I didn't. I gave your body a surge of energy that it used to enhance your own healing power. Lotician thinks that since our ability to heal so quickly is one of our greatest assets, your body chose to use my magic to speed it up further. That's why it hurt so badly; it shrank the time your body took to heal, so you felt all of the discomfort at once."

"So what does that mean?"

"That I could help another werewolf heal faster, probably, but probably not any other species, and not if they're too far gone to restore themselves at all."

The apprentice warrior looked back into his bowl, thinking about what Silver Wolf had just said.

"At—" The caster quickly cut off the word as his brother shot him a glare. They'd agreed to shed their names and were now going by the simple monikers of Black Wolf and Silver Wolf, or whatever variation of that their masters decided to use that day. Black Wolf, of course, had taken to his new title much quicker. Silver Wolf was still having trouble remembering not to use their names, even to each other.

"Brother," he began again, "how long do you think we'll be here?"

The dark twin looked up with a raised eyebrow. "What do you mean?"

"We've been here a few months already. I've learned a lot, and there's so very much more to learn. Only we have no idea how long we actually have. How long do you think we'll be here until the darkness comes? If destiny needs us to finish our apprenticeships first, that could take lifetimes. I need to learn and control all five elements, but I'm being taught by a being who's been alive for over two hundred years, and even he says he's still learning. What if I don't have enough life left to finish my apprenticeship?"

"We know the darkness will come before we die." His brother chuckled without humor. "Though I get your meaning. I need to defeat Dexus in a fight, after all, and to your point, dragons also measure their lives in centuries."

The mention of the dragon sword master again brought an old question to his mind. "Why does he use weapons anyway?"

"Curiosity, he says."

"Curiosity?" That was what Lotician had said too.

His brother shrugged. "Dexus doesn't talk much."

"So why is he here? Why make the trip all the way from Rhovan? Was it curiosity about you?"

"Maybe," he said, clearly considering it. "He did say the ryong dragons offered him a sword."

"A sword? That's it?"

"Dragons don't make swords," he emphasized. "They are good with metal, but dragons don't use weapons. The fact that the dragons living in the City of Sky Fire offered to make him something like that was very tempting to Dexus. I also think he's pleased that someone has acknowledged his skills."

The younger twin cocked his head to the side. "Acknowledged his skills?"

"Dragons don't use weapons. Why would his people care if he was skilled with some useless tool?" he explained patiently. "Then someone, one of his own kind, asks him to use those skills, to teach those skills. It must've been gratifying."

The pair spent another moment chewing in silence, thinking on all that had been said, before Silver Wolf veered back to their previous topic. "So how long do you think we have?"

His brother paused, staring as though he could read the future in the wood grain of the table. At last he said, "I don't know."

"What do you think the darkness is?"

The older replied again, "I don't know."

"And that doesn't bother you? All of this uncertainty?" In a fit of frustration, Silver Wolf tossed his spoon into the bowl, sloshing the broth, and threw up his hands.

"It's no different than anything else in life." The larger boy shrugged.

"I think looming darkness is a little unusual."

Black Wolf blinked at him before replying. "It is unusual. This is better."

"This is not better than our life before," the younger one said. He felt the growl rumbling at the back of his throat and the hairs on his neck begin to rise.

"We lived our lives in hiding."

He looked away, unable to refute the comment. "It was still better than this."

"It was good," Black Wolf nodded. "But it was selfish."

"What?"

"We were born different, stronger. It would've been selfish not to use those gifts, especially when we knew others would need them."

"So the cards claim," replied the caster sullenly. "Only it's hard, you know? Hard realizing that, even if we do defeat this mysterious trouble, we'll never be able to go home again. Hard knowing that we've left it all behind."

His brother offered him a small smile and a mock punch to his shoulder. "You haven't left it *all* behind."

## CHAPTER 28

# *A Balanced Education*

"Do you intend to stay that way all morning?" the warrior-in-training asked, a spoonful of porridge halfway to his mouth.

"Yes," Silver Wolf groaned, his head resting on his folded arms and his own empty bowl of breakfast porridge sitting just in front of him. The small black pot it'd been brought in, still smelling of the oats and dried berries it had contained, sat empty and cooling in the center of their little table next to the ceramic pitcher of fresh spring water brought to accompany it. They'd yet to have any milk during their stay. As clever as the dragons were about foraging and planting to satisfy their varied diets, domesticating animals was apparently a step too far.

"I think your spell master would have something to say about that."

Silver Wolf was quiet, imagining Lotician breaking through the door with blasts of fire to retrieve his wayward student. "Fine." He pulled up his head.

"Sorcerer training isn't that difficult," his brother snorted, finishing the last morsels of his breakfast.

He sat up with a sigh. "Training with magic is exhausting enough. You know, it actually takes more energy from the caster to do it the 'right' way? Yes, you get better results, but by Varro I didn't think it would be so"

His addled brain couldn't find the right word, so he changed tack. "And then there's all the other training we do."

"Other training?"

"Lotician says it's not enough to just practice with spells and talk to spirits. I need to improve my mind. So he's been teaching me math and science and the philosophy of all things."

"Sounds terrible," the other boy smirked. "It also sounds like you could use a little endurance training."

He gave his older twin a scowl. "And Dexus only teaches you about fighting?"

"And works on my breathing, endurance, strength. You think you're tired?" Black Wolf snorted.

"Must be nice."

"Come on." The bigger wolf tossed his spoon in his bowl and stood, carrying the tray to the door and leaving it in the hall. As heroes of destiny, they weren't required to do their own dishes anymore.

"Yeah, yeah." Silver Wolf pushed himself up from the table and followed his brother out into the hall. He emerged just in time to see the black tip of his brother's tail disappear around the corner, clearly having tarried with his younger brother enough. Of course, he reflected, Dexus would probably make him do another thousand sword swings to punish him for being late. On that note, he hurried down the hall, just in case Lotician decided to be equally creative in his punishment.

He jogged through his teacher's open door, finding the silver-haired elf back at his desk, taking notes next to another book.

Without looking up Lotician said, "Cutting it close this morning?"

"Sorry. My brother and I were just comparing our lessons," he said offhandedly, looking for his pile of rocks.

"Oh?" His teacher looked up from his book, one white-silver brow arched.

"He said my training didn't sound very difficult. I just sit around, either moving my energy from hand to hand or with my nose in a book."

Instead of getting annoyed as Silver Wolf had, his teacher gave a little smirk. "Those who rarely use their minds lack the experience to know how very tiring it can be to expand it." Then he added, returning to his book, "Though I'm sure that doesn't describe your brother, nor his esteemed dragon sword master."

The apprentice caster didn't know how to reply to that. He found his pile of rocks and sat down cross-legged before them, readying to begin his typical warm-up.

His teacher spoke again. "You are looking a bit ragged." He'd turned around fully on his stool, regarding his pupil. "Perhaps a trip outside and a little sunlight might do you some good."

The youth was surprised by the suggestion, but not opposed. "Sure," he smiled, getting up off the floor and moving back to the stone portal.

Lotician rose from his stool, only he didn't grab his cloak hanging on the hook as he passed. It was cold out on the peaks without the heat from the mountain's heart flowing up through the vents to offset the temperature, nor did he have a fur coat to protect him from the wind.

Silver Wolf didn't have any more time to wonder about it as Lotician was already walking down the passageway. Jogging after his teacher, he also noticed that this wasn't their typical route to the outer gates. When they'd gone there before to study the wind spirits, they'd left by the palace's front gates, through the city, to the central landing area, the reverse of how they'd come to this place the first time. Only now his teacher was leading him through back hallways, still within the smaller guest wing. Perhaps he'd found a balcony or someplace where they'd not have to worry about being underfoot.

Then Silver Wolf heard the sharp smack of wood on wood. He heard it twice more in quick succession before a third, louder *clack*. The noise sounded like a sheep trying to dance—chaotic, but not totally absent of a sort of rhythm.

His teacher appeared to be approaching the noise. Then the hall opened up to a larger chamber with higher ceilings, smooth floors, and in the center of it, within a rough circle of ropes, Dexus and his brother stood across from one another, sparring.

Only Black Wolf wasn't a black wolf. He was sparring in his human form, clad in only a pair of shorts, with the much larger dragon; both were armed with a wooden practice sword. Sweat was running off of his forehead and chest. It seemed so long since they'd worn their human skin that it had taken Silver Wolf a moment to recognize the other boy.

Human shape or not, his brother was fast—strike, dodge, strike-strike in quick order, dodge the other sword swinging for his head, and strike again. Still Dexus was ready for him. With each strike there would be a replying parry, a turn, or a snap with his tail. At one point the boy charged, no doubt frustrated with all of his work being turned so easily. He ducked the swing from the dragon, jumped the tail as the great being swung at his legs, only to get smacked in the face by a wing and thrown to the far side of the area. The apprentice hit the rope and bounced forward, falling to a knee and panting to catch his breath.

It was at this point that the claret drake took notice of their visitors. "Good day." The greeting was fairly grunted.

"Good day to you as well, Master Dexus." Lotician returned the grunt with a pleasant smile and a nod. "And how goes the training? Are the repeated beatings bringing the desired effects yet?"

The comment caused the large reptile to still and straighten himself up, making him look even bigger. "This is how a warrior prepares for a fight, building up strength, endurance, and resilience." The accompanying smile revealed his matching rows of sharp teeth.

"Yes, of course, that's how a hero would prepare, assuming that the coming darkness is something you can hit with a stick." The elf gave a dismissive glance to the mock sword in the dragon's hand. "Only, if that were the case, why would the dragons, being so much larger and stronger than the rest of us, need such tiny assistance?"

One reptilian brow lifted in response. "You believe the darkness will not be a monster."

The sorcerer shrugged. "Oh, I don't know. It could be. It could also be a natural disaster, the volcano exploding and releasing a cloud of ash into the air, or poison in the spring. It could be political in nature, a sect of rebellious servants bent on relieving the regent of his throne in the City of Sky Fire. It could be a sorcerer, bent on mastering the dragons to use in his own nefarious plans."

"Would that be you then?" Dexus laughed, derision clear in his tone. At this point the young warrior had recovered enough to stand behind his teacher, mirroring the young sorcerer.

Silver Wolf didn't know if he liked where this was going.

"Me? No." Lotician shook his head, a smile still on his lips. "I'm much too busy studying the collected histories of the dragons to want to conquer them."

"Too busy, too lazy, or too weak?" Yellow eyes flashed a challenge to the elf.

"Too weak?"

"If we knew the darkness was one of your ilk, I'd say I was pushing the pup too hard. He'd have no troubles with the likes of you, especially considering your defender is the runt of the litter."

The apprentice sorcerer pinned his ears, unable to meet the dragon's disapproving stare. Lotician turned to study Silver Wolf as though noticing him for the first time. He looked to him and then his brother, still in human form but standing straight, a grim look on his dark, youthful features. Lotician then turned his marigold eyes to Dexus, who was twice as big as his pupil and still another three heads taller than the elf.

"Smaller, I'll grant you, but weaker?" He let a slow smile spread across his fine features. "Especially not if we can use the pair of us as a comparison."

This caused the sword master to rear his serpentine neck back, eyes wide in surprise. "You think you're stronger than me?"

"Strength is a relative word and one with many meanings."

"Only one that matters." Dexus leaned in toward the magic teacher, and even Silver Wolf felt the hot blast of air as he snorted. "Strength means being able to fight your enemies and being able to walk away from the conflict. Being the only one to walk away."

"Yes." The elf kept smiling, unintimidated by the great beast leaning in closer. "I believe we're talking about the same matter."

"And you think you could stand." Dexus loomed over the smaller figure.

"I do," Lotician responded, not moving, his smile still pleasant.

"Against any enemy?"

"Yes."

"Including one like me?" Dexus's grin exposed his sharp teeth again, tendrils of smoke drifting up between them, hinting at the inferno building in his gut.

It was Lotician's turn to grin, and the younger twin was shocked to see it, so feral, a glint of mischief in his teacher's eye to accompany it. "Of course."

"Wolf," the dragon boomed.

"Yes." Black Wolf stepped forward.

"Give the elf your sword."

The sword apprentice walked forward and extended the practice sword, hilt first, toward the sorcerer.

"That's quite alright," Lotician said, putting a hand on the pommel and lowering it.

The dark-haired boy looked confused until Dexus called, "It's on his own head. Step out and give us some room."

Silver Wolf's twin ducked the rope, sword still in hand, and came to stand next to him. Silver Wolf had the barest moment to realize he was taller than his brother for the first time this way, he as a wolf and his twin as a human. The thought fled quickly as he watched his master duck the rope and step into the makeshift arena. Dexus had backed up to the center. Lotician walked over until he stood opposite him.

"What are the terms?" the elf asked.

"Fight to a standstill, to a mock killing blow."

"And the rules?"

"None. You may use whatever tricks you have at your disposal."

"Very generous of you," the sorcerer said, giving his opponent a nod.

"Not at all," the dragon replied, spinning the wooden blade in his hand. "We may not be able to cast, but you know that's because we don't need to."

"Yes, I saw your tussle with the boy. Your extra appendages do come in handy."

"As do our powers of flight and fire."

"Yes, I'm prepared for all of that."

"Then let us begin."

"As soon as your boy signals."

Silver Wolf's brother didn't have his wolf hearing, but both of the teachers were speaking loudly enough that he was sure he'd heard.

Both boys stood perfectly rigid, staring at the combatants with bated breath. The elder shouted, "Begin!"

Dexus launched himself forward with a gust of his wings. Aggressive and quick, his long arms lengthened by the reach of the blade, the warrior sliced through the air toward his opponent.

A gust of unseen wind exploded throughout the room from no obvious source. It pushed Dexus from behind, adding to his original burst and knocking the dragon off balance, forcing him to tumble forward. The same wind picked up the lighter elf like a leave on the breeze and carried him a safe distance away. Dexus used his fall, landing on all fours, sword still clasped in one fist, and sweeping out with his tail, to strike against a stone spire the elf had suddenly conjured from the ground. Undaunted, the warrior continued to spin, whirling up to his feet and raking his claws on his free hand through the air, smashing into the pillar and turning it into chunks of flying rocks the elf had to duck and dodge.

The slighter combatant used his own momentum to spin away, opening up space between them. Only Dexus strove to keep the pressure on. The deep red beast rushed forward again, wooden sword in both talons, low to the ground and ready to slice the willow of a man from root to crown. Lotician threw up a hand, a matching appendage of stone erupting from the floor right next to his aggressor, grabbed the sword, and held it steadfast. The unexpected jolt and impediment to his attack gave the charging dragon a second of pause. With little thought he let go of his tool and struck out with the weapons Varro had provided his kind. The dragon slashed at the sorcerer with his claws, sweeping out with his tail, trying to buffet him with his wings, but the elf danced away from each blow, appearing for all the world as though they'd rehearsed the battle.

Enraged by his lack of a quick victory, Dexus burst out with a wing, hitting the caster squarely in the chest with the limb's bony wrist and sending him staggering back from the force of the punch. The warrior then followed up his attack with a slash from his tail. While Lotician leaned back, trying to dodge, the appendage was too long to evade and its razor edge sliced through the flesh at his temple.

The blood, even against the elf's flushed complexion, stood out like a beacon and Silver Wolf saw it almost as well as he could smell its metallic tang from across the room. The scent of iron mixing with the sharp sweetness of the magic all around them made his head spin. Though it seemed the sword master had achieved the upper hand, the match's rule wasn't to first blood. There would be more to come, and he knew Lotician hadn't yet showed his full prowess.

Eyes squinting, blood sliding past and streaking the sorcerer's silver-white hair, Lotician's hands instantly started to radiate a golden-orange light. The elf's apprentice recognized the level of power his teacher was calling. The softer the light the less energetic, but at that moment, his master's hands were glowing like twin stars.

The ground beneath their feet began to quake.

"A quake?" Black Wolf asked.

Dexus felt it too, opening his massive wings and taking flight an instant before the floor erupted into a field of giant, stone spikes. The students jumped back as one, even as the rock spires ended before the edge of the rope circle. They could see the sword master knocking back stone points jabbing up toward him, dodging others as they grew, centered on him like thorns in a hedge.

The spikes had driven the reptile nearly to the ceiling of the cavern, but his forced vantage had apparently afforded him a view of something. The young sorcerer saw the dragon take in a deep breath, and he could smell the smoke before the beast opened his mouth and shot a quick ball of flame toward the far side of the arena. In one heartbeat the stones crumbled and in the next a shining dome of the same yellow-orange light formed over the master sorcerer, taking the brunt of the fireball and dissipating it to nothing. Before the flames' glow had fully dissipated, Lotician's hands were glowing again, and he launched a bolt of lightening back at the warrior.

Moving with the speed of light, Dexus couldn't dodge the bolt striking him right in the chest. Sparks flew and tendrils of cracking energy flowed over his shoulders and down his limbs. The dragon's head rocked back, the spell clearly causing intense pain, but his wings didn't skip a beat.

The elevated warrior shook his head as if to clear it before shouting down at the sorcerer. "Seems your scholarly study missed an important point—dragons may not use magic, but we're highly resilient to it."

"I know."

That was all the warning Lotician gave before he started running. Before him more towers of stone appeared, only stopping at precise heights as the elf leapt from one to the next, climbing into the air to achieve his opponent's height. It caught all who watched him by surprise, including Dexus, who could only stare. It was just the moment the caster needed. The master sorcerer pulled back his hands, still bounding upward, palms glowing brilliantly. Achieving his desired height, bringing him eye to eye with the sword master, the elf let loose a blast of wind right into the webbing of the warrior's left wing. The sudden gust spun him into a tight series of circles. Unable to keep himself aloft, Dexus fell out of the air and plummeted toward the cavern floor, the sorcerer diving after him.

Silver Wolf heard the colossal impact when the dragon hit. Scales or no, the werewolf was willing to bet that hurt. It delayed the winged serpent for only a moment. His brother's teacher achieved a kneeling position almost at once. His reptilian eyes grew wide and he reached out, retrieving his discarded wooden sword.

The apprentice caster felt his twin tense next to him, as rigid as he felt his own muscles to be, while holding his breath and watching his teacher fall through the air.

Dexus swung upward to meet his aggressor with the wooden weapon. Lotician dodged only by way of a well-timed blast of air. Soft boots clacked on the stone, the elf absorbing his landing by taking a knee. The sword master, holding his blade in two hands, ready to stab down on the crouching sorcerer at his feet, froze.

Silver Wolf gasped. He could see the blade ready to split his master's skull in two, but also the spike of stone extending from his teacher's fist, the tip aimed at the dragon's neck, right at the softer flesh between jaw and jugular.

They held. Both weapons were poised for the killing blow. Even though it was only a mock battle, Silver Wolf felt very real tension crackling in the air. There wasn't a sound in the hall; there wasn't a movement. He didn't even think anyone blinked.

Then Dexus let out a loud bark of a laugh, shattering the silence. "Well played."

"You as well," Lotician said, still crouching, still with the spike to the dragon's throat, but grinning in return.

Lowering his wooden sword, Dexus extended a hand to the elf. Lotician stood with his typical fluid grace and accepted the shake, his smaller hand fitting only halfway around his opponent's wrist.

"I was told the pup doesn't have the talent to cast, but I acknowledge your point about studying for the possibility of encountering a magical opponent."

"Thank you. Does this also mean I have your blessing to instruct your student in other topics of my choosing?"

"I'm sure he could benefit from any wisdom you'd care to impart." He smirked, not showing off his razor teeth this time. "Only you'll have to give me the same opportunity to improve your runt. I may not be able to turn him into a celebrated fighter, but even a tactician should be light on his feet."

"I wholeheartedly agree. I've been paying too much attention to his mind, growing his power and skill in that matter. Growing his body through strength and vitality training will open up other avenues for improvement within the magical arts."

"Twice a week then?"

"My thought exactly."

The teachers shook again, smiling at one another.

Unnoticed by their professors, Black Wolf leaned closer to his brother, whispering just above an exhaled breath though his lupine ears easily heard it. "And you thought you were tired before."

# CHAPTER 29

## *Even Better*

"" Silver Wolf counted each push-up as he reached its zenith, arms fully extended, sweat dripping from the tip of his nose to join the tiny puddle beneath him. He, like his brother, was training as a human, pale skin gleaming with perspiration, bright hair hanging about his face. He'd not thought to get a haircut in all those months of traveling.

Dexus, it seemed, believed in starting with a person's weakest point, to get right to the root of the matter and remove it. For a werewolf, the dragon estimated, that would be the human form. Clawless, flat-toothed, and undersized, humans did seem to have drawn the short stick when Varro handed out attributes. The warrior said if they improved his human side, his werewolf form would reap even more benefit, since the shift appeared to enhance whatever prowess the human started with. Of course a bit of the wolf bled back into the human, lending that form some of its endurance and strength, which was why Dexus had him doing the push-ups with an enormous rock sitting on his back.

"Ninety-nine..." He grunted. As hard as it was, Silver Wolf knew that if his back dipped at all out of its perfect plank position, he'd receive a snap in his side from the tip of his teacher's tail as a reminder, and it wouldn't tickle. His instructor paced the floor beside him, hands clasped behind his back under his folded wings, twin swords hanging from his belt.

"One hundred." Silver Wolf pushed up one last time on shaking arms and locked his elbows for a bit of rest. Much as he'd have loved to collapsed right there on the floor, rock and all, the warrior would've considered it a show of laziness, and there was no way he was going to make that mistake again.

"Good." Silver Wolf thought the rumble from his teacher sounded more bored than pleased. "Do a hundred more."

"Ugh," he grunted, falling to his side, the rock tumbling from its perch on his shoulders and rolling a bit away. He lay on the floor panting, arms screaming, bare chest and face dripping. "Can't I have a break?"

"You believe you've earned a break." Dexus lifted one scaly eye-ridge as though he doubted that.

"Yes," he shouted as loudly as he could with what little breath he could get. He didn't care that he was being rude. Maybe if he were lucky, Dexus would take offense and just kill him there on the floor. As it was his lungs were taking such greedy gulps of air, he might choke on it and end both their suffering.

The sword master shook his head, but stepped over to their break area anyway. It wasn't much—a pair of benches, a couple of towels, and a bucket of water with a ladle to fill up the pair of ceramic cups sitting next to it.

Dexus took one of the benches, picked up a cup, and poured water as Silver Wolf staggered to a slumped sort of half stand and wobbled over. The dragon held out the filled cup to him, which he accepted gratefully, gulping it greedily as he half fell to the floor. The master poured himself a cup before dipping the ladle back in for a third time and offering Silver Wolf a refill. Having finished the first, he held out the mug to accept.

The sword master sipped at his own drink as calmly and slowly as though he were drinking tea. Silver Wolf studied the dragon over the lip of his own mug, thinking about what he knew of the master and what he didn't. Half out of curiosity, and half to have an excuse not to go back to their training right away, he struck up a conversation.

"Master Dexus," he tried.

"Hmm," Dexus rumbled in reply.

"I asked high sorcerer Lotician a while ago why he came here. He told me that it was to study the dragon archives and also that he was curious about who the gods had selected to be their chosen heroes. Why did you decide to come?"

"To train your brother, and now you." Dexus took another slow sip, not bothering to look at the young man.

"But why? They said you came all the way here from the City of Stone Fire. That's on the east coast of Rahovan, practically on the other side of the world. Why would you travel all that way?"

"Regent Feng Ryok requested a sword master."

"But why from the dragons? Why not from the elves, or the nokken, or even the dwarves?"

"It was a necessity that the dragons summon an elf to instruct you to use the magics of Eris." Yellow eyes snapped up to Silver Wolf's face, pinning him with a glare. "Dragons do not use the world's energies the same way as some of the other Eight do."

"Yes." He used the one word to try and coax a little more out of the dragon.

Dexus set down his cup, looking directly at his pupil. "Your brother and you have come here to aid the dragon people because it was foretold. It is our duty to make sure you can fulfill that purpose."

As much as the glare made him want to squirm, he couldn't stop now, not when the stoic drake seemed to be in such a talkative mood. "But why a dragon from Rahovan? Why couldn't they've found one here to train my brother and me?"

"Fire drakes are created similarly to humans and werewolves, unlike the ryong."

"The ryong? Is that what Sonju and Yielle are? And you're a fire drake? So you mean you're better to train us because you walk on two legs instead of four?"

"Both the ryong and azdah walk on four legs—only the fire drakes walk on two, freeing up our hands for much more of the time. Neither of the other two subspecies of our kind would be suited for the skill."

"Azdah? Is there a third type of dragon?"

Dexus only stared at him.

He tried a different question. "Are there other sword masters where you come from?"

"No." The one word was clipped.

"Why? Why are you the only one?"

"They don't see the artistry in it." Dexus sighed and picked up his cup, taking another sip.

"Artistry?"

"Tools are evidence of a certain degree of intelligence among all species of the world. Art and artistry are the dominion of only the Eight, and not even all of them."

"So you think swords are a type of art?" The confusion and doubt were obvious to his own ears, and when the dragon pulled the long sword from its scabbard, the silver werewolf was worried that he might've offended him. Only his teacher didn't stand to attack; instead, he stayed sitting on the bench, the sword held in the palms of his open hands, his eyes intent upon it. It reminded him of the look his brother had given the short sword from their mother, like it was made of gold.

"Dragons are the finest artists on Eris. Dwarves may make such things with delicate patterns or glittering stones, but hold it too tight, or drop it on stone, and it shatters. Dragons, born next to the flaming heart of the world, understand metal in a way the others could never. When a dragon takes up a piece of metal it is always in the attempt to improve it, not just to change it."

His words and the way the drake was looking so lovingly at the sword made Silver Wolf stand up, his limbs no longer screaming thanks to his quick werewolf healing, and gaze at the sword himself. It was long, four feet at least, the red-wrapped hilt a third of that. It was smooth and slightly curved, sharp on the long edge, blunt on the reverse, unlike his brother's short sword that had cutting edges on both sides. Despite that, his twin's weapon didn't have the restrained strength that this long fang of a blade seemed to radiate. As beautiful as the blade was, though, it was the pommel that caught Silver Wolf's full attention. It was in the shape of a drake's head, sharp featured, with horns jutting back toward the two-handed hilt, mouth open in a snarl, tiny teeth picked out with excellent precision, and two bright eyes. They were rubies, reflecting the light from the sunstone that provided light to the cavern, but the crimson glow made him shiver nonetheless, remembering another such glare.

"This is artistry, more than a simple tool to hack something into smaller pieces, and that is how it should be regarded."

That was all the warning he received as Dexus stood, leaving him to scurry out of his path. The dragon took the sword in one hand and walked out to the center of the floor. He sliced the sword through the air, and Silver Wolf could feel the breeze respond. The sword master cut and swept and ducked and spun. The boy wouldn't have called it delicate, but there was a sort of brutal beauty to the drake's movements, a dance fit for a warrior. Dexus and the sword began to resemble one being, the weapon an extension of him, he the power behind the blade.

When the martial instructor finished his series of movements, his pupil could've sworn a soft smile curved the drake's mouth. Dexus sheathed the weapon and turned back to the apprentice caster, any hint of a smile having vanished.

"That was amazing," Silver Wolf said.

"I'm glad you liked it." Nothing about his countenance said he was anything like glad.

"Is my brother learning that?"

Dexus gave a short bark of a laugh. "That pup can barely hold a sword and keep both pads on the stone. No, he's a far way from doing anything like what you've just seen, though not as far away as you." He added the last bit with a snarl. "Now, your break is over. Get back to it."

## CHAPTER 30

## *Fire Root Tea*

"Wake up."

Silver Wolf felt the pillow hit him in the face as his brother said the words. Filled with a downy sort of plant fiber, it wasn't the most awful of projectiles, but it was still a rude way to wake someone.

"Why?" he grunted, not even bothering to remove the pillow from his face.

"Breakfast's here." The sound of a tray being set on the table accompanied his words.

"I need my rest if I'm going to challenge Dexus to duel to the death today."

"Oh, are you?" Black Wolf didn't sound like he believed it. The distinctive sounds of bowls and spoons being set on the table was an indication that his younger brother was getting only half of his attention.

Silver Wolf pulled the pillow from his face and let it slump to the floor. "Hardly. It's been months and he hasn't even given me a sword yet, not even a wooden one."

"Are you that eager for one?"

"Not really. You're clearly the warrior here." He punctuated the sentence with a sniff. "I just thought that that was the point of this shared training."

"I'm not learning any spells."

"That's different. You can't use magic, but anyone can use a sword."

Silver Wolf's twin shot him a dark glower. He backtracked, propping himself up to look at his brother. "What I mean is that anyone can hold a sword, not use it well."

Somewhat mollified, the larger boy went back to dishing up breakfast, which was porridge again, this time with the distinct smell of wild honey and strawberries.

"So if I'm not learning swordsmanship and you're not learning magic, what is Lotician teaching you?"

"To sense what's coming, to recognize the feeling and that scent."

"That part must be pretty easy."

The older boy nodded but didn't look at his brother as he spooned the porridge into the bowls. It felt like Silver Wolf had touched another nerve.

"So why did I have to get up? The porridge would've stayed warm for a while and it's our day off, the one day a week we can do whatever we want, like sleep in." Silver Wolf laid back down and turned his back to the other boy. He pulled the sheets up for good measure, though partly to see if he could distract his twin from whatever he was thinking.

It seemed to work in a way, as Silver Wolf heard the smile in his voice when his older twin replied, "A nap might not be a bad thought, not since we'll only have half a day free."

"Half a day?" He looked over his shoulder, ears perked.

"Lotician didn't tell you?"

Now Silver Wolf could see his brother's smug smirk as he ate a spoonful of breakfast. "He tells me a lot of things, usually between flipping the pages of a dusty, old book. But no, he didn't mention anything special about today. It's our day to rest. What could we possibly be doing?"

"It's also a year to the day since our arrival here."

Silver Wolf's eyes lost focus, as though he were staring at all the moments between then and now. "It hasn't really been a year already, has it?"

The smirk leaving his face, Black Wolf replied, "It has."

"And we've seen what? Nothing. No clues to the nature of the darkness, no hints we're getting any closer to this destiny everyone keeps going on about."

"Nothing that I've seen," his brother confirmed. "Though that could be what today's summons is about."

"Summons?"

"Sonju wants to see us."

"Sonju?" Flashes of the old blind dragon zipped through the caster's mind. It'd been a year since they'd seen him too, a year since they'd gotten a ride from Yielle and come to the City of Sky Fire. "You think he's seen something?"

"Why else would he have called us?"

"Your sparkling personality?"

Black Wolf gave him a flat look.

"Right." Silver Wolf flipped the sheets off his bed and swung his feet to the floor. "When do we see him?"

"This afternoon."

Silver Wolf looked out their window to the sky, still low to the ridgeline, indicating that it was still early morning. "That's hours away."

"Which is why we have time for that nap you proposed," his brother said with a stretch, spoon still in his hand.

"Who could sleep now?"

"Me. Don't wake me with your pacing." The big wolf stood, placed his spoon on the table, and walked back to his bed to lie down, his back facing his twin.

"Stop it," the younger boy said, picking up the discarded spoon and lobbing it at the warrior's exposed back. Still sticky with the slowly congealing remains of their meal, the spoon stayed lodged in his dark fur.

His brother laughed and sat up, reaching over his shoulder and plucking the utensil from its perch. It came away sporting dark furs in the golden, creamy mess. The bigger wolf tossed the utensil to the tray, to be dealt with later.

Seeing that and hearing about the summons, the caster had lost his appetite. "Let's go into town," he suggested. "I don't want to sit here the whole time."

"Fine." His sibling shrugged his massive shoulders.

The bright sunlight momentarily blinded Silver Wolf when they first exited from the palace walls and he had to blink to clear the spots from his vision. From the regent's home they could see the entire expanse of the City of Sky Fire, sitting atop its peak, shrouded in clouds and appearing to float among them. It looked so otherworldly, so beautiful.

The older twin had already started walking down the incline and the younger had to jog to catch up. They approached the main gate, which stood open. The plum-colored steward, Hiensun, was speaking to another ryong. A wide set of horns indicated he was male, his scales a dusty sort of copper color. Behind him stood a cart full of fish, some as large as the werewolves.

"Yes, it looks to be a good catch this morning," they heard the purple dragon say to the other as she jotted down something on a little board in her claws. "Take it around to the kitchens," she instructed, waving with her reed pen.

They'd be having fish soup for dinner, it appeared.

Watching the sepia-colored dragon wheel in his delivery, the steward's gaze locked with the younger twin's as he waited for the gate to be cleared. One lip, pulled back in disgust, revealed some very white, very long teeth. "Be sure the cook checks the fish when you arrive. I think I caught a hint of something undesirable," she added to the vendor though her eyes were still on the werewolf.

They hurried past her with respectful, if brief nods, nearly galloping onto the main thoroughfare.

Silver Wolf had worried that they'd be trampled the first time they'd gone into the city on their own, being so far beneath most of the citizens' eye levels. It turned out that only half of the city's residents ever walked anywhere. Since their flight didn't require the use of wings, floating above the street didn't cause nearly the same disturbances. Without great outstretched or flapping appendages, far less wind was generated and far less space or effort were required. Most of the dragons, especially the younger ones, just soared from shop to shop or out into the wide blue sky, just for the joy of it. He envied them that.

"Hungry?" his brother asked.

He wasn't; his stomach was still in knots as he wondered what Sonju could possibly say to them. He shook his head.

Shrugging in response, Black Wolf walked over to one of the massive carts without him. The cart in question was painted a bright orange, and a mountain goat, hide, and curved horns dripping a dark sauce were depicted in the center. It smelled of roasting meat, the accompanying sounds of sizzling and popping further confirming the cart's purpose.

"Starlin," Black Wolf called up. From over the top of the grill a greenish-beige-ish head appeared, light green fur ringing a pair of rather plump cheeks.

"Ah, the black and silver werewolves are back," the merchant said with a broad and particularly toothy grin, making his cheeks appear even fuller. He was one of the rougher-looking dragons the apprentice sorcerer had seen since their time in the city. His green hue was muddy at best and his ruffled fur, which often bore splatters of grease in its tangled strands, made him appear unkempt. Still, his smile was infectious, the sort that made others want to smile back. It was a combination of that smile and the delicious sauce he put over his roasted goat that made his stall Black Wolf's favorite.

"I've got some very nice goat today." Starlin gave them that smile again.

Smirking, because even the stoic warrior couldn't resist, Black Wolf said, "One please."

"Nothing for you?" the dragon asked the caster.

"No, thank you. My stomach's not feeling too well right now."

"I could give you a hoof to gnaw on, or a bone. Always helps me to crack into something when something's on my mind. And a boy like you has got to eat if he's to get any bigger. See how big your brother's gotten off my goat?"

Silver Wolf smiled, not bothering to point out that his brother had arrived in the city already being that much bigger than him. "Thanks, not today."

"Suit yourself," the dragon shrugged.

Grabbing a haunch of goat sizzling off the cart's metal flattop with his bare claws, Starlin ripped a chunk of it off, slapping both pieces of meat back down on the scalding grill. The merchant then leaned down and, opening his mouth, released a quick gout of flame into the cart's innards, causing the food atop it to pop and sizzle all the more vigorously. Finally, the green-brown serpent took up a stick about the size of a three-year-old pine sapling, snapped it in two, and then stabbed the smaller bit of meat. He took the skewer and, dipping a ladle into a pot sitting on the ground beside him, drizzled it with a thick sauce that smelled of ginger, salt, and sweet black garlic before he handed it over to Black Wolf. Black Wolf nodded his thanks, accepting the cut of meat that was nearly as large as his head. The roasted flesh dripped a viscous combination of sticky-sweet sauce mingled with goat grease onto the rock below their feet as the werewolf tore into it with obvious delight.

"It's good," he said around the mouthful. A puff of steam accompanied each of his words like he was a dragon about to breathe fire. "Thank you," he added once he'd swallowed, wiping his mouth on the fur of his free arm. Their mother would've been appalled.

The ryong only chuckled. "Take care then." He waved to them without asking for any coin and looked back to the streets to see if anyone else was interested in a meal.

The whole city knew the werewolf brothers were guests of the lord regent, though very few knew why. Whatever the reason, it was understood that the regent was a generous host and would pay for anything his guests required. Settling the bill therefore, would be the responsibility of the steward. Silver Wolf smirked as he thought of the annoyed expression on Hiensun's face when she received the invoice for their goat snack.

They walked on, Black Wolf ripping off mouthfuls of the fragrant thigh meat. Ordinarily, Silver Wolf would've gladly joined him, only with the mood he was in even smelling the thing was making him nauseous, as were all the other food sellers in the market.

"Dragons love to eat," he said, feeling another wave of unease as they passed by a vendor selling eels out of a barrel.

The older twin shrugged, swallowing his latest bite before replying. "They don't wear clothes. They don't own much furniture or many tools. Not much to trade in a dragon market apart from food."

"Or art," he replied, nodding to a window where finely crafted golden ornaments sat in the open air, gleaming in the late morning light. Dexus had said that dwarf craftsmanship was more intricate, that their works were all loops of thin metal and jewels. Only looking at the fine weavings of golden strands of the dragon-made bracelet on display made him wonder if such a thing were possible.

"Baubles." Black Wolf dismissed the jewelry with a sniff.

It was the younger brother's turn to shrug. "Dexus said that well-made swords were like pieces of art."

"Dexus meant that a blade may be crafted to complete a fighter, to fit with him, to strengthen him. It's art with a purpose, not just something to set on a table."

They passed a shop selling pottery works, the indigo dragon inside stoking her kiln, a raw set of delicate teacups set nearby, ready to be fired. They passed a shop that sold silks, not for the dragons to wear, but for decorating their homes, the swaths shining in as many hues as the dragons passing by. Food was important to the dragon culture, but it was in every culture. The dragon sword master had been right. Those of higher intelligence, those Varro had blessed, had other thoughts for their lives—to fill them with purpose and beauty.

"Not much use to it," Silver Wolf's twin said as they passed a shop selling jewelry.

Dragons didn't wear clothes because what was the point? Their scales protected them in any inclement weather, and since they walked on all fours and often hunted amongst the rocks or through the trees, cloth or leather would just get in the way and likely tear. Jewelry, on the other hand, was more durable. They never wore necklaces or anything that hung too loosely, but cuffs to go around wrists or ankles, charms that swung from horns, or piercings of softer skin around the nose, whiskers, or ears were the height of fashion. It was how they could bring attention to their best features for possible mates, and how they could show their status to rivals.

"You don't see a use because you're not cultured enough." Silver Wolf smirked. "Though a gold ring in your ear would be striking."

Black Wolf wrinkled his muzzle and twitched his ears, probably thinking about having a trinket weighing one down.

By the time they reached the music shop, the melody of a wooden flute floating out the open door on a stirring breeze, the sun was nearly at its zenith.

"It's about that time," said the younger twin, his ears slightly back.

"Yeah," replied the elder boy, looking up and confirming the position of the sun for himself.

The brothers hurried along the streets, clinging to the side of the main thoroughfare, dodging boxes and barrels with the grace of hunters on the trail. The gates were still open, and they rushed through, passing the plum dragon without giving her time to sneer. They raced up the slope, the larger of the two easily outstripping the smaller, but never leaving him too far behind. They ran down the corridors, avoiding servants cleaning or bringing things from room to room, until they came at last to the seer's door.

They knew Lord Regent Fen Ryok's quarters and audience chamber were further back in the complex. Set higher toward the summit, it was the jewel at the peak of crown that was the City of Sky Fire, while the seer's chambers were at its heart. The future-telling Sonju's rooms were positioned straight over a central shaft that led all the way down to its molten core. Maybe the builders of this palace had done that so that the ancient dragon would be in the warmest possible spot in the entire city. Or was there more to it? Sitting above the heart of the mountain, did that mean he sat above the heart of Eris too? The heart of Varro? Did it help his visions to be so close to two of the elements—fire and stone? Did that make it easier to communicate with the gods, depending on which provided the visions?

Silver Wolf wished he knew more, but could he ask Sonju? Did the seer even know what, if anything, effected his prophecies? Would Lotician know anything about visions?

The sight of the door snapped him back to the moment. Once again, it stood ajar just wide enough for their smaller frames to enter. Feeling his shoulder start to creep up, the young caster forced himself to remain calm.

It could be that the old dragon was summoning them to say that the darkness would be there tomorrow and their time to prepare was at an end, only a year into its beginning. Only Sonju hadn't said it yet. He couldn't allow himself to panic over possible futures, not until he heard Sonju confirm it.

Black Wolf entered first, swallowed up by the shadows nearly at once. Following behind, Silver Wolf waited for his eyes to adjust. He thought maybe it took less time as he knew what to look for. The room was still shadowy, still glowing sinisterly red from the fire in the mountain, the light blurred by the steam passing through the cave. Only this time, it wasn't nearly so terrifying as it'd been on that first day. They'd been there before. They knew what to expect.

The twins walked toward the light source, down the spiral path, coming quickly to the grate. They saw Sonju, his head laid on one of his coils, his milky eyes shut. Was he asleep? Should they come back? The door had been opened, though, and his brother had been told they'd been summoned.

After a moment, when none of the three had moved, the larger of the pair leaned over and whispered in his twin's ear, "We should return to our rooms. We'll wait there till he sends someone to get us."

"Not at all," the seer said, opening his eyes. "There is no need to leave. Come." The old dragon raised himself up as the boys started across the grate, till his shoulders were above the main coils of the rest of his body and his front claws rested on them. Putting padded feet to the reception deck, the old ryong stood fully erect, gazing toward the entrance with his unfocused eyes.

"Hello," the smaller twin called up when another moment had passed without movement.

"Greetings once again, Children of Bain." The seer shifted his head down toward Silver Wolf's voice.

"Seer Sonju," Silver Wolf's brother asked, too eager for niceties, "what have you seen?"

"A great many things," the ancient serpent replied, a slight cock to his head.

"Will the darkness be here soon then?" The younger werewolf couldn't keep his shoulders down any longer and he felt his flattened ears brush them.

A shake came from the wizened, white head, limp whiskers waving with the movement. "I have seen nothing more of the impending darkness."

"What?" they said in unison, gazing up, mouths slightly parted.

Finally Black Wolf asked, "Then why are we here?"

"To celebrate this first year of your training, and for you to tell me how your progress is coming along."

Black Wolf made a sound in his throat, somewhere between a grunt and a growl.

"Please, sit," said the seer, extending one talon to his right. "I have had the palace staff prepare tea. In your tongue you would call it fire root, I think."

The younger twin hadn't noticed it there before, but there was a low table next to the dragon, though more like a tray to one his size. There was a huge teapot and teacup upon it, cast in bronze, beautiful designs etched all around both pieces.

"We didn't come here for tea," his brother said, sounding like he wanted to say even more, but was holding himself back.

"Oh?" Sonju asked. "Is there another drink you would have preferred?"

For some reason this made Silver Wolf think back to his time on the mountain. It'd been a particularly frigid winter. As a special treat their mother had splurged on a strange scrap of bark bought from a spice vendor she'd met in the market. When shaved and steeped in warm sheep's milk and honey, the bark made the tastiest treat—sweet and warm and a bit spicy all at once. He remembered it warming him all the way to his toes.

He thought he could smell traces of that bark now. His chest squeezed at the memory.

"No, we didn't come here to drink or celebrate." His brother tried to clarify. "We came because you summoned us."

"Yes, I did. So that you could share a drink with me." To demonstrate Sonju dipped his long neck down toward the cup of steaming tea he'd picked up from the table. Using both claws, the weary old dragon lifted it to his bent head, taking a sip and then sighing contemplatively, a smile curving his mouth in satisfaction.

Silver Wolf thought he could've bathed in that teacup.

"Why?" his brother asked flatly.

"Because I thought that maybe you would like to chat."

"Chat?" the older boy asked, brows furrowed. "About what?"

"I am a seer of things. Both a great many things, and many great things. Past and future. I have had a number of centuries to acquire these visions. You do not think I may have a story or two I could impart?"

The caster felt his eyes grow wide and looked to see his brother's were much the same. They'd only been thinking about the darkness, only thinking about their duty, but this wasn't about that. This was the only thing that hadn't been about their destiny since they'd left home. What mysteries did this dragon know? What would he share? The possibilities could be as numerous as the stars.

"What kind of stories?" the older boy finally asked.

"I have seen as far back as the dragons discovering time, elves stumbling upon the Well, the War of the Waves. I have seen the passing of your progenitor, Bain."

The younger twin piped up. "Do you see only big, important events, or little things too?" They could find out about their mother's past, about what became of their father.

Sonju frowned a little at that question. "My visions see only the things the gods choose to show me. This world is vast. I would be overwhelmed if I were to see all things, all at once, every moment, everywhere. So the gods show me only what I must see."

Crestfallen, the caster asked his next question. "How far into the future have you seen, then?" His ears were back when he said it. Sonju might not be able to see the darkness clearly, but could he see the outcome of their struggle?

Ancient lips pulled up at the corners again. "I do not like to reveal the future until it has a direct impact on the present. I do not like to ruin the ending of stories." His chuckle sounded dry and unused. Silver Wolf wondered when the last time he'd used it was.

"So, what's the point?" his twin broke in again. "These visions, where do they come from? You said the gods send them to you, but why? The gods wouldn't need to inform anyone of their plans; they could simply move us into place. What's even the point of the future when the gods have already decided it anyway?"

"Ah." The old dragon let out a sigh, the smile still on his lips. "That is a big question. Are they messages from the Five Gods? Are they dreams of the old god Varro? Are they shattered fragments of time, spinning through the void to be glimpsed by hapless beings? Who can say? Without knowing who has sent them, their purpose cannot be understood."

"So because you can't know if the visions are really from the gods, you can't tell us their purpose, but you also won't share them with us because you don't want to ruin the surprise?" His exasperation was evident in his words.

"I do believe that they are sent to me by the gods of this world." The dragon put one claw to his chest for emphasis. "There has always been debate, conflicting stories, but I believe in my heart that they are divine. I believe the Five Gods do send them together to those who listen, who are still, who wish to hear."

"But why?" Black Wolf pressed again.

"To give us hope." Sonju returned his claws to the still steaming cup of tea as though warming them, though his lair was warmer than any summer day Silver Wolf could remember on the mountain. Sonju tilted his head back and gazed sightlessly toward the sky. "Sometimes the visions are terrible, sometimes very tragic, only often with a bright spot. I have seen the darkness, only I have seen the pair of you as well." His face tilted down again and he gave the twins a gentle smile, almost grandfatherly—proud and loving. "I tell the things I see in the future when the present is at its darkest. When we all need hope."

It moved something in Silver Wolf, and on some level, he knew this blind seer, only glimpsing life and stories from afar, never living them himself, felt as alone as they did, so very far away from everything they'd ever known. "Tell us a story about hope," he asked. "Please? Maybe one of your favorites?"

Black Wolf gave his brother a sideways scowl, but placed a gentle hand on his shoulder, looking up at the giant leviathan with sympathy and understanding.

"Ah." Sonju breathed again after another sip of tea. "There are so many, but I think I will start with one of the finest adventures from the past. It was during the War of the Waves between the nokken and the elves. It was a dark time, very dark. Death and destruction were everywhere, with the promise of much more to come. It was then that hope appeared. You see, at that time, there was a young nokken boy, Sedry. He was a typical youth of the breed, though he needed to be called to greatness very young, younger than the thirteen years you two have managed—"

The brothers sat down behind the low tea table, which had also been set with a teapot and two cups sized for them. The younger of the twins poured as the rumbling voice of Sonju, like a distant thunderstorm, swept them away to long-ago times and faraway places.

Silver Wolf couldn't help but be reminded of the fairy tales their mother used to read to them, only these were true—underwater cities, magical battles, strange beasts from the depths—all true, but so long ago they might as well have been just stories. The twins drank the tea, the fire root warming them from their noses to their toes, which was welcome even in the humid room, as they hung on the seer's every word. Their breaths stilled when they came to an exciting part of the story; their hearts sank when the story turned sad, only to soar again when Sedry had his victory.

Later, the tea and snacks long ago consumed, Sonju finished his story, and the boys were both grinning from pointed ear to pointed ear.

"That was amazing," Silver Wolf said. "And it's all true?"

"A seer does not lie. It all happened as I saw it and as I have told it."

"And our story?" Black Wolf asked. "Does it end as well?"

The ancient shook his head, his drooping whiskers waving with the motion. "As I have said, I have seen nothing further of the darkness, and the future is ever more shrouded than the past. I do not see the ending of your story, not yet."

Black Wolf frowned, but didn't push.

"Now," said the seer, setting his empty teacup down. "You have had tea with me, and we have celebrated a year of your training, and you have had a story too." His lip quirked in a quick smirk. "I think you must have more training to do. You may go."

They both stood and bowed and were turning to obey when the younger boy paused and looked back. "Could we come again?" he asked.

Sonju's smile was gentle as he gave a single bob of his head. "Of course. Next year we will celebrate again."

"Maybe sooner than that?"

"You are welcome to come whenever you like."

## CHAPTER 31

# *Trembling Stones*

"So, what're we doing today?" Silver Wolf asked with a yawn and a stretch, strolling down the palace corridor.

"Go into the mountains," Black Wolf grunted.

"Don't get enough exercise on your regular training days?" the younger brother asked with a raised brow.

Grimacing, the elder boy replied, "Just looking for some quiet after being berated for my stances yesterday."

"Well, Dexus must have a point if you don't know them after six years of training with him—"

"Were you hoping to spend your free day alone?" his brother growled.

"Alright, alright, sorry. Still, let's stop in town first to pick up a few of those sweet buns. Then we can seek solitude in the mountains, if that's what you're after."

"Fine." Black Wolf flicked his tail. "A hero of destiny with a sweet tooth," he muttered in disapproval.

"I'm sure all the best ones have them," Silver Wolf chuckled.

"Clearly not."

A bit of the play fell from his features. "Can we even call ourselves heroes of destiny?"

His brother merely shrugged. "We will be one day."

"But when? We've been in training for six years now. Six years. I've summoned and made pacts with all four types of elementals. I feel I'm close to flying for all Dexus's physical training. We're eighteen years old, not our masters' equals yet, but still, are we going to be waiting in this place forever?"

"Not forever, just until the right time."

"The right time? Who decides that?"

His brother shrugged massive shoulders. "The darkness? The gods? Fate? Destiny? Varro? Take your pick."

They'd grown larger still in the six years since they'd left home. Black Wolf was still larger, taller, more heavily muscled, but thanks to his own training with the drake sword master, Silver Wolf had filled out a bit himself. He wasn't a warrior like his brother, but nor would he imagine anyone calling him the runt of the litter anymore, except maybe Dexus.

Thinking on their teachers, the caster sighed, tilting his head up to gaze at the pearl stone pillars and wooden beams supporting the roof. He remembered those colors, the white and the red, gleaming in the light of the setting sun on their first day in the City of Sky Fire, when Yielle had flown them through the open gates. He remembered meeting the steward Hiensun, who still gave a cutting remark and curved lip when she saw them, but who would also occasionally smirk when she thought they weren't looking. She'd taken them to see Sonju, who they now thought of like a grandfather. They still visited him once a month on their free day to drink fire root tea and listen to his stories of heroes from long ago, but more recently he had told them about his own life before his sight left him, when he was a young buck out in the great wide world. Dexus hadn't softened any, but he did seem to dole out a bit more praise these days, when he thought they'd earned it. Lotician—there was too much there for the Silver Wolf to think. They'd never known their father and the elf didn't feel like that, but he was an older, male influence, like an uncle or a much older brother. He'd taught him so much, not just about spell work, but also about the world, its history, and its secrets he was uncovering in his books.

"It hasn't been so bad," he said, smiling at the memories.

"It hasn't," his brother agreed.

He opened his mouth to say more when he noticed that something was amiss. It was subtle, odd, and it took a moment to identify what he was feeling. He felt a tiny tremor coming up through the thick pads of his feet, and he stopped to be certain about the sensation. He didn't have to wait long. It was growing stronger.

"A quake," Black Wolf confirmed.

"This has never happened before. Is the mountain erupting?" His fur bristled just thinking about the molten fire burning at the heart of this peak, the burning heart swirling just below their friend. "Sonju!" The younger werewolf burst out. Without another word, the caster took off down the hallway in the other direction, the warrior matching him step for step as the tremors increased, the palace shaking all around them with the vibrations.

Roof tiles fell and shattered like red rain to either side of the open corridor, spraying the running wolves with chips of crimson ceramic. The quake was getting stronger still, and spiderweb cracks crawled over the supporting columns and around window openings. They hopped and danced on ground that rolled beneath their feet like crashing ocean waves. It was only due to their natural agility and training with Dexus that they were able to stay upright at all.

The twins saw the door to the seer's hall, once again standing only slightly ajar. The shaking reached a bone-jarring crescendo, and Silver Wolf, stumbling, arms wind-milling, willing himself not to fall, was the first to reach it.

"Look out," Black Wolf called. Before the younger wolf could react, he felt the weight of his older brother crashing into him, pushing him into the open doorway. Around them, the structures began to crumble. The pillars supporting their section of the hall finally lost their battle with the tremendous quake and collapsed, stone, wood, and ceramic all crashing around them. The destruction cascaded in a line, skipping the strong circular doorframe, but they could hear and see the huge chunks of stone falling from inside the seer's room. There were little supports within the natural tunnel, and it seemed not all of the stone was of equal strength; house-sized chunks fell from the ceiling and walls with deafening crashes. Braced within the portal, they heard the devastating impact deep below, mixed with an anguished cry.

"Sonju," called Silver Wolf.

"Stay," boomed the other as they braced themselves against the worst of the rocking.

It seemed to the younger brother that the shaking lasted for an hour or more. All the while he tried desperately to penetrate the gloom and detect something of the ancient dragon within. Yet the stones must've covered much of the grate that allowed the room its only illumination, for he couldn't see anything at all. He strained his ears but heard only the trembling stones and collapsing buildings further in the distance. He could detect no signs of life from within the dark chamber.

When the tremors halted, they stayed still a heartbeat longer. Even that was more than the smaller wolf could bear. He bolted from their shelter, calling, "Sonju."

"Watch for afterquakes," Black Wolf called, but he entered quickly behind his brother despite his own warnings.

Silver Wolf picked his way quickly through the rubble, down the curved path to the seer's den. He tried to be careful that where he placed his paws would at least bear his weight and not send him into the burning heart of the mountain, but he took time for little else as he scrambled and stumbled his way forward. He saw some light ahead; the stones had not covered the grate entirely, and he could hear weak breathing, giving his feet extra speed.

"The grate," called Black Wolf in warning.

Carefully, but swiftly, the caster started toward the prone form of the seer while the warrior studied the pool of churning fire below.

"The levels haven't changed," he called. "This isn't an eruption."

"Sonju." The light twin had reached the seer's side and pressed padded digits up against his ancient and brittle scales. He could hear the great heartbeat inside the leviathan's body, feel his sides expand and then contract with each breath, and yet he was still struck with the horror of the scene. The prophet lay stretched out upon the grate. A clutch of massive stone, larger than the dragon's own head, pinned him to the spot, crushing scale and timeworn bone to fine powder within the old leathery hide. His breathing was ragged and labored.

"Sonju," the sorcerer said again, trying desperately to keep the wobble from his voice.

"Silver Wolf," the seer said in a strained, quiet voice, the thunderstorm reduced to a summer's drizzle.

"We're both here," Black Wolf said, coming to stand beside his brother.

"Of course," said the seer with the ghost of a smile creeping up into his milky eyes. "Your bond is the source of your strength."

"Sonju—" The younger brother faltered. "You're hurt. We'll go get help."

"No, young wolf. I am dying and there is nothing more anyone can do to aid me now."

"No, we can still save you," he insisted.

"You must conserve your strength to fight the source of this destruction."

"'The source of this destruction'? But it's only a quake."

"Brought on by the darkness," coughed the ancient beast.

"The darkness?" The older twin surged forward at his words. "Can you see it?"

Sonju nodded his head where it lay, giving an exhausted puff as he did so. "Finally, I can see it clearly."

"What is it?" asked the warrior, while the younger's light dimmed further, his concentration completely consumed by the conversation.

"It is a demon," rasped the seer. "A greater demon." The sorcerer's light was fully extinguished with that pronouncement.

"It can't be," said Silver Wolf.

"It must be," his brother said in a quiet voice, his body visibly straining against whatever emotions were coursing through him. "It makes sense. What other darkness could be great enough to threaten a nest of dragons?"

"And what are we supposed to do in the face of such a darkness?" the younger brother asked, whirling to face the elder. "What are we supposed to do against a greater demon? immortal. They're second only to the gods themselves."

"And it is from them that you must seek aid," interrupted the seer.

The younger wolf turned back to the injured ryong. "What? Help from the gods?"

"How?" the elder wolf asked, standing his ground.

"Lord Regent Fen Ryok has the power to send you to meet the gods; only it is up to you to obtain their help."

"And how are we supposed to do that?" the caster asked.

"This close to death I can see much, and very clearly; only now it is my hearing that seems to be fading. Though I see you in audience with the gods, I can hear not a word of your conversation. Only do not despair. You are bold and clever beings. Otherwise, you would never have made it this far."

"Sonju—" The sorcerer struggled to find the words to express his gratitude for getting them so far, for teaching them so much, for his company and his stories. He felt stifled with grief at the old seer's pain and fear at this new turn in events. Both strong emotions clutched his throat, choking all words from him.

Sonju must have sensed his struggles because he said softly, "I have always had faith in the gods and that the visions they would send me would always show the path to the best possible future. I simply never understood, until I met you, quite how generous they were capable of being. I have been honored to know you. You have given me and my people comfort in the face of a great danger yet to come, and for that I thank you. May you carry my gratitude with you long after I have departed these world-weary bones."

The younger brother's jaw was working, trying to squeeze the words past his unwilling mouth, when Black Wolf spoke. "And thank you, Sonju, for your counsel, guidance, stories, and kindness. We will do what we can to ensure that no further harm comes to this place or its people."

The caster wasn't so sure. He looked from his brother to the ancient dragon, trying to articulate the torrent of feelings ripping through his heart. Then he saw the smile on the lips of the blind seer, the look of gentle pride, of grandfatherly love.

He pushed down his panic, his turmoil, his grief, and his fear, for just that moment, understanding that they were heartbreakingly near the end of this sage and kind dragon's long, long life. It was best to send him off with a smile of his own.

"Thank you, Sonju, for showing us our path and for the hope you've given us and all your people. Thank you." His words faltered as tears ran rivulets through his sleek fur. "Thank you for giving us a place to rest from our training, for your stories and fire root tea. Thank you for your company and your belief in us." He reached out a shaking hand and laid it on the seer's head, letting him know he was there, and close. His brother came and placed his hand next to his. Sonju wasn't alone, and they wanted to make sure he knew that.

The three stayed there, in reverent silence, listening to Sonju's labored breaths, each one softer than the last, accompanied by the occasional hiss of the dragon's oozing blood meeting the molten core beneath. It was a strangely comforting reminder—they were born of the Old God's body in the form of this world of Eris, nurtured by it, and to Eris they all returned in the end.

A dozen breaths more, a score of heartbeats, and the colossal leviathan, the ancient seer, their friend Sonju, ceased to be.

# CHAPTER 32

# *Conviction*

Silver Wolf wasn't sure how long they stayed that way. The weight of grief made each intake of breath a struggle. He couldn't name all of the emotions churning in the pit of his stomach, but at that moment they all seemed dulled, forced down by the same heavy sadness.

His brother's voice cut through his contemplations. "Time to go."

He turned to face him. The warrior's violet eyes were steely and determined. The way he stood, the way he carried himself, proclaimed that he was afraid of nothing, neither demon nor deity. He looked every inch the hero, the chosen of the Five Gods, the savior of the City of Sky Fire. Silver Wolf, though no longer the runt he'd once been, did not feel equal to being the other half of the divine set. His voice sounded distant. "Go where?"

"To see Lord Regent Fen Ryok."

"So he can send us to the gods?" The words dripped with scorn. He looked back at the seer, impossibly feeling that this was somehow partially his fault, for telling his brother to do this mad thing.

"Yes."

"And then what?" He spun back to glare at his twin. "We go fight a demon? And not a lesser demon, mind you. Not even a whole pack of lesser demons. We're supposed to fight a greater demon?"

His brother actually shrugged. "Explains why we've been training for so long."

"Are you listening to yourself? It's a greater demon! We could spend our whole lives training and it wouldn't matter. Greater demons can't be killed."

"You're only saying that because no one ever has killed one." There might have been a ghost of a smile as he said it, but the younger twin was having none of it.

"It's not possible. There are no books, no artifacts. Sonju never even told us any stories of someone actually killing a greater demon, and do you know why? Because it can't be done."

"That's why we need to speak to the gods."

"And what are the gods supposed to do? Because unless they're going to fight for us, I can't see how any of us will survive."

"We'll understand once we've asked. Now let's go."

"No." He nearly laughed at the absurdity of the request, anger bubbling up inside him. "What was the point of all this? Of surviving the trek through the mountains, of training for six long years, when we were just going to end up having our souls rent from our body by an immortal creature of evil?"

"This isn't the time for cowardice," his brother warned.

"You're right; it's the time for sense. If you thought about this for one second, you'd see what a colossal mistake this is."

"It's our destiny."

"And what if I say it's not? Who's left to tell me I'm wrong? Sonju's dead. Our mother's dead. And I don't think you've got a Deck of Destiny on you. No one is going to stop us if we just decide to walk away."

"I would." There was a low growl in those two words.

"Be reasonable, At—"

Before he even knew what'd happened, his brother had shot toward him in a blur of motion. The massive black wolf slammed him up against one of the huge stone blocks that had fallen from the ceiling. Bells rang in his ears and his head swam from the force of the impact. Shaking off his daze, he found himself looking into his brother's snarling face, white teeth flashing and eyes blazing.

"That is not my name." He said the words slowly, as if he were pulling up each one from a great depth. "Our destiny has finally come, and I intend to meet it. I'll not let all of the sacrifices given to bring us to this point be wasted."

"We'll be wasted if you persist," he said back, but the blow from his older brother had knocked out some of his bite.

"Have you no faith in destiny?"

The question caught him off guard, and Silver Wolf couldn't find the words to reply right away, but his brother went on.

"I, for one, am grateful for this destiny. It's given me the purpose I thought I'd lost that day when Mother passed." Silver Wolf could hear the waver in his brother's voice, but his twin swallowed past it. "But then you found that letter. After I read it, I knew. I knew that our lives, her death, they meant something. That we were meant for more. That I was meant for more."

"Your ego is going to get us killed." He tried to argue, but his anger had faded and only his tired sorrow was left to fill the void.

"And helping these people? Is that ego? Isn't it right? Isn't it our duty for all—"

"And if I can't?" The words were squeezed out of him in a way that had nothing to do with his brother pinning him to the wall. "You've always been the strong one, the one who looked and acted like the god-chosen hero you're meant to be, but me?" He looked down at his slighter frame. "I've always been the runt of the litter."

"You have power—"

"That's helped who? When you were bitten by that snake, you didn't need me. We're werewolves; you would have survived the bite fine without my magic. In the mountains, my power didn't kill that demon-mountain cat. It called it. And with Mother, there was no way your talents could've stopped her from falling off that cliff, but my magic should've been able to bring her back. And yet again I couldn't do anything. I've gotten stronger. I've made pacts with elementals for Varro's sake, but against a greater demon? What if it just wants to eat my power? What if my power is what called it here? I could be the reason the dragons are in danger in the first place." With his rant running out of steam, he sagged and finished in a softer, more resigned tone. "I don't deserve to be the other half of this brotherhood. We saw it in the mountains. I'm more likely to get you killed than to help you fight."

"Then why did the gods choose us both?"

He barked a laugh. "I can't even begin to imagine."

"Then why don't we ask them?"

The suggestion brought the younger brother up short.

Black Wolf straightened, loosening his grip and allowing Silver Wolf to do the same. Their mother's ring, hanging by a chain at Silver Wolf's throat, had spilled out of his shirt in the tussle. He'd worn it every day since his brother had given him the cord and told him to. When they'd arrived in the dragon city, Lotician had required that the fledgling caster get himself a proper chain to put it on if he insisted on wearing it during their practices.

Black Wolf looked at the gem catching the dim light and tapped it with a knuckle. "She understood it. Perhaps it's time we did too."

They locked eyes, a bit of challenge and mischief coloring Black Wolf's gaze. "Are you ready to find out?"

Silver Wolf looked down at the ring hanging around his neck, a bright spot of light and color in the gloom, just like their mother had been.

She'd set them on this path because she'd believed the seer's words. "Yes," he said. If it meant he could finally understand why he'd been chosen, the reason for all his hardships and losses, he would go on. "I think I am."

## CHAPTER 33

# *The Audience*

The damage to the palace had been extensive. As the brothers trotted through the devastation, they took pains to avoid the sharp roofing tiles that littered the ground in red rivers and to circumvent hallways that had completely collapsed. Still they hurried, higher and deeper than they ever had, toward the section dedicated to the great regent of the City of Sky Fire.

The destruction lessened more the higher they went. The walls bore fewer cracks, the ground split less, making their way easier. It was as if the regent himself had somehow forbidden the tremors from marring his personal rooms.

The apprentice sorcerer felt a flash of nostalgia as he noticed who sat before the doors of the regency's quarters. He didn't know how, but Hiensun, the plum dragon steward from the palace gates, was coiled before the barrier. The courtly dragon looked the pair of them over with her accustomed curled lip as though she'd just bitten into an unripened apple.

"You two," she said, shaking her head.

"I believe we're expected this time too," the younger twin smiled up at the steward.

"Indeed," she replied, showing more teeth. "The regent has anticipated your arrival and thus has left me here to see you in; however, I suspect that he will be even less pleased to see you than I am."

Her words took a little light out of Silver Wolf's grin. He supposed that if he'd been the regent, he wouldn't be very happy to see them, the harbingers of darkness, either.

"Then he'll want to be done with this quickly," Black Wolf replied.

"Of course," agreed Hiensun briskly. "This way." Bending away from them, she pulled at the doors blocking their path. They were made of metal, not stone, and though still circular, still ornate with scenes of flowers and birds molded into them, they felt more ominous for their darker hue.

Silver Wolf was struck speechless as he entered behind the gatekeeper and saw the grandeur of the room beyond. Where the rest of the City of Sky Fire had felt light and airy, this room could only be called ethereal. All the stone was still white, carved like the rest, only in this room it had subtle veins of pink cutting through. The clouds drifted across the chamber in banks that would obscure and then reveal, adding mystique to its splendor. In the center of the room was a long pool of perfectly still water, the pillars that supported the ceiling ending beneath its depths. White and pink water lily clusters grew around the base of each column, their stone likeness continuing up each stone column. It was warm too, the same vents were cleverly carved into the border of the pool, another decorative element hiding a utilitarian purpose. The room felt calm, it felt peaceful, and despite the trouble outside Silver Wolf could feel a little of that ease trying to seep inside him. That is, until his eyes reached the far end of the hall.

At the other end of the long pool was a dais, tall and grand, carved from the same white-and-pink stone, the base of it depicting more carved white lilies, but upon it lounged the largest dragon the fledgling caster ever seen. Flame-red and gold, the majestic, terrifying creature lay glaring at the pair with bright yellow eyes. His crimson scales reflected the light of the sunstones around him, sending shards of ruby illumination dancing through the clouds. His wild mane of yellow fur framed a head both regal and savage and ran in an elegant cascade down an impossibly long body. The horns upon his head were long and curved, innumerable points forming a crown of dangerous regalia, and onyx claws rested just at the surface of the water, still as the stone he sat upon. Rings, bracelets, and chains glittered on every appendage, a clear display of his wealth. There could be no confusion as to the identity of this colossal titan of the skies; he could only be the great lord regent, Fen Ryok.

"Ah, the Children of Bain." The bass of his tone sent ripples skidding across the surface of the clear pool. "I've heard a great deal about you—twin stars meant to lead us through the darkness." It was the nicest description of their futures Silver Wolf had heard, though the caster noted the regent didn't sound pleased as he uttered the words.

"Lord," the older twin said, "we've come on instructions from the seer Sonju. He said that you would send us to speak with the gods so that we may ask for their aid against the coming of this greater demon."

Fen Ryok's full attention snapped to Black Wolf, his yellow eyes blazing, the sudden movement causing his claws to rake through the water's surface, sending small waves into the once-still pool. "And why should the gods listen to a pair of insignificant hounds when they've turned deaf ears to their chosen sentinels?"

The fledging caster took a step back at the heat in his words.

The warrior didn't even flinch. "We do not claim to understand the gods' plans; we can only follow the path as it's been laid out for us."

"Or cause further harm by angering the deities with your impertinence."

"Sonju saw us speaking with the gods. He believed this is how we are to aid your people."

"Prophecy is not memory," said the regent. "Call the seer," he snapped at an attendant. "I'd like to hear for myself this new turn in his vision."

"Sonju is dead." Black Wolf's tone was flat, impassive, and factual, but he'd had some practice at it.

This pronouncement stilled the red behemoth, his brows rising as he regarded them.

"So," the leviathan said, settling. "That part of his prophecy has come to pass. He once told me, nearly a decade ago now, that two whelps brought in from the mountains would one day make the difference between our survival or annihilation. He claimed their path would be laden with hardship and death, but these boys would be tempered by it as metal is by flame. It would be through this forge of pain that their will and skill would be hardened and honed to a cutting edge. He went on to say we would all be required to lend them our strength and wisdom for the battle to come, and I would know my time when his had ended. And here you are, telling me his time has passed." There was a softening to his voice as he said, "And so it is that mine has begun." The ruler gazed at them, weighing them, the wisdom of centuries heavy in his metallic stare. "Sonju said I was to deliver you to the gods?"

"He did." Black Wolf nodded.

Shaking his head, waving golden-tipped whiskers, the serpent said, "I have prayed for guidance and received only silence in return."

"Because you are not their chosen champion, Lord Regent," said a new voice, one that Silver Wolf recognized.

Lotician and Dexus stood to one side of the pool, obscured before by a pillar and the mist. "If you'll take my meaning, Your Lordship," the elf gave a low bow. "You've very little to lose by sending these two. The worst outcome could only be a similar silence."

"Or the gods' wrath," replied the regent.

Lotician grinned. "Properly directed, that too could be a boon."

"Send them." This came from the fire drake. "We were all called for a reason. If not for this, then what?"

The leader of the ryong gave a snort, his brows furrowed, then let out a breath between clenched teeth. "For all our sakes, I pray the seer saw this vision clearly. I will send you as far as I'm able. It will then be on you to obtain your audience. Now, look into my eyes and don't look away."

Both werewolves came to stand at the edge of the pool, shoulders almost touching, with their eyes fixed upon the regent's as instructed. Slowly, gracefully, the ruby dragon began to float above the dais. He uncoiled his impossibly long body as he drifted almost lazily over the pond. His golden belly was reflected in its waters, but the regent's eyes were too transfixing to notice anything else. They started out as lanterns glimpsed through the misty clouds, but as they drew nearer and nearer, they became bright as bonfires, and then as blinding as the sun itself. There was nothing save the dazzling light of those eyes, and then everything faded to black.

## CHAPTER 34

# *In the Presence of Divinity*

When the apprentice sorcerer opened his eyes again, the blackness was still there. He felt himself standing upright, but on what, he didn't know. He strained to see something, anything, only, unlike in Sonju's hall, it wasn't that it was too dim to see properly. Instead there was literally nothing to be seen. They'd left their world and found themselves in—nothing.

A hand touched his shoulder, but he didn't jump at his brother's touch this time. Silver Wolf felt quite proud of himself, that his age had given him a degree of backbone, until he turned around. Then he jumped. In turning, he could see the warrior clearly, not just as a silhouette either, but clearly lit as though under a midday sun, despite the lack of any obvious light source.

The dark twin wore the same look of confusion that the light twin must've had on his own face. "Where are we?"

"I'm not sure," confessed the caster. "This reminds me of some of my mental training, only—"

"It feels like I'm dreaming."

"Exactly. Think of this place like a way station between your waking and sleeping mind. Lotician showed me this place before, but he never mentioned reaching the gods from here."

"So how does that help us?"

"I don't know if it does." He looked around again. On every side was the same dull black, the void stretching out into eternity, except for one small speck of slightly less black over his right shoulder. "We should go that way." He pointed to the lighter speck.

Black Wolf only shrugged in reply, extending his hand. "Lead on."

They walked toward the lightness. Silver Wolf wasn't wholly convinced about how they could be walking at all. There was no discernible ground beneath their feet, no texture or solidity to even hint at a floor. It was like walking on thick air, yet all they could do was simply keep walking. There was no way of telling distance either, as everything was the same shade of nothingness. Had they actually walked any way at all?

He heard his brother ask from over his shoulder, "How far will we have to go?"

"I have no idea. I've never been to see the gods before."

As their seemingly endless walk continued, the younger twin couldn't help thinking about the dragons fighting the greater demon while their prophesied heroes were somewhere in the blackness, very likely walking in circles. Faith that they'd find the gods, that they'd find anything, was difficult to maintain in the face of a featureless void.

The caster was almost to the point of telling his brother that they should head back, try a different approach, when he realized the substance beneath his feet had changed. He looked down and saw they were walking on something—a black-and-white, checkered, tiled floor. The normality of the thing in such an odd place made his brain feel numb. The space around them, while still black and endless, started to have an odd, closed-in feeling, and then there were pillars on either side of them at intervals as they continued walking. Within the black walls, small twinkling lights appeared, and then Silver Wolf saw that they were in a hallway lined on either side by clear glass panels looking out onto the night sky itself.

"What is this place?" the older brother asked in hushed reverence.

Shocked himself, Silver Wolf took a moment to answer. "I'm guessing this is where the gods dwell. Or at least where they deign to speak to mortals."

The world outside was limitless. Stars, some larger, some smaller, many white, but others of blue and red, twinkled all around them. A flash jolted the brothers as a rock on fire streaked past them and continued on its way through the night. They walked on because as amazing as all of it was—the lights and the stars and the strange planets with shining rings—they had to keep going. Lives were riding on the outcome of their mission. They would not fail them.

They walked until they could go no farther. The corridor simply stopped, and in nothing so mundane as stone or another wall of glass. The hall ended in a solid barrier of black, a black darker than the void before it, as dark as ink spilled on white paper, but more disturbing than its pitch was that the wall was moving. It roiled like the liquid stone they'd seen beneath the City of Sky Fire, undulating and bulging, but never leaving its confines at the hall's end.

The brothers stood before the pulsing obstacle and examined it.

"Now what?" the caster asked aloud.

"This is supposed to be your field of expertise," answered the warrior.

"I suppose we wait." He wasn't particularly pleased by their proximity to the throbbing wall of dark.

"Can we afford to waste the time?"

"I don't think we have a choice," he said, sitting down before the throbbing panel. It made his flesh crawl under his fur to see it, a reaction lessened only slightly as his older brother joined him on the floor.

They waited and waited, neither speaking nor moving for what felt like an age.

This time, it was Black Wolf's turn for impatience. "The battle must be lost by now." He raked his claws vigorously through the fur on his head in frustration. "The demon will have slaughtered every last dragon in the city and we're just sitting here."

"Let's hope not. Though I don't think it's likely."

"How can you say that? It feels like we've been in this place for months."

"I don't think time moves the same way here. I mean gravity and light don't seem to."

His brother only shook his head with another growl.

"Besides, I think we'd know if the demon had already won."

"How would we know that from here?"

"I don't think this place is as far away as you think it is."

"How's that?"

"I don't know; it's just a feeling I have. If something catastrophic were to happen back home, I think we'd feel it here."

When his twin didn't respond, Silver Wolf turned to face him, only to see that he wasn't looking at him. Instead the warrior's wide eyes were on the living wall.

A twinkling, shining light had appeared within the undulating surface like a distant star being born. It grew bigger, taking on a bluish hue as it drew near, and bigger yet, closing the apparent distance rapidly. Then it multiplied. It split into two stars, a blue star and a gold one, then three, adding a green, and then—

The brothers took a step back as four orbs of light soared out of the barrier and into the corridor. The four lights, shining like differently colored lanterns, shimmered and pulsed, hanging in the air before them with illumination dim enough to be admired. The younger twin couldn't help but be reminded of their mother sitting in the kitchen with the pulsing orb of magic between her hands. None of these lights were the same color, but the way they pulsed in time with his heart, glowing softly, made his heart ache with the memory.

The first light, the blue one, floated toward the pair. Silver Wolf had opened his hands to receive it when suddenly and without warning, the orb of light exploded. The blast was blinding. The dark world turned alternating shades of electric blue and white. When his eyes could see again, the view had not improved. The caster was faced with a wall of water, a massive wave whipped up by a storm behind it, surging toward them. They were surrounded by an ocean, the brothers suddenly standing on a stone jutting up from the water, waves and storm clouds in every direction. Wind streaked with icy crystals that flashed in the lightening tore at Silver Wolf's fur and thunder emitting from the gray clouds rang in his ears.

Neither werewolf moved, unsure how to escape their predicament, when the wall of water broke, crashing around the stone they stood on, narrowly failing to wash them out to sea. In the passing of the tsunami, the clouds parted, illuminating a figure walking over the waters to meet them.

It was a fox, a werefox, walking upright on two legs, with fur as white as snow and paws as black as onyx. A long, cobalt robe edged with golden symbols hung about its thin frame with a fluffy, black-tipped tail just visible beneath the back hem. It was the size of an average werefox, thus shorter than the werewolves, but it hovered above the ground, bringing it up to their eye level. As it reached them, the waves and the clouds faded, the light dimming once again, until the hall was as it had been before, only this time with three glowing orbs and a hovering werefox.

The second, yellow sphere drifted toward them next, and Silver Wolf tensed for what was to come. It burst much like the first, only this one expressed its power in a torrent of winds and howling gales, stinging his eyes and pulling at his clothes. He flung one arm up to protect his sight. All he could see around him was a cyclone of swirling air. Rocks, trees, and brush alternated, appearing and then disappearing within the currents, demonstrating the destruction it must have wreaked in its passing.

When the surge had passed and the raging winds had softened to a light breeze, he lowered his hand to see another were, a raven, dressed in vivid yellow robes with similar golden detail and trim. Its sleek black feathers shown almost blue, in stark contrast to its clothing. The breeze continued to blow, but not from the flapping of the raven's wings. They floated, like the fox, without any visible effort.

Then the green orb broke to their left, all the more startling for it not being in the center of things. The hall vanished again for a moment, revealing a sun-soaked canyon, great towers of banded stone around them. From the canyon floor and the ridge, stones began to rise. They swam through the air, orchestrated by some power the brothers couldn't see. The younger twin saw a large chunk of rock sailing in his direction and ducked, though it only passed him lazily to join the others gathering in the center of the scene. It was a gentler display compared to the other two, the pieces of stone collecting sedately around a werebear in concentric rings, like one of the strange planets glimpsed through the corridor's walls. As the stones circled and weaved about, they occasionally struck one another, sometimes splintering off tiny pieces, sometimes holding together to make larger planetoids. The ursine at this galaxy's heart took no notice as the bangs produced lights that illuminated its chestnut fur in dapples.

The last, the crimson red orb, didn't wait for the canyon to vanish. It flashed more rapidly than the rest and erupted at once into a torrent of flames, wiping out all indications of the previous scene. Silver Wolf felt his fur and lungs instantly scalded by the heat. Both werewolves ducked their heads, covering their eyes and noses to protect themselves from the intensity of the heat. A bonfire roared and flared aggressively at the center of it all, the world around them nothing but flames. Where there had been canyons before, now there was a scene of erupting mountains, spewing the same fire-red rock that was at the center of the world. The temperature was nearly unbearable. Unable to breath, unable to escape, Silver Wolf thought he would pass out, when it all vanished. The hall went back to its original coolness, the flames and lights vanishing with the heat and leaving them with the stars and darkness once again. He looked back up to see the last of the fire parting before it faded entirely, revealing a massive male lion cloaked in deep red robes, its full, coppery mane dancing like the flames.

Heads still ducked, the brothers lowered their arms to gaze upon the four assembled deities. Despite the inherent differences in size, due to their varied species, each god hovered a proportionate amount off the floor. The levitation aside, the caster might've thought the four of them to be regular weres, maybe strong sorcerers, with their impressive entrances, which had been dramatic. Only there was something else, something that made them more otherworldly—their eyes, or their lack of them. Instead of regular white-and-black-colored orbs in their skulls, each being sported two holes where its eyes should've been. The empty sockets could blink and move as if there were something to fill them, and he supposed they weren't truly empty. Each pair glowed with an eerie light emanating from deep within their forms, as though someone had lit a bonfire inside of a cave and it was shining distantly out of the cavern's mouth, like they were made from light and only wearing the forms of mortals.

"Who dares to come, to disturb the Gods of Eris, here within our Hall of Dreams?" the raven asked in a deep and melodic but clearly feminine voice. The magical twin hadn't noticed before, but there was a delicacy to her clawed hands, a slenderness to her frame and how she moved it, though partially hidden by the indifferent robes, that practically shouted female. He wasn't sure how he'd missed it on his first glance, though the hurricane winds might've had something to do with it.

Black Wolf nodded to him as if to remind him this was still his realm of expertise. The sorcerer's ears flattened for a moment before he stepped forward. "Pardon our intrusion, great beings of Eris." He bowed so low he nearly bent in half. "But we have come to plead for your aid."

"Then speak and make your plea," the wind goddess cawed in her beautiful voice.

Silver Wolf had never spoken to a god before. He'd prayed to the gods and he'd spoken to elementals, perhaps a combination of the two. "Please, great Gods of Eris, hear my request," he began, bowing again to the raven-woman. "Hear me, Belkis, Goddess of Wind." He turned to the white fox. "Pendry, God of Water." He faced the bear. "Arden, God of Stone." He directed the next acknowledgment to the glowering lion. "Indris, God of Fire. And Enoch—"

Here the sorcerer faltered. He hadn't realized it before, what with the lightening and wind and fire, but there had been only four orbs of light. They were in the presence of only four gods. Where was the fifth? Where was Enoch, God of Light?

"Our brother is not here," growled the lion, intuiting the meaning behind Silver Wolf's sudden silence. "Say what you've come to say and do so quickly."

"Lords." He tried to recover himself with a bow, but he couldn't stop his mind from spinning. Why wasn't Enoch present? His mother had thought him the strongest of the gods, so what did it mean that he wasn't there?

"Speak," the lion roared.

"Lords," he started again, "my brother and I have come to ask for your help."

"So you've said," snapped Indris, tail twitching beneath his robe. "Why should we give it?"

"Please," Silver Wolf tried, "two seers now have told us that we're to save the dragon people from a great darkness. We know now that that darkness is a greater demon and no power on Eris could destroy such a creature. No mortal could stand against it, not without help. That's why we've come to you. Please lend us your aid in defeating this monster."

Indris snorted derisively, causing little embers to swirl in the air before him, blazing brighter as they passed through the beams from his empty eyes. "Fool."

"Lord." Black Wolf spoke, stepping forward to stand beside his twin.

Indris waved an impatient paw. "You said it yourselves—nothing on Eris can bring down a greater demon."

"That's why we've come to you," the younger brother said urgently.

"We will offer no aid," Indris clarified.

Silver Wolf was struck speechless for a moment, his mouth working, but with no sound emerging. Shaking himself, he rallied. "But we were chosen by you to fight this thing."

"Presumptive." The lion shook his mane as though to clear his own thoughts of such ridiculousness.

"What were the words that convinced you that we might help?" Pendry asked. Like his smaller size implied, his tone was light, his question curious.

Why was he asking them that? Was it a test?

"The dragon seer Sonju told us that you'd sent him a vision of this audience."

"Ah, yes." Pendry nodded as though confirming the words. "And did he tell you what form our assistance would take?"

"No." Silver Wolf's ears fell back.

Pendry shook his head as though disappointed. "A pity."

The caster felt as though he were failing their test. "But he said you would. You would help us defeat the greater demon and save the dragons." Near panic colored his voice.

"It isn't quite as simple as you may think," Belkis said.

"Why not?"

"Only the power of the divine can harm one of those creatures," she answered, scowling in distaste. "And since our laws forbid us from interfering too directly in worldly affairs, I'm afraid our hands are tied."

"Could Enoch help us?" he found himself asking.

Indris looked ready to pounce. "Enoch is not here. And even if he were, he is restrained by the same laws as the rest of us."

"Then give us the divine power so that we may use it against the demon," Black Wolf spoke up again.

"Oh, yes?" Belkis raised a brow in reply. "And how much would you like?"

Neither of the twins could offer an answer to that.

"Too little," she continued, "and the demon would swallow you both up like splendid treats. Too much and you'd shatter like ice crystals in a hailstorm."

The sorcerer swallowed hard, remembering his master's demonstration with the jar. He didn't doubt that a god's power could shatter a mortal's body completely.

She shook her avian head sadly. "No, giving you a divine gift of our power is not the answer you're looking for."

"Then how?" Silver Wolf asked.

She shrugged prettily, head tilted to the side, palms upturned.

"There is no way," Indris snarled, punctuating the point.

"No way?" Silver Wolf asked in the barest whisper. He didn't know how to feel about it. Should he be happy? He wouldn't have to fight the greater demon. No one could expect him to do anything so crazy, not if the gods wouldn't help.

"No way?"

Silver Wolf heard the echo from beside him and saw his brother's fur standing on end. He had to look up to see Black Wolf's expression, but he thought in that moment, even with the frustration and raised fur, that his brother looked smaller. The warrior looked confused, lost even. Their whole life had been building to this, building to nothing? It couldn't be true.

"Then why are we here?" Silver Wolf asked before he'd realized the words were on his tongue. "Why did Sonju see us speaking to you? How could he have seen us helping them if it's not possible?"

"I wouldn't say it wasn't possible." The goddess cast a dark look to her fellow deity before her demeanor grew more thoughtful. "It would certainly require divine power. The question is how much and how to bestow it upon you." She pondered aloud, tapping a talon to the side of her beak, considering the riddle.

"It could be possible," Pendry said, one black paw running along the underside of his long muzzle.

The goddess looked up. "Oh, yes?"

"If the problem is the amount, we could connect ourselves to the world through a mortal, providing a small, constant stream of divine energy into a willing host."

"What would that do?" Silver Wolf asked.

The blue god turned his hollow sockets to regard the caster. "Our power would link with yours. Just as you draw on the magic of Eris to add to your spells, you would draw on our energies."

"Like a pact with an elemental?"

"Not precisely. As a mortal you are tied firmly to Eris. You drink her waters, you trod upon her stones, you breathe her air. You are in constant contact with Eris and thus with the elementals that dwell within her. Your ties to the divine are not so clear. We'd have to forge a connection through the Basilar."

"The Basilar?" the caster echoed.

The white fox waved away the question, but did answer quickly. "The weft and the weave of existence. Threads that deliver energy throughout the worlds and tie it to its source."

Before he could ask more Belkis spoke up again.

"That could work," she said. "Presumably—and mind you this linking has never been tested before—the connection would increase a caster's magical abilities while also giving their spells that little extra something. There would be a few other, tiny side effects of course."

"Side effects?"

She shrugged an elegant shoulder. "They might be a bit sturdier, for example, a bit more resilient. And of course time would stop for them—"

"Time would stop?" Silver Wolf interrupted, his violet eyes widening as he looked from the yellow divinity to the blue.

"Oh, yes," she said, unoffended by his outburst, for which he was thankful. She looked up and blinked those uncanny eyeless gaps at him as though she'd just remembered he was there at all. "Like we gods or the greater demon itself, time would simply pass you by. You'd still be mortal, insofar as anything that would kill a werewolf outright would still kill you, but with our great power flooding your body, old age would no longer be a consideration for you."

The caster didn't know what to make of that. He didn't have much time to ponder it either because the fire god spoke again.

"More fools." Indris snapped like a splintered log too long in a blaze. "You speak about possibilities and theories, but it's pointless. The power is ours. Only we hold dominion over the divine."

"It would come close to the law of interference, but would not cross it," Arden said, nodding.

"That's not the point. We don't simply give away our power to any mortal who's foolish enough or reckless enough to ask for it."

"At least not to any mortal who wished to see the other side of such a contract." Arden fixed Silver Wolf with a meaningful gaze, though he found the look hard to understand without eyes to focus on.

"What do you mean?" he asked. "She just said I wouldn't age, I'd be stronger, I—"

"Pendry's not mistaken, though neither is Arden." Belkis waved a talon to further grab his attention while also cutting him off. "We could bind you to us, giving you access to our divine power, and thus adding it to your own—"

"Only such a bond would undoubtedly prove fatal to the one bound," Arden finished for her. "Our power flowing into you would sustain your form during the linking, though when we inevitably withdrew the link, your body would sustain irreparable damage. Your own strength would not be enough to recover from it. You would die."

"Die," he heard himself echo dully.

"A body, once bolstered by our divinity, would collapse in on itself once we took that power away." Belkis nodded sadly.

"Why are we even wasting our breath on such an inane conversation?" Indris asked, spreading both hands. "Even if we gave him divine power, there is no way a mortal could even use it to strike a greater demon."

"Why not?" Silver Wolf's brother asked, which was good because he was too numb to even form coherent thoughts.

"Ignorant dog," the god snarled. "Because demons consume magic. Due to that, even the lesser kind are somewhat resistant to its effects. With a greater demon, all magics, save for a direct attack by the divine, would simply slide off its scaly hide without making a mark. Your sibling's pitiful form isn't even capable of containing the magnitude of power it would take to overwhelm such defenses."

Silver Wolf blinked, half hearing the words and remembering the demon-mountain cat they'd fought in the mountains. He hadn't been able to hurt it with his wind spell at all. The energy had drifted to the side when he had tried. He'd had to throw his strongest spell at it, focusing on the fire, and even then, it had still only annoyed the thing. If a greater demon had even more resistance—

"Unless you had a way to deliver the spell past its barrier." Arden shifted his gaze to Black Wolf as he said the words.

"Lunacy." Indris rolled his eyeless sockets skyward, though who'd he be asking for patience from, Silver Wolf didn't know. "Why are we still discussing this?"

"What do you mean?" the older brother asked Arden directly.

Belkis looked surprised again but explained for her fellow god. "A demon's natural barrier extends around it as a shell encases an egg. This invisible shield protects the demon from magics, but only magics. This shell cannot deflect physical objects. The creatures would not be able to get close to their prey if it were so. It also would not be able to drink the power flowing from their victims if it rejected magic so close to it. So this natural defense does not repel magic already within its confines. If you were able to wrap a spell around a physical object, a spear or pike perhaps, then you should be able to deliver the spell past its magical barrier and strike the foul beast with it."

This comment made Silver Wolf think back again to the fiend in the mountains. His magic had slid right off while his brother had pierced the demon and ultimately killed it with his blade.

"If it isn't immune to physical attacks, couldn't we simply slay it with a sword?" Black Wolf clenched his fist for emphasis.

Pendry shook his head. "You could kill a lesser demon in this manner; they're much more a part of Eris. Greater demons are altogether different, more powerful, immortal beings. As previously discussed, you'd need the power of the divine to do it."

"So, if my brother wrapped a spell around my sword, and then I struck the monster," the warrior asked slowly to make sure they all understood the plan, "the weapon would strike the demon with the divine energy and destroy it?"

"Yes, that is the theory." Pendry nodded.

"Not with that, though." The green god nodded to the warrior's belt, where the image of his short sword hung. Silver Wolf hadn't remembered it being there before, but Arden didn't give him the time to contemplate the mystery. "A human-forged blade would have difficulty withstanding the power required for this undertaking."

"There are greater blacksmiths among the other Eight," Pendry supplied.

"The demon is here now," the apprentice caster said. "How will my brother get another weapon in time?"

Black Wolf reached out and touched his shoulder, ending his objection. "I will find a greater weapon, one that is fit for the task, only if we do this, my brother will die?" The dark twin looked to the bright twin and then to the gods.

"Yes. If we connected with your brother, if we shared our power with him, he would die the moment we ceased to provide it," the dark-winged goddess confirmed.

"And you couldn't keep this link in place?" the warrior asked, a note of pleading in his deep voice.

Arden shook his head. "We would not sustain the spell past this battle. It would draw too heavily on our powers."

"You are the Gods of Eris," Black Wolf protested. "Surely you have a bit—"

"This is not the only threat that demands our attention," Arden said, his voice even and flat, but stern.

"We are fighting a greater demon," scoffed the older twin. "What greater threat could there possibly be?"

"Do not presume to question the gods," Arden boomed in response, a glower etched deep into his features.

The sorcerer looked into the angry eyes of his older brother, glaring daggers at the four divinities, but for his part, Silver Wolf only felt empty disbelief. They'd come all this way, had struggled and trained, had lost so much so that they could do something important. Now it looked like he wouldn't even be able to savor his victory, even if they somehow did win. Somehow it didn't seem fair. None of it did.

"There must be another way," he heard the dark werewolf protest distantly.

"I do not see one," Pendry said with upturned hands.

"Don't look so crestfallen," the goddess said, shaking her head and ruffling her blue-black feathers. "It wouldn't have worked anyway. Indris is correct. We couldn't possibly interfere in this struggle. Arden says we're close to the barrier of the law—best not to risk overstepping it. Besides, we don't even know if the mortal's body could withstand the connection anyway. The thought was intriguing, but pointless at the end."

"That's it, then? You're not even willing to try?" Black Wolf asked, suddenly finding himself off his guard.

"A moment ago, you were concerned that we'd be taking your younger brother before his time. Now you want us to attempt it?" The goddess looked surprised again.

"No." The warrior shook his head, trying to get his thoughts in order. "I don't want my brother to make this pact, but I don't want to give up either. I want you to find another way for us to save the dragons and stop this demon."

"There are laws that govern this world—" Pendry tried to explain.

"So you'll sit back while a greater demon wipes out an entire city?" growled Black Wolf.

"It'll only kill those foolish enough to challenge it," Indris added with a sniff. "Once it gluts itself and its followers, it'll leave the rest alone."

"Followers?" Both werewolves spun their heads to the red god.

"The greater demon has brought a horde of its lesser brethren with it," the water god explained.

"A horde?"

"You think the demon's come to feast?" Arden asked, arching one brow.

"Of course. Why bring so many otherwise?" answered the fire god, both gods ignoring the mortals.

"You know what else that mountain holds." The bear's voice was low.

"Oriehada," Belkis whispered, her eyeless sockets stretching wide.

"What is Oriehada?" asked the werewolf warrior in a tone demanding attention. Only the question failed to reach the deities.

"The demon will not reach Oriehada. The dragons are not the only guardians of that holy place," Indris shot back.

"And you don't think the demon considered that? That the multitude of guardians could be why it has brought so many others with it?" Arden suggested.

"Regardless, we're done with this conversation." Indris turned with another sniff. "Dismiss the mortals; you said yourself that they are unfit for your idiotic schemes."

"But the relic," Belkis hissed. Her feathers lifted as she spoke, visibly upset for the first time.

"What relic?" The older brother asked, pitching his voice to be heard over the others, still trying to gain purchase in the conversation.

"None of your concern," snapped Arden. Then to the red god he said, "There is more at stake here than the survival of one mortal city. If a greater demon were to gain the artifact—"

"The dragons stand guard. The guardian at Oriehada is in place. What more do you suggest? These dogs are not going to make that kind of a difference, with or without our help."

Silver Wolf, for his part, had stopped listening some time ago. The echo of the gods' pronouncement was still ringing in his ears. He'd known since the day he'd found his mother's letter that it was his destiny to fight a great evil, and in doing so there would be a chance that he'd die. There'd always been that chance, even before the letter. The humans in Vidar could've learned he was a werewolf or a caster. He could've fallen off a cliff or been trampled to death by the sheep, theoretically. He couldn't even think about the number of times he'd almost died just in traveling to the City of Sky Fire.

Only he didn't want to die. He hadn't been given enough time. Eighteen years. He'd been on Eris for eighteen years, and most of that time had been wrapped up in training with his mother, Lotician, or Dexus. It just wasn't enough. What was his alternative, though? He could run. He could flee into the mountains and hide until the demon left with whatever this relic was. He could leave the dragons to take care of the demon—surely they'd do better than him, and if they needed magic, they had Lotician, an elf who'd been practicing sorcery for nearly two centuries. If they needed a fighter, they had Dexus, a stronger, more skilled warrior than his brother was. Looking over at his brother's worried face, he wondered if he could convince him to run with him.

Then he remembered what his twin had said back in Sonju's cave, which made him then think of the old seer. He'd believed in them. Their mother had believed in them. So many others—York, Lotician, Dexus, the lord regent, and everyone else who'd helped them along the way. His brother had said they'd ask the gods why they'd been chosen. Now those same gods were claiming that it'd all been pointless, but did he believe them? Did he really believe that all the talk about the future, all their training to meet it, and all of the sacrifices along the way were for nothing? Even if it meant he would die?

"Why so scared, Lord Indris?" Silver Wolf heard himself ask through his daze.

"What did you say?" Each word the red god spoke was punctuated by a plume of smoke.

"If you're truly an immortal being of unfathomable power, then what are you worried about in aiding two lowly mortals? Scared we'll gain this artifact after we've dealt with the demon and come back for you?"

"Listen to me, you miserable cur." Tangible heat radiated from the deity. "We fear nothing."

"Then you wouldn't be afraid to give us the power we need to defeat this terrible monster coming straight at your precious treasure. You have nothing to lose in this bargain, whereas I, I have quite a bit."

"Brother," the warrior said in a harsh whisper, grabbing his arm. "We'll find another way."

"We don't have time to find another way. This is the way."

"You'll die."

"We all will someday," he said, trying to smile. "I might as well make my death mean something."

"I—" Silver Wolf saw his brother's throat work as he tried to swallow. "I can't lose you," Black Wolf said, still gripping his arm. "Not you too."

"You're the hero. You're the one who has to end this. I'm the support, the one who'll help you accomplish the impossible, but expendable at the end of it all."

"You're not expendable."

"You said it yourself: what would be the point of these powers if we didn't have an obligation to do something with them? How could I ever face Sonju or Mother if I chose to save myself when so many more were out there dying and I had the power to stop it?" It was like everything his brother had ever told him just came tumbling out of his mouth, only this time the Silver Wolf felt like the words were his own. After all the questions, after all the doubts, he'd finally come to understand his part in their shared destiny. He could be the lightning rod to direct the gods' power on Eris and give it to his brother.

"Of course," Black Wolf said, his hold loosening and then reasserting itself. "But I won't let you face this alone."

"Of course you won't," the younger wolf said, smiling for real this time.

Turning his attention back to the gods, Silver Wolf said with all the formality he could muster, "Please, oh gods of this world, make the pact with me so that I may borrow your power and help my brother defeat the evil threatening our allies and the temple of Oriehada." He looked at each deity individually as he spoke, his eyes locking with each of their glowing, hollow gazes.

Arden was the first to nod, solemnly and slowly.

Pendry looked surprised when it was his turn, with his ears perked and his fur bristling. Hands pressed together, he nodded a quick bow of acknowledgment. "We will try."

"To protect the artifact," Belkis hissed with hushed urgency and a firm dip of her long beak, "we will accept your sacrifice and make the attempt to join our powers to yours."

When at last it was Indris's turn, Silver Wolf looked to see the lion seething and smoking, little yellow flames escaping from between his teeth to vanish amongst the darker golden strands of his mane. "Your presumption, the arrogance—" The god seemed to be working himself into a torrent until he glanced at the other gods' faces, some pleading, some laced with censure and meaning that Silver Wolf couldn't begin to understand. Only it appeared to convince the fire god of something. "Cur, if you try one trick outside of putting down this cretin, I'll tear your soul apart with my own hands."

"After we've dealt with the threat, it is your right to take my life," the bright twin agreed with a respectful nod.

"It's decided, then," the wind goddess announced, throwing up a dark talon that made her robe swirl around her. "We, the Gods of Eris, will make the connection with you, Silver Wolf, and share our power so that you may defeat the greater demon before further harm can be done."

The four gods floated toward him, forming a circle around and above him, each with a single hand outstretched. Black Wolf had to take a step back, forced from the circle, but he didn't go far. Silver Wolf could see him past the deities, their violet gazes locked, their worried smiles matched.

He could feel his heart throbbing in his chest, faster and faster. Excitement, fascination, pride, and admittedly a good dose of fear coursed through his veins while the gods about him began to glow. They showed their colors—green, yellow, blue, and red—and yet somehow the light that bathed the apprentice sorcerer was white. It grew brighter, a blinding brilliance that blocked out the stars, the hall, his brother, everything. It grew brighter and brighter until it consumed the whole world.

## CHAPTER 35

## *Slayer*

Silver Wolf's next conscious thought was that he was lying down, his eyes closed. Was he asleep? Could everything he'd just experienced have been a dream?

Once he opened his eyes, he knew the truth. Gazing down at him were the cat-slit pupils of the lord regent, studying him as though he'd never seen a werewolf before. Putting that aside for the moment, he turned his head to the right and found his brother in much the same position, lying flat on his back at the edge of the regent's pool, staring at the ceiling and looking just as bewildered.

"You've done it," the great red dragon said in a low voice that he could feel rumbling through his bones. "I can feel the touch of the gods upon you." With that pronouncement, the lord regent turned from the wolves and floated back across the pond, presumably to give them room to stand and reorient themselves. Only the great ruler swung about, rippling the water with his passing, hovering just above it and his dais in clear agitation. "Tell me what happened."

Silver Wolf picked himself up. "The gods made a connection with me," he replied in a disbelieving evaluation. He marveled at the energy he could feel just at the edges of his consciousness. He could feel his power moving inside of him; he'd learned to recognize it since his mother had started teaching him. He could feel the energies of Eris, feel the workings of the elementals, the spirits, and all the living beings around him, but something had changed. The power within him was his power, but there was more, only slightly more, but now it shined. He couldn't think of any other way to explain it. Like the sheen of oil on the surface of the water with which he'd washed the dishes after dinner, the power shined as it ran through him. "I'm to channel this divine power gifted by the gods and give it to my brother so that he may use it to slay the demon."

The dark warrior stepped up next to him, but didn't touch him. The steel was back in his eyes. "I'll need a better sword." His hand went automatically to the sword at his hip, his actions and words faltering for just a moment. "The gods have informed me this won't be enough."

"Take mine." Dexus stepped forward from the side of the pool where he and Lotician had been standing and pulled the long, thin blade from around his middle.

"Slayer?" was his brother's stunned reply. "That was your reward—"

"For training the gods' chosen champions," Dexus finished. "Such a weapon can have no greater use." A smile, a mere crack in the dragon's impenetrable stoicism, slid over his features as Black Wolf took the blade reverently from his master and into his own hands.

Silver Wolf had never seen the sword exposed before, and he couldn't tear his eyes away from it as the glittering metal sang while coming free of its black-and-red sheath. The blade was long, thin, and slightly curved, reminding him of a snake's fang, poised and ready to strike. On the pommel, the head of a roaring dragon looked back at its wielder. It was not the goliath weapon he'd been expecting, but a savage and efficient-looking killer nonetheless.

"Thank you, Master," the dark twin said, gaze wide and tone low.

"Bring it back to me once you've taken his head." Dexus nodded in return.

Lotician broke in, striding over to join them. "And on that note, now that you've returned intact with the divine blessing, we'll lend our own support to the conflict." He finished by giving a stately bow to the lord regent.

"How goes the battle?" Black Wolf asked, strapping his master's sword to his belt. The warrior removed the short sword in turn, laying the gift from their mother gently, reverently next to the lord regent's pool.

"It's not been joined long," Lotician reported, "but it's already a bloody mess."

He was relieved to know they hadn't been in the Hall of Dreams for the weeks it'd seemed, but even minutes meant lives lost.

"Go and bring an end to this darkness," commanded Fen Ryok, his words echoing through the halls.

## CHAPTER 36

# *Demon Siege*

The light and dark wolves loped over the high terrain. The battle was raging along the ridge of the mountain, just a few miles before and below the City of Sky Fire. Behind the city, past the very seat of the regency, upon the very summit, supposedly sat the resting place of the gods' relic, the one the dragons were guarding—the shrine of Oriehada. To claim it the greater demon would have to march his army right through the city, no doubt killing any they found in their path.

Dexus and Lotician had entered the battle from the lower end of the slope, the flatter part of the terrain, where the majority of the battle was being waged, all the better to support the lord regent's armies. By contrast, the wolf brothers would approach from the height of the spine, as it was their job to deal with the greater demon at the exclusion of all else. They climbed a steep formation, giving them a clear view of the battle below.

The sight was like nothing Silver Wolf could've ever dreamed of. It was like watching a dark sea crash against a colorful shore. The demon horde, all muted colors and shades of gray, twisted and more numerous than trees in a forest, were throwing themselves against the brightly colored bodies of the dragons around them. The shining serpents, though far fewer, breathed fire, reaching out with claw and fang, snapping and tearing their way through body after body, leaving mounds of mangled corpses, and yet still the demons came in near overwhelming numbers. The sinister horde returned the abuse with strikes of their own, sometimes with simple teeth and claws of their own and sometimes with poison and acid, scaling, tearing, melting, and yet still the dragons held their line. Each side bled upon the ground, splashes of crimson and splashes of ink, until the rock was so slick with red and black it seemed the very ground was made of it, and still the sides fought for purchase, gaining and losing their ground.

"Which one is he?" Black Wolf called.

Silver Wolf had been searching the crowd. There'd been massive creatures with bull horns and savage monsters with six arms, but none had felt powerful enough to the sorcerer to represent the true threat. They were all nightmares, beings of darkness and terror, but none strong enough to feel like the king of nightmares. He imagined that such a creature would feel like death walking.

He tried to let his feelings and magic flow out of him across the field, brushing against warm dragon and cool demon. He didn't really know what he was doing, but it felt right—he was able to tell friend from foe and could feel none so powerful that they could be their invincible enemy. That is, until his power brushed up against something terrible. It felt massive, it felt dark like the living wall of black within the Hall of Dreams, and it felt oily, as though even his magic slid right off of it. Revulsion surged in the pit of his stomach. The sensation made him want to retch, only fear constricted his insides, ensuring nothing moved until he released the source of that terrible energy.

"What is it?" his brother asked, laying a hand on his shoulder, snapping him from his trance.

"He's out there," he replied in a gasp, finally free to breathe.

Suddenly, the pitch of the battle changed, drawing both of their attention.

As though by unheard command, the demons, who'd been fighting ferociously, all turned as one and began retreating. The dragons, loathe to relinquish the sudden momentum, pursued the demons for a few paces more, taking the opportunity to fell their foes wherever they could. The nightmarish creatures didn't even defend themselves as they blindly scampered to their predetermined destination. Unnerved by this unexplainable behavior, the dragons stopped their pursuit, staying to their side of some invisible line.

The field split with bright dragons on one side and darkly muted demons on the other. It looked as though the battle hadn't even started yet, the enemies standing across a barren section, though the illusion was ruined by the splatters and pools of blood that coated the scene between them. An eerie stillness held the scene, all upon the field seeming to hold their breaths in anticipation until one figure separated itself from the demon line.

The being was not what Silver Wolf had been expecting. Roughly man-shaped, though stretched tall and thin, with skin and points like a thornbush in winter, it stood no more than a head taller than his older twin and was terrifyingly familiar to both brothers. Kaliton, the monster from the mountains, came strolling toward them, passing the demon horde and dragon army as though they were daisies lining a meadow path. He was just as the younger twin remembered him: dark, twisted, terrible, and so at ease with himself.

One dragon, a great jade-green beast nearly as large as Yielle had been when they'd last met her, rumbled at the passing demon, smoking and twisting, clearly aggravated by the nonchalant air of their aggressor. It surged forward quicker than a striking snake. The ryong reached out with open maw and snapped down on the demon, meaning to crush him between gargantuan jaws. Only the demon was not smashed. The immortal passed through the dragon's mouth as though it were no more than an illusion, no more than smoke, appearing half above and half within the dragon's snout once his jaws had snapped closed. Seemingly unfazed by the attack, the greater demon continued his stroll and passed right through the stunned beast with hardly a pause. None dared to strike at him again after that.

Kaliton continued his unhurried progress up the incline, the brothers clearly his objective. Halfway up the hill, he began speaking, pitching his voice so they could hear him. "I didn't expect to find a sorcerer on the battlefield today. Imagine my surprise when I sensed two. The dragons must've gone far afield to recruit allies. An elf all the way from Rahovan and a werewolf? Two werewolves," he corrected when he reached an angle where he could see them clearly. "I hadn't thought your breed had spread this far east yet. Although you would be the second set I've seen in these mountains. Why, not long ago I was having a lark with a set of puppies I ran across and—" The demon let his words trail away as he finally reached their level, scrutinizing the twins for the first time with narrowed eyes. The demon then tossed his head back and laughed a long peal of surprised, manic delight. "It's you, isn't it?" he managed through his mirth. "The pups from before? I didn't expect to find you here nor to see you again so soon. Though I suppose to look at you, it's been longer than I realize," he said contemplatively, putting a long claw up to one cheek in thought. "Mortal lives are such fleeting things, so inconsequential." His smirk spread over his slash of a mouth at their shared joke. "How is it that you find yourselves all the way out here? And for the gods' sake, why?"

"We've come to stop you from slaughtering dragons," Black Wolf answered. It was obvious that he remembered the demon too, judging from the way his ruff stood on end. He showed no other signs of fear or hate, though. Only his hackles and his hand, gripped a little tighter around the hilt of Slayer, betrayed his tension.

"Oh, really?" the demon asked with some surprise. "I believe all the snakes here have come for that very same reason, to little effect. What makes you think you'll fare any better?"

"We've been training the past six years to do just that," replied Black Wolf, unsheathing his sword, the blade gleaming even on so cloudy a day.

"Ah, well, then. Please, by all means, demonstrate to me what you've learned."

Faster than any of them could utter another word, Black Wolf struck out. Kaliton anticipated the strike, raising one clawed hand and catching the sword in his open palm.

The demon looked disappointed. "I do hope that wasn't it."

Silver Wolf had used his brother's distraction, calling a wave of fire that, once his brother had leapt away, flowed toward the greater demon. The brilliant crimson and golden flames surrounded the dark figure, who lifted his hands to protect his face from the heat, but he sneered in contempt as the spell flowed around him like a stone in the river.

"That was—" Kaliton was cut off as his first opponent dove back in, skirting the fire and slashing his blade across the demon's back, shoulder to hip. The sword struck true, slicing through the flesh and leaving a line of ink-black blood upon the ground that sizzled and hissed where it landed. Kaliton whirled with long talons, but Black Wolf had already dodged away. Silver Wolf readied his next attack, even as he watched, his mouth going slack, as Kaliton's wound ceased to bleed and closed before his eyes.

"It had no effect," the sorcerer said.

"We cut him. He can't do his smoke trick if he doesn't see it coming."

"But he healed the wound instantly and my spells don't even hit him."

"They will." The warrior bared his teeth, spinning the blade in his hand once, loosening and then retightening his grip.

The demon straightened, stretching out the newly sealed skin on his back. The casual way the creature stood and twisted set Silver Wolf's teeth on edge. It sent its message clear enough—there was no threat here.

When the demon was satisfied, he turned back and fixed the brothers with his crazed stare once again. "Now I can see some of that training. You've become quite strong, for mortals," he added with a smirk. "Only, if that is the extent of your powers, then I'm liable to become bored, and rather quickly." His smirk twisted into a gleeful sneer.

"We wouldn't want that," Silver Wolf said, hands already glowing and unleashing a series of concussive bolts of water. They tumbled and swirled toward the demon, only, like the fire, they slid past him and around his unseen barrier, smashing to the rocks behind him. The last bolt, aimed squarely at Kaliton's head, couldn't miss, its aim too true to slide off in either direction. It burst a foot before its intended target, five long, straight talons ripping the orb of water apart. The remnants dripped down Kaliton's hand and fell in tiny, harmless droplets all around them.

The demon brought his sodden, undamaged hand to his face and, darting out a long, slick, black tongue, licked the water from his claws. "Divine power." His voice dripped with disdain like the water from his weapons, the glee absent from his sneer now. "I thought I detected something off about your particular taste of sorcery. I don't know how you've managed it, though," he amended in a slightly lighter tone, "it does make you slightly more interesting. It is unfortunate that you're unable to do much with it, though."

The sorcerer blinked and Kaliton was before him, the creature moving much faster than the caster could've anticipated. Talons raised, he slashed down at Silver Wolf, who barely had time to raise his hands to block.

Silver Wolf felt no pain, however, as he heard the blow ring on steel. Black Wolf had arrived and blocked the attack, holding his assailant back with Slayer. Kaliton's red eyes narrowed; he was clearly annoyed by the interruption. Silver Wolf scrambled out from beneath them and turned just in time to see the demon pushing the warrior away with little effort, sending him sliding over the painted battlefield. Silver Wolf shot back at the demon with a flurry of cast stones, distracting Kaliton and giving him the chance to run over to his brother.

"This distraction is becoming dangerously dull," the demon called out in warning.

"Time to test the gods' plan," the older brother said, his eyes still fixed on the demon.

"I don't know if I can." Silver Wolf shook his head. "I've never put a spell on anything before."

"Try," the elder brother urged. "Coat this in water." He held out the bared blade to him.

"You can't honestly be finished already?" the demon asked, strolling in their direction.

"I'll try." The light twin placed his hands to the flat of his brother's blade, calling the water to his hands, droplets dripping from his fingers, and ordered it to flow around the weapon. Immediately the sword absorbed the spell, sucking in the water and its energies like a cloth and beginning to glow bright green.

"If you'll not be coming after me—" Kaliton called from thirty paces away. Then in a blink, he was right beside them. "—then I'll have to come after you instead."

The sorcerer scrambled to get out of the way while his brother shot forward, slicing the demon's chest, even as Kaliton brought his claws down and raked them over the warrior's back.

Red and black blood poured out from the combatants as they broke apart. The demon snarled, his inky blood running through his fingers, while the hulking werewolf backed up a few paces, his bared teeth forming half a growl and half a grimace.

Green light flowed over Black Wolf's wounds; the sorcerer hurried back over to help repair the damage, only Kaliton's injury was healing just as quickly without any magical aid.

"It didn't work," said Black Wolf.

"The blade was glowing," his brother insisted.

He shook his head. "Not when I hit him with it. It must need to be cast at the same time as the strike."

"And how am I supposed to do that?"

"Cast your spell and try to hit the demon at the same time I do."

"I'll hit you."

"Aim carefully." Then the warrior was off, charging the greater demon who stood ready for him.

Mind racing, fingers fidgeting, the sorcerer thought through his spells. Wind was powerful but difficult to direct. Water was precise but not as powerful. He saw Black Wolf pull back his sword, the strike imminent. No time to think. He shot forth a dozen flaming arrows, bright, intense, and furious. Each streaked past his brother, who was already in mid-swing.

In a moment of contempt, Kaliton turned his attention toward the barrage of flaming ballista, leaving himself wide open to the sword attack coming from his left. It was a clear message to the warrior that the creature considered him no threat at all. What the monster didn't see was that two of the caster's arrows had bent toward the weapon in his brother's hands and bled into the metal, causing it to glow first green, then white as a star.

Black Wolf aimed the shining weapon directly at the demon's right arm. The blow passed the invisible magical barrier without resistance or a moment's hesitation, passing through its target like a soft cheese.

Kaliton's arm fell to the ground, rolling some ways away down the slope, oozing black blood. The greater demon watched its retreat in blatant disbelief, frozen in shock. Then he screamed, crying out in pain and fury, his free hand clutching the blackened stump of his right arm, cauterized by the magic's intensity.

Not wanting to lose his momentum, the warrior followed up the strike by plunging his sword deep into his opponent's gut. This cut off the monster's screams, doubling him over with further pain, but the sword had lost its glow. Kaliton shifted to smoke in the next instant, passing his body around the weapon and his attacker, rematerializing behind the wolf-man.

Face contorted with rage, Kaliton appeared behind Black Wolf, swatting him away with the back of his remaining hand, sending the warrior careening away, rolling down the slope like the severed appendage. Silver Wolf leapt up and charged after his brother, standing before him where he finally landed. He could hear his brother coughing and spitting behind him, the metal tang of blood floating in the air. He needed time to recover. Looking up the slope, the sorcerer saw the demon approaching, slowly walking down the slope, fury and vengeance carved into every line. He was pleased to note that Kaliton's arm hadn't come back after his smoke trick—it seemed the wounds inflicted by god-power weren't so easy to mend—but that didn't mean he wasn't still dangerous. Silver Wolf's hands began glowing, ready to defend his brother, or at least distract the monster, until the creature started speaking.

"Now that," panted Kaliton, sounding winded for the first time, "was unexpected."

"Why are you doing this?" the younger twin called back. He was partially trying to buy more time for his brother's werewolf strength to heal him, but also to understand, from the demon's perspective, what this was all about.

"Why?" The dark figure paused a step, head cocked in contemplation of the question. "I am a greater demon, one of the oldest creatures on Eris, with powers beyond mortal understanding. Why would I need a reason for anything?"

"You have to have a reason," the caster insisted. "Even the gods have their wants and motivations. Demons have to be the same, and this attack is too specific, too deliberate to be random. Is this all for the artifact? For Oriehada? Why do you need it? You seem strong enough."

"Strong enough," the demon echoed softly, as though not understanding, and then threw back his head and laughed long, mad peals of mirth. "You don't even know what the relic is, do you? This is not simply about power. It's about relevance."

"Relevance?" It was Silver Wolf's turn for confusion.

"Demons are dying," Kaliton said with a sour smirk on his lips and his eyes boring into the brothers. "Not we greater demons, of course, but our lesser cousins dwindle by the day."

"We saw plenty of you monsters on the way here," Black Wolf grunted, coming to stand beside him, though he still gripped his side. The caster wondered if he'd broken a rib.

"The decline is slow, but I assure you it's been going on a long time. Faster now, since your breed showed up." The demon spat something gelatinous and sickly yellow on the ground. "Your progenitor was barely around then, but once there was a time when there wasn't a corner of this world that didn't house some dark spawn or other. Demons of every shape, size, and nightmarish description crawled and hunted in every shadow, and now they're merely clinging to its fringes."

"Good riddance," said the elder brother.

"But why do you care?" the younger twin asked, stepping a little further in front of the injured werewolf lest he draw his ire again. "You brought so many lesser demons with you and they're getting slaughtered by the dragons. If you wanted to save them—"

"I don't care about saving them." Kaliton shook his head as if to dismiss the notion.

"Then why—"

"I brought them here so that they could distract the dragons and they've done that fine enough. You are correct that I'm only here for the relic."

"But why?" Silver Wolf urged.

"Because I wondered that myself—why?" Kaliton said it with narrowed eyes. "Why are demons dying out? Why are only demons, dragons, elves, dwarves, and nokken disappearing yet your kind and the humans you breed through are immune? Humans and weres. Why only those two? If all the rest of the Eight are marked by slow death, if the powers that be have picked their favorites, will the greater demons be the next to go extinct?"

"Dragons, elves, dwarves dying?" Silver Wolf shook his head. He didn't understand what Kaliton could be implying. "The other species are dying? What are you talking about?"

"Oh, the effect is slow, incremental, barely noticeable for the moment." Kaliton was looking skyward, a faraway look in those claret eyes. "The others most likely don't even realize it yet, but given enough time, they'll figure it out." A soft, mirthless chuckle escaped him." By that time, though, we'll all be nothing but memories and dust." He threaded his talons through the air as if waving goodbye to their existence.

"Now," Kaliton said in a more engaged tone, shaking off whatever mood had come upon him, "this may all be a part of his grand scheme—"

"Whose grand scheme?" Silver Wolf wanted to understand, wanted to know what the demon did, but the monster wasn't about to be so accommodating.

"But why the humans and why the half-beasts?" he continued as though the sorcerer hadn't asked a question. "Why wouldn't demons, the strongest of the Eight, be chosen?"

"Isn't that obvious?"

"Obvious?" Kaliton blinked at him.

"Demons eat magic, the magic that's in all of us. If there were too many demons, they'd drain the life of every living creature on Eris. Eventually the world itself would become a wasteland. There'd be nothing left for them to consume and they'd all starve to death. Either way, your kind is dust. With humans and weres, at least Eris would have a chance to survive."

Kaliton chuckled. "Oh, there's no hope of that. We're already spinning toward oblivion, whether you can feel it or not. There'll be far greater players wagering on that outcome. I simply want to see if the variables can be changed. If we're all doomed, I want to be the one who sets fire to this sinking ship. I want this world of Eris to go screaming my name into that endless night." His eyes closed, a smile spreading over his slash of a mouth as though savoring the vision of it. When he opened them again, he said, "I'll not be made irrelevant by anyone, not by a mortal, demon, or god." Kaliton looked at the twisted digits of his remaining hand and sneered. "The relic," he said glancing up toward the misty peak, "that's how I'll claim my infamy, my relevance. With the last of my lesser brethren spreading my good works further and faster, our collective, bolstered by that strength, will make one sensational bonfire."

"We won't let you get that far," barked the warrior, stepping back in front of the caster.

"Then it's a good thing I'm tired of playing with you." The demon looked back to the brothers, his left arm dropping to his side. "Let's get on with the business of destroying each other, shall we?"

Both werewolves tensed, ready for the attack, but Kaliton surprised them. The creature, still a ways up the slope, sank to his knees in the bloody, rocky soil, threw back his head, and screamed.

## CHAPTER 37

# *Uphill Battle*

Both wolves clasped their hands over their ears at once. The shrill, piercing scream echoed off the cliffs, making the sound seem to come from every direction, a sonic attack. The creature's voice, seemingly fused with the death cries of a thousand shrieking rats, almost made Silver Wolf fall to his own knees. Only, as terrible as it was, the caster couldn't fathom its use. It didn't appear to be a distraction. The demon was still, not attacking or running, and as much as it was uncomfortable, it wasn't inflicting any real damage, so why?

In the next moment, Silver Wolf felt a trembling beneath his feet. Was Kaliton calling another quake? Was this how he did it?

His brother's hand clamped down on his shoulder and spun him around with such force that he almost toppled over. Then he was staggered by a new reason as he saw what his brother had. Beneath them, the quiet battleground was no longer still. The lesser demons, the ones that Kaliton had brought with him as his distraction, appeared to be going mad. They roared and thrashed and struck out at anything around them, which quite often were their fellow demons. Sprays of blood and flailing limbs cluttered the air about them. Was this the purpose of Kaliton's scream? To drive his followers insane? But why?

Like a river bursting its banks, the horde of lesser demons broke from their line and charged straight up the hill toward the twins. Silver Wolf staggered back in shock. Black Wolf gripped Slayer in both hands, readying himself for the onslaught. Only the horde's charge was not unchallenged. The dragons, apparently freed from their own trance, struck out at the fleeing monsters. Whole legions of them fell to dragon teeth, claws, and fiery breath, though, for all the death raining down upon their numbers, the demons seemed to have lost all concept of self-preservation or retaliation. They ran on without returning a single blow, not even pausing when one or more of their own were cut down just beside them. Their only goal was to climb the rise, mindlessly, unstoppably, unceasingly, to keep climbing until they gained the summit or died trying.

Silver Wolf stared down at the sea of writhing, screaming, crazed demons, thousands of flashing red eyes staring straight back. They were coming at them, a never-ending stream of teeth and hands and wings and pain, and he found that he just couldn't move, he was so transfixed by the coming horror.

A sharp shove to his left shook him from his stupor and send him fairly flying to his left. After launching him, his brother leapt to the other side, sword never lowering, ready to face the charging mass from his new perch.

Only the horde of lesser demons ran straight past them, sparing them not even a glance as they ran straight toward the still form of Kaliton. Red eyes unfocused, mouth still wide, screaming his unnatural scream, the greater demon didn't even seem to notice their advance.

They swarmed him. Body after twisted body threw themselves onto the form of their master, and the next on top of them. They weren't just pinning him, either. Silver Wolf watched in horror as the nightmares bit into the charcoal-gray flesh beneath. Ripping, tearing, screaming, howling—the terrors converged on the greater demon like an avalanche of the worst kind of pain and fear and unimaginable torture.

The young caster clasped his hand to his mouth at the savagery. Nausea churned in the pit of his stomach, threatening to bring up bile. Kaliton's minions, his army he brought to fight the dragons, had turned on him and were now devouring his immortal flesh. Why? How had this happened?

Only the screams could be heard, ironically muffling the sounds of the worse violence happening beneath. He couldn't be sure if the greater demon's voice were still among them or if the horde had succeeded and he'd been silenced. Silver Wolf felt his grip on reality slacken as more and more twisted bodies piled on top of the mound, the dark heap of squirming, crazed forms becoming difficult to recognize as individuals. As he watched, unable to tear his attention away, he thought the nausea must be playing havoc with his eyes too, because the demons appeared to be melting into one another. He shook his head to clear his vision. It must be a warping of his sight—that or the warping of reality in that moment.

Then the whole mass of them quivered as one. With no further warning, huge spikes jutted out through the pile. The beings were impaled, one after another, on each long spear. The mound had taken on the look of the head of a mace half-buried in the dirt, points jutting out at every angle. The lesser demons, the ones he could still see, began to slow their once frantic movement. Each looked as though they were swimming through tar as their flesh fused into the flesh of their fellows beneath.

The mass of demonic bodies solidified, stilled, shuddered, and then laboriously began to unfurl itself like a grotesque flower. First one arm stretched out, impossibly long, bulked, and tipped with five sharp knives at the end of each gnarled finger. Then two legs, thick as tree trunks, hoisted the mass aloft. It boasted no head above broad shoulders, its resemblance to one of the mortal races having run out. The new, unified coalition of lesser demons stood twice as tall as Black Wolf, thick, solid, and imposing. Spikes as large as saplings jutted out from its shoulders and crowned the place its head should've been. The dagger fingers on its one hand twitched, light winking off their tips, while the other appendage, just below the elbow, was a single, long, broad blade.

Examining the thing more closely, Silver Wolf could see individual faces throughout the form, demon faces frozen in a rictus of pain and madness, covering the body's skin in a grim tableau. At its heart, stationed at the core of the new horror, was Kaliton. The greater demon opened his wide, mad, red eyes and smiled, revealing a mouth full of knifelike teeth.

"Blessed by the gods you may be, but you're still no match for me," the demon intoned, and as he did, the other faces covering his skin spoke with him, moving their lips and lending their voices to his taunt. The eerie chorus sent shivers screaming along the sorcerer's spine, raising all the silver fur down his back from ruff to tail.

"Now, I've had quite enough of you two," the massive demon said, taking a step toward the brothers.

"The feeling's mutual," Black Wolf said, leaping as high as he could and bringing his blade down, straight toward the abomination's chest and the greater demon nestled within. The construct caught it easily on its own sword-arm.

His twin's words had snapped Silver Wolf out of his shock and he began calling a spell. It had worked before. All he had to do was imbue his blade with a spell and Black Wolf would cut straight through that sword. He was lucky the warrior had drawn him off a few paces. Kaliton was too far away to strike at him, especially while the swordsmen clashed, distracting one another.

Only it wouldn't be that easy. The creature, while still holding Black Wolf at bay with his arm-blade, flung back with his free hand in the general direction of the caster. Lesser demons, about a dozen of them, flew from the arm, dissolving it for a moment, only for other creatures to shift and reform the appendage. The newly freed fiends charged straight for the sorcerer, eyes blank and wild, spittle or venom dripping from their mouths.

Silver Wolf pivoted, selecting a new target in his mind, a new spell, no longer arrows, but unleashing his gathered energy into a wave of flames. The spell covered the ground, spilling from the caster like a spigot, widening as it ran. The lesser demons struck the divine-magical fire, now a blanket of conflagration covering the terrain before them, and instantly caught the blaze. They screamed and cried as they fell to the ground, charred, blackened, and smoking, but still reaching out with brittle hands toward their intended prey.

His own assailants dealt with, Silver Wolf looked back toward his dark twin. Black Wolf was trying to overcome the giant demon, but it was a contest he couldn't help but lose. The thing housing Kaliton threw its considerable weight behind its next blow, knocking Black Wolf off his feet, soaring away to tumble down the hill again.

Having dealt with the immediate distraction, the monster turned to look at Silver Wolf, the brother with the much-detested gods' blessing. He saw his brother, down the field, leap to his feet, racing back up to engage the nightmare anew. Only the greater demon seemed to be through with him for the moment.

More lesser demons sprang from the collective's back, creating a void briefly before sprinting into battle. They fell upon the charging werewolf without hesitation, totally ignoring the several feet of steel he brandished. Surrounded, Black Wolf slashed out. He hacked at all manner of nightmarish things that reached for him with fin, wing, or snout. None touched him. The warrior sliced them to pieces before they inflicted so much as a scratch, but killing him hadn't really been their objective.

Kaliton walked purposefully across the field, elevated by the bodies all around him to tower over the smaller wolf, but Silver Wolf refused to be intimidated. He'd spent the length of the creature's stroll to gather more power. He knew he should have felt more exhausted after all of this casting, all of the pulling of his resources. It looked like the gods' pact was more potent than he'd guessed.

Taking his gathered energy, Silver Wolf slammed his open palm to the ground, sending a surge rippling through the dirt, breaking and splintering the rock beneath the giant's feet. He hoped to catch him in a pit or trip him up, only the bulky thing was more agile than he'd accounted for. It avoided all pitfalls, bounding over the cracked stone with little effort, coming at him quicker now.

Next, gathering power as quickly as he could, the sorcerer sent a flurry of water spheres. These he aimed directly at the central form of the greater demon. Lesser beasts flew from the torso, throwing themselves before the projectiles and absorbing the force that may not have even hit their target, considering his shield. The dozens of pulped corpses littering its path had been pointless; Silver Wolf had thrown the spell just to delay the greater threat, but by sacrificing his minions Kaliton didn't even break stride as he approached him.

A gale of wind came to Silver Wolf's hands next. He was pulling deep now. The gods' link was strong, but it was only a trickle—he was casting too quickly for it to keep up. He'd be out of options soon. He needed to make this one count. Pulling up every scrap he could, the sorcerer werewolf tossed blades and scythes and sickles out to slice the grim horror to ribbons. He could almost see the magical barrier when his winds hit it. It stopped marching for just a heartbeat, the wind flowing around it and over it but never touching the flesh beneath. When the wind had passed, it moved again.

He took a step back and found rough stone behind him. Exhausted, he put some weight to the barrier penning him in. He spared a glance to check on his older brother. Black Wolf had dispatched the first wave of lesser demons some time before, but there were more. Beyond his seeing, Kaliton had most likely sent more and more from his back. Their opponent had recognized the danger and was keeping them apart, effectively it would seem.

With no help, his back butting up against the cliff, and the hulking demon looming over him, Silver Wolf could feel cold dread gathering in the pit of his stomach, only dulled by his fatigue. How had they—how had the gods or anyone else—ever dreamed that they could kill an immortal?

Kaliton seemed to read his mind. "Honestly, you didn't think this would end any other way, did you?" He raised one massive hand, stretching out the tension of the moment before he cut the caster down.

"Yes, I did, and I still do." He opened his hands, palms together and stretched out, a brilliant bloom of flames bursting from the padded digits. The spell was close, but not too close. It wrapped around the monster's chest, flowing off its natural shield, only it wasn't just heat. It was so bright, so intensely gleaming, that it momentarily blinded the greater demon at the heart of the construct, the other faces around it crying out in surprise.

It didn't end there. In the next moment, a flash of metal cut through the flames, absorbing the power, stealing its light, and slicing into the flesh golem's mottled gray side. The resulting gash gushed gore onto the rock in a tsunami. Kaliton cried out in surprised pain, echoed by the chorus of demonic skin-faces.

He could see Black Wolf's white grin flash through the dissipating sparks and smoke. It was a deep wound, surprising the foul beast and knocking it off balance, sending the colossus falling away. Except the hulking horror proved itself more capable yet again.

Using the momentum of the dark twin's blow, Kaliton whirled his construct, swinging wide his right hand and catching the warrior with four of its long, blade-tipped fingers. They sliced easily through fur and flesh alike. Garish red trails of blood flew like banners of war in their wake. Black Wolf collapsed to his knees, Kaliton continuing his spin and staggering away from them.

The dark form steadied itself, the face at the heart of the creature radiating hate, staring blazing eyes toward them as though they alone could burn them to ash. "You just don't know when to lay down and die."

The demon reared back a giant hand, knees bent, ready to leap back and take another gouge out of Black Wolf's hide.

Silver Wolf was tapped. His reserve of energy was drained, exhaustion was pulling him down, and even as he felt the gods' energies trickling back in, it wouldn't be enough. He didn't have the energy to save his brother, but those talons were falling.

Without thought, his training with Dexus kicked in. He hadn't learned much from the drake outside of using his own natural strength and agility, but he had learned he could trust more than his magic when it came to a fight. His fingers wrapped around the grip at his belt; like the ring around his neck, this piece of metal was a constant companion. He pulled the silver blade from its leather sheath, gripping it tightly in his hand and running at the sinister titan, the weapon flashing at his side.

The caster plunged the dwarf-made hunting knife into the still-open gash in the creature's side. The silver vanished up to the hilt, cutting through muscle and softer tissues and pushing out more black ichor. Kaliton bucked, arching his back and screaming in pain, his swing going wide and missing his target.

Silver Wolf lost his grip on the blade, Brywyn's labor vanishing into the demonic mass, but he had one more trick. He didn't have much power, but perhaps he had just a trickle. Sucking in a breath, squeezing his eyes shut, and flexing every muscle, Silver Wolf planted his palm to the stone. In response, pillars of stone jutted upward, one, three, five. They slammed into the towering body, still reaching for the metal thorn in its side, and thrust it away down the slope, rolling and tumbling and kicking up dust and ruble in its wake.

The caster dove to his twin's side. "Brother. You'll be alright. Get up."

"Go," he snarled in reply, blood seeping out between his fingers where he clutched his fresh wounds.

"What?"

"We can't beat him this way. Need to get away. Regroup. Now go."

"Fine. Then get up and we'll find a place to hide and heal."

"I'll be right behind you."

"No. You didn't leave me in the forest; I'm not going to leave you here. Come on." Silver Wolf grabbed his brother by the arm. He'd hoist him to his feet if he had to. They'd hide and then they'd come back. They'd— His thoughts were cut off as he felt a jolt from behind.

## CHAPTER 38

# The Demon of Blades

Silver Wolf's guts burned. He felt like he'd swallowed the sun, like he was on fire—sharp, hot fire. He couldn't imagine what could be causing it, what was making him feel so much pain.

He looked down. A wide, dark plane of metal, nearly half as broad as he was wide, protruded from his torso. It glistened wet in the light, wet with blood, his blood.

He looked up. Two sets of violet eyes connected then, both filled with pain and confusion, unable to understand what was happening. His brother looked to him, asking what he should do, only Silver Wolf didn't know.

Before either of them could say a word, the caster was pulled off his feet, hoisted skyward in a wide arch by the sword through his middle. The greater demon lifted the younger twin aloft for all to see, like a grisly banner proclaiming his victory.

"I am Kaliton, Demon of Blades," he roared, "and now I've shown that not even the gods are an obstacle to me." With his free hand the demon pulled the silvery hunting knife from the wound at his side and cast it away, the blade pitted and half-melted from its exposure to demonic blood. The slice that the knife had caused ceased bleeding almost instantly, but the gash Black Wolf had caused was still there. The monster was breathing a bit heavier. The cut on his side hadn't vanished, but he showed no other signs of damage, no other signs that they had even bothered him. In the end they hadn't been able to kill a greater demon.

Hanging limply, feeling the burning radiating from the hole in his gut, eyes squeezed tightly, Silver Wolf heard a voice in his ear, words spoken only for him. "I am sorry you'll not be here to witness the wreckage I make of this crumbling shambles of a planet. Regrettable, but don't worry. The world won't be far behind you."

Stunned silence filled the field, or at least that's how it seemed to the sorcerer. Kaliton was so sure of his words, so sure he'd already won. Had he?

The sorcerer opened his eyes and gazed into the sky and was disappointed to find it gray. Puffy storm clouds covered the sky like a pall over these grim proceedings. Perhaps it was his own funeral shroud. He didn't want it to be, and he didn't want gray to be the last thing he saw. If he were going to die, here, like this, the gods could've at least given him a blue sky, bright, brilliant, and endless.

Pain roared through him. He couldn't argue with that. Only there wasn't as much as he thought there ought to be. Maybe he was just starting to lose feeling in his extremities, but the sensation felt hollow, distant, as though he were feeling the echo of someone else's anguish. Padded digits went to the sword through his middle, checking that it was still there. It was.

It felt wrong to be dying in such a way, wrong that he should have a living sword sticking through his abdomen, wrong that such a thing should even have existed. He didn't have the strength to deal with the demon, but this abominable thing, he thought he could do something about.

He pulled, the agony of which cleared his head some. He dug deep, summoning the dregs of his strength, every scrap of energy he could, and gathered that power—of him, of Eris, of the gods—pushing it onto one hand. Blazing light like an otherworldly green sun enveloped both himself and his attacker, and Silver Wolf pressed his open palm to the flat of the blade and released its power.

"Not yet," he said softly.

That close, past the magical shield, with physical contact, the energy couldn't miss. The blade shattered. Dozens of black shards and inky ichor flew from the explosion. Kaliton reared back and Silver Wolf, with nothing left to hold him up, fell.

It was like a dream, time moving like tree sap in autumn, falling with bits of black stars twinkling all around him. It ended sooner than he thought it should have. He landed hard on the ground a moment later with a bone-jarring *thud*.

Kaliton was letting loose a series of wild screams of agony as he pulled back a bloody stump where his sword-arm had been. Silver Wolf wanted to feel some satisfaction, but he hurt too much. Hands on his shoulders, rolling him to his back, brought him back to the moment.

"Brother." Black Wolf held him, one arm supporting his back and head, the other hovering above the ruin of his guts. "What can I do? Tell me what to do."

"Nothing to do," the younger twin ground out.

"There must be something. If I can get you out of here, you'll have time to heal."

"Can't." He shook his head, which was a mistake. Then he clarified. "Can't heal this."

"You're a werewolf; you can heal this scratch."

"Poison."

Silver Wolf felt the arm holding him tense.

"What poison?" his dark twin asked him in a quiet voice.

"From the blade."

He watched the warrior look him over, hollow horror reflecting in his eyes. The hand that'd been hovering over his torso a moment before descended then. There was a sharp stab of pain that he barely recognized over the multitude of other parts that were screaming at him, and he saw his brother holding a piece of glistening, black, living metal. His twin held the shard of Kaliton's sword between his thumb and forefinger, turning it in the dim light, the artifact dripping black from each oozing edge. Realization dawned on him then, a realization Silver Wolf had already come to.

"The sword is of his body," Black Wolf said quietly, slowly. "Demon blood is acidic, poisonous."

"There are more shards, more blood, more ichor," Silver Wolf said grimly, putting his bloodstained hand to the edge of his gaping wound. "And it burns."

Black Wolf had been looking at the shard but turned his eyes back to him when he spoke. "It's because you shattered the blade." He dropped the cursed thing; it made a chiming *clang* sound when it landed, just like real metal. His brother took him in both hands, shaking him just a bit. "You should've left it. I would've made him put you down. I could've gotten to you—"

"My choice." He sighed painfully against the agony. "I had to take that thing away from him. Now you, you have a job to do. I took his sword—you need to take his head."

"I can't defeat him. Not alone."

Silver Wolf's breath was heavy, labored. "I don't think I feel up to fighting anymore today. It has to be you. It was always—always going to be you."

"You have the power; I only have a sword. Kaliton can be defeated only when both of us are together. That's why we were born twins."

"Can't be, because I'm dying and we're not done yet."

"Right," his brother said, giving his shoulder another shake. "*We're not done yet.*"

"Have you no faith in destiny?" He smiled, a sickly ghost of a thing, but he hoped his twin could understand.

"Brother." He could hear the word sticking in his throat as he said it.

"I have faith in you. You'll kill Kaliton. You'll save us all."

"I, I can't—"

"You can. I know you can and I know you will. I'll just wait for you here."

Silver Wolf could feel the venom racing up from his shredded guts toward his chest. It wasn't just that it was dissolving his insides—not that that wasn't bad enough—but it had a far sinister plan. Silver Wolf's blood would use his own body against him. That black plasma had gotten into his bloodstream and would travel straight to his heart. As the traitorous organ cycled blood throughout his body, it would pull the darkness into it and burn him from his core. Werewolves were a robust species, and Silver Wolf even more so with the gods bolstering him, but not even he could live without a heart.

"Goodbye, brother."

He shut his eyes then. He was tired, he was hurt, and he was done. He shut his eyes to show his brother that he wasn't afraid, that his dying was almost like he was going to sleep, and he shut them so that he wouldn't have to watch his brother's heart break.

He felt his brother pull him in, felt him press their foreheads together, and felt two drops fall on his own cheeks. Then he heard him whisper one word. "Aaron."

## CHAPTER 39

## *The Fires of Rebirth*

Even with his eyes shut, Silver Wolf was staggered to discover that he could still see. It was hazy and not quiet "seeing"—more of a dim sort of comprehension—but he was still aware of everything. He "saw" his brother, holding him, silently weeping over his still form.

His chest tightened. He hadn't wanted to see this. He'd wanted to give both of them this moment of weakness, unwitnessed, but still together—him dying and his brother his moment of grief. The sensation of these raw emotions, the extra feelings that observing them caused, pulled the poison nearer to his core as his heart clenched with its own kind of pain.

The whole world stilled while the brothers mourned, or so it seemed to him. The world held its breath, his brother's tears flowed, and his heart beat its last rhythm. Only time never really stops for anything.

In his strange half-perception, Silver Wolf could see something else. It was a figure, a dark shadow looming up behind his dark twin. Kaliton, wild red eyes focused on his brother, all of his faces contorted in rage, raised his left hand. Even though he'd taken his sword, the Demon of Blades would never be unarmed and the five daggerlike claws were poised to strike.

He couldn't allow this. He wouldn't allow it. He wanted to cry out, he wanted to warn his brother, only his body wouldn't respond. His insides were half melted, his abdomen was flayed and open to the sky, his very blood was laced with demon blood racing toward a very fragile, very vital organ, the last thing keeping him alive. His body had nothing left to give. There was no breath and no energy left to him to shout his warning. Kaliton had beaten him utterly. The younger wolf may not be dead yet, but his body was nearly there, shattered and useless. It was over. The greater demon would win, the dragons would be slaughtered, Eris herself could be in danger, and they were both going to die.

A different sort of heat, apart from the poison, came to his attention then, a heat emanating from his chest instead of his guts, a burning emotion: anger. Silver Wolf was suddenly flooded with righteous indignation at a world that'd placed them in such an impossible situation and expected them to succeed. It was absurd. Even the gods, who'd sent the seers their visions of this miraculous victory, had said it was impossible, and now he and his brother were going to die for their own arrogance in believing in someone else's folly. Anger, that simple, primary emotion, burned within him, hotter and hotter, adding to the conflagration brought on by the venom. It would consume him, burn him up so that there'd be nothing left to bury, nothing left for Kaliton to desecrate. He would simply blow away on the breeze.

Only his thoughts changed again. It was a stupid, delirious thought brought on by the heat no doubt, but what if they could? What if the impossible dream was, in fact, true? The anger within him paused at the notion, as did his breath and his heart. Did he have faith in his destiny like he told his brother? What if the prophecy were true and they could do what the seers had said? What if they could defeat a greater demon? What if they could save the world from this one nightmare? Not just his brother, but both of them. What if he mattered too? What if they were strong enough to defeat the darkness? Together?

It was crazy, stupid. He was dying and his twin was a breath away from his own death, but the question remained, ringing in his mind. What if they could?

The heat built again, but not the flame of anger, which seemed to have fizzled out somehow, but a new flame. Each successive thought added fuel to this new fire, burning in his core. It was different from his anger, and it had nothing to do with Kaliton's filth. It was warm, but not burning, not scalding. This fire was not dark—it didn't mean to turn him to ash—but bright and gleaming, a flame to light his way. Hope pulled at the sorcerer's power the way his heart had pulled at his tainted blood. He hadn't thought he had any energy left, but the gods still fed him that trickle, and he knew from his training that a body could never fully deplete itself. So the energy gathered from the tips of his ears, from his fingertips to his toes, from the edges of his shoulder blades to the length of his tail, all collecting, concentrating in his very center, over his faithful heart, until it seemed to burst in a brilliant green light.

His temperature continued to rise, feeling alight with it, but not in a painful way. He could feel the heat running joyfully through his veins, feel the moment it made contact with the dark poison, and he had the sensation that the noxious liquid boiled at its touch. The caster could feel the demonic blood turning to vapor, propelled along by his still beating heart and purging itself from his system, fading away like smoke on the wind, until he couldn't detect it at all.

Free from the blight, he was surprised to find himself, despite his egregious wounds, buoyant, almost like he was floating. It was a wonderful sensation, especially compared to moments before when he'd been sure he was dying, and filled with the glow of possibilities. Was this what dying felt like? No, the poison was gone, his heart felt warm and strong, his brain had suffered no injury, and he was a werewolf. As long as he had those two organs, theoretically he could live through any injury.

He floated higher, lifted by the warmth and the energy. Turning and looking down at the world tinged with a green hue, the sorcerer locked eyes with his brother. He was on his feet, staring up at him. Disbelief was etched into the dark wolf's every feature. The younger twin chuckled to see it. No doubt his older brother was shocked by his miraculous healing. Still, there was no time to be impressed. They had a demon to slay.

Silver Wolf swiveled again, casting his eyes for the behemoth. He found him not far away, but paused in his trek back to their position. The demon seemed momentarily frozen to the spot, staring at him much like his brother had, each face along his skin reflecting the same surprise.

Then Kaliton shook himself and snarled. "I don't know what trick you think you're trying now, but it won't be enough to stop me. I am Kaliton, a greater demon, the Demon of Blades, an immortal, and you two are nothing but sheep driven by those in power that you can't even see."

Silver Wolf hung there, feeling a strange mixture of calm and disgust for the being standing below him.

When he didn't answer Kaliton took another step forward and continued his rant. "I won't be stopped here. I won't be killed, and I won't fade into the obscurity of the dark. I am a force unto myself. I have the power to effect change, and once I have the relic I will have more. I will change this story. I and every other demon will not vanish into the void with nothing but a whisper!"

He shook his head almost sadly. Maybe it was his higher vantage point, but Kaliton looked smaller to him now. Without responding, he looked back to the black werewolf. He looked less surprised now. He looked ready, Slayer clasped tightly in his fist. The twins stared into each other's eyes, a whole conversation exchanged without a single word. The possibility that they could defeat this scourge existed, and all of them knew it.

Without any clear signal, the warrior spun to face their enemy. Kaliton took one final glance at the sorcerer before directing his attention back to the brother wielding the weapon.

"I'll not be making the journey to that oblivion alone," the Demon of Blades said darkly.

They charged. It was like watching two titanic forces of nature, avalanche and forest, sea and surf, pitting themselves against the other, both bent on the destruction of the other.

The sorcerer glided down to fly alongside his twin, joining his headlong rush toward the hideous nightmare. They'd face Kaliton together.

Out of the corner of his eye, Silver Wolf saw Slayer begin to shine. He thought it a trick of his green-tinted vision, but it wasn't. The weapon shone as brightly as though he'd thrown a spell at it and increased its intensity the nearer he came. He moved as close as he could, and the whole mountain lit up with their light. Light with dark, the twins moved as one.

Kaliton lunged, his massive blade-tipped hand slicing at the opposing force. Black Wolf ducked. The talons shredded through the air just above his head. The warrior grabbed his sword in both hands and thrust upward.

The sorcerer glimpsed just a moment of stunned surprise in the demon's wide eyes before the gray wolf drifted with the blade on its path toward the dark flesh. He embraced Slayer, giving the tool every ounce of his intent and strength. The blade made contact with the demon's chest.

The sword pierced the spot as easily as cutting through paper. The skin around the strike was instantly charred and curled away from its edge as it plunged deeper. Blood boiled and muscle shriveled deeper and deeper. Silver Wolf shared his wish with his brother, with Slayer, with the world—to cleanse this blight from their lives. They found the strength to reach the center of Kaliton's core, his chest.

The space felt more hollow than he thought it should. The demon's chest was like a dried cave with the bellows of his lungs billowing in the back and the great stalactite of his heart hanging out above dark depths. There was little time to observe as the sword's tip pushed forward still and found Kaliton's heart. The dragon steel connected with the shadowy, twisted thing that pulsed with malice, and it shuddered with the impact. Silver Wolf took one moment to regard it, then stretched out fingers of flame to burn it away even as Slayer cut straight through. The organ stopped beating, solidifying, burning, crumbling at their combined touch, and still they would not cease. Drawn on by the conviction that there should be no trace of the demon left, the caster surged ahead followed by the sword, past the detritus of the heart, tearing through the lungs, through and through until they burst forth, sword and sorcerer, straight out of Kaliton's back.

## CHAPTER 40

# *Visions of Another Age*

The caster, freed from the dark, soared high into the air and spun around. He hovered, waiting, watching to see what Kaliton would do next. Only the enormous beast stood perfectly still. Everything seemed to stand still, as if history itself were waiting to see the outcome, and perhaps it was.

After that moment, after that eternity, Kaliton fell to his knees. From his vantage, Silver Wolf could see the twin plumes of dust kicked up by the impact, viewed through the hole in his chest. Immediately after, the body began to crumble, breaking into pieces and particles like ash. The faces vanished and the bulk of the thing split and broke and shattered until the greater demon was reduced to a pile of fine dust.

The wind danced a solemn waltz as it picked up specks of the once greater demon and carried them away. The warrior stepped forward and pushed through the ashen hill at his feet with the blade of Slayer, still dark with Kaliton's blood. The sorcerer thought he saw bits of charred bone, even a skull, the jagged teeth bared below sockets void of their mad red light. All of it crumbled like an illusion in the snow, leaving nothing to attest to anything being there at all.

Grimly satisfied, Black Wolf sheathed the sword and gazed up at his brother. They stared wordlessly at one another until the older twin gave one sure nod.

The light twin's heart nearly burst with the joy of it. They had defeated the darkness. They'd defeated an immortal greater demon. They had saved the dragons' city, the gods' relic, and quite possibly the world, and both brothers were still alive.

His joy carried him higher, flying, soaring into the misty sky. Driving up and up, he rose until he broke through the heavy clouds and glimpsed the bright blue sky, clean and crisp and full of light. The clouds, so fluffy and light from his vantage, reminded him of their flock, of his youth, of the stories their mother had told them, and of hope. He felt that hope, warm and secure, in the center of his chest.

He dove back down, returning to the shadow of the overcast sky, but the bright green light was ever at the edges of his vision, making things appear a little less dim. Using this new power of flight he'd somehow acquired, the sorcerer plummeted back toward the ground, exulting in the speed and the freedom of it, swooping up just before the ground. He hovered, feeling himself grinning from ear to ear, and glanced to his twin to see his reaction. The black werewolf, still standing straight as the warrior, his face still set, still grim, showed no signs of joy or triumph. The younger brother glided closer, giving his full attention to his elder.

The darker twin studied him in turn. He didn't speak, didn't move beyond his eyes scanning over him, filled with concern and reflected green light. What could possibly trouble him so badly? Silver Wolf wanted to take his shoulders and shake him, to scream at him that they'd won, that they'd proven themselves to be true god-chosen champions, and that they'd won, but that look, his brother's clear worry and confusion, stopped him. He wanted to ask about that too, but before he could the dark werewolf turned and ran back toward where they'd begun their mad dash to vanquish the demon.

The sorcerer easily kept pace with him, lighter and faster than he'd ever been. He followed until his older brother halted abruptly, catching sight of something that stopped him like a stone wall. He'd flown a little further and turned back. Black Wolf was staring, mesmerized by something on the ground, his look changed from worry and confusion to a grimace of sheer pain.

The caster turned to look, somewhat afraid of what he might see, but too curious not to. What could have caused his indomitable, fearless hero of a brother such pain? When he'd fully turned, when he'd seen what his brother had, when he understood, Silver Wolf felt his breath catch in his chest.

It was him. His body, broken and gutted, lay there on the battlefield, oozing blood and looking as dead as the stones around it.

The sorcerer couldn't understand. He wasn't dead. He was there; he'd helped his brother kill Kaliton. He couldn't be dead.

He glided closer. His eyes were closed like he was sleeping and his chest moved, so he knew he wasn't dead, but the rhythmic breathing seemed shallow. He wasn't dead, but was he dying? And if he was dying, if that was his body, where was he? What was he?

The implications sent ripples of panic surging through him. There were questions he couldn't answer. Pains he didn't feel. Things he'd done, but had no idea how he'd done them. Was he some kind of ghost?

Suddenly, the sorcerer started to feel something. It was a pull, a strong jerk at the very core of his being. Was this dying? Was he being pulled into the afterlife, to the realm of the gods? But he hadn't even spoken to his brother yet. He couldn't die without telling him how proud he was of them both, of how hard they'd fought to survive. The more he raged against the pull, the more the drag intensified. Struggling, fighting, screaming inside his mind, he was drawn by the pull down into darkness, into nothing. He tried to thrash, to scream, and yet nothing seemed to affect the dark. Then he heard a soft *click* echo in his ears. At least he thought he'd heard it. He might have felt it, a sound like something fitting back exactly where it belonged.

Against all hope or sense, the caster opened his eyes. He blinked blearily until Black Wolf's concerned face filled his vision.

"Brother," Silver Wolf rasped through blood-crusted lips.

Without answer or warning, the older twin pulled him into a sudden embrace. There was relief in that embrace, and joy, and love. The younger returned it as fiercely as his broken body would allow. The pain was forgotten in the exultation of the moment. They'd done it, and they were both still there.

After a second, after an eternity, they pulled apart from each other.

He had to swallow to moisten his parched throat. "Are you alright?"

Black Wolf gave a puff of laughter and a lopsided smile, but he wasn't looking at him anymore. He'd seen something when his brother's shoulder had heaved, something behind him, that stole all of his attention.

A bird, hanging effortlessly in the air with only the occasional flap of its wings, studied the brothers serenely. To call it a bird was inaccurate, though. It was massive, its wingspan as wide as Silver Wolf's own outstretched arms. With a long and graceful neck and thin legs, the creature sported a long tail that flowed behind it in feathers reminiscent of ribbons. Yet the most startling detail was that it was composed entirely of green flame glowing steadily as a hearth in midwinter.

"What is that?" he whispered.

His twin turned to look at the bird and then back to his brother. "Shouldn't you know?"

"How would I know? I've never seen anything like that before."

"Because it came out of you."

"Out of me?" he asked in alarm, looking at the speaker and then back at the bird. As if summoned, the bright creature flapped toward them, leaving a soft green afterimage in its wake. The warrior moved aside and let the bird alight on his brother's raised knee despite the sorcerer's clear trepidation.

It didn't burn him. In fact, he didn't feel any heat, at least not any more than he'd expect from any other living thing. The younger twin was also surprised to find that the bird weighed so little, and then he was surprised again that it weighed anything at all, for all that it was made of fire. As large as it was, this close he could swear the bird would stand up to his hip. The avian felt like no more than a songbird perched atop his knee. It leaned in toward him, giving the caster a close view of its sharp, hooked beak. It regarded him, blinking smooth, pupilless eyes. They were like jade-green marbles in the flaming face, the only part of the animal that seemed wholly solid aside from that hooked beak and talons. This was no mindless killer, though. There was intelligence in those glistening orbs; that was abundantly clear based on the intensity with which it stared at him. It looked expectant, as though waiting for him to do or say something. But what could he possibly say to a bird? A bird he'd never seen before, a bird made of fire—

The answer was suddenly obvious, seeing that the thing was on fire, but there was more. "It's a construct. I summoned a construct."

His mind whirled with the thought, his vision narrowing down to the bright green creature and its ever-shifting plumage. He'd called a construct, though with no memory about how he'd actually done it. If he had called it, then it should be composed of his magic, and it was clearly his spring-green color, but fire too. How did that work?

The caster stretched out a tentative hand. He felt his brother tense beside him, clearly nervous that he'd hurt himself, but he didn't interfere as he made to touch the creature's chest.

The caster drew his hand back immediately, but out of surprise instead of pain. The bird had been cool to the touch. His fingers hadn't met anything solid, instead passing right through the feathers, like trying to touch mist as opposed to fire. He looked at his digits to see if anything had changed with them. The construct gave a cry, clearly annoyed at Silver Wolf's timidity.

"What are you trying to tell me?" he asked the magical creature, shifting from one foot to another as it stared at him. It glared at him. "Then tell me."

The light twin reached out again. He put his hand back to the construct, not recoiling at the chill this time. He let his hand sink below the magical flames, only the avian didn't seem to be made of anything solid. Was the creature truly only fire? No core at all?

The creature parted its wings, welcoming the wolf to delve deeper. Steeling himself, he pressed on, feeling his fingers descend into the body of the construct. It felt like his arm was traveling farther than the bird should have allowed, but then again magic often played by its own rules. Then, suddenly, he found a momentary resistance. Did it have a core after all? He felt around it, trying to decide if it was a sphere or if it actually had any kind of organs. He pushed a little deeper, through the resistance, through the barrier, and found nothing—no resistance, no mist, nothing cool or hot. The inside of the bird appeared to be a void.

At once his mind was flooded with light and images. He no longer saw the bird, or his brother, or the mountain; only light and color filled his vision, filled his mind, so much so that there was no longer any room for input from the rest of his senses. His heart raced and his breathing was clipped and shallow as his body struggled with the sudden onslaught.

It took him time for him, for his mind, to adjust, to start to make sense of the things he was seeing. The first image he recognized was of the bright green bird swirling around him and his brother, wrapping them in that bright green light. The scene skipped, and they were in Fen Ryok's reception room, then the Hall of Dreams in the presence of the four Gods of Eris. He and his twin were speaking to them animatedly, the gods responding much the same, only there was no sound to these images. Whatever they were discussing, he couldn't hear the words. Then he was pulled from the darkness of the hall and into the blinding sun. He saw a ship riding the open seas, silent spray and gulls flying through the bright air. His brother stood at one of the rails, black hair and tan skin shining under the sun and kissed by the sea breezes as the ship cut through the dark waves. He looked deep in thought. The young man closed his eyes, pulling in a great lung full of the salty air, and let it out, opening his eyes again, focused ahead to the course of the ship, toward their destination.

Silver Wolf wondered at these images, wondered why he was seeing them and what they could mean, but he had very little time to contemplate it as the scene changed again. The images flew faster now—him in a great library, him in the forest and then a village, him in human form. Faster and faster, the scenes changed until the vision was as a raging storm of faces and places, of people and time beyond knowing. He could scarcely breathe for the intensity of the feelings that accompanied each flash. Satisfaction, joy, love, pain, focus, determination—the emotions ripped through him, felt with such passion and conviction and then forgotten as the next asserted itself. Each feeling, each face was an individual he knew well and yet had never met.

Just when Silver Wolf feared his mind would explode with so much knowledge and so many questions, the images began to slow once again. They settled for a moment on a clear picture of a white-covered landscape, barren and frozen. The sky was clear and blue but as cold as the land wrapped in a blanket of deep snow. The land showed few details— mountains in the distance, a rock standing above the white here and there, but no trees, no signs of life, except for between a cluster of larger stones in the center of his vision. He saw his brother, older, but how much he couldn't tell, his black werewolf fur coat insulating him from the chill. He was standing in a sort of doorway sheltered by the boulders. Some breeze slipped past the stone barrier as Silver Wolf saw the fur stir around his hard violet eyes. The great warrior stood in the snow, regarding a trio of visitors standing on his doorstep. A man and a woman in fine clothes and cloaks stood with a child between them, both with a hand on the youth's shoulder as they spoke with his brother. The boy, who couldn't have been more than ten years old, remained silent. Only the sorcerer could see the clear and determined look in his intelligent, golden eyes.

Then the scene changed. He still saw the snow-covered hills, only now the man and woman were gone and his brother and the boy were out standing in it. The boy stood shin-deep in the white, cloak discarded as he crossed wooden blades with the black wolf. When the practice swords touched he saw his twin speak. The child nodded, face furrowed in concentration, swinging again and again and again.

The vision jumped again. The world was no longer the bright white of the field, but the darker tones of the forest, though the forest floor still bore signs of the frigid temperatures. The boy, slightly older, was running blindly through the trees, snapping branches and tearing his way through the undergrowth. The sorcerer sensed pain, raw and fresh and aching, radiating off of the youth like heat. Silver Wolf wanted to close his eyes against the feelings, feelings he recognized and knew so well. He wanted to reach out a hand, to reassure the young man that this surely was not the end of his story, that there was so much more to look forward to, only he was an observer. He had no voice, no body, no self in this place.

The boy disappeared in a flash, taking his painful emotions with him. This time Silver Wolf found his perspective showed him the top of a mountain, blue skies above him, clouds below him down the gray slopes of the mountain. He could tell at once that he wasn't in the Shei Denti. He was in some other mountain range, and he wasn't alone. A little girl, golden hair whipping about her face, illuminated by the shining light of the dawn, sat on the edge of the peak, facing the rising sun. She was also wrapped in a cloak, bundled well against the high altitude and mountain winds, all of her except for her hands. She held out her tiny, bare hands, holding them a bit apart. The sorcerer's eyes grew wide as he saw her begging to collect power between open palms. Dazzling sky-blue light, the exact color of her widening eyes, lit up her face, perfectly highlighting her wonder and joy.

The golden rays of the sun and the blue of the girl's power battled to be the brightest, until all he saw were the two colors, gold and blue.

The vision surged on after that, again going so quickly that Silver Wolf couldn't make sense of most of it. There were more people, more places, more emotions, and then he began to notice flashes of the youths—an image of the boy, a flash of the girl, and then a scene of them together in the darkness of a rain-soaked forest. The vision seemed to follow them more closely. He couldn't pick out much, the moments and colors always changing, never settling on one. He'd see them laughing with friends, fighting terrible creatures, speaking with dragons, and dealing with gods. Their lives flew through his mind so fast that he felt exhausted, his insides churning with all of the thoughts and feelings that traveled in their wake. There was so much story between these two, full of victories and losses, jubilation and sorrow, sweetness and pain.

Then the vision stopped. Everything was black, though not the darkness of the gods' void. This was the ordinary sort of darkness that comes of being hidden from the sun. He waited, knowing he was still in the vision, and then he saw the sky-blue light. It illuminated a cave and a river running through it. The girl sat with her hands raised, radiating the cheery glow, in a tiny boat hurtling down the underground river like a leaf in a gale. She shared her vessel with seven other occupants, all of whom were on guard, some with blades drawn. The boy, a man now, was at their head, his teeth and sword bared, and Silver Wolf saw why. On that river beneath the surface of the world, they were beset by a horde of lesser demons. The creatures were hard to see in the gloom despite the girl's attempt to show them. Red glittering eyes and hooked claws reached out from the shadows toward the watercraft. The sorcerer felt his own heart race, in part sharing the terror of the others, in part remembering his own battle so recently fought. The demons were all around them, outnumbering the boat's occupants and threatening to swamp them on that advantage alone, until a new color was added to the twilight. The blue light was bolstered by this new color in holding off the gray shadows, and the bright twin gasped when he glimpsed it. His own familiar green flames, clinging to the roof of the cavern, shot forward with purpose and intent and flooded the cavern with heat and light, bringing the noonday sun into the darkness of the cavern's interior.

Everything was wiped away—the girl, the boy, the demons, even the flames—in torrents of images, lights, and bursts of emotions. It reached a screaming, howling crescendo of knowledge and information and emotions, filling him to the very brim of himself, and then it popped. Like a soap bubble in a wash basin, it ended, was gone so quickly, so abruptly. White replaced sight, replaced knowledge, there was nothing and he was nothing in the white.

## CHAPTER 41

# *Something New*

Silver Wolf fell back against the stones, panting. He dropped his hand to support himself when he fell, leaving the bird still perched on his knee looking at him with a satisfied expression.

"What happened?" Black Wolf asked, coming close to his shoulder while still giving the construct a wide berth.

"How long was I gone?" He panted, still spent from the experience. It'd felt like days.

"Gone?"

"In the vision."

"You put your hand in it and then froze. You had a vision?"

"Yes. How long?"

"Minutes. Five, maybe seven."

"That was all?" His breath slowed marginally.

"What did you see?"

"Too much." He shook his head. "I need to sort through it."

"Alright. You've never had visions before. What is that bird?"

"Her name is Kelseya," the younger twin said automatically. It startled him that he now knew both the construct's name and gender. It appeared he learned more than even he'd realized inside his altered state. "She's my construct, an embodiment of my power."

"As close to death as you were, you were able to call such a spell?"

"Not on purpose."

"'Not on purpose'?" Black Wolf echoed.

"I don't know exactly what happened, but I think when Kaliton nearly killed me a part of me knew I wasn't finished. I was so angry and frustrated. We'd spent our entire lives preparing for this moment and I was going to die without finishing it. And then I thought about all the people who said we could, and I thought they couldn't all be wrong, but what if I could? He laughed at himself. "Just that one, simple thought made me feel so hopeful, so optimistic, I must've been near delirium. Then my emotions took over what was left of me and kind of ran away with my magic, calling this version of me, this construct, made from my energies to do what my body couldn't."

The warrior blinked at him. "So you created a new creature out of your magic?"

"Not exactly." He sighed, knowing he was explaining it poorly. "She's not alive, not really. Lotician said that when you make a construct, it exists only as long as you're feeding power to it. So, if I stop sending her energy she'll just vanish, break apart. Same as when I send out a blast of wind—the air and energy just dissolve back into the ambient flows." The sorcerer felt an ache in the pit of his stomach. He couldn't help seeing the parallels between himself and his connection to the magical bird and his relationship to the gods. The gods were feeding him power, and when they eventually withdrew it, he would crumple like the stone tortoise had. Just as Kelseya would eventually vanish when he stopped casting. Only—

"That's strange."

"Indeed." His brother grunted.

"No." He shook his head as much as he could from his prone position. "Lotician said constructs are taxing to maintain, that they are huge drains on a sorcerer's energies because they need a constant flow of energy, only I don't feel like she's draining me. In fact, I don't feel her drawing power from me at all." Silver Wolf stared at the construct, who poignantly avoided looking back, pretending instead to clean her fire-feather wings.

The warrior shook his head in turn. "How's that? She is your power, isn't she?"

"Yes, of course." The sorcerer nodded, eyes still on the green figure on his knee. "I feel a connection, only—"

The sorcerer shut his eyes, drifting to the space in between the worlds, to the Basilar, and felt the connection, the thread the power followed to create and sustain his construct. It was strong and distinct, just like a string leading from his chest to the bird's. She was what she appeared to be, a construct made from his magic, only there was no pull, no tension on the cord like he would've expected if she'd been drawing on him. He moved to his other connection for comparison to the thread that connected him to the gods. It was taut, and he sensed and saw, in his way, the glowing, sparkling, divine power that ran down it like the patter of drops off of a melting icicle. The cord was vibrant, strong, secure, just like the one he shared with his construct. In fact, it even ran alongside the same path.

"That's it!" he shouted, trying to sit up further and wincing at the pain before slumping back down. "She's drawing power from the gods."

"What?"

"We're all—you, me, that tree, the dragons—connected to Eris, and the planet is connected to the gods."

"What?"

"Threads connect mortals like us and everything else living on Eris's surface to the planet that brings us life, that gives us energy, that we return to when we die. In turn the gods are connected to the elementals and the world. They're the bonds that connect us, that sustain us, that make everything live and grow."

"I don't feel a connection." The warrior ran his hand over the back of his skull and scratched his shoulder, not quite searching for a string, but clearly unnerved by the idea.

"You can't feel it, not without training, and you can't see it. All the threads exist in the Basilar, a space in between this world and the gods, kind of stitching them together if you want to think about it that way."

"So if all of these threads connect us to our sources of power, then how are the gods supplying power to the construct you created?"

"Because they're connected to my magic and she's connected to my magic. Because of how close they are, and I'm not sure anything like this has ever happened. The strings got twisted together. So as the gods are sending me power, they're feeding her, as a part of my magic, at the same time. Kelseya doesn't need to drain magic from me; she's quite contented taking all she needs from the gods."

"So the gods are supporting you both? They're going to love that," Black Wolf said under his breath. "Are you going to call her back to regain that piece of your energy?"

Kelseya gave an indignant shriek at the suggestion, her wings half-flared.

"I don't think she wants to," the bright twin replied. He reached out a tentative hand to stroke her wing, which she leaned into with a soft coo, apparently placated.

"So, if she's staying out here, you'll lose control of that part of your power?"

Looking at the bird now nuzzling at his hand, he replied slowly, thoughtfully, "No. When you were fighting Kaliton, I was seeing it happen through Kelseya's eyes. We were doing it together. We're still connected. I can still work with her, but she can also act on her own."

The warrior hung his head, scratching the back of his neck. "As long as you're keeping track of all the rules." The dark werewolf looked around them at the carnage plastered over the stones, at his own tattered and bloodied clothes, at his other half. "I'm just glad we both survived." Letting out a deep sigh, Black Wolf smiled at him with relief and then instantly grimaced in his next breath. He already knew the direction his brother's thoughts had taken before he said, "At least for the moment."

The reminder of their agreement with the gods was enough to draw Silver Wolf out of his study of their new companion. He'd seen the visions of what was to come next. He knew there was more that they needed to do. The caster just wished they'd have more time to rest, to celebrate their impossible victory, only he wasn't sure time was a luxury they had.

Responsibility and resolution taking over his thoughts, the younger brother said, "We need to get back to the dragon city." Struggling, he tried to push himself up. He needed to stand if he was going to go anywhere, but pain shot through him, reminding him of the bloody mess that was his abdomen. The demonic poison might've been completely purged, but the damage it had caused was still there, not to mention the hole the sword had carved through him, severing muscle and bone alike. He wouldn't die from the wounds now, but nor could he hope to move anywhere on his own for a long while.

"Stay," his brother ordered, putting a hand to his shoulder. "You're tearing at your wounds. You'll rip them open if you're not careful." He looked to the field and down the slope. "The city's miles away. I could carry you, but that would take too long. We'll have to see if any of the dragons will take us back."

The older brother bent down and Silver Wolf could see his wounds, still red and barely sealed. They were both in a pretty sorry state, but he didn't think they'd have the time to rest anymore. So when the elder bent down, the younger hooked a gray arm around his neck, causing Kelseya to hop off of her perch as his colossal brother lifted him to his feet. The pain was just as intense, worse in some respects. He worried that being vertical would let all his innards fall through the gaping wound, but the muscles and sinew he still had seemed to be doing an admirable job of holding everything in, even if his organs did feel like they were drooping lower than they should.

From a nearby rock, the green fire construct screeched in annoyance. They both turned to look at her, only Kelseya was staring poignantly at her creator. It was only then that the light twin remembered the first scene from his vision.

"Wait," he said through clenched teeth, the pain causing places in him to jolt and spasm uncomfortably. "She can help, I think."

"Help how?"

"Just wait," he grunted. If he'd been human, he'd be sweating, but as he couldn't, his tongue lolled out to relieve some heat from his exertions. "Will you help us. Please?" He gasped at the pain of talking, but it seemed worth it.

The construct gave a long trilling call, almost a song, and flapped into the air, floating just like an ember on the wind. She flew high and then turned, sweeping low, her brilliant plumage leaving a glowing afterimage in her wake. She swooped around the brothers, wrapping them in ribbons of her light, bathing them both in her brilliance and power. Energy filled the air, hairs rising all over him, sparks jumping between the strands. As the cocoon of light grew thicker with each pass, he could sense the energy flowing into him. It was just as he'd been able to heal his brother. Silver Wolf had not been trained formerly in healing magic, but he had picked up the trick that sorcerers could lend others their energies to give their bodies a boost to help their own bodies heal quicker. It wasn't as effective as instructing the body about how to heal correctly and then working together to bring the subject fully back to health, but it would help some and worked particularly well with werewolves, who had advanced healing powers anyway.

The pain in his abdomen lessened. The hole was closing over, the muscles beneath working to knit back together. He could feel the greater damage, the melting the poison had wrought, working on fixing itself, but it was slow. Glancing at his brother, he could see that his wounds too were shrinking and sealing, quicker than his own, deeper injuries. All the while, Kelseya spun, danced, and spun again around them, sharing her energy until both wolves were standing on their own, their physical damage no longer visible. Then the construct glided on a breeze over to a taller stone where she settled, too tired even to flap.

The first thing Silver Wolf did was to feel where the sword had pierced him. It was tender, still painful, but no longer open. Under the fur, his fingers traced the ridge of scar tissue that ran the width of him. Werewolves typically didn't scar, their advanced healing able to clean up most injuries completely. He considered himself lucky to have faced off against a greater demon and to have survived the encounter with only a scar for his trouble.

After his inspection, the caster looked to the bird. Her head hung low and she looked completely spent. He was disturbed to note that her light was a little less bright and her green was a little less vivid. He walked over to her and extended his arm, offering it as a perch. She stepped over to it, grateful for the mobile rest. She worked her way up his arm and to his shoulder, where she nestled into the crook of his neck contentedly.

"It looks like my power is a little more potent outside of my body." He grinned, stroking the back of Kelseya's neck.

His brother didn't look as pleased. "I can see that, though she's not looking too well. Are you worried she might use herself up?"

The sorcerer studied the bird and slowly shook his head. "I clearly can't know, but I think she'll be fine as long as she gets some rest and we can maintain our connection to the gods."

"About that." His frown deepened. "We should get back."

# CHAPTER 42

# *Homecoming*

When they reached the City of Sky Fire, they found its streets eerily empty. There were no towering ryong walking from store to store, no merchants enticing customers, no children flying through the air like brightly colored ribbons.

The main force of the dragon army had stayed behind on the field, some to tend to the wounded, some to search for demonic stragglers, and some to collect the dead. The corpses of the demons would be thrown over the cliffs to vanish through the mist and be lost in the valleys below. The fallen dragons would be placed in a sacred cave where their physical forms could rest and slowly break apart, while their souls would return to Eris.

Those citizens who couldn't join the battle waited in their homes for news of the outcome. Curious youngsters and solemn elders peered out at them from within their homes. Awe and disbelief both reflected back to him in their eyes, along with the green shine of Kelseya's light. His construct was still riding on his shoulder. None approached or even spoke to the trio, not knowing they'd been the heroes of the day. He was glad. The quiet march to the palace gave him time to think.

They passed through the palace gates that stood open to them and through the shattered hallways until they once again reached the chambers of the lord regent. The plum steward was there, looking down at them with a thoughtful expression. She opened her mouth to say something, then shut it, instead only nodding her head respectfully and opening the door without a word.

"You've done it," Fen Ryok said before they'd even entered the room. His voice was heavy with respect and gratitude. "You defeated the demon and protected the relic."

"How do you know that?" Silver Wolf asked. "Just because we came back alive?"

"That, and the guardian of Oriehada saw the moment of the danger's passing and my few guards and myself."

"'The Guardian of Oriehada.'" Black Wolf repeated the title, though he couldn't read from his face what he thought about this mysterious individual. He recalled the gods mentioning another guardian besides the dragons and themselves. Now wasn't the time to ask about them, though.

"We of the City of Sky Fire owe you both a great debt." The lord regent bowed his massive head in acknowledgment, jewelry clinking and glittering with the movement. "Whatever you wish, name it and if it is within our power to grant, you will have it."

Before more than a heartbeat passed, the sorcerer said, "I would like to request a favor."

He felt his brother's curious stare land on him, but there wasn't time to explain.

Fen Ryok looked both surprised and bemused. "Name it."

"We seek a second audience with the gods. Please send us to the Hall of Dreams."

He felt Black Wolf's gaze go from curious to demanding, but Fen Ryok merely nodded as though he expected the request.

"A simple matter. I will not count this as your boon and offer this service as a gift." He fixed his blazing yellow eyes on the pair. "As to your audience, good luck. I hope, for the sake of your plan, that the gods are in a generous mood."

With that, the great red beast rose from the dais. Bright yellow eyes blazed like suns as they stared, waiting for the moment when everything went black.

## CHAPTER 43

# *A New Bargain*

Silver Wolf opened his eyes again on the expected nothing.

"Why are we back here?" his brother asked, finally giving words to all his previous glances.

The younger twin turned to face the older, seeing him and his furrowed brow clearly even in the nothing. "Because there's still more to do."

He saw the warrior's throat bob as he swallowed. He knew his twin thought they were there so Silver Wolf could fulfill his end of the bargain and give his life up to the gods, but there wasn't time to discuss it just then.

Turning again to face the dark, he found himself missing his construct's green light, even though he knew it wouldn't actually illuminate anything. Kelseya hadn't followed them into the trance, whether she'd chosen that or wasn't able, the caster wasn't sure. He felt an ache in his chest at her absence, in the same spot where she'd originally burst from, like he was missing something besides his body. He shook his head to clear the thought. He didn't have time for his own musings either, striding toward the slightly less black.

The trip to the hall was near instantaneous this time, the pillars and stars appearing after he'd taken his next breath.

"Is that because we've been here before or are the gods as eager to speak to us as we are to speak to them?" he wondered to himself.

The hall felt shorter too, the brothers coming to stand before the living black wall in only a few steps. He wanted to wonder about the perception and concept of space in this place, but stopped himself.

"Stay focused," he whispered.

Neither of them bothered to sit. Both siblings radiated anticipation for the next part in their story and fixed their attention to the portal.

The gods appeared a short time later, again as orbs of light coming through the undulating black wall, directly from the other world they were thought to reside in. Unlike their first appearance, the deities chose to dispense with the greater show of their power as they entered the Hall of Dreams. Instead, each globe merely stretched and grew into their were-avatars—the fox, the bear, the raven, and the drake. There were still only four.

"You did it," Pendry said with a smile and a nod of his vulpine head.

"Yes," Belkis added. "You've slayed a greater demon, and even with our help, that is no small feat. You fought and protected the shrine of Oriehada well, and for that we are grateful."

"Yes, good job." Indris's words were clipped as he hovered toward them. "Now that this little skirmish is done with, we'll be taking our power back." He opened a hand full of black claws as though he intended to reach into the sorcerer's very soul and rip out the connection himself.

Black Wolf glanced to his brother, alarmed, but Silver Wolf took a step toward the feline, straight, eyes turned to the god's frown and spoke. "Not yet." His voice rang out against the glass panels, the tremor in it barely perceptible.

Indris curled one furred lip, showing sharp, white teeth. "Groveling isn't going to do you any good. You knew the terms. We've upheld our end of our understanding, now you—"

"I don't mean to go back on our agreement, only to extend it."

"Extend it?" Indris snorted.

"Oh, but we cannot." Pendry shook his head sadly. "We regret that you will forfeit your life; however, we cannot afford to lengthen your existence."

"This isn't about my life." He extended a hand back to encompass his brother. "Our destiny isn't fulfilled yet."

"The demon is dead," Arden pointed out in his deep rumble of a voice. "The City of Sky Fire in under no threat and the holy shrine is safe. Your task is finished."

"Killing Kaliton isn't our only duty."

"It's the only one we have a care for," snapped Indris.

"There's one more you'll care about." The ghost of a smile played over his lupine features, though it didn't quite reach his violet eyes.

Indris crossed his arms over his broad chest. "And that is?"

"The death of the Eight."

"What are you talking about?" Arden asked when none of the others did.

"Kaliton said it, and I think you know it too. The elves, dwarves, nokken, dragons, even the demons and the people of this world are dying, and if they do, Eris isn't going to be far behind. That was the other problem you mentioned before, wasn't it?"

The gods didn't answer; their eye sockets narrowed at the impertinence of the question.

"What do you think you know?" Indris asked after a moment.

"And you believe you can stop this?" asked Belkis, almost on top of her fellow divinity's question, one graceful brow raised.

"Not us," he clarified, choosing to answer the goddess's question out of the two. "There will be—" He paused, looking for the word he wanted. "—another."

"What other?" asked Arden.

"A boy, a werewolf with golden eyes. He's going to save Eris and its people."

Indris spoke, brows even lower. "If someone else is going to save Eris, then why do we need you?"

"He's going to need help. I've seen the troubles he's going to face. This boy is going to need skills and guidance to make it through them. I've seen him training with my brother, and I've seen myself advising him."

"Have 'seen' him?" scoffed. "Are you claiming to be a seer now as well as a demon slayer?"

The caster shook his head. "Merely a glimpse, a gift of a vision maybe. My reward for such a hard-fought battle? I'm not a seer, but I know what I saw will be true."

"Let's say that what you saw is going to happen," Belkis said almost lazily. "What will you require to move this little prophecy along?"

"Time," he answered simply.

"Of course," Indris said, but the rest of the gods seemed to think on his words more carefully, studying the pair. Black Wolf's face was an unreadable mask, but Silver Wolf was standing as tall as he could make himself, willing them to believe him.

Finally, Belkis asked, "And how long will it take to find, train, and lead this hero to perform his miracles?"

"I don't know," Silver Wolf said, shrugging his shoulders.

"You don't know?" Indris echoed incredulously.

"The vision didn't give me anything so clear as a specific time or day. It could be six months from now, six years, or sixty," the caster answered, again with a shrug. Of course, thinking about the vision and the cyclone of people and places he'd seen, it seemed too many future memories to be able to have glimpsed them all in a single lifetime. "You may have to extend our lives past their natural limits."

The assembled gods looked surprised at this pronouncement.

Belkis was the first to recover, asking in her lyrical voice, "Our?"

"Yes. You'll need to make the same pact with my brother that you've made with me. We need the time to find this hero and help him. If we do, I've seen an end to the conflict that threatens the Eight."

"What you're asking for isn't simple. The drain on our power to sustain the lives of two mortals for an indefinite amount of time will be considerable," Pendry informed him.

Silver Wolf nodded his acknowledgment. "Yes, I understand that. I understand that this will necessitate an acceleration of time in which you'll need to—" He paused to think of a suitable word. "—replenish yourselves."

This comment sparked a reaction. Indris snarled, embers floating out between bared fangs. Belkis placed a delicate claw over her beak while Pendry and Arden looked on in surprised and attentive silence.

The sorcerer could feel his brother's confused eyes on him in response to the gods' discomfort, but he couldn't explain it just then. "This is not an easy path. He'll need help, not just from us, but from so many others along the way. Give us the time we need to help him."

"And we're just supposed to believe you?" Indris snarled. "That you've seen a vision, even though you admit to not having the Sight, where a mysterious boy will come and gift us the very thing we need? And yet somehow this miraculous cur will require your help, which conveniently will have the added benefit of delaying your inevitable deaths? We could sit here forever waiting for this miracle. Meanwhile, you and your brother live comfortably long lives, practically immortal. This all seems a little too convenient, doesn't it?"

"We cannot," Pendry said again. "The energy required—"

"I know what the relic of Oriehada is." Another wave of shock filled the hall at this sudden and striking declaration. Wide-eyed stares were focused on the young sorcerer like spotlights, but he knew what to say next. "It may be safe for now, but there will be a day when this youth will need it."

The red god again spoke for the group. "No mortal is ever going to lay hands on the relic."

"And yet he will."

"A mortal couldn't get past the guardian, let alone survive contact with it—"

"And yet I know he does."

Belkis spoke up, the first of the other gods to find her voice. "How? What will this boy do with the relic?"

"It's not possible," Indris persisted.

"He's correct," the blue god said, supporting the red.

"What if it could be?" Arden wanted to know.

"It's not," Indris said.

The caster broke into the divine conversation. "I've seen the end of the turmoil we now find ourselves in. Kaliton told us Eris is on the path to being destroyed. This boy, with the relic in hand, could stop it. Isn't that worth extending our lives for? So that we can help ensure he does?"

"It would be if we could trust the words of a greater demon and the delusions of a mortal magician." The fire god grunted the words.

"Isn't it worth the risk, even if I might be lying, if there's even a chance I'm not?"

The hall was silent.

"I believe in what I saw, with all of my being. I know the future can be changed, that we can save Eris, if we help this new hero."

Each of the gods exchanged thoughtful glances with the others. Their eerie, orb-less eyes were difficult to read, but each burned brightly with unvoiced thoughts, opinions, and doubts.

Though they might've been conversing with each other through some means that the brothers had no way of hearing, Silver Wolf was grateful for the reprieve. His heart raced hard and his breaths came quick and shallow. He felt he'd run the length of Jenoha. It'd taken every ounce of his will and courage to speak to the gods the way he had, but he'd known he was right. Those images, those feelings, felt true, felt earnest and honest. He had to make them understand.

At last Pendry turned back and addressed him. "Very well. We will make the pact with your brother."

"For the sake of Eris's future," Belkis said, her accompanying glare fierce. "We'll see that you're able to aid this champion."

"This contract won't last forever," Arden clarified. "The hero will arrive, then your service will be at an end. There will be no second reprieve. We will settle this agreement and take back our link."

"Of course." Silver Wolf bowed his head in acknowledgment to the stone gods, but also in sheer relief and gratitude. Even though he'd seen the future, there was nothing to say that one small action couldn't alter that preferred path. After all, he was trying to bring about the path he'd seen over the one Kaliton had predicted.

Then the light twin turned to the dark for the first time in this conversation with immortals. The taller wolf stood stock-still, staring back at the younger sibling. He said not a word, but the caster could see the questions in his eyes. "Are you alright with this—"

Indris broke in, his voice full of command and colored with disapproval. "There is another condition. As a way to guarantee your sincerity and limit your potential malice, you two must separate."

The warrior spun to face the red god, but the caster only closed his eyes.

The lion continued to speak to both in turn. "Your task is to guide and your brother's is to train, tasks that don't require the presence of the other to complete. Separating you should not impede your duties."

"But why?" Silver Wolf heard his brother ask so quietly he had trouble understanding the words.

"Of all the mortals crawling on the world, you two represent the greatest threat to the tenuous balance we have left." The fire god narrowed his eyelids and curled his lip. "If you are lying, we need to ensure you twins can't cause any further damage."

"We wouldn't—"

"Your blade and your magic will not come together, not ever again." His roar boomed through the darkened hall, cutting off the older werewolf's words.

"He is correct." Pendry nodded, though without the malice of the other god. "Your power together is too great. A force with the ability to topple a greater demon would represent an unstable factor in our calculations. We would have no way to predict your actions."

"Or your loyalties," growled the lion.

The older brother stared, mouth hanging slightly agape, but he merely looked at the checked floor. He'd seen that too.

"So my brother and I will never see each other again?" the larger werewolf asked.

"If you desire our power and more time to wait for your champion, then no," Indris replied.

"It won't be as bad as you think," said the younger brother, trying to sound lighthearted through the ache in his own chest. Growing more serious, he added, "But I won't force this on you either. You've heard what needs to be done and why, but I won't make you form the pact against your will. It could be a long time to wait alone."

His stalwart brother didn't speak right away. He could see doubt flicker for the barest moment over his steely gaze. He knew how he felt because he felt it too. They'd never been alone in their eighteen years. They'd pulled each other through the worst moments of their lives and now they'd never see each other again. Only Silver Wolf had seen the future; he could have no doubt about this choice. He needed his brother with him. He needed him to trust him and stand with him, just like he had when they'd challenged Kaliton.

The dark werewolf looked at him, uncertainty wavering in his eyes for a heartbeat more, and then his resolve returned, his glance shining bright like the spring sunlight after the winter's gloom. A smirk spread over his features, steadfast steel behind his expression. "If that is to be our purpose, then so be it."

He smiled back, letting out the breath he hadn't realized he'd been holding. Turning to the gods, he said, "Great lords of this world, please make the pact with my brother and give us the time we need to help these heroes of another age."

One by one, the gods drew near with their right arms outstretched, forming a circle around the dark werewolf. The light was burning, brilliant and almost terrible in its brightness, sealing their pact and the brothers' future.

## CHAPTER 44

# *A Path and a Name*

When they returned to the lord regent's hall, Silver Wolf sat up first. The great red dragon, Fen Ryok, his expression grim, hovered over his pool of lilies, close enough to observe, but far enough to be at a respectful distance. He searched the cavernous ceilings. Kelseya, who'd been perched at the top of one of the pillars, nestled on the snout of one of the carved dragons, opened her wings, and glided down to him. He obligingly lifted an arm for her to alight upon. She touched down, the coolness of her talons seeping through his fur, the weight of her just enough to make him sure she was there but not enough to dip his arm under the strain. He reached out his other hand and stroked the feathers at her neck. The gesture reminded him that she was real, the bird in turn leaning into his touch.

"How fared your audience?" the dragon asked in a quiet rumble.

"It's done," the younger brother replied, looking back to the lord regent while his construct walked her way up to his shoulder.

"I can sense the divine aura around you both now." The dragon nodded to his older brother, who'd not yet lifted his head from the marble floor.

He could see that the warrior was awake; he was just laying there, blinking with deliberate slowness. He could only imagine what he must be feeling. He'd been a caster for almost all his life, had learned how to sense the magic, how to move it, how to use it, but his brother had never. As far as the warrior was concerned the energy that had flowed through his body since birth had been as innocuous as his blood, but now that the gods were feeding him a stream of new power, he'd be feeling things very differently.

Black Wolf lifted his hands to stare at them, flipping them over, most likely checking to make sure he wasn't glowing.

"Will I be able to do magic now, like you?"

"No," he replied. "As far as I understand it you're either born with the ability to use magic or you're not. Having a new source of it shouldn't change that, even if it is divine."

"And why would you need more divine power?" Fen Ryok asked. "The demon is defeated."

"This power is not for us. It will help others act when the time comes." Silver Wolf glanced to his brother, who returned his look with a nod.

"All of that hard work and training, only so that you could pass the job onto someone else," called the voice of the elven sorcerer.

Lotician strode in through the open doorway, his clothes and exposed skin flecked with blood, both the red of his own and the black of his enemies' stinking with an acidic tang. Silver Wolf saw him limp and a nasty scratch marred his pale cheek as he walked over to them.

"Did I just waste all of those years training you two?"

He chuckled. "Master Lotician, I'm glad to see you."

"And I you." He smiled at his apprentice wearily but warmly. "As soon as the lesser demons fled the field, we knew you'd taken care of their master. I wish I could've seen the killing blow, but alas, I had other distractions." As he said it, still walking, the elf slid one glowing hand down his damaged face. In their passing, his glowing fingers seemed to wipe away the injury, clearing the blood and healing the wound, leaving only smooth, unmarked flesh.

"What on Eris is that?" The master sorcerer stopped in his tracks and pointed at the bright green bird on the werewolf's shoulder.

"This is Kelseya."

"A construct? My congratulations for controlling such a high-level spell, but why is it still here? You can't have a reason for keeping such a demanding summoning in place, not this long after the conflict."

"She's a little different than your average construct," he said, stroking her under the chin.

The elf smiled, lifting one questioning eyebrow. "Oh, yes? I want to hear that story."

He laughed. "We'll have plenty of time for me to tell it." His smile dimmed as he realized the unintended gravity of his words.

"Pardon the interruption," Black Wolf said. "Have you seen Dexus? I'd like to return Slayer to him. The weapon did its job well, just as he said it would." He patted the sword in its sheath for emphasis as though rewarding a well-behaved pet.

Lotician visibly flinched as though staving off a jolt of pain before recovering himself and answering. "Dexus is dead."

"What? How?"

"Killed by the demon horde," Lotician said with a heavy breath.

"No."

"It's true. I didn't see him fall, I only found his body later among the dead." He closed his eyes. "It was too late for me to do anything for him."

Black Wolf let his arm go slack, his face draining of emotion till it became as unreadable as stone. The room was quiet, save for the occupants' breathing, while they allowed his brother to absorb and grieve this news in his own way. He wanted to reach out, but he knew this was something his twin would not want to be comforted over, not yet.

When the moment had stretched for some time, Black Wolf lifted his head, his hand returning to clutch at the hilt of Slayer. "Dexus was a strong warrior, a great dragon, and a master of the blade."

"And he will always be remembered as such," Fen Ryok promised solemnly. "He will be present in our writings and songs. His legacy will live on."

Looking up at the red dragon, the warrior marched up to the edge of the reflecting pool. Undoing the scabbard's fastenings, Black Wolf held Slayer up. "Keep his sword alongside your writings."

"I would've thought you'd keep it," Lotician interjected.

"He lent it to me for the battle. It wasn't a gift. Upon his death, the blade should revert to its creators." Striding the last step forward, he bent down and left the sword at the water's edge. Once done, the dark werewolf turned his back to the regent, instead going to the pillar where he'd left his short sword, the gift from their mother, before the battle. Silver Wolf could sense his brother's pain, not in giving up the sword he'd slain the greater demon with, not in picking up the familiar if lesser weapon, but because it was another death and another weight he'd carry with him until the end of his time, however long that turned out to be.

His older brother strapped the short sword back to his hip, and Silver Wolf couldn't help but think how right it looked back in the place it'd been since the day he'd pulled it from the sack.

"We will keep the blade in honor of Dexus until the time it is needed again." Fen Ryok bowed to the warrior.

"Even if you don't intend to use it, why not keep it with you? Won't these new heroes of yours need it?" Lotician asked.

He shook his head. "I don't know what will happen to Slayer. Maybe it still has a part to play, but it won't go to the hero I saw. There will be another blade intended."

"What do you mean you saw? What is this hero you keep talking about?"

Before he could go into the long explanation of his vision and conversation with the gods, Black Wolf looked up from his quiet reflection upon switching swords. "Thank you, Lord Regent Fen Ryok. My brother and I appreciate all of the years you've housed and fed us and called our masters from across the seas. Now that our task is finished here, I'll be leaving your hospitality at first light tomorrow."

"Leaving?" Lotician echoed and looked back to Silver Wolf.

Silver Wolf put a hand on his teacher's shoulder. "It was part of the bargain. While this bond with the gods exists, and while we wait for the new champion, we have to remain separated."

"Why?"

"The gods demanded it. My brother will travel to Rahovan and wait to train the hero there, and I'll stay here and wait to guide them to their next step on the path."

"Rahovan?" the elf exclaimed. His brother's eyes widened too. Maybe he'd not told him that part of the vision.

"Cutting a family apart seems like a rotten way to reward servants for their good works," Lotician scowled.

"It'll be worth it in the end."

"I'll have to teach you to speak through the flames then," grunted the master sorcerer. "That way, at the very least, you'll be able to see and speak to your brother."

"That's a possibility?" Black Wolf asked, brows lifted at the first pleasant surprise they'd gotten since they'd killed Kaliton.

"Of course." The elf crossed his arms and sniffed. "How do you think sorcerers can speak to each other over long distances?"

"Thank you," he began. "Master Lotician, I—"

"I think we can dispense with the 'master' talk." Silver Wolf merely blinked at his teacher, making the elf laugh. "You've defeated a greater demon, something I could never do."

"But the gods—"

"Whether or not the gods gave you a bit of assistance is irrelevant. You've shown yourself to be more than a competent sorcerer. I'll still teach you, of course. The gods know you've plenty left to learn. However, as of this moment, you may consider your apprenticeship over."

He felt his mouth open, but he couldn't think of a thing to say.

"Which means," Lotician continued, "as far as I understand these dragon traditions, you may reclaim your name."

The younger twin blinked. It'd been so long that being called anything other than Silver Wolf or Brother seemed so strange. He'd earned his name, but what name should he take? Should he concoct something new, something that spoke of his magical prowess or the fact that he'd killed a greater demon? Should he take a dragon or elven name to honor those that had taught and guided him?

He grinned at his brother, the smile going so wide it almost hurt, and undid the chain that always hung around his neck. He removed the ring, admiring it in the soft light of the hall, before sliding it over his smallest finger. "Aaron," he said, looking at the green stone.

His wild grin still in place, his eyes sought out his older brother's. "Brother, you too. What name will you take?"

But Black Wolf only shook his head. "I never surpassed my master. I haven't earned my name."

"Dexus, for all that he was an astounding warrior, couldn't have done what you did," Lotician said. "Surely that amounts to the same thing. No doubt he'd agree with me."

Again the dark twin shook his head. "His words were clear. My apprenticeship will be over only once I have defeated him in combat."

"But Dexus is dead," pressed the elf.

"Then I suppose I'll never find my name."

"But—"

Aaron dropped his hand on his teacher's shoulder again, cutting off his words. "Let him be for now. He'll have time to think about it."

"But—" The elf tried again, only for the regent to speak over him.

"The future is a place we may never truly know," rumbled the great red dragon, "even for those who do see hints of it. Your paths appear to be set. Is there anything more my people or I can do to help you with what's to come next?"

The twins shared a look. "No." Aaron spoke for them both, his brother's hand on his shoulder lending him strength. "We began this journey alone, and we go on just the same."

## CHAPTER 45

## *Across the Seas*

The brothers arrived together in Gahar Barea. The seat of King Gilberto, Gahar Barea was a massive port city gazing out at the shining ocean and the heavy merchant vessels bobbing at anchor. The beating heart of High King Castlewall's empire across the sea, the city was the gateway for all goods traded to and from Rahovan. It was said that you could purchase anything from its markets from the latest fashions to the finest lamb brains or a full set of dragon claws.

The pair walked through the crowded city in their human forms, though it might've been an unwarranted precaution. They passed elves in the streets who were as tall and lithe as Lotician, clutching books to their chests or selling charms of protection and luck. He spotted a cluster of dwarves setting up a stall packed with all manner of metal objects winking in the sun, from a delicate gold necklace to a heavy battle-ax. Aaron lost a step when he spotted a nokken hauling crates of fish from one of the ships. The man looked and walked like a human, only there was a bluish cast to his skin and webbing between his fingers and his bare toes. His nose was nearly absent, no more than two slits where the nostrils should be. As they passed, the sorcerer observed three ridges, gills he supposed, behind small sail-like ears, pulsing open and then shut with each intake of breath.

Though a few more of the Eight were present, Gahar Barea was a human city. There were no dragons either walking amongst or flying over the crowds, no demons certainly, but no weres either, none that weren't disguised as they were, anyway.

Even without seeing any of his own ilk, he would've liked to stop and watch this microcosm of Eris. They'd spent so much of their lives isolated in one mountain range or another, to be out among the regular people, the ones they'd just saved without them knowing, called to him, though he knew they were on borrowed time.

The gods had demanded that the brothers should separate and never see each other again. Aaron could only credit the other four gods' calming influence for the fact that the fire god hadn't raged at them during the months it'd taken for the twins to reach the port city. He thought it a small indulgence, considering the time that stretched out before them.

They veered off the main thoroughfare, taking the west gate exit out of the city. Unlike much of the surrounding area outside the gates, which was filled with the dwellings of the less affluent or wealthy residents, the southeastern outskirts offered a more hilly terrain. Hiking up a particularly steep slope, they reached the summit and turned to take in the view of the harbor and much of the sprawling metropolis. The view was a kaleidoscope of colors—the blue-green sea, the brown-gray docks, the houses in their many shades of pinks and yellows or dark blue and further in the shining gold of King Gilberto's palace. The ships docked in the harbor were just as diverse, showing everything from tiny rowboats, to speedy schooners, going all the way up to stately caravels. Only one ship caught Aaron's attention, a tall, three-masted ship with deep mahogany wood polished to a shine and silver winking from stern to its gunnel. The ship from his vision.

Swooping out of the sky, the sun at her back, Kelseya joined them on the slope.

"There you are," the sorcerer said, lifting his arm to receive her.

"A little too flashy for the streets?" Black Wolf asked with a mocking lift of an eyebrow.

"Some species are more tolerant of magic than others." Aaron stroked her neck and she walked up his arm, taking her accustomed place on his shoulder.

Against his will the caster's eyes drifted back to the harbor, back to the dark ship on the bright water. His mouth was dry and his mind was blank.

Black Wolf broke the silence. "How long do we wait?"

"Visions don't appear to be very precise when it comes to time," he replied, his attention on the boat holding for a moment longer before he turned. "I wasn't lying to the gods about that, but I think it's going to be a long, long time."

"What will you do?"

He shrugged. "Receiving the sum total of all of Lotician's teachings should be enough to occupy me. He's been at it a couple hundred years, after all. And you?"

It was his twin's turn to look out over the ocean before replying. "It isn't just this boy and girl who are important to the future." The elder brother nodded to himself as if confirming his thought. "While I'm waiting, I'll pass on Dexus's training to as many as I'm able."

"It's a worthy tribute to Dexus, and a few practice apprentices before the golden-eyed boy appears will probably do you some good. It sounds like we'll both be busy for a while."

"Yeah." The older boy said the word on a great exhale of breath that was almost a sigh.

"I promise the speaking spell will be the first I learn."

"See that it is," the tan-skinned man replied sternly. Then he added less harshly, "Will you be alright on your own?" Before Aaron could answer his brother shook his head, letting his dark hair fall over his forehead, and corrected himself. "Of course you will. You defeated a greater demon, after all."

"We did."

"Keep him out of trouble." The words were directed to the bright bird on his shoulder. Black Wolf tapped her playfully on the beak with a knuckle and Kelseya let out a cry of agreement.

"And you? Will you be alright?" Aaron asked.

"I will."

The younger looked back to the ship that would take his family across the Karnak Sea, away from everything they'd ever known. Turning back to the larger man, he wrapped him in an embrace. The other returned it. Kelseya extended her wings over both of them as if to protect the moment, the sun shining down on them all tinged green by her fire.

When they stepped back, the dark twin nodded. "Take care till I see you again."

"Same to you," Aaron replied with a small smile.

The young man shouldered his pack, obvious muscles hefting the weight easily, made even more so without the fur to obscure the lines below his short shirtsleeves when he flexed to lift it. It reminded Aaron of the strong sentinel his brother had always been, and he felt the knot in his guts ease just a bit.

The champion of the gods, the slayer of the Demon of Blades, his older brother gave him a wave over his shoulder and walked down the hill. Despite all that lay before him, Aaron could see that his steps were light. Clearly he was looking forward to the challenges ahead—a new land, a new quest, a new purpose. It made him smile to see it.

As the boat threw in its mooring ropes, gulls calling their harsh cries and sails filling with warm, salty air, his dark twin came to the railing. He found him on the rise and waved. The light twin waved back.

He and Kelseya stayed silent as they watched the ship sail over the horizon until the tip of the mast vanished, until the sun was low on the horizon, until he could no longer see his brother.

# EPILOGUE

Aaron stood on the bank of the Nyoak Riol, watching the river's waters spill in tumultuous rapids from the mouth of a deep crack in the side of the plateau. A warm breeze ran over the stubby grass and up into his silver fur. The sun shone brightly, the steps bathed in its glow, and yet he felt a chill coming from the yawning maw of that cavern and the underground river flowing out of it. Kelseya sat on his shoulder shifting her weight from foot to foot and rustling her fiery feathers in anticipation. He smoothed a hand over her wing.

"We've waited this long; we can wait a bit more."

His words didn't seem to calm her any as she continued her swaying. Smiling at his construct's impatience, he looked down at the book in his hand for what must've been the thousandth time. He'd found a use for the tomb that was their mother's last gift to him.

After he and his brother left the City of Sky Fire and began their journey back west toward the port city that was his brother's path to Rahovan, Aaron used the evenings before sleep to write down every detail he could remember of the vision Kelseya had shown him before they started to fade. He'd wondered over the years if their mother hadn't received a vision too and thus knew what he'd use the book for, or if the seer in the marketplace had told her something, or if she'd just merely wanted to get something of equivalent worth to his brother's short sword. Whatever the reason, Aaron thanked her for it every day as he continued to fill in the pages over the years with more notes and stories, adding detail to the lengthy list of sights and people he'd first glimpsed in that future memory so very long ago. Each one except for the last had been checked off that list.

His ears swiveled on his head as he began to notice another sound over the tumultuous current. Quiet at first, it grew quickly and aggressively. It was a sinister, maddening, chattering noise. The noise grew louder and louder, emanating from the pitch-black portal.

"It's time."

With a flourish of his hand, the book vanished. Aaron held up his wrist for Kelseya to alight upon and she hopped eagerly on the appendage. He flung out his arm, launching her into the sky. The bright green fire-bird gave a wild cry of delight as she flew high, getting lost in the sun's rays before swooping back down toward the dark opening of the cave. She darted upward and smashed herself into the ceiling of the cavern, becoming a blazing spring-green flame that burned as it streamed into the hole, bathing the roof in an eerie glow.

Aaron waited. It didn't take long before he heard an explosion of furious chattering and screeching. The sound of objects striking the water echoed down the river, shattering the peace of the surrounding hills. Malformed black shapes, bulbous round things with too many legs, floated out of the tunnel first. The caster didn't need to look closer.

Then a boat hardly larger than a dinghy burst into view. Small, scratched, and barely afloat under the weight of its six occupants, it broke fully into the light, leaving all of its passengers to blink as their eyes adjusted to the new brilliance. Then they were up, looking around and behind them to assure themselves they were out of danger.

Aaron barely noticed any of the other five at first. His violet eyes were immediately drawn to the shining, golden hair that rippled in the summer breeze. The woman, for she was no longer the girl she'd been at the beginning of his visions, was sitting on the bench, looking back at the cavern's mouth and the green fire coalescing there.

Kelseya followed the boat, having charred many of the chattering fiends and meaning to deter any further conflict. Coming back to the mouth of the cave, she resumed her form as the great bird and flew over the tiny vessel. The woman followed her path through the air as she winged to him. Aaron lifted his arm to receive her, and Kelseya landed gently, giving a self-satisfied chirrup of triumph. Aaron stroked the back of her neck, pressing his forehead to her and letting her know he agreed with her self-praise.

The golden-haired woman turned in the boat. Her sky-blue eyes, just as he remembered them, widened further when she caught sight of the silver werewolf standing on the bank and holding the firbird. Those bright eyes found his and Aaron smiled.

If you liked this story, there are many more to come in the Guardian series. Please take a moment to review Heroes of Another Age wherever you buy books to help more readers like yourself find and enjoy it.

If you want to learn more about what's coming up next in the world of Eris—visit my website, and don't forget to sign up for my email newsletter while you're there.

**BLMOSTYN.COM**

## ACKNOWLEDGMENTS

There are so many people who have helped make my dream of becoming a published author a reality. While I can only name a few here, know that my gratitude extends far beyond this page. Thank you all.

To my family—my mom, dad, and sisters, Layne and Tess—your unwavering support means everything. To my husband, Matt, and our children, Alexandra and Samantha—thank you for cheering me on every day and believing in me even when I doubted myself.

To my incredible Beta Readers—Brent Hesse, my very first fan, Alex Mader, Natali Mader, Sean Kozo, Leslie Goetsch, Linda Zetter, and Tarleen Weston—your feedback and encouragement have been invaluable.

A heartfelt thank you to the professionals who guided me through this journey: the team at BookBaby for helping bring this book to life; Robin LeeAnn, my dedicated freelance editor; and Sarah Fox from The Bookish Fox, whose keen insights helped refine both my story and my craft.

And finally, thank you, dear reader. The individuals above helped shape this book, but you brought it to life by picking it up and reading it. Taking a chance on an unknown author is no small thing, and I am deeply grateful. I hope my story brought you something meaningful—even if it's just a smile.

## ABOUT THE AUTHOR

B.L. Mostyn's life passion is telling stories—either in her novels, through her art, or in coming up with unique explanations as to why her coworker is really on crutches (alligator wrestling). She currently resides in Maryland with her fellow dreamers— her husband and two children.